HALE'S FIRE

Book Two in the Hale's Storm Series, by

ALISSA BRIGHT

This book is dedicated to my favorite fly boy,
James Kerr, also known as 'Grandpa Jim'.
There is so much of you in this story;
your struggle through childhood,
your love of flying,
and your legacy of correcting my grammar.

ONE

"One's coming in hot," crackles through the speakers in my leather helmet. "Request to engage."

"Roger; engage," another rough voice confirms in my ears as we break through a thick white cloud.

Jack furrows his brow, and I know that he's heard the same thing in his own leather helmet. His hands move mechanically with the levers, and I'm thrown sideways in the small cockpit as his plane, Missy, nearly turns on her side. He maneuvers her with expert grace, his eyes determined under his flight goggles.

"Roger," Jack hums into his radio mask.

Like a pack of wild geese, a perfect V of American fighter planes forms in front of us. We fall seamlessly into its lines. Under his goggles, Jack's eyes glaze over in a steely look I don't recognize. His shoulders and neck stiffen, bracing. Squished uncomfortably between his seat and the window, my body responds with an outpouring of adrenaline.

"Jack, what's g--" I begin, but I'm quickly interrupted by the whistle of another plane whizzing directly past us. Missy's belly turns up toward our assailant. I throw my hands up to brace myself, realizing that I'm not strapped in at all.

How can Jack be this careless with me? I wonder. *This isn't like him. Where is my buckle?*

I barely have time to search the tight space around me for a restraint before Jack throws Missy's nose downward, and I topple over him. My chest slams into the control board. Pressed against the glass, my hands absorb the rat-a-tat shudder of bullets pinging off of Missy's frame. As he pulls hard on the lever, I fall backward. My hip stings where I've smashed backward into the door. I scramble onto my knees, clinging to whatever supports my hands can grasp.

Ping!

"Enemy line! Peel off!" urges the speakers in our ears.

Jack's brows furrow, and we roll sideways. As my face squishes hard against the glass, all my eyes can see is the landscape below. Planes whizz below us, nearly hitting one another.

Rat-tat-tat-tat. Ping!

Fighting; we're fighting. This is it! We're engaged in a firefight!

"Jack! Can I help? What do you want me to do?" I yell to him, eyeballing the untouched gun perched between his knees.

"Savvy is hit!" Jack grunts into his radio, circling back. "He's going down!"

"Savage, bail out!" crackles frantically through the speakers.

"C'mon, Savvy," Jack urges under his mask. "Jump." It's not difficult to pick out the plane that must be Savage's. It sags lifelessly in the air as it drops toward the greyish earth below us.

"Savage!" I scream under my own mask, knowing that this endangered pilot is someone's son, perhaps even someone's husband. I watch helplessly as his plane relaxes into a spiral, carelessly drilling its way down with a thin line of black smoke trailing behind.

"Bail out! Savvy, bail out!"

"C'mon, Savage!"

Our craft jerks suddenly to the right with a shudder, drawing a curse from Jack. We've been hit.

Rat-tat-tat.

His left hand wraps around the gun as his right brings the craft back around. Facing the enemy plane, his arm shudders as the gun fires. *Rat-tat-tat-tat-tat. Rat-tat-tat-tat.*

A small shower of glass rains into my hair where a hole has been shot through the fuselage above me. Jack's jaw sets, his neck stiff, his eyes aflame in the heat of the action. Confidently, his hands

2

maneuver the levers and the trigger simultaneously, and I feel grateful for our many weeks apart that he spent perfecting these techniques.

An enemy plane charges toward us, and we dip evasively low toward the ground. I feel our craft shudder as the other plane whizzes over us. Just before Jack pulls us sharply upward again, I catch sight of Savage's plane, broken and still in the marshland. Jack must see it too, because he immediately clicks the comm buttons at his throat.

"Savage down. Repeat, Savvy is down."

"Jack!" I scream as we nearly collide with an enemy plane, but the sound is muffled under my air mask. Both our plane and the hostile roll sideways, and my rattled bones absorb the vibration of two engines passing in the air.

Rat-tat-tat-tat-tat! Rat-tat-tat!

"This is Jack-o calling in a hit," he reports, and just then I notice the plume of black smoke trailing from our nose. *We've* been hit, right in the engine. "Repeat, Jack-o-Lantern hit."

Ping! Ping! Ping!

Jack fires back, sweat rolling down the bridge of his nose. The plane's engine sputters. As we hang dead in the air, the metal housing of the vessel absorbs another round of flak.

"Mayday! Mayday! Jack-o-Lantern's going down!"

"Bail out," the crackling speakers command. "Repeat, Jack-o; bail out."

Jack reaches for a green bag beside him, firing with his free hand. My stomach drops as I feel the weight of the plane pulling us down, see the smear of color on the landscape drawing nearer.

We're going to end up just like Savage, I realize as my heart stops.

An enemy plane swoops down and flies at us. *Rat-tat-tat! Ping!* Another shower of glass rains into the cockpit. I hear the thud of a bullet sinking into Jack's flesh; his grunt on impact. He stiffens in shocked pain. My fingers have no difficulty finding the wound under his leather jacket, as a maroon oval rapidly spreads at his shoulder. I hold his sagging face up, but his eyes won't focus on me.

"Jack! Wake up! How do I land this thing?" I beg him, ripping the mask from over my mouth. "Jack! We're gonna crash, Jack! What do I do?"

His eyelids flutter. He's clearly passing out.

"Jack! Stay with me! Tell me what to do!" I let go of his jaw, and his body slumps over in his seat. Fighting panic, I turn to the controls on the dash, the levers and gun between Jack's knees. He groans.

"Aaaagh! Jack! Help me!" I push the mask back up to my face and squeeze down the button at my throat with trembling fingers. "Mayday! Mayday!" I shriek. My fingers grasp the yoke, and I push it forward. Nothing.

Please! I scream inside. I pull backward on the lever, toward Jack's body. The nose of the plane lifts briefly before the whole system peters out. My hands claw desperately at the controls, which give me about as much response as Jack does: none.

I can't look away from the grass below us as we freefall toward it. We're going to hit. We're going to crash, right now. My muscles brace themselves, stiff as rigor as I wrap myself around Jack. The blur of the green earth transforms into individual blades of grass rising from the dark brown marsh. I'd scream if I could breathe.

Thud.

We hit the ground so hard that my brain bounces around in my skull, blurring my sight to a muddy darkness. I feel the tail violently swing from side to side as we buck over the uneven ground. Our bodies tumble forward as the plane jerks to a sudden halt. We must've collided with something solid. *A building? A tree?*

In the sudden silence, my ears ring as my palms search for Jack's skin.

"Jack? Jack," I pant, and I know that I've found him the moment that my skin makes contact with the warm wetness at his shoulder. My eyes strain to see, finding only dark smudges before me, but my nose registers the acrid burn of smoke.

"Jack, we need to get out. The engine is on fire. Jack! Listen to me! *Jack!*"

The door of the plane swings open, offering a blast of clean air. I turn my body toward our escape, but feel Jack's body sliding out from under my fingers.

"C'mon, Jack-o," the rescuer grunts. I crawl toward his gruff voice.

"Savage?" I call out.

"Oh, sheesh, how'd you get a *dame* in here? Miss, you've got to get out, now!" he urges. "The engine's about to blow!" I cling to his outstretched arm.

I tumble to the damp grass and claw my way to my feet, screaming hoarsely, "Jack!"

"I've got him," the other pilot assures me. "Get out of here! Go!" I hear him grunt under Jack's dead weight as I blindly stumble away from the plane. "C'mon, Sharpe, don't make this so difficu-"

BOOM!

My spine arcs forward with the blow of the blast, forcing me face first into the grassy soil. White-hot flames eat through the skin on my back, and all I can think is that if I'm this badly charred, Jack and Savvy have been completely incinerated.

A tortured cry rips from my chest. They're dead.

He's dead.

Jack is gone.

TWO

February 24th, 1942

I burst through the veil of sleep into consciousness, gasping hungrily for breath. With my body tangled up tightly in my sheets, I have to wrestle my hands free to reach out and feel for Jack's body. Beside me, his empty spot feels as cold as ice against the lingering heat of my skin.

I wipe a slick sheen of sweat from my forehead. A square of dim light from the window provides enough of a glow for me to realize that I'm in my bedroom in our apartment. I'm alone, and I'm not soaked in Jack's blood or coated in wet soil.

I swipe my hand under my collarbone twice to be sure, inspecting my palm in the dim light. My palm angles left and right as I strain to see the dark smear that must be there. It's not blood or dirt, but I realize that I'm completely covered in my own sweat. I can't seem to draw in a deep enough breath to satisfy my lungs, which suck oxygen greedily through my gaping mouth.

It was just another dream, the voice of Sense soothes me in my head. *Only a vision; it's all right.*

More like another nightmare, grunts the Imp inside me from her opposite perch. These voices in my head follow me everywhere as my closest companions.

It takes a moment for consciousness to fully take over, for my racing pulse to slow. I gulp the glass of tepid water on the night table, attempting to wash down the bitter taste of that dream. *How long can Jack possibly last in a war like that? How could I have let him go?*

Gulp.

As the sunrise starts to warm the windowsill, I realize that I do know one solid thing: worrying about this isn't going to get me anywhere. But I must do something with this nervous energy that vibrates through my limbs, and I need to hear from Jack.

Snowy fields roll alongside me in my peripheral vision, the morning sun glinting off of their endless white blanket as I steer my way toward the farmhouse. Jack sends his correspondence to me to the farmhouse as insurance that I won't keep myself lonely and cooped up in our apartment. In order to get his letters, I have to go home and visit my family.

It still surprises me how quickly I can get around in a car, as opposed to walking or endlessly waiting on the trolley schedule. Driving Jack's shiny black Mercury feels much like having a superpower. I pat the dash gratefully as I pull up to my old home, and the engine purrs in response before I shut it off. My sister, May, bounces through the rickety farmhouse door and down the snowy walkway before I can extract myself from the low seat.

"Hiya, Sis!" she chirps to me. Cautiously, her bright eyes sweep the snow-covered yard before her jacket sweeps open like stage curtains. She sticks out her chest proudly.

"May! Oh my, *May*," I giggle, savoring the burst of endorphins her stunt provides me. "You have a *bosom*."

"Finally getting somewhere!" She breathes out a sigh it seems she's that been holding throughout her pre-adolescent years. The plume of her breath in the frosty air punctuates her dramatic revelation, and her shoulders shudder from the sudden exposure to the chilly air.

I don't remember coaxing my chest to grow like my little sister does. I caught her once with a page torn from a ladies' magazine, demonstrating exercises that promised to '*perk your bustline!*'. Today, I catch her in a hug, and hear a soft crinkling as we embrace. May wrinkles her freckled nose.

"What's that in there? Toilet paper?" My challenge materializes in the cold air, a puff of steaming words.

May sighs deeply enough to depress her shoulders and her smile. The sparkle in her green eyes dims as she digs a handful of white from inside her shirt like a flag of surrender.

"Yeah," she admits with a deep frown. "You're no fun at all, Pene*lo*pe."

"Slow down, Mayhem. Growing up isn't all it's cracked up to be," I claim as we cross over the creaking floorboards of the one-room house.

"It's not *my* fault, P. Ma won't buy me a brassiere of my own, and the few you left behind are way too big for these disappointing little buds of mine!" She pulls at the loose fabric of the empty cup under her shirt. The perky point of the fabric sinks into an odd lump when she lets go. Now my own freckled nose wrinkles up.

"And Mama's underthings were made for nuns," she grumbles.

"Then how about you let your big sister take you shopping for a proper one? One that fits those 'disappointing little buds' of yours."

May's countenance perks back up like her single tissue-stuffed cup. She hastily arranges the handful of toilet tissue back into her empty one.

"Well, until then, I can't go lopsided, can I?" She examines her faux chest.

"You could just go bra-less," I mumble, but May looks stricken by the idea.

"I may not fill your cups, but I do have *something* blooming under here," she insists as we walk through the house and out the back door.

On the back porch, I start at the sight of more than a dozen people crawling all over the farm. "Who are all of these people?"

Hammers ting against nail heads in rhythmic bars where six of them seem to construct the frame of a new barn.

"They're the Victory Corps, P. We're war farmers!" she announces keenly.

My eyes go blank as I try to make sense of her words.

May sighs and elaborates, "Mac is leasing this land to Uncle Sam to grow crops for the soldiers. They just showed up this morning."

I follow her gaze to a stranger riding Ollie, our ancient tractor, through the snow in Tilly's old pasture. As he tears up her old grazing grounds, strips of dark brown, newly-turned earth contrast sharply against the fluffy white snow.

"Preparing for Spring," she finishes.

"Oh," is all I can say, surprised that something as unchangeable as Mac's old farm and his stubbornness have progressed. "They sure are early. They're gonna break that thing."

"Yeah, you should have heard the suits pitching Mac about making the switch. He stood there when they started with his arms crossed over his chest, a huge scowl on his face. All it took 'em to change his mind was a wave of some greenbacks under his nose!"

We laugh together, imagining Mac's mood swing.

"Now he brags to the neighbors about how he's doing this for his country! *'As a patriotic American,'*" May mocks with low brows, her finger under her nose, imitating Mac's mustache, "'*It's my duty to make sure none of our brave soldiers are crippled by hunger. It's simply the right thing to do!'*"

We laugh together. Every grumpy old farmer has a price.

"May, they're just kids!" I gasp as I take a closer look at the workers, spindly young boys straining to carry lumber through a foot of snow. My stomach turns.

"We used to do chores like that as kids. Remember?" she reminds me.

"Yeah, but we didn't have a choice," I say. Just as pictures of my young self wielding a shovel in the deep snow form in my head, Mama appears on the sagging porch with a half-empty basket of biscuits, and interrupts my flickering memories.

"Hello, Mama," I greet her, straightening my neck. My body seems to hold itself in regal posture around Mama, as if to prove that I am thriving with the mistake she thinks I've made in marrying

Jackson Sharpe, Socialite turned Patriot.

"Why hello, Penny. Biscuit?"

I choose one from the basket, still warm, and hug her. Bread is one of the only things that sits comfortably in my stomach these days, but I wouldn't dream of admitting to Mama that I feel sick more often than not. She gives me an extra squeeze before she pulls back. Her eyebrows shoot up in surprise.

"Hmm. Looks like your airman's salary is large enough to put food in your belly. You're filling out!" she comments.

Peripherally, I notice May cave in her shoulders and cross her arms over her enhanced chest. If Mama is this keen to a change in my body, May had better hide her extra padding under her winter coat.

"Thanks, Mama," I answer as I bite into the warm biscuit. A stream of eager steam escapes from it and rises in the cold air. "It's true, I can't count my ribs when I bathe anymore."

"And thank goodness for *that*. How is it sleeping in your own bed, all alone?"

"Cold," I laugh, and a shudder runs down my spine. "You two can join me any night and keep me warm!" Perhaps with my family snuggled up next to me, I wouldn't be plagued with such wretched nightmares. Even with a radiator in my bedroom, I feel fairly hollow without my husband's body warming the bed beside me.

"Until Jack comes home on leave," May giggles.

Mama's eyes grow wide as she pulls a face. "We wouldn't dream of that," she insists. It still seems strange to trust her happy opinion of my husband, as he represents my single act of rebellion against her. "You're welcome back here any night, Penny."

"*Every* night," May amends. "There's a draft in the corner. Guess you used to block it for me." She grins wickedly.

"Hey, speaking of leave, any word about Max coming home for R & R?" I ask hopefully.

Mama gulps and scratches her eyebrow.

"He'll surely be sent home for rest and recuperation when he wakes up, Penny." She manages to plaster an uncomfortable smile across her face, but her gaze drops to the ground.

"He's still in the coma," I deduce. Her nod is almost imperceptible. "He's in my prayers, Mama." I hug around her stone-still body. "Every day."

"Ours too, Penny. We just haven't had the best of luck with these matters in the past, no matter how fervent our petitions."

Daddy. Eddie.

"Say, why are all these laborers so young?" I shift the subject as a short young man runs out of the skeletal orchard. "They're like little puppies running all over the farm."

She takes my bait.

"All the fellas of age have been drafted to fight," she points out. "These 'puppies' are just stepping in and doing their part where they can."

"Oh," I realize solemnly. "They're here for their fathers." I would break my back in a field to ensure my daddy had all the fresh food he needed in battle. I would do it twice, no matter how sick to my stomach I'm feeling. My heart swells with new respect for these young boys. "Well, I hope you're at least letting them use the bathroom instead of the old outhouse."

One of the boys approaches Mama, and she extends the basket to him. He gratefully scoops up a biscuit with grimy fingers and tips his cap to her. His eyes flick quickly to May. A goofy grin stretches across his mouth before he moves along his way.

Young fellas. Teenage boys, pumping with newfound attraction to females, crawling all over the farm. And only one pretty teenage gal to zero all of their interest on, Imp whispers in my head.

Suddenly, the thought of my little sister's developing bustline terrifies me. I look warily to Mama, hoping for a reflection of my realization in her eyes, but she moves on with her basket to the other laborers. When our mother is out of earshot, I pounce on my little sister.

"May." Her name fires sternly off my lips in a puff of steam as my fingers hastily button up her jacket for her. "Stay away from these fellas, alright? They're nothing but trouble."

"Whatever you say, Sis."

I can feel her eyes rolling, even though her face has turned away from mine.

"What's this all over your mouth, anyway? Have you been getting into Mama's lipstick again?"

May scowls and wipes the back of her wrist across her lips.

"It's just beet juice, P."

"You're pretty enough without it," I insist, and frown. "Actually, that's what worries me."

My brows gather together in a scowl as I stare warily at the workers. Another curious young boy grins at my little sister as he saunters past us, his eyebrows wagging.

"Hey you!" I bark at him. "Eyes on your work, eh?"

The fella dips his cap over his eyes and skitters away from my words as though I'm a vicious dog with my hungry eyes on his rump.

"Sheesh! You sound just like Mama," May complains.

Good. I'm soothed by Mama's awareness of the unbalanced ratio of boys to gal here.

"I mean it," I growl. "And on second thought, Mayhem, just let these boys use the outhouse."

When I'm certain that every last ogling teenage boy has gone home for the day, I decide that it's safe to abandon my post on the farm as May's bodyguard. My keys jingle as I slide under the steering wheel and head home to my lonely apartment. All day, I've been eager to devour the sealed letter from Jack in my fist; however, I've learned that it's futile to try and have privacy with his words with May around. So, I'm headed home with a plan that includes my hot radiator, a steaming bubble bath, and the warmth of Jack's words. At the stoplight near the apartment, I unhook my binding brasserie in anticipation. My ribs sigh gratefully at their new freedom.

But when I step out of the car, I quickly cross my arms over my chest to hide my loosened brassiere from another of my building's residents as we pass in the common entryway.

"Hiya, Lottie," I call to my wild-haired neighbor, trying to appear casual.

She mumbles senselessly as she brushes by, and I'm unsure if she even notices me and my unkempt underthings. But before I release my arms, I notice my cousin, Claire, folded against my door, rhythmically bouncing the back of her head into the wood without regard for her perfect hairstyle. Tiny as a forest sprite, she looks rather delicate and helpless folded up on the ground.

Though Claire is my dear friend, our relationship hasn't always been chummy. For years, I'd assumed that after my dad died and her mother threw the rest of our family to the wolves, keeping the spoils to herself, Claire thought she was better than that bunch of her farmhand relatives. But I was wrong.

"Oh! Hello, Penny," she greets me, rising into her ladylike stance and smoothing the back of her hair. Claire is an heiress, and heiresses don't often sit in hallways.

I grimace as she hugs me hello, hoping that she won't detect my loose underclothes.

In my doorway, she doesn't move over the threshold in my small apartment. I peer into the front room, modest in size but filled with fine furniture, wondering what keeps her from entering. After too long, I realize that her finishing school training prevents her from sitting without an invitation. I roll my eyes, drawing a parallel between 'finished' gals and vampires, who both must be invited in before they can enter.

"Make yourself comfortable, Claire," I invite her, gesturing inside. "And I do mean comfortable. Kick off your shoes! Oh, and lose those gloves, would'ja? You make me feel like a regular scrub over here." I examine my naked hands, and touch my untamed mane as I drop into one of the cushy chairs that's more suited to Claire's gloves than the dirt under my fingernails.

"I have to admit that I released my girls from their shackles before I knew I had a guest waiting for me," I confide, shrugging. Sometimes its easier to accept you're just not proper than it is to try to keep up with the society gals. I slip my brassiere out from the arm of my blouse and toss it toward the bedroom. It lands on the corner of the rug.

Ever the lady, Claire pretends not to notice. But her body responds eagerly to my invitation of comfort, and she shakes off her jacket with haste. But when she perches herself daintily on the sofa, I scoop her legs up and swing them over its curved arm. On her back, she giggles freely, and her carmelly curls cascade off of the stiff cushion.

"Penny," she laughs. In her natural state, she reminds me of the young cousin I used to play with.

I lay Jack's letter carefully on the glass-topped coffee table, internally pining for the moment I can drink up his words. Alone.

"I just came from the farmhouse. There's an awfully nice toilet there now." After years of enduring my most private comforts in an outhouse, a good Samaritan mysteriously upgraded that old place from small wooden box with a hole over the ground to a fully functioning, flushing toilet. I heavily suspect Claire as the benefactor.

"Oh, that's wonderful, Pip." She twirls a strand of her hair around her dainty finger. The soft pink of her fingernail peeks out the top of the coil. "No more outhouse, then?"

"Yeah, someone just sent in a construction crew one day. May and Mama don't know who," I continue, my voice thick with false curiosity. Her gaze carefully avoids mine, alternating between the tin tiles on the ceiling and the mint green kitchen chairs. "They say the crew was sworn to silence. Or *paid* to it, I s'pose."

"My, how peculiar," she offers, picking at her skirt with her right hand.

"Yes, our generous Santa Claus doesn't even want the credit! It's so odd!"

"Mmm, strange," she agrees, chewing at her polished fingernail on her left hand.

"I'm just dying of curiosity over who would be so incredibly magnanimous as to fund such an expensive project," I say with pointed emphasis, purposefully trying to make my cousin squirm enough to admit her part in funding the bathroom a mysterious guarantor built onto my family's tiny farmhouse. "Plumbing from scratch, construction…"

She stiffens on the couch. I stop talking and stare at her, allowing the seconds to tick by on the mantle clock.

Tick.

Tick.

She gulps.

Tick.

"Oh, please, Penny!" she explodes, pushing herself up to a sitting position. "Stop that! You're making me ruin my nails!"

"What?" I ask, all too innocently. I've popped her silence bubble, and I like it.

She rolls her eyes upward. "I'd wanted to keep my hand in that a *secret*," she complains, running her thumb over her newly-ragged nail.

"I'm sorry, Claire. But, can I ask why you did it?"

"It's absolutely selfish, really. I did it… I mean, we did it; it was actually Bentley's idea, to soothe my own guilt."

My eyes examine my cousin quizzically. Claire didn't throw us away, her mother did.

"Ever since you told me the truth, anytime I'd see a toilet, I'd tear up. It haunted me, you know. An outhouse? *Hales* using an *outhouse* for all those years? It's *wrong!*"

In my opinion, anyone forced to do their business in a hot wooden box is wrong, wealthy or not.

"Kindness isn't selfishness, Claire."

"Oh, but it *is*, Penny; in my case anyway," she insists, pulling a nail file from her handbag. She holds up the pocket-sized emery board with a pointed tip. "Do you mind?"

"Naw, go ahead," I permiss, and she smooths the chewed edge

of her nail against its rough edge. A fine powder rains down over her skirt.

"Well, you know; Bentley and I were willing to try anything to help the, um, *baby stuff*," she whispers, blushing. "My doctor referred me to a psychologist. Please don't tell anyone." Her blush deepens into levels of mortification.

"I'm not crazy, Pip; it's just that sometimes, when a woman is having trouble with, you know… Well, the pressure society puts on a gal to have children can actually stifle her fertility; the doc said that stress makes a woman's body a hostile environment for a little baby.

"He said I need to clear my mind, and to relax about it; as though I need to build a nice cozy nursery inside me for the little thing. Calm, warm."

She blows away the dust around her nail and looks at me with her eyes wide. Seeing the confusion in mine, she continues, "A belly full of guilt is no place to host a sweet little baby."

"The only guilt you should feel is that you waited to build that bathroom until after I'd already left home. I never even got to use it!" My lips turn upward into a smile.

Her shoulders stiffen briefly before she realizes that I'm teasing her.

"How did Bentley feel about the expense of construction? It must have been substantial, Claire." I glance at Jack's envelope; lonely on the glass.

"Oh, that was his idea!"

Bentley? A Sharpe, loose with his riches? That sounds like Jack, who'd I'd always assumed was the black sheep in that household. Something a boy would do out of rebellion, which doesn't fit my impression of Jack's stiff older brother at all.

Apparently, my face reveals my skepticism, because Claire hurries in with, "Bentley would do anything for me, you know."

"Well, you know men. When a gal bawls to them, they go into shock and scramble for any solution to make it stop, right?" I quip, and Claire grins briefly before staring off into space.

"I think he'd give it all away if it would make me happy," she whispers longingly.

I admire her romantic outlook on her marriage, but I know that their union is a financial arrangement to benefit both parties, with two attractive faces pasted on the neatly-wrapped package. If either of them had been free to choose their own partner, then Claire might really know what love feels like. The real thing is a deep, abiding satisfaction that soaks into your very bones. I shudder as fresh thoughts of Jack tingle pleasantly up my spine.

I consider what she said about the pressure society places on a woman to be a mother. *Is that what's expected of me, now that I'm married? Am I a waste of skin if I don't bear children right away?* That sort of expectation rattles me.

Sure, I've always dreamed of having children of my own, and more recently I've dreamed of having children with Jack, but the dreams were always a projection of the future. The *far* future. I still have so much training ahead, and well, babies aren't often made when the would-be father is off fighting a war. We'd need to be together for that. I blush just thinking about it.

As if you've ever cared for the opinion of society, Sense reminds me.

I don't have any desire to do things the way someone else tells me to, but I know that Claire does. Being perfect in every way is required of her.

Claire huffs and sits up on the sofa. "Anyway, before you distracted me by raking me over the coals, I was going to tell you something." Her eyes brighten as though a lampshade has been removed from them. "Can you keep a secret?"

"That depends," I tease. "I write Jack every week, and I could really use some new material for him."

She scowls at me.

"Don't worry," I assure the wrinkle between her eyebrows. "The postal delay takes a lifetime anyway."

"You have to swear to keep this to yourself," she insists, her slim hips dancing to the edge of the cushion, where she sits regally upright. Her chin points down as she watches me from under her serious brows.

"You have your spit-sister's word," I vow, holding up my palm stiffly.

"I think I'm, um…" Claire's cheeks flush as her words trail off. "Sorry, I haven't said it aloud yet. I think I'm… I'm expecting."

I jump to my feet. "The toilet worked!" I exclaim in a squeak. "Your nest is guilt-free!"

Claire tries to contain her excitement, but it glows around her like a halo. "I suppose it did."

"How do you know?" I wonder aloud. "I mean, did the stork come knocking on your door with a notice or something?" We giggle together.

"No, no," Claire laughs, giddy; "my monthly bill hasn't come for ages. I wasn't even paying attention; I never expected this! We haven't even started the doctor's treatments yet!"

Hmm, I wonder to myself, digging up an old memory of health class and the signs of pregnancy. I've never had much of a monthly bill, or 'the curse', as some gals call it, but none of the underfed, skeleton-thin public school gals were really nourished enough to have a regular one anyway. Public Health mentioned something about iron deficiency suspending menses, and I have never complained about missing out on the curse!

"Bentley doesn't even know yet. Oh, he'll be ecstatic, Penny!" she squeals with a dainty clap of her hands. "I can't wait to see the look on his face!"

"When will you tell him?"

"Friday. I'm taking him to the very tip top of the Empire State building to give him the news. I was going to burst waiting that long, so I just had to tell *someone,*" she gushes.

"I'm glad it was me!" I beam. "And I promise, I won't even tell Jack."

"Oh, go ahead," she allows with a flick of her thin wrist. "Come Friday, I'll be shouting the news to all of New York City! He may as well know he's going to be an uncle."

"That's just swell, Claire! Wait a minute, hasn't Bentley been drafted?" I wonder aloud. Every young, able-bodied fella seems to have been plucked by Uncle Sam already.

Jack swore his mother would break her sons' legs herself before letting them into the belly of the beast, remember? Sense reminds me. Part of me wishes she had; Jack wouldn't be gone.

"No, we've been lucky so far," Claire shares.

"Well, thank goodness for that. Your little one will need a daddy."

"It's funny how having to wait has made me really want to be a parent more than anything in the world. I mean, I'll have to wave goodbye to my waistline, but who cares? I'll be a mother," she coos, her eyelids drooping dreamily.

"And I'll be an aunt!" I grin. I find that I'm truly happy for her. My eyes flicker again to Jack's letter on the table, as though attracted to another source of happiness.

"Well, I suppose I shall be going," Claire says, standing upright and fixing her jacket over her shoulders. "I've got to pick up some champagne for Friday's big reveal!" Another squeal escapes between her lips.

Carefully, I arrange my face in disappointment. "Leaving already, Claire?"

"Oh, I'm sure you'll want to be alone with your beau, there." She points her dainty nose toward the letter on the table as she pulls her snow-white gloves over her small hands.

My cheeks grow hot again; I ache to devour his words.

"You've been eyeballing that envelope ever since you came home. I'm sure I'd do the same if Bentley were away." Claire snags one of Lyla's crocheted doilies and stuffs it into her pocket before stepping into her heels.

"I think that's the last one of these dreadful things," I tell her as she moves out into the hall.

"Oh, just wait until Christmas," she grins over her shoulder.

"That woman has nothing but time on her hands to tat these rags! You'll be restocked."

"Bye, Claire."

"Goodbye!" she chirps, a new bounce in her step as she saunters down the hallway.

I feel guilty for celebrating Claire's departure as I run for my bathroom and eagerly twirl the hot water handle on the tub. Water gushes out of the spout and splashes against the white porcelain. As the little tiled room fills with steam, I ceremoniously set a glass of water, Jack's letter, and a letter opener on the soap tray. When the tub is half full, I slide into the silky water. A satisfied shiver rumbles up my spine as the liquid heat permeates my skin, and I roll the knob to 'off' with my toes. Water is my happy place.

Steam rising from the bath clings to the bathroom tiles, wraps around the belly of the claw foot tub, and curls the edges of the precious paper in my hands.

"To My Dearest Penelope,

Hiya, Darlin'! Happy Valentine's Day! You probably won't read this for at least a week, but know that I thought about you every second of every day today, the day of love. This is my favorite time of the week, writing you and letting our memories flood my mind. The diner, the creek, your hair, your face, the curve of your lips. I get to remember all of the things that keep me going; I get to remember my real life. I hate to be apart from you, even though I know I'm the one who gets to have all of the fun, flying a plane around all day, while you're stuck back in Saratoga.

How is your candy striping going? Are you a nurse yet? Ha ha. Hang in there, Doll. Your dreams are on their way. If you're reading this, it means you've been back home to the farm. Hopefully, sending my letters there every week helps bait you off of the sofa. I don't want you to develop a bad case of the lonelies."

Too late, I think. but a grin stretches across my lips. Even though he's away, he's still looking out for me.

"Home is great medicine for loneliness, and I miss ours terribly, Pip. I'm there every time I lie down and close my eyes at lights out. I see you lying beside me with your endlessly long eyelashes resting on your cheeks, your shoulder and hip forming a beautiful mountain range as you sleep. I can almost smell your strawberry-scented hair all the way over here on base. That is, until I breathe in and the overpowering scent of twenty pairs of boots brings me back to the bunk.

I miss you. I miss you so much and I am so proud of you. I'm proud of your training. I'm proud that you've been so brave. I can't wait to hold you again, and wake up next to you in our apartment."

Curse you, Jack! I scold him in my mind. I can manage just fine alone until I read his mush, at which point a lump balls up in my throat and tears prick my eyes. This is when I feel the most alone; when he reaches out for me through his words.

He may be proud of me, but I'm not. The only thing I want more than Jack and Max's safe return is to prove to Mama that I didn't stop chasing my dreams when I got married. However, it's hard to press forward when I only have a few good hours each day of a settled stomach.

I sink lower into the tub's soothing warmth, so deep that the short curls at the nape of my neck dip below the surface.

"They really push us in every aspect, physically, mentally, and emotionally in training. Why, just the other day after our PT (Physical Training), I just about lost my breakfast! Not that I would have missed it much; like I've told you, the chow here is not all that great. I'd do anything for one of your mama's hot biscuits with homemade peach jam. (Please excuse any drool marks I may have left on the page while dreaming of that). Sarge just keeps barking that we're not as ready as we think we are, and pushes us that much harder.

Tomorrow, we set sail as pilots headed to our first mission. If I told you where, I'd be thrown in the pen; even though it's all just guesses at this point. What I do know is that all of our planes will ride aboard a ship like cars taking a ferry. Perhaps the chow will improve with a little salty sea air! Hopefully I can find my sea legs for the trip, since it sounds like you've been vomiting enough for the both of us lately. The best part about the open ocean is that I'll get to take Missy out for a spin over it. Blue above me, blue below. I can't wait."

I smirk at his use of his plane's nickname, 'Missy'. He named her that just to tease me for referring to it as his mistress; he even painted the title across the tail of the plane. However, my superficial grin is just an accessory to the simmering fear deep in my gut. My husband is actually doing this; he's headed to war. There's a very real possibility that my nightmare will come to pass, only, I won't be there with him when it happens. While I soak here, it's likely that he's already halfway over the Atlantic ocean, careening toward the possibility of an awful fate.

"I've got to get to bed. We never know if we're going to get woken up at two a.m. for a six mile run! I love you, Darling. I'll be back before you know it. And as they say in the Force, 'fly low and slow'."

By the time I reach the bottom of the page, the tub water has gone cold. As I trace my damp finger over his signature, I hold his image in my mind. He's been away three times longer than we've been together since we were wed, and I fear that if he's gone much longer, I'll forget his face completely.

Come home quickly, Jack, I urge the image in my head. *Come home.*

The next morning, my nose wrinkles as I breeze through the familiar wall of antiseptic smell that greets me inside the doors of Saint Christopher's Hospital. I'm tired of letting Jack have all of the fun while I waste away at home, and I've come to push an official end to my sick leave. I crave the cold metal trays, rows of clean white bandages, even the cranky patients; they're the vehicle to my future career. Without them, I'm just some hollow shell of a gal, waiting, waiting...

Waiting.

"Hiya, Hale! Er, Sharpe... whatever we're calling you these days," Doris greets me, rolling her big brown eyes as she stands up behind the wide wooden hospital counter. With her cap nestled into her hairdo and her apron pinned tightly around her waist, she makes the candy striper's uniform look almost fetching.

She appraises me from head to toe. "You look like death!"

"Thanks, Doris. You've never looked better, yourself," I respond, shifting my feet over the green and white checkered linoleum and leaning into the counter. My fingers absently run over the nicks on the wooden surface.

"Aw, thanks, Honey," Doris grins, jutting out her hip. "It's got to be the new glow I'm sporting... the glow of George Quinn," she breathes, placing her right hand delicately on the countertop. Her ring finger is wrapped in a gold band encrusted with glittering jewels. A ring.

"You're engaged?"

"Not yet. This is just a promise ring," she sighs through puckered lips as she examines her wiggling fingers. She leans in and whispers, "I'm making him work for it! I've got him crawling on his knees, Penelope... but I'm keeping my legs crossed this time! I'm sure he'll be putting a ring on my left hand soon enough."

"Make him buy the cow," I grin, and she giggles in response. I'm pleased that in six short months, Doris has bounced back from Doctor Sweeney's ruthless attack.

"So, what are you still doing here?" I wonder aloud. Doris never was one for voluntary work, and she had only signed on as a volunteer here to troll for a wealthy husband. "A kept woman doesn't need a career, ya know. No use wasting your time here if George is a sure thing."

She sighs and plops into the squeaky chair behind the desk, rolling the ring on her finger in circles.

"I know, but Mama says that this gig gives me 'character'. And, Georgie likes the uniform," she grins, poking her tongue through her lips. "Anyhow, you'd better clear outta here before Adler sees you and puts you to 'verk'!"

"Too late, Miz Abernathy," Nurse Adler grunts behind her. Before I even see her stout figure step around Doris, I recognize her rough bark and heavy accent. Her beady green eyes sweep up to me, and she grunts "Miz *Hell*," which is her way of pronouncing my last name while asserting her opinion of me.

"I sink you coot use a little verk to perk you back up. It's being all alone en zet leetle apartment zet has met you seeck!" Her ample cheeks jiggle as she shakes her head at me.

"Well, if she's got something awful crawling through her, I sure don't want to catch it!" Doris claims, quickly snatching her hand back to her apron and wiping it. "Or the patients," she adds in phony concern.

Doctor Bodily catches our conversation as he passes, and stops short.

"She's right," he agrees, his handsome face clinical and emotionless. "Stripers are invaluable help around here, but not if they're spreading infection to the patients."

Adler nods to him with the familiar pinch of her lips that tells me she has changed her mind. "Miz Hell," she addresses me, "Do not step foot een zis hospital until you ah fit ez a fiddle, un-duh-stend?"

I nod to her.

"Not seeck et *all*," she asserts.

"Why don't you meet me in exam room two?" Doctor Bodily offers. "I'll give you a quick once-over, so Nurse Adler can have you back on board as quickly as possible. I'll just need to wash up." He winks at Adler. I watch the tiniest of smiles twitch the outer corners of her thin lips.

"Thank you, Doctor," I nod to him. Hopefully, he'll clear me to return here as Adler's minion so I can get back on the ladder.

Alone in the exam room, I perch myself at the end of the table and swing my legs. When the doctor enters, he clicks on the bright exam light, and I squeeze my eyes closed against its glare.

"Open up," he prods, and I obey by dropping my jaw. I gag as he presses a wooden depressor against my tongue. "Now say 'ah'."

"Agh," I retch.

The doctor chuckles as he removes the stick from my mouth. "That was good enough. Your throat looks pretty red and raw back there, Penelope."

"I'm been vomiting a lot," I tell him.

"So I see. Let me look in your eyes." He shines a small flashlight into each eye, and I try to hold them open as my eyelids struggle to squeeze shut. "Hmm, I thought yellow fever, maybe," he mutters as he turns my chin sideways in the bright light; "but thankfully you're not turning yellow on us. We'd have an epidemic on our hands! Tell me, how long has your vomiting persisted?"

"Several weeks. More than a month, actually. Maybe two months? Hang on..." I hold up my palm as I count in my head. I realize with shock that I've felt under the weather since November! "Four months."

His eyebrows rise toward his hairline. "Oh, my; that's odd. It could be influenza. Sometimes a weak immune system has trouble recovering from a bad strain, and one is susceptible to new diseases. I'm certain that working so closely with our patients has exposed you to several varieties of germs. It can seem like one long illness, but it's actually several overlapping; the body has trouble fighting them all off at once. Regular hand washing will help with that, you know."

"Weak?" I wonder aloud. I don't like being referred to that way.

"Well, you know... sometimes children from less, um, less-fortunate families develop health concerns from improper nourishment." He shifts uncomfortably while I absorb the label he has branded me with. Poor hygiene and... just plain poor.

"I'm afraid you'll have to rest until this passes, so give this to your parents," he instructs as he scribbles on a pad and tears off the top sheet for me.

I stare down at his hasty scrawl. It reads, "Bed rest required." 'Required' has been underlined for emphasis. "Plenty of fluids, and no duties for one week or until symptoms disappear."

Give it to my parents, indeed.

"Looks like you're going to live, Penelope," he grins as he ushers me out the door. He calls to Doris and Nurse Adler, "She's going to live!" and raises his hand like a magician.

"But Doctor Bodily, I'm here to train for a nursing career. I can't do that from my sofa!" I complain, stopping in the doorway.

He purses his lips. "I have a shelf of textbooks in my office. You may borrow them for your sabbatical if you promise to make good use of them," he offers. "Knowledge of human anatomy is essential in a healthcare career. This will set you ahead of the pack once you return."

"Thank you, Doctor," I murmur as we head back to Doris and Nurse Adler at the front desk. The books seem like a consolation prize.

"She'll live, but first she'll need a sabbatical," he informs the pair. "Perhaps the rest of us can do more to pick up the slack in her absence," the doctor suggests, slapping his hand on Doris's shoulder. Her eyes widen as she's thrown forward. I giggle under my cupped hand.

Doris's face sours and she sticks her tongue out at me. Though I'm disappointed to be stalled, the corners of my mouth can't help but turn upward.

Go ahead, Jack, I think. *Have enough fun for the both of us.*

THREE

March 15th, 1942

I toss a cold pebble over the icy river's surface. It bounces over the thin ice until it reaches the middle of the channel, and sinks down into the chilly depths. Three weeks ago, Doctor Bodily ordered rest and relaxation, and there's nowhere on Earth I can rest better than my escape from the world, the Spot. The familiar ground under me is cold enough to worm its chill through my clothes, so my bottom feels nearly frozen through, but the isolation out here relieves me of the pressures of expectations. Not even a bird or a squirrel interrupts the peace in the canopy of naked branches all around me. Out here, the rest of the world doesn't exist.

However, even the sound of rushing water an the icy surface does little to settle my nerves today. I haven't had a letter from Jack arrive since he'd announced his fleet's departure across the Atlantic. I'm not allowed in the hospital, so I can't curl up next to the radio and wait for a news broadcast. The papers have been dry of war news. As a result, my nails have been chewed down to ragged nubs, and I wake in a cold sweat several times each night when my nightmares send my heart beating so rapidly that I'm nudged into consciousness.

I send him eager correspondence almost daily, urging him to be careful up there in the air and to come home as quickly as possible, but each time I lick the back of a postal stamp, it feels as though I'm sending useless letters fluttering over the open sea. They fall to the surface, soak up saltwater, and sink down into its dark depths.

Mama assures me that the postal delay from another continent takes weeks, and I should relax. She's certain that several of his letters are en route to the rusty farmhouse mailbox. I have a standing invitation for dinner every night, and we all know that I'm there to check for a letter more than I'm there for company. My nervous stomach can't handle much more than a few bites anyhow.

Restless, I swipe the cold from my bottom and make my way back to the waiting Merc. Seven of the doctor's textbooks sit perched on the passenger side of the bench seat, already read and nearly memorized. I climb in and drive over dusty back roads to the farmhouse, throwing out my arm to keep the stack of books from flying off of the seat as I turn onto road that leads to my home. It wouldn't hurt to carry one or two textbooks inside so Mama knows I'm still on track.

As I roll past the old outhouse, I nod a salute to its aged wooden planks. A sense of satisfaction overcomes me when I realize, *I will never have to go inside that thing again!*

The spongy front steps flex under my weight as I climb to the door of the old farmhouse and push my way inside.

"Hiya, Mama. What's new?" I call to her as I stride across the wooden floor, full of nervous energy. "Any word about Max?"

"Yes, but it's just a quick note from Phineas," she answers, pulling a folded envelope from the pocket of her apron.

My heart leaps; *news!*

"You can read it if you like."

Eagerly, I take the wrinkled envelope in my fingers and dig a page from inside. Phin's scrawl barely fills a quarter of the page.

"Hello Missus Hale,

I don't know if the service is keeping your family updated on Max, so I thought I would send you a quick note. I write from his bedside, where he still lies without a twitch. His chest rises and falls, and his face has color, like he's sleeping; but the nurses tell me he still hasn't woken up yet. I've pinched him for you to try to help things along.

I visit him every day if I can, so I'll write again as soon as there's good news to report.

Yours, Phineas "

I sigh as my shoulders slump. "I sure hope we get some better news soon."

"You and me both," she agrees.

When I fold the page and slide it back into the envelope, I notice a small brown, shriveled lump inside.

"What's this?" I ask with the curious object pinched between my fingers. "A leaf?"

Mama shakes her head. "I don't know what it is, but smell it," she encourages. "It's divine."

I lift the mysterious item to my nose and breathe in. My eyes close of their own volition as a sweet, flowery scent fills my nose.

"Mmmm. Is this what their island smells like?" If only I could be there myself, drawing in deep breaths of this heavenly scent and shaking my brother's shoulders. I want him to wake up.

"I imagine it must. Without winter there, the plants probably never die," guesses Mama.

"Lucky fellas," I mumble, dropping the lump back into the envelope.

"Come here, Penny," Mama invites me with her arms held open. I embrace her, hoping my hug is convincing enough to hide my real motivation for coming home. I'm going nuts waiting to hear from Jack, and this is where his letters are posted to. Over her shoulder, I notice three sets of dishes in the sink.

"You had company?"

Mama flushes, batting her long lashes as she straightens her neck. "The Reverend stopped in. I felt obligated to provide sustenance for a man of God."

My eyes narrow into slits. "I think you like that 'man of God'," I tease, and she quickly turns away and begins scrubbing the plates with unnecessary force.

"Oh, please, Penny," she argues, shaking her blonde head back and forth. "You know your father will always be the love of my life, rest his soul."

"Oooo-kay," I sing, rolling my eyes. "I'm sure Daddy doesn't expect you to live the rest of your days alone."

"I'm not alone," she insists with a slender, stiff neck. "You and your brothers may have abandoned me, but May's still around."

Her dig sends my eyes rolling heavenward again.

"Say, where is Miss May?" I wonder aloud.

Mama's light blonde hair dances around her head as she turns her chin to me. "She brought out lunch to the Corps awhile back." The mention of the young boys reminds me of their appreciative glances at my little sister. "She should be back any minute, if you just want to... hey! Penny, where are you going?"

I allow the bang of the screen door to serve as my reply as I scurry out the back of the house. The cold ground crunches beneath my shoes while I track my little sister like a hunting dog. If I know her at all, Mayhem is up to no good.

The fields are empty. I find most of the laborers finishing up their sandwiches, staggered around on hay bales in the newly-constructed barn, but the only greeting I offer them is my focused glare as my eyes rake through them for May's freckled face and curly brown hair. Back outside, I search the orchard. The naked branches make it easy to see all the way to the back row of peach trees. A frustrated puff of air blows out of my mouth as I climb up the tree house ladder. I find the small space up there empty of everything except for half-melted drifts of snow.

"Gah!" I murmur and drop back down to the cold, hard ground. *Where is she?*

Nell's stall? Sense suggests, and I turn on my heel, making my way toward the wooden outboard structure.

Crunch, crunch, crunch, the dirt and snow under my feet sound. Just outside of the aged wooden building, I hear a giggle, so I quiet my steps to a slow creep. I pause, balancing mid-step on one foot, and strain my ears. Muffled words make their way through the slats and into my hungry ears.

"Only if you want me to," a voice too low to be May's purrs coyly from inside the stall.

Quickly, I shuffle to the entrance and peer around the corner. Nell stands lazily in the hay, oblivious of her two companions. A young man, no doubt one of the Corps workers, leans against a stall wall on one arm. The hay shifts below him, and I notice May in front of him, her back pressed up against the wooden slats.

What is she doing in here with a boy?

The boy dips his head down and leans toward her.

"*Mayhem!*" I grunt forcefully, startling the pair and the horse. Nell neighs and shakes her mane with annoyance.

The startled boy stands up straight and brushes at his shirt, mumbling, "Oh, um…"

"P!" May frowns, and her companion makes to scurry out of the stall. "No wait, Peter, you don't have to go!" Her brows gather sadly as she reaches her arm out after her companion.

"I'll catch you later, May," he promises as he escapes.

May throws her hands on her hips. "You just interrupted my first kiss, P," she grouses. "Well, what would've been my first kiss, if it weren't for my nosy sister!" Though her green eyes glare fiercely at me, her freckled nose betrays her youth.

"You really want your first kiss to be over a pile of horse apples?" I contend, comparing these circumstances to my kiss in the steamy alleyway with Jack. The strings of my heart pluck out reminiscent notes as that delicious moment replays in my head, in stark contrast to the sour smell of horse poop and ankle deep hay around us.

"Well, we were alone here until you showed up," May grumbles. "It was kind of romantic, being all by ourselves out here." She blushes.

"With a Corps boy, surrounded by horse fudge? Max is in a coma, May; I have to be the bulldog around here until he gets back.

What would he think of this? How old was that kid, anyway?"

May's face sours. "What's wrong with a farm hand? I'm a farm hand! You were a farm hand! Anyhow, Peter's not a Corps boy; I met him at the factory. And he's sixteen, if you must know. Hardly a kid."

"*You're* a kid, Mayhem! Wait... what factory?" I challenge.

"The steel mill. I sold him a war bond last week."

"You're moonlighting as a bond girl?" I clarify, my head spinning. Bond girls wiggle their hips through factories wearing huge, lipsticked grins and entice the workers to invest in the war effort by flashing their smiles. My stomach turns as I imagine May flirting her way through a factory. "Does Mama know about this?"

"Yes," she claims. "Well, no, not really. With the Corps here, I don't have much to do anymore, and I want to be able to buy some things of my own, P! You weren't very careful with the clothes you handed down to me, you know," she whines.

"Sorry," I offer, knowing that my tomboyish shenanigans were hard on those clothes. "Wait, those weren't mine," I insist, pointing to her very new-looking skirt and blouse.

May blushes as her hands smooth the fine fabric of her skirt. "Claire brought these by, along with a bunch of other outfits. She said she didn't need them anymore, with a baby on the way."

"Claire came by the farm house? Was Mama nice to her?" A spark of worry fizzles in my stomach. Claire can be as fragile as a bird's nest, and Mama's claws can be sharp.

"Yeah," May answers. "She better have been, since Claire brought the clothes along with a *real* mattress for us."

"Wow, she sure is laying it on thick," I mumble to myself.

"Now I can use my earnings for practical things, like a swell pair of heels to go with this skirt. Or maybe a handbag..."

I roll my eyes, but my chest swells a bit with pride for my little sister. She's forging her own way in the world.

"I just don't think war bonds are a good way to go about that, Miss Mayhem."

"It's easy money, P."

"That's not what I mean," I argue. "I don't like the idea of you using your figure to make a buck."

May touches her chin to her shoulder.

"So, you admit I have a figure?" she giggles, striking a film star pose.

I groan. *Mayhem.* I'm going to have to keep a close eye on this little pistol.

"May? Penny?" Mama's call sounds through the wooden slats of Nell's stall. "Are you out here?"

"If you say a word, I swear, I'll hide your next letter from Jack," May threatens, narrowing her dark-fringed eyes at me. "Or worse, I'll read it to Mama."

The skin from my hairline to my neck flushes instantly. Jack's words inspire a rush of such deep affection in me, I would be horrified to have those feelings exposed to my *mother!*

Oh, I love him. I miss him! I'd give anything for a morsel of his words, or better yet, the feel of my back pressed against his chest with his strong arms wrapped around me as he whispers his warm words into my hair, and they drip all the way down to my toes like warm honey.

"We're in here, Mama," I respond. "Has the postman come by yet?"

Mama shakes her head as she enters, oblivious to the deep scarlet shade of May's cheeks and mine, and saying, "You wouldn't believe it, but we have a post woman now. It seems every red-blooded male of age has been drafted!"

Except for the wealthy ones, Imp adds, and Bentley's face flashes in my thoughts.

My brows lift hopefully, reminding Mama of my question: *a letter?*

"She just came by, but there nothing from Jack," she amends, and my heart drops to the bottom of the ocean amidst my soggy letters. "I'm sorry. I hope you'll stay awhile anyway."

"Only if you tell me more about your visit with the Rev," I tease, forcing my spirits to stay light. I place my disappointment and affection for Jack just to the side, so she won't see them burning in my eyes and occupying my thoughts. We all shuffle sideways past Nell and out of the stall. I have to tell my knees to lift to make a step as I teeter shakily over a pit of anxious depression. *Why haven't I heard from him?*

I whisper to May, "See? There are respectable jobs for gals out there. You could even work for the U.S. Postal Service."

May grimaces. "I don't think the perks are quite the same, Sis."

"There's more to life than boys, May," I insist sharply behind my hand.

"Oh really?" she replies, flipping her mane of sun-streaked brown curls over her shoulder and placing a hand on her hip. "And how are you faring without your beau?"

I won't admit it to my little sister, but she's right. With Jack away and with no communication from him, I am indeed living just half a life. His well-being consumes my thoughts. Even when I leaf through the doctor's anatomy textbooks, I imagine every one of the pictured injuries on Jack's wounded, bloody body. I feel as though I'm teetering over the face of a cliff, the very edge of insanity, and the wind pushes hard at my back.

Against the warnings screaming "No!" in my head, I've decided to ask Jack's family if they've heard from him. I scan the backroads for familiar landmarks as I drive the Merc to the Sharpe's impressive home; the large green house on the way, the giant oak tree at the corner I should turn right at.

I'm not sure if visiting them means that I'm desperately trying to avoid falling over the edge, or that I've already tumbled down into the depths of insanity. No right-minded soul would willingly place herself within the reach of Ruby's venomous claws.

But the risk is worth it to me; I have to know if he's alright. My knees quiver as I urge them up the steps toward the grand, sweeping archway at the entrance.

The Sharpe's maid answers the door, her apron starched and gleaming white. She studies me a moment, barely stifling her surprise when she places my face. The last time she saw me, when I came to meet Jack's parents for the first time, I was a little more put together and glowing with sparkling hope all over my face. Nothing like the pale waif with stringy hair and a sheen of sweat and worry that I am now. She falters, unsure of what to do.

"Hello, I'm looking for Mister and Missus Sharpe?" I push through the lump in my throat. Thankfully, my voice sounds strong. I hope it will stay that way.

She nods and leads me over marble flooring toward the sitting room. Ruby Sharpe's exquisite home makes me feel as shabby as a vagrant circus worker in the midst of its blinding opulence, punctuated by the tiny sound of dirt grinding under my heels as we walk.

The longer my eyes drink in the details in the entryway, the more my ears ring with the sound of a cash register. Seven fresh floral arrangements placed around the two front rooms flanking the entrance: *cha-ching!* Two women on their knees, polishing ornate grooves in the woodwork: *cha-ching!* Five chandeliers, dripping heavily with brilliant sparkling crystal, leading down the entryway to the rest of the home: *cha-ching!* Deep, luxe rugs, commissioned portraits, fine vases, rare books, and an unmistakably precious painting of the swirling night sky: *cha-ching, cha-ching, cha-ching.*

In the sitting room, the carpet is so cushy and thick, it nearly swallows my feet in its pile. I sit on the very edge of the closest chair with ants crawling down my spine. My breaths become shorter, shallower.

I hear the staccato click of Ruby's heels on the marble before they round the corner, and my breath completely disappears. The set of Ruby's hardened lips tell me that her maid has given me away, and she's had ample moments to arrange her features into the sneer she wears now. Behind her, Mister Sharpe wears a vacant expression.

"Penelope," she greets me coldly.

Her husband nods his hello.

The chill of her tone washes me in ice. We haven't spoken since she blew fire at me in City Hall on my wedding day, and I ran from her like a convict. My limbs seem to freshly remember the hummingbird rhythm of their trembling on that occasion, repeating their nervous tremors here in her home.

"Hello," I begin, my voice wobbling over just two syllables. I stand as she enters. I can't remember if that's what you're supposed to do when someone enters a room or not. Maybe it's just the men who are supposed to stand when a lady enters? I make to sit down again.

"I... I came to--"

"As much as you'd love to waltz in here, uninvited, whenever you please," she interrupts with a voice as sharp as a blade, gliding across the carpet toward me; "...you are *not* recognized as a member of this family, and certainly can't just--" she pauses abruptly as her molten-hot stare shifts down to my left hand.

"*What* is *that?*"

"Dear, please," Mister Sharpe quietly soothes his wife, with hints of his soft southern accent riding on his words. "She's our guest. Let the girl speak."

"Hugh! Look at this!" she hisses, jerking my left hand upward for him to view. I may as well be a mannequin as she moves my finger in the light. The diamond sparkles in the daylight that tumbles in through the large windows.

"Your mother's!" she shrieks at him, her voice echoing with scandal. Her chest heaves, caving in dramatically and puffing up with each breath.

I try in vain to squirm my hand out of her grip. Her claws hold me very tightly. She huffs and sneers, vocalizing her disgust without words.

"Darling, I gave that ring to you, but you traded it in for something bigger," Mister Sharpe points out.

"I didn't trade it; I gave it to our Bentley as a gift!" she insists.

"Whose wife found the carat count unsatisfactory as well," he returns. "A cast-off."

"An *heirloom*," she corrects him. Ruby sets her mouth in a tight line, turning the accusatory finger back my way.

"The last time I saw you, you promised you weren't hoping to marry my son! Now look at you! Parading around town with my rock weighing down your grimy finger!"

I keep to myself the correction that the last time she saw me, at the courthouse on our wedding day, she'd chased after me and Jack with flaming pitchforks of anger.

"Ruby," Mister Sharpe says, but his wife doesn't seem to hear him.

"You are a slimy little gold digger of a girl, aren't you?" she growls through her teeth, wiped clean of all traces of the southern hospitality former Georgians should have ingrained in them. Her husband places his palm on her shoulder.

"Naturally she wears a family ring, dear; she is our daughter-in-law," Mister Sharpe replies in a lazy chuckle.

Ruby gives her husband a searing look, dropping my hand. I rub it to regain the blood flow where her angry fingers have pressed my skin ghost white, feeling the half-moon indentations from her fingernails.

Ruby hisses at him, a wordless lecture.

"*Daughter*-in-law? Please! That girl is not our *daughter!*"

"I don't need to be your daughter, Missus Sharpe. I just have somethi--" I try to interject.

Her fierce gaze swings back to me. "Whatever it is, the answer is most definitely *no!*" Ruby shouts as her husband gently restrains her with his arms. She tries to squash me with the weight of her anger, and I expand like a threatened blowfish in response, puffing up my ribcage.

"I just wondered if you had heard from Jack since he'd gone overseas."

Ruby's jaw bounces wordlessly as she absorbs my statement. "O- overseas?" she repeats, her eyes bulging out of their sockets. "He's gone over... overseas? To the... in the war?" she stammers.

Oh, I realize. Jack really has kept his distance from his family since they shut him out. They had no idea. I nod, holding my neck as stiffly as I can against the billowing force of her stare.

"He's a Naval Air Force pilot."

Her soft jaw drops. "You!" she growls, a shining sharp fingernail trained at my eyeball. "You let him enlist?"

Defensive anger bubbles up inside of me, spewing out through my lips. "He enlisted on his own! He's always wanted to be a fly boy! He is a person, you know. He can make his own choices," I growl back at her, for the first time feeling proud of allowing Jack to go. If it were up to this woman, her sons would be marionettes on strings and she the puppet master. She would simply yank a string to tell them who to marry and pull another to insist what they do with their lives.

"Clearly," she hisses in sarcastic agreement. "He made his own choice to run off with a milk maid." Her head drops into her splayed fingers as she shakes her head, radiating disdain.

You're a source of embarrassment for her, Imp giggles. This knowledge sits inside of me very uncomfortably.

"A fighter pilot?" Mister Sharpe asks.

"Yes," I confirm.

The corner of Mister Sharpe's mouth twitches upward before his brows crumple in concern.

Ruby's head snaps back up. "And you're here because you haven't heard from my son? How long has it been?"

"Three weeks. His last letter was posted just before they shipped out on the Atlantic," I tell them. The grim possibilities settle over the room with a thick silence. "I'm so sorry. I thought you knew. After... after the courthouse, I sort of thought you had eyes all over town, Missus Sharpe."

The silence breaks as Ruby chuckles.

"I had hoped that maybe you'd heard from him," I say softly, cowering.

Her tittering builds into maniacal laughter. "He's just... he's realized that he has made a huge mistake! He's not writing to you because he doesn't want you anymore! The thrill of the hunt is over now, Penelope." I grimace, and her eyes dance with glee. The lashing of her laughter whittles me down where I stand.

Are you just going to stand here and allow her to whip you with her words? Sense prods.

"I can see that I've wasted my time here. Good day," I say in parting, wading through the thick carpet back to the hallway. As my shoes click across the marble floor on my way to the door, Ruby's taunting laughter rings through the home.

You're just going to leave? Give that wench a piece of your mind! Imp prods me.

I open the large wooden door, and make to step outside, but a cutting comeback pops into my head. I turn back into the home and close the door. As soon as the wood settles into the jamb, Ruby's laughter stops.

"Oh, Hugh; what if something's happened to our boy?" I hear her say. If Ruby, so sure and confident, is worried, then trouble is at our heels. Her worry echoes in my chest.

I abandon my comeback, and slip out the door. I nestle it soundlessly into its frame and lean my back against it for support. My eyes search the clouds above me.

What if he hasn't written because he can't? What if he really is injured, or... dead?

Doris's breaths come rapid and angry as she sits rigidly on the edge of my couch. I set a glass of water on the table in front of her, and nestle my bottom on the other cushion of the couch.

"Your cousin is a real jerk," she blurts out after gulping down half her glass. She pants like she's just run a mile.

"Oh?" I reply as I settle in to listen.

"George *Quinn*, Mister Good-For-Nothing," she mutters as she shreds a handkerchief in her fingers.

"What happened?" I prod.

"Oh, I don't want to talk about it," she claims from under low brows.

"Alright, then we'll talk about something else. Tell me about the hospital! Have you run into--"

"*Apparently,*" Doris interrupts, and the words waiting in my throat fall away; "George thinks that I'll just hang around for years and years until he finishes college, and then we can 'think about where this relationship is headed'." She imitates his low voice with her fingers forming quotation marks in the air. "Like this stupid ring is going to keep me stringing along! Like I have nothing better to do with my life than watch him become a useless drunk like his father!" She wrestles with the promise ring on her finger, and tosses it into the corner. It rolls next to a dust bunny and falls flat on the hard wood.

"He's moving a little slower than you'd like?" I confirm.

"He's not moving *anywhere*. We're done," she claims while her nostrils flare rapidly. "I can't waste my best years on some creep who's too blind to know what he has."

Quiet seconds pass as her lips twist in and out of angry expressions.

"Well," I begin responding.

She interrupts me again, and I wonder if she would even notice if I slipped out of the room.

"Do you know what a no-good jerk that boy is? Do you know that he's just like his father?"

"His father?" I repeat.

She scoffs. "Exactly. Mister Quinn doesn't love anything on the face of the earth more than he loves the drink. And when he's drunk, he just leers at me across the dinner table like I'm going to be his dessert. Georgie thinks I'm crazy, but his father makes my skin crawl." Her shoulders shudder. "I mean, I thought it'd be worth it to put up with his dad because marrying into that family is like hitting the jackpot! But George told me that once, his father nearly gambled away their entire fortune, just for the thrill of it. It almost broke them! They would've lost everything, their home, their land, their *standing!* And the kids were so little at the time! Can I trust my future to the son of a creep like that? The future of my *children?*"

The dusty cogs surrounding my thoughts of the Quinns creak into action. I didn't realize that my uncle Harry was a sport gambler.

"And," she continues, "...you know that fellas put their best foot forward when courting. But if I do wait around and we finally get married, will he drop the romance and turn out just like his father? I can't risk that!"

I can barely hear her reasoning over the roar of my thoughts. If he'd driven Madge face to face with destitution, she'd become desperate for a windfall.

Desperate enough to kill?

Doris is in no shape to be questioned about this, but I've caught the scent of something that makes my mouth water with desire for answers. I need to know exactly when Uncle Harry gambled away his fortune. *Was it, perhaps, just before my father's "accident"?*

"Give George a break," I tell her, though I can feel the weight of dishonesty on my chest. "Why don't we all get together sometime and work this all out? You, me, Claire, George. I'd *love* to talk with him."

FOUR

March 17th, 1942

It seems that instead of rest each night, my mind must drag me through horrific nightmares, leaving me more depleted of energy than when I'd settled down to sleep in this lonely bed.

As I wake, I start to wipe the thin sheen of sweat from my forehead, but a knock at the door startles me. I groan; I don't want to pull myself to the door. Though it's just a room away, I still feel weak and woozy from this persistent strain of influenza, and an endless string of unsatisfying nights of sleep. The morning is always the worst.

The heavy rapping sounds again. With ferocious plans to give the annoying person behind the door a piece of my mind, I drag myself to the door on my knees, and stretch a feeble hand up to turn the handle. As the door falls open, a short, stocky man in a white uniform stares down stoically at me without any salutation, and my argument melts away in the face of the oddity of his greeting.

"Can I help--" I begin as I make to stand, but he shoves a long white envelope into my hand before I can rise, nodding curtly as my fingers close around it.

"Th--thank you," I call as he marches away, a little slighted by his impoliteness. He made me crawl all the way to the door, and didn't even say a word.

I watch him leave, tearing the envelope open blindly with my index finger. I unfold one white, thick sheet, emblazoned with the U.S. Navy's seal.

"Mrs. Penelope Sharpe,

We regret to inform you... missing in action... presumably deceased... please contact to arrange..."

My back bangs into the door jamb, and I crumple in the doorway under the weight of the message before I can finish reading. The familiar trappings of our apartment disappear as a fuzzy circle of white blossoms widen before my eyes. I fight the faintness.

No, no! This can't be. Wake up, Penelope! I must be tangled in the thick of another nightmare. This vision is merely the worry in me coming out to play as I sleep.

You're awake, Sense claims. I note the ache of my knees against the hard wood beneath me, something only a conscious person would feel. My nails dig into my skin as I pinch my arm.

No, really, this isn't just another vision, she insists.

I gulp. On my hands and knees, I lose control of my breathing and start to hyperventilate. My eyes can't focus. Strangely, I realize why the man had been so brief with the delivery of the letter. He knew what it contained, and how I'd react, and he didn't want to stick around to witness my horror as my world crumbles around me. Perhaps he's made that mistake before.

"No, no," I murmur, inches from the linoleum. Sweat beads on my forehead and lip while I imagine the terrible scene, just like I'd dreamed; only this time, Jack endures it without me squeezed into the cockpit with him.

Rat-tat-tat! Ping! A shower of glass rains into the cockpit. A bullet sinks into Jack's flesh with a thud; he grunts on impact. A maroon oval spreads at his shoulder; his eyelids flutter as he passes out. His plane spirals downward, his eyes vacant behind his goggles as his head flops over. The underside of the plane shrieks as it grates across the marshy earth and...

The nightmare I'd suffered through was real. The picture becomes fuzzy and dark, and the linoleum strikes my cheek as I fall into it; as I tumble into total darkness.

When I come to, my odd neighbor Lottie pats my cheek. Her wild hair is aglow, but it is hard to see her backlit face in my peripheral vision. I know it's her; no one else wears their hair so unkemptly.

"Penelope? Penelope!" she croaks urgently.

I groan. My cheekbone aches where it was squashed into the floor. The dread rolls through me, head to foot, as my fingers crinkle the paper in my hand. Tears spill from my eyes and pool around my cheek. I groan and roll onto my side. Thick tears hurry over my nose and down into my ear. My face feels swollen. My vision is fuzzy.

"Umph," I whimper.

My fingers extend the letter. She takes it, squinting at the typed words. Her eyes comb over the first line, and she gasps. It's a small sound, but it resonates through me like I am again hearing the awful news for the first time.

"Oh no!" murmurs Lottie.

As she melts with sympathetic grief, I rise to my elbow to comfort her. My mind tells me this is backwards, but my heart is fresh with anguish and longs to soothe hers. The curling tentacles from her head brush my face as we embrace.

Suddenly, my heart strengthens, encased with a thick protective shell and my weeping ceases. Though my ear still holds a pool of tears and tear tracks stain my face, I feel resolved to action. I stand, leaving Lottie kneeling in my doorway, and feel for the hook just inside the door. My fingers close around a key and slide it from its place.

"Sorry, Lottie," I begin. "I've got something I have to do." I follow the path of the cowardly messenger down the hall, but my steps are sure and decided. I am going to drive across town.

My surety wavers a bit as I drive, aching for the comfort of my family. The thought of facing Ruby again rattles my very bones. I have to will my hands to keep the steering wheel on track to my destination, but my resolve wavers much more than a bit as I stand on the grand front entrance of the Sharpe home.

I give the wrinkled letter in my hand a squeeze, though I am the one who needs the reassurance. I hope I won't pass out again.

The apologetic Sharpe's maid asks me to wait on the porch, and leaves the heavy entry door slightly ajar as she skitters away to find the Sharpes. With a sigh, I plop onto the top stone step. The thick white paper becomes translucent where my sweaty palms hold it. I wipe them on my skirt and smooth the paper in my lap. My legs bounce nervously, so I smooth them as well.

My heart continues pumping only on the tiny shred of hope that Jack is only missing, 'Missing in Action', but somehow still alive. It's such a dim thought that I barely register it's there, even though it serves as my lifeline.

Moments later, I hear Ruby's snarl escape through the crack in the door, "We haven't heard a word from our son, Sarah. Tell the tramp to leave!" The potted topiaries that flank the entrance shudder as the heavy door slams with a 'bang'.

Before I can collect the shattered bits of my pride littered across the steps, the door cracks and the timid maid pokes her head outside.

As she opens her mouth in dismissal, I shout, "Wait!" and scurry to my feet, holding out the wrinkled notice.

Her eyes widen as she absorbs the seal at the top of the page.

"It's a notice…" I pause. Her calm nod urges me on. "About Jack--Jackson. This letter…from the Air Force..." I stretch across the stoop and offer the damp, wrinkled paper. A fresh wave of grief washes through me at the sight and my tears spring up again, wetting the salty crust that lingers in my lashes.

Though I'd expected the notice to serve as my ticket inside, the Sharpe's maid nods a silent farewell to me and quickly eases the thick door closed. That's it. Ruby has what she has always wanted: I'm officially out of the family. No ties whatsoever to the Sharpe dynasty. Their heavy, ornate door has been shut on me.

Had it ever been open to me in the first place?

But even through its buffering thickness, Ruby's wrenching

howls penetrate the outside air. I marvel at the pity I feel for her. My body shakes as I turn to take the steps. Sobs rack my chest, and I trip over my feet, unbalanced. When I make it to the car, my eyes swim with moisture, obscuring my vision. Now that the task of telling his parents is complete, my heart resumes its painful breaking. I can barely breathe through the agony of my heart ripping into jagged pieces, and plopping into the searing pain of realization. It burns; oh, it burns.

I throw myself down toward the seat, misjudging my position and smacking my forehead into the metal frame of the door. Pain explodes through my skull, pulling the focus away from the excruciating torture in my chest. My vision goes black, though points of light flash through the ink. My bottom somehow finds the seat and I lean into it while a sheen of cold sweat breaks out all over me. In moments, I go unconscious. I let go and fall gratefully into the slippery, ink-black of nothingness.

The last thought I register before it all goes black is gratitude for the hard door frame, which has provided me with a break from the unbearable pain in my heart.

Thank you.

FIVE

Beep.

    Beep.

    Beep.

Rhythmic beeping. Soft shuffling. Noises that don't fit anywhere into the horror scene that's been playing on a loop in my head again and again: Brave Jackson Sharpe flying through a sea of enemy planes with steeled blue eyes, fighting with honor. Enemy fire hits his shoulder. He gasps, passes out, and slumps over the controls. Unguided, his plane careens toward the earth at full speed. The sickening crash echoes through my bones, followed by a short delay before the entire craft is eaten up in a bright explosion, destroying the remains of my husband. My husband, and my best friend.

    Beep.

    Beep.

What is that endless *beeping?*

"She's stirring," I hear. The female voice is unfamiliar.

"Hmmm," A man's low assent.

My eyes flutter. In the flashes of vision they allow, I can see that my body has been placed on a hospital bed. A hospital bed? How have I gotten here? I don't remember carefully laying my legs side by side under this taut sheet and thin blanket. I'm usually curled up on my side when I wake, not posed as delicately as a doll like this. My head swims as I try to place the reason. Bathed in sweat, I raise a feeble arm to my brow.

"Ha-ale," the female voice coaxes, taunting like we're in a game of hide and seek.

"Pen-e-lope," she says a little louder as my lids work to stay open.

I feel weak; woozy. Her fuzzy face swims in circles. I blink hard to steady it.

"There you are," the gal praises when I'm finally able to hold her gaze.

I can't place her face with a memory as it swims in circles before me. I will my brain to search for a name, but when my eyes finally focus on her head, I notice her cap and apron, and finally realize that she's a hospital candy striper.

"Hello, Hale, it's me! Doris!" the striper urges with a hint of annoyance riding on her words.

I stare hard at her and suddenly it makes sense why someone in charge of nurturing a patient would be slapping my cheek so hard. Doris will never be described as 'gentle'.

"Wake up!"

My eyes flit around, and to my surprise, Mister Sharpe sits in a chair near the bed.

"Nurse! She's coming around!" Doris calls toward the door.

Jack's father offers me a feeble, crooked smile when I focus on him. That smile reminds me of... Jack. Without his usual flat expression, the resemblance to Jack becomes so clear that I could see that even with age, Mister Sharpe is a knockout.

"Penelope," he greets me in his mellow manner.

"Mister Sharpe," I croak. Speech grates my dry throat. The sandpaper must be audible, because the nurse is quick to place a straw to my lips. The fresh moisture in my mouth is a painful pleasure.

Too afraid of the grating pain in my throat to speak, I allow my gaze at Jack's father to serve as my greeting to him. He's handsome, though wiry white hairs push through his brows here and there, and tired lines etch his rugged face. Perhaps Jack would've aged this well if he'd been allowed. I note his familiar sharp jaw line as he speaks again.

"Pip, Jack always calls you," he smiles. "Drives Ruby nuts."

My lips curl into a grin, matching his.

"Well, *drove* her nuts, anyway. Call me Hugh, Dear. You're a fine, brave gal for coming to us in person," his smile is a little sad as he looks down. "Even with crushing news."

"Wh--why…" I try to speak, but the sandpaper remains poised in my throat, ready to grate my vocal chords when I speak. I need to know how I came to be in a hospital. In a hospital *bed*. As a *patient*. I'm usually on the other end of things here.

He's keen to my unspoken question.

"Sarah, our maid, found you collapsed on the seat of the Merc. I think you passed out; you've got a nasty bump on your head."

The goose egg on my forehead throbs in response and I nod, putting together the sequence of events that landed me in this bed.

"Doc came by and gave Ruby a tranquilizer to calm her down; she was pretty hysterical. When Sarah came running in, I brought you here."

I smile at the kind man, feeling a rush of affection for him.

"Couldn't pass up an opportunity to drive the ol' Merc." Apparently he shares Jack's dry sense of humor as well.

I marvel that he'd enjoy the standard features of the car over the luxurious Cadillac, or the ostentatious Rolls Royce in front of his house when he purrs, "Vee eight," sounding just like Jack.

Doctor Rife enters, rubbing his clean hands together, with Nurse Adler trailing after him. He takes a perch on the side of my bed to poke and prod my head and arms.

"You've been out for quite some time. Almost three hours," he speaks in his clinical voice as he checks me over.

My eyes flit to Mister Sharpe. *Has he been sitting with me that long?*

"We've run several tests, though that knot on your head explains enough," the doctor continues. I try to look upward at my own forehead. He shines a small light into my eyes, lifting my lids. I squint counter-productively against the beam.

"Lab only got us two results back so far," he continues. "You definitely don't have scarlet fever, and, um…"

His eyes dart quickly to Mister Sharpe, and he raises an eyebrow before he tells me, "The other test confirmed your pregnancy. You don't seem to have any bleeding, so we are sure the fetus is just fine, despite the spill you took when you passed ou--"

"Excuse me?" I shriek, my raw throat screaming back in protest. My body shoots straight up with my exclamation. My feet muss the blanket with my jerking movement. I peek over at Jack's father, who looks surprised and bashful. My cheeks flush with color.

"Yes," the doctor smiles at our awkward exchange, "and you seem to be just on this side of four months… you weren't, uh, previously aware then, I take it?"

I shake my head and groan, slumping forward into my hands.

"Are you sure? Doctor Bodily examined me less than a month ago and he said that my illness was just influenza. How could I be… Doctor, my husband is deployed. I mean, he was," I sputter.

Doctor Rife's eyes skitter between mine and Mister Sharpe's, and I let my head fall sideways. I don't have the oomph required to convince the doctor that I've been a faithful wife.

"You must have experienced some symptoms, Missus Sharpe. Dizziness," he starts.

Yes.

"Vomiting…"

Oh, boy.

"Excessive tiredness…"

Check.

"Strange dreams…"

Like you wouldn't believe.

"Heightened senses, such as a keen sense of smell?"

Well, that explains a lot.

"Perhaps mood swings?"

I'm an idiot!

A nurse would have known. A *woman* would have known; but

even though I'm the poster girl for the doctor's pregnancy checklist, I can't believe that anything good and sweet and tiny could possibly reside in the same body as all the tumultuous torture inside me right now. Scanning myself for some tiny blip of sweetness within me, I come up empty. I am full to bursting with rancid agony; no room for fresh new life. Doctor Rife must be mistaken.

My heart pounds. My forehead beads over with sweat, and my breaths become rapid. And then, I throw up right into the doctor's lap. He jumps to his feet as my vomit tumbles down his pants. Doris and Adler rush over like doting servants to clean up the mess. Flustered, he continues speaking while they furiously dab at his pants.

"I see you won't need to take any pains to inform your, eh, beau here…" he gestures toward Mister Sharpe.

Jack's father and I begin a chorus of negating, and my blush deepens. This is the loudest I've heard his voice all day… or, ever, really. Doctor Rife's skeptical gaze bounces between us. His face, ripe with disapproval, clearly suspects some sort of shady affair between us, but he brushes it off. Mister Sharpe sure doesn't look like your standard soldier.

"I'll just change my slacks, ladies, thanks anyway," he tells his assistants.

Simultaneously, looks of relief fall over their faces and they immediately drop their cloths over the mess on the floor.

"Send in Bodily with a mop; he was the goon who misdiagnosed this patient," the doctor mumbles as he moves through the doorway.

"I'll send in ze janitor," Nurse Adler promises in parting. She and Doris leave together.

"I'm sorry; I'm sorry," I mumble into my hands. Vomiting is one of life's most humiliating happenings. You can quiet a burp, stifle a sneeze with your finger under your nose, uncomfortably hold back gas; but when your stomach decides to spasm uncontrollably to rid itself of its contents, it's a rolling stone that can't be halted.

Jack's father just witnessed it all, and he's still here.

What is he still doing here?

"Um, Penelope?" he begins timidly, reverting to my proper name to assert the distance between us.

I think we were both terribly embarrassed by the assumption that I've become pregnant by the senior Mister Sharpe. All of a sudden, I realize what he's waiting for. Ruby must have sent him to retrieve it, though his timing sure is rude for a man who was raised as a gentleman. I can only imagine her command: *Rip that ring from her filthy hand, Hugh! Chop off the entire finger if you must!* Weakly, I wrestle the wedding ring from my trembling finger.

"I suppose you'll want this back," I murmur quietly as I offer him the circle of precious stones. I sent Jack to war with the four-leaf clover charm he'd given me. Though I know that the charm and the ring are mere objects, when his father takes my wedding ring, I won't have any tokens of Jack to carry with me. "Being a family heirloom and all."

But Jack's father doesn't take the circle from me. He doesn't even twitch.

Maybe he was raised with manners, after all.

"Oh no, Penelope," he protests. "You are family as far as I see it. Jackson put that ring on your finger. It belongs to you. My mother adores you, so does--ahem, so did--my son. It's yours."

I slide the ring back toward my knuckle without breaking eye contact with him. He acts so radically different from Ruby that I find myself very interested in what he's like.

"I tucked the Naval notice into your glove box for you," he adds. "I imagine you'd like to keep it."

My eyes well up with tears. I can only manage a timid, "Thank you."

"You're expecting, Penelope. That's marvelous news! It's a lot to take in in one day, but I can't think of a thing that could soothe this old soul any better." He rests his palm over his heart, shaking his head slowly. "We've lost a son today, but we'll gain a grandchild."

I can't hear the sense in his words through the thick sludge in my heart, my head, my ears. We lost Jack today. We lost Jack.

Jack, lost.

A cold wind blows through the hollow of my insides.

"A grandchild!" he laughs, and his eyes shine with wonder. "A bit of Jack," he whispers, and tears spill down his cheeks. "You have no idea how Ruby has ached for a grandbaby. And now she'll have two!"

The thought of pleasing Ruby does little to please me.

"P!" chirps a breathless voice from the door. May rushes in, her cheeks bright pink against her flushed, freckled skin. She pulls a strand of hair from her sticky forehead as she hurries toward me.

"Watch out for the…" Mister Sharpe and I warn in unison as May's shoe lands in the puddle of my sickness.

"Vomit," he finishes quietly.

May hastily kicks the soiled shoe off of her foot and lets it drop to the cold linoleum. She curls up next to me on the bed.

"P, I've been looking everywhere for you! A messenger came to the house looking for you. I sent him to your apartment, but then Mama told me that messengers dressed like that can only mean one thing, a bad thing. She thought he'd come about Max, but then I realized, if they were only looking for you…" Her eyebrows fold with sympathy.

"So I hopped on my bicycle and rode all the way into town, but you weren't home! I asked everyone on your block where you'd gone, until your crazy neighbor told me what you'd said… so I rode back home, thinking you'd gotten the bad news and come to the farmhouse. Nobody there had seen you, so I came back into town and checked here…" She pants, searching my face.

"Is it true, P? Was it… that kind of messenger?"

I nod, and May squeaks in horror.

Mister Sharpe stands and places his hat on his head.

"I'll just be going, ladies," he whispers, nodding to us. "Give you some privacy."

"You don't have to leave, Mister Sharpe. This is my little sister, May."

She wipes her free hand on her hip and offers it to him.

"Pleased to meet you, Miss. I just need to clear up the bill with the front desk, and I should check in on Ruby," he insists.

My lips are frozen in place. I can only imagine which of the astronomical charges I'd often seen on patients charts was billed to my case. An emergent entrance, tests, admittance to a bed... Mister Sharpe is a generous man.

"Thank you," I mouth to him, not able to trust my voice.

"Please be in touch with us, Penelope. Don't let Ruby drive you off."

May strokes my hair until we're alone in the room.

"Are you okay?" she asks, her clear green eyes wide and waiting.

No. Not at all.

"I'm fine," I tell her, my voice warbling under the thin lie. "May, the doctor did a test, and he said that I'm apparently, um, on stork watch."

May stiffens. Her fingers grasp my face and she turns it until we're eye to wide, beaming eye.

"You're going to have a baby?" she squeaks, hopping onto all fours over me. The thin bed frame rattles underneath us as she bounces excitedly.

"May, we're going to roll away if you don't stop that."

"But, I'm an aunt? I'm an *aunt!*" Her head looks as though the glee inside of it will explode any second, her eyes blind behind the thick blizzard of sparkles in them. She hops up and down on her knees, jiggling my limp arms with joy.

"And Mama's a grand... does Mama know? I'll go home and get her!" she promises, bolting upright off of the bed.

"No, May, please," I beg, gripping her wrist.

"Come on, Sis! She'll want to know the big news right away!" She pulls stubbornly against my grip. I have no doubt May will have the news in every paper and written in the sky before I'm released from the hospital if I don't restrain her now.

"May, I'm still absorbing the idea myself. Please, just let me be the one to deliver the news to Mama, okay?" I force my face into the most pathetic expression I can muster, which turns out to be similar to my current expression.

"O-*kay*," she reluctantly groans, surrendering onto my pillow like a falling corn stalk. "Can I please be there when you tell her, at least? Please, P?" I can't imagine that the news will be as bright and cheerful to Mama's ears as it is to May's, but I nod in agreement anyhow.

"Fine, Auntie Mayhem. You can be there."

"I'm an *aunt*," she breathes again. "Will you name your baby after me? May for a girl, of course, and May...son for a boy? Mason?" She blows upward, sending a lock of hair flying off of her forehead. She crinkles her freckled nose, and I see a thought bouncing around behind her eyes.

"Wait, P, are you saying you're actually surprised about this? I mean, I hummed as loud as I could through Mama's explanation of the birds and the bees, but even I caught that, um..." She pauses as her eyes sweep the room, and her voice drops to a faint whisper. "...making whoopie will make a baby. Are you thick or something?"

But you took preventive measures. And you were examined, Sense protests. *Mislead.*

"May," I remind her gently. "My husband is dead." I wince at the stinging in my eyes as they fill with thick tears.

"Oh, sorry, Sis."

I feel bitter at this spoiled moment. A gal's first child should be joyous news to spread. It should have been joyous news for me to learn.

The janitor's rolling mop and bucket rumble over the linoleum into the room.

"Hiya," May greets the old man. "Say, is she okay to leave now? Can we go home? Bill's paid and all." I can feel the wattage of her dimples turned all the way up, even though she's turned away from me.

The janitor bares his slimy teeth in a return grin.

"I ain't no doctor, Miss," he answers, chuckling. "But I think your man just paid for another day's stay. Ol' Addie was selling him some line about head injuries requiring a full night of observation." The odor of hard liquor grows stronger with every word from his lips.

"Okay, thanks," May replies, dimming.

"Cheer up, little Miss, I'll be done here in a jiff." The thick wet mop plops onto the ground with a splat. The janitor barely wrinkles his nose as he cleans the floor.

May brightens again. "Say, if we have to stay here all night, would'ja mind flipping off the light as you go?" she coaxes. "So we can catch a little shut-eye?"

"Not before I get you an extra blanket, little Miss," the janitor answers, stumbling a bit as his knobby fingers carry a folded blanket from the empty bed across the room to her.

"I'm forever grateful," she beams to him, throwing the extra blanket over herself and nestling into my shoulder. The janitor wears a goofy grin as he rolls the bucket out the door.

The room goes dark. We lie in silence as the squeaking of the bucket's wheels fades into the distance.

"You don't have to stay here with me, Sis," I whisper in the darkness. Part of me wants to be alone, but the other part knows I'll crumble to ash the moment I am. I need my little sister right now.

"I wouldn't want to be anywhere else," she purrs into my shoulder. It could maybe feel similar to cozying up in our old bed, if it weren't for the bizarre truths this day has revealed; one bleak and terrible, the other beautiful and terrifying.

I've become a widow, and a mother. All in the same day.

Every hour, an unwelcome nurse comes to pry open my sleeping lids and shine an overly bright light into my pupils. I can't help but begin to plan each of their gruesome murders in my head as I'm torn from the peaceful comfort of sleep- I'll heave that nurse in front of a speeding freight train; the next will die of strangulation under my vengeful fingers--and then I'm abruptly left in the dark with my vile plans when they leave. I'm barely conscious of the fact that my anger over losing Jack is being funneled toward these innocent women.

"Have I proven that I'll stay alive yet?" I mutter to one of them in the dead of night. "I know I'd rest much better at home."

"One more hour of observation is required," the nurse whispers back. "Then you're free."

This one can stay alive, I mentally allow.

I silently vow that once I'm granted this freedom, I'll do anything to keep out of harm's way so I'll never have to submit to this cruel torture again. Being a patient is really no better than being a prisoner.

As soon as I drift to sleep, an irritating noise yanks me back toward consciousness.

"Hell," Adler whispers. "Hell, vake up. I net to check your pupils."

I rub my eyes and pry my eyelids apart. They grate over my scratchy eyeballs uncomfortably.

"I'm afraid de grapevine moves qvickly in dees place," she reveals. "You've been fired, so eet seems."

I grimace as I swim through a sleepy cloud to grasp her words.

"But... what? I'm not even paid! How can a hospital fire a volunteer?" I grumble.

"You ah a liability now, as you ah on the nest," she explains. "Zis hospital does not vant to be responsible for harming a voman who ees expecting. But not to vorry, ve vill git by; ve've done vithout you for some time now." She cracks a grin, and the ample apples of her cheeks gather. "Eet seems you veren't riddled vith disease, after all."

My eyes fall to the metal grate in the center of the room, a small drain dimly lit by the light from the hallway, and I watch my future circle around it. My hopes, my dreams, and my plans sink through the grate; lost.

"Harumph," I grunt. This has been a horrible day.

Adler gently lays her hand on my belly. "I know dees feeling. It feels like disease, doesn't eet?" She has my attention. Nurse Adler has never mentioned having a child; I'd assumed that this hospital was her only love in life since her husband died.

"Beck en Germany, I vaz ripe vith child seven times," she murmurs with glazed eyes. "Christoph vas alvays so happy; so hopeful. But zeh leetle ones vere alvays too eager to arrive." Her shoulders rise and fall in a heavy sigh. "Zey jest came too early to thrive."

"I'm so sorry, Nurse Adler."

"Four months vas the longest I carried a child. Zet chart says you ah nearly zere, so I'm sure zis child vill stay right vere eet shoult."

She pats my belly again. My eyes fill with hot tears, a liquid manifestation of the overwhelming turns today has taken. I've lost my husband, I've learned I'm expecting a baby in just five months, and I've been fired from the hospital; fired from my dreams. My world has imploded in a day's time.

Her eyes flicker to May, but it seems that not even the rigid Nurse Adler can stomach kicking out my stowaway visitor.

"Aw, cheer up, Hell. You hev better things to think about now than clearing bedpans and spooning gelatin! You shouldn't vaste your time vith zese trifles ven you vill be very busy for several decades. Your nursing career vill just have to vait."

Being a parent has always been my dream, of course, but that dream included a husband. If parenthood is the gift that everyone claims it is, then this gift is incomplete. Like getting only one shoe, it's completely useless on its own! *How can I walk straight wearing only one? How can I possibly maneuver through life without Jack by my side? How can I raise this child all alone?*

I blink as I stare into the nothingness of my future.

Your mother seemed to do alright with a bunch of left shoes, pipes in Sense. I suppose that depends on one's definition of 'alright'. I'm sure that even Mama would agree that raising four children on her own, hand to mouth, was never how she had dreamed her adult life would play out.

"I suppose it will," I agree, forcing my lips to turn upward in a false smile.

Her cheeks gather again into a grin before she takes her leave.

When I've convinced the doctor that I'm fit to check out, I rouse May just enough to get her to move her own feet out the doors and into the car. Under the weight of all of these new revelations, I can't possibly carry her, as well. She shuffles alongside me with her arm draped across my shoulders, too dozy to insist we hail a cab.

"Auntie May," she slurs sleepily as I drop her into the passenger seat of the Mercury.

Once I sit behind the wheel, I take new notice of the slight bulge below my belly button. *Expecting*, ha! I'd thought I was just well fed.

You're in no shape to drive, Sense warns me.

I pull the Navy's letter from the glove box and press it to my chest, deciding to ignore her. I will my eyes to keep themselves propped open for one short ride to the farmhouse. Under the inky cover of night, I'll have to rely on the yellow glow of the Merc's headlights on the road to find my way home.

May slumps against her door. I shake my head at her; Sleepyhead. Without her chirping to keep me awake, I find my own eyes fluttering, heavy with exhaustion. After a long blink threatens to steal me from consciousness, I have to pull the steering wheel hard to the right to straighten out on the road. I shake my head. *Keep it together, Pip. We're almost there.*

Dangit! Red and blue lights flash behind me, bright against the dark nothingness in my rearview mirror. *Can't a gal make one mistake while driving without getting caught?* I sigh and pull onto the muddy snow on the side of the road with new adrenaline holding my eyes open.

"I thought I recognized this old heap," says the officer as he kicks the back tire. It's Officer Dalton, Jack's old buddy who'd ratted us out to Ruby on our wedding day. He drapes himself over the window with a toothpick playing between his lips.

"Hello, Officer Dalton. You sure have the ache for flipping on that siren, don't you?" I reply in a hushed voice, hanging my head halfway out the window so as not to disturb my little sister.

"Keeping the peace, Ma'am. Keeping the peace. Can't have inebriated women swerving all over the road, can we?"

I wipe both my eyes. "I'm not drunk, just exhausted."

"Hmm," he smirks, flipping the toothpick in his lips. "Just as bad, seems."

"If I could just borrow that toothpick, it could hold one of my eyes open for the rest of the drive," I joke, just before a yawn arrests my face. "Actually, I'm glad to run into you, Dalton. I wanted to thank you for your beautiful music at my brother's funeral. I'm sure you can imagine I was in no state at the services to offer my gratitude." I gulp down the memory. "But it was very nice. Soothing to our weary souls that day."

Sickly, I realize that I'll be attending another funeral soon.

He smiles. "All those music lessons ought to be worth something, I s'pose."

"Speaking of worth, may I ask, Officer Dalton… I mean, Jack had given me the impression that your family was quite well-to-do. It just makes a gal curious why you'd be working a night shift instead of… well, I don't know…"

"Instead of staying at home, counting my gold coins?" He smiles.

"I was thinking, sleeping soundly under your quilt sewn from hundred dollar bills, actually," I quip.

"Well, Missus Sharpe, can I show you something?" He gives May's sleeping form a quick glance.

May's lids flutter a bit, and I slip out into the night air as quietly as I can manage, barely nestling the car door into the jamb. I steady myself on the Merc in its cold, slick tire tracks.

Dalton digs into his pocket, retrieving his wallet. He pulls out a photograph.

"This is my family," he explains with the beam of his flashlight illuminating the photo. Two smiling parents stand regally over a herd of children. "Guess which one's me?"

I poke at one of the blonde heads in the crowd.

"No, Ma'am; that's my older brother. That's me," he says, pointing to a much younger boy. "I've got four older brothers, see. My father is in investments, which can be tricky business after the crash."

I nod in agreement.

"Not too many of those gold coins around these days. Those that have 'em, well, they don't want to let them out of their sight. My brothers are in the family business, but my father says I'm much more useful to him as a man of the law."

He raises his brow suggestively. I shake my head, until the meaning pops into my head, and I gasp.

"Is your father doing something… illegal?"

He stares at me. Without expression, he flatly offers, "No. Never." His words ring false, because his eyes speak so much louder. His look suggests that Dalton is the pawn that runs interference between his father's illegal dealings and the law. Policeman are respected members of society, aren't they? At least, they should be.

I pull away from him, but he catches my arm in a tight grip.

"I'm sure you won't run off telling people what you think you know, now, will you, Kitten? 'Cuz folks want to believe a lawman before they believe some scrub gal crying wolf all over town."

"I don't care that much about you, Dalton; I have bigger things to worry about. I wouldn't waste my breath." My skin crawls where he touches me.

"Oh, but you've got nothing but time right now, don't you? Waiting for your fella to fly one of them planes back home to his ol' lady?" With his hand free, he grabs my other arm.

"Let go of me, you creep," I snarl, squirming under his grip.

He shoves my back against the Merc and leans his head in so that his words are a hiss in my ear.

"C'mon now, Kitten; now that you've had a taste of a man, and he's been gone *oh so long…*" He presses his wet lips against my neck.

I cringe, freshly remembering my unwelcome attack by the creep in the alley who'd been after Nurse Adler, and wrapped his slimy self around me as his hostage. Only, out in the backroads of town under the cover of darkness, Dalton isn't playing to an audience; he's playing for himself. With double the revulsion I'd felt back then, I shove him away.

"Okay, okay, Sweetness. I can take a hint," he chuckles, unfazed.

The clammy skin of my face meets the cold air uncomfortably as I swoop back down into the car, moist from our struggle.

"You creep!" I spit at him. "I will report you," I vow through my clenched teeth. Dalton just laughs, sauntering back to his cruiser in the dim yellow glow of his headlights.

May's sleeping head rocks as the car bumps up over the edge of the asphalt and onto the road. I press the pedal all the way down to the floor, and peel away from the dirty snow on the shoulder with my fingers clamped around the steering wheel.

She stirs.

"You okay, Sis? If you're falling asleep, I can drive," she offers sleepily, yawning.

"Oh, I'm wide awake," I declare, fuming behind the wheel. I hope she won't notice in the near-darkness how my body trembles with belated adrenaline.

The sun's glow just barely begins to hint in the eastern sky as I pull up to the farmhouse. The song of every rooster on the block floats on the morning air when I crack the car door.

Mama rushes out the front door to us, clearly wide awake.

"Oh, thank goodness, Penny!" she exclaims when I stand, and wraps her arms around me. "We've been so worried!"

"We?"

"Yes, *we.* When I saw that messenger here, I fetched Reverend Bell. Are you all right? What's happened to you?" She palms my cheeks as her large eyes inspect my face. "That's a nasty bump on your pretty forehead!" Her long fingers slide down to my wrists.

"Hiya, Mama. Hello, Reverend," I call to the serene man standing in the farmhouse doorway.

"Hello, Penelope." His nod and wave are small; humble.

"Will you unravel the mystery for me already, Penny? What's happened to you?" Mama coaxes. In the sincerity of her eyes, I fold like a small child and lean into her chest for support. "Your cheeks are so blotchy, Dear."

A young farm laborer rounds the house and tips his hat to May. An eager smile breaks out across his face as she blushes and smooths her hair. I break away from Mama's soothing arms and charge at the boy like an angry bull.

"You stay away from my sister, do you hear me? Stay away!" Angry tears well up in my eyes, blurring the confused boy's face as he slinks back. With the fresh recollection of Officer Dalton's slimy fingers running over my body, I have no patience for the appreciative leering this fella has for my little sister. "Don't you lay a hand on her!" Panting, I feel a large, gentle hand rest on my shoulder.

"Let's move inside, shall we? Your mother made tea," Reverend Bell coaxes.

"Okay," I agree, wiping my eyes and using my clear vision to shoot one more nasty look at May's admirer. "I told you to stay away from those doll-dizzy saps, May!"

"You may have noticed that the Hale gals don't exactly do as they're told, Penny," Mama laughs.

The Reverend smiles at her, and turns his kind eyes to me.

"I get the sense that not everything is right in your world, Penelo--" he starts.

Mama cuts him off. "*Penny.* She hates Penelope."

"My apologies, Penny." He whispers behind his hand, "My first name is Herman, so you can see how I was so eager to change it to 'Reverend'. I can understand a certain amount of unrest with your proper name." He coaxes a small smile from my angry mouth. "War is a troubling time for many. I'm sorry to hear that its trouble has fallen so greatly upon you."

I nod in reply as he pats my hand.

"I hope you'll stay for breakfast, Reverend. We have bacon," coaxes Mama with a singsong voice and wagging eyebrows.

Bacon? We've never had bacon around this table.

"Then thank goodness I'm a Reverend, not a Rabbi!" he grins as he settles into a creaking chair. The wrinkles around his eyes fold happily. "Meat from an animal with a cloven hoof would be considered unclean to consume."

"This old farmhouse seems to be turning into the Ritz Carlton Hotel in my absence," I mutter in the wake of his quip.

"The government sends crates of food here to feed the workers," May explains, yawning widely enough for us to peer all the way down her throat. "The most deliciously dirty bacon you've ever had, Rev. Wake me up when it's ready." She disappears behind the hung sheet that conceals the upgraded bed from Claire.

"Ahem, may I, um, use the facilities?" Reverend Bell asks. Mama smiles her assent.

"Have you been up all night, Mama?" I ask when we're relatively alone.

"Yes, I've been worried. I almost climbed behind the wheel of that thing to come and find you," she scoffs.

"The tractor?"

"No, the car that Claire gave to us," she clarifies. "That was only Tuesday; I guess you haven't been by since then to hear the news."

"Claire gave you a *car?* A whole car?"

"Why yes, Penny," Mama affirms as my mind blows. "Her husband bought her a new one, and so she passed her old one along to us. She has been quite generous to us of late."

I'll say. The bathroom, clothes, a mattress, a *car.*

"Though, I haven't driven a car in so long that I've forgotten how. That's why I called on Reverend Bell; he's the only soul I thought I could disturb before the break of dawn, and I needed someone to man the wheel."

"Oh," I whisper, trying to wrap my head around the idea. "Well, you can join May for a catnap. I'll cook breakfast," I offer, though the mention of raw, fatty meat sends my tender stomach rumbling. However, if I don't do something with my shaking limbs, I worry that my despair will swallow me whole. I gulp down the rising lump in my throat and sink into a wobbly chair at the battered kitchen table, my head dropping into my hands.

"Penny," she replies gravely, waving away the thought of breakfast with her hand. "What's happened?"

Pictures flash through my head, coupled with emotion: My annoyance at the messenger, losing my breath when reading the notice, being rejected on the Sharpe's doorstep. The discomfort of the hospital, the depth of my anguish. The grease-slick blonde hair on Dalton's head, the dirty grin he wore, his body forced up against my back.

My eyes go glassy with these thoughts, but I don't realize it until I feel the light pressure of a hand on my shoulder.

"Penny?" she breathes. "A man came here; did he find you? What did he say?" Her voice is soft, soothing; motherly. I stand here, stunned, as my mind heaves yesterday's revelations to the forefront of my mind, stifling Dalton's attack.

"He…" I begin. "He didn't say anything at all." He was silent, as silent as Death.

My fingers find the folded letter in my pocket. I offer it to Mama. It crinkles just as I did when I opened it, when I naively dived into this dark place of loss. That piece of paper has changed my world.

Her clear blue eyes widen, and a look of dread mars her pretty face.

"Oh!" she gasps, folding herself into a rickety kitchen chair as the notice floats toward the grey floorboards. Her hand cradles her heart. "Oh, Penny."

Her rough, beautiful hands reach out for me, and I fold my adult body into the size of a child's in her lap. My face rests at her neck, her collarbone, her chest. Her fingers smooth over my hair, again and again as we rock gently. "I'm so sorry, my darling girl. I'm so sorry."

When the slick tear tracks on my face slide against her wet neck, I sit up.

"Mama, there's more. It seems I'm, um, *expecting*..." I feel her body tighten. She swallows. "...a baby. And its father is dead."

She nods, pulling me back to her, and I muffle my sobs with her skin. I don't want to raise a child like Mama had to raise us.

"I've known for months, Penny," she whispers. "I wanted to let you be the one to tell me, once you figured it out for yourself."

"What am I going to do?" I cry.

I feel her swallow a thick lump in her throat. It moves against my cheek.

"You can move back home. We'll help you raise this child right here in this house; nothing we haven't done before." She looks to the walls appraisingly.

"I don't want to be a burden here, Mama."

"Well, Honey, I'm afraid you don't have much choice in the matter anymore."

I draw myself away from her.

"You made your bed when you married that boy," she teases lightly.

"I didn't want him to *die*, Mama," I defend. I sniff and wipe under my soggy eyes.

"I know that, Dear. I'm just saying…"

"Just saying 'I told you so'?" I stumble to my feet to break our close contact.

"Perhaps I am, Penny," she returns, looking perplexed by our sudden explosion.

"Oh, so you're pleased that things didn't work out, aren't you?" I sneer, holding my palm at my leaky nose.

"I did not say that," she claims, her neck stiffening.

"Oh, it didn't need to come out of your mouth, Mama; it's

written all over you!" I growl.   She's been waiting to wag her all-knowing finger at me since she first gave me her warning about marrying Jack.

"You're being ridiculous, Penelope; I would never wish for a young man to lose his life.   I just told you to move home here, and I'll help you take care of your baby--"

"P!" May shrieks, appearing from behind the dividing fabric to the bedroom.   It sways in an echo of her disruption.   "You said I could be there when you told her!"
I roll my head toward my little sister.

"Go ahead, May; tell her then," I allow.

She swallows and clasps her hands.   Glistening sparkles replace the annoyance in her eyes as she draws a long breath to deliver the news.

"Mama, you're about to become 'Grandmama'," she grins, once again appearing as though her excitement will cause her head to explode.   Clearly, she's thrilled to have been able to vocalize one of her carefully practiced lines of delivery, even though Mama already knows; even though the air in this room is as thick as cheese with tension.

"Well, Edith!" Reverend Bell calls as he walks out of the bathroom doorway.   "I don't think you look at all old enough to be called 'Grandmother'!"

"'Grand*mama*'," May corrects, prancing about, giddy with the joy of becoming an aunt.

The reverend seems to echo her delight.   "Well, a scandal all the same for a pretty young thing to gain the 'grand' title," he amends, his grin out of place in the hostility.

Mama's lashes beat against her flushed cheeks.

"It's wonderful news," she affirms, grinning at him.

Wonderful?   It doesn't feel *wonderful* to me.   I feel cheated, not 'wonderful'.

"Yes, Mama; isn't it wonderful that it'll be born without its father?" I mutter.

"Penelope," she scolds, her eyes icing over in the Stare.

I throw my arms out dramatically. "Ain't it just grand that you'll get to spend this kid's entire life rubbing 'I told you so' in my face?"

"That's enough," Mama chastens, her eyes hardening into the Stare.

"It's true," I grumble.

"Well, is 'I told you so' so misplaced in this situation, young lady? You jumped willy-nilly into the arms of the first fellow who paid you any attention, and then life wasted no time before showing you how unfair it can be!"

"Young lady?" I return in exasperation. I'm not twelve any longer; I've flown the coop. She can't treat me like a child! My chest heaves in and out while familiar adrenaline courses through me. I hate it when my anger takes me over like this.

"P," May follows, disappointed. The Reverend looks at me sadly as well.

Mama adds, "And I did warn you, Penelope; I told you this could happen."

"And if I move home here, you'll tell that to me every single day." With the crushing weight of my losses, I don't need to add a heavy lecture. She'll hang it over my head for the rest of my existence. I'll be stuck in a gallows. "Well, I don't believe I'll ever be giving you that pleasure, Mama," I vow in a hiss. I won't come back to this farm with my tail tucked between my legs like a sorry dog.

"Fine!" she hollers flippantly. The anger in me wants her to hurt, so I draw back a flaming arrow and aim it straight for her heart.

"I won't raise my baby like you raised your children! All hard work and scanty food living in this tiny house! Survival, is what it was; merely scraping by!" A flood of those feelings rushes through my chest: uncertainty, grief, hunger, worry.

Mama looks like I've slapped her with an open palm. Her eyes shine with tears. Her pain is evident.

Good, Imp assures me.

"Do you think I had any other choice?" she whispers through

her teeth, but I've already drawn another arrow from my quiver.

"Remember the week after we moved here, and that night May wouldn't stop crying because she was so hungry?"

"Yes," she whispers in horror, her fingers flying to her mouth. We don't speak about that.

"Two days; It had been two entire days since we'd had a scrap to eat, and we all just lay there on the bed hoping she would just fall asleep, because we were too lethargic to soothe her?"

At that point, we hadn't learned yet that lying flat on your back makes the hunger pangs worse. We know now that an empty belly can be somewhat soothed by curling up into a ball, like a roly poly.

"Don't you think I did everything I could to fill your bellies?" Mama defends, her hoarse voice wavering. "That I did as much as I could myself to lighten your loads?"

My eyes comb over her sun-spotted skin, her early wrinkles, and tattered clothes and her rough, cracked hands. I remember the times that the crate boys brought home aging fruit for us, fruit that was too close to spoiling to be sold. Mama never ate any, she always just leaned against the sink and watched us dig in. Her thin neck and hollow cheeks have barely filled in since then, and still appear unnaturally slender. These reminders start to calm my fury.

That is, until she adds, "When you left us, you became a spoiled brat, Penelope."

The Reverend and May stand by with wide eyes, shifting uncomfortably in the webs of the strain as anger rumbles up my legs, through my belly and out of my mouth.

"Having a decent meal and a bathtub isn't spoiled, Mother!" Mama hates it when we call her that.

"Well, you won't find either of those here, Princess."

The title stings me like a slap. I've never considered myself spoiled or a princess, not even as a child, when I actually was.

"Well I won't do this child the disservice of lying in that bed," I hiss, pointing to it behind the sheet, "too afraid to fall asleep because it won't know if it'll ever wake up again."

Mama's chest stiffens as though my arrow has speared her through the heart. We don't talk about those early hungry days, even though I remember quite clearly stuffing the corner of the sheet into my mouth and gnawing on it, just to feel something between my teeth. I know that the economic depression has passed, and that our desperation has since fueled creative ways of obtaining food. But I also know that bringing it up stings Mama in an ugly place. Her nostrils flare over her tightly set mouth. I can see that her humiliation has tripled with the Reverend as our audience.

"Please leave, Penelope. Feel free to come back when you're ready to accept our humble offerings," she jeers, rolling her wet eyes.

I stomp over the grey floorboards toward the front door, wading through the thick discomfort that fills the tiny house.

"I won't bother!" I vow. "Goodbye, Mother. May; Reverend."

As the door slams behind me, I realize that I may never hear that sound again. I may never come back.

SIX

I have no trouble peeling away from the farmhouse with reckless abandon, fueled more by the adrenaline and anger coursing through me than the gasoline in the tank.

Me, spoiled? Who has the ostentatious hand-me-down vehicle parked on her farm? How dare she kick me like that when I'm down?

However, the closer I roll toward the apartment I shared with Jack, the less fervently I press down on the gas pedal.

Can I even return home there? I wonder as my white knuckles grip the steering wheel. *Can I look at the things that are his and ours and feel anything but horror in my gut?* My foot slips completely off of the gas pedal, and the car rolls forward on momentum alone.

Where else could we go? Imp's question weaves in with my own thoughts. Seems to me we burned a bridge back there, to a crisp. A smoldering, crispy pile of ashes.

I pull carefully into a parking spot right in front of my building, as closely as I can to the cement curb without scuffing the white-walls on the tires, and squeeze my eyelids tightly against the thought.

Mama would take you back, insists Sense.

Ha! Not without a healthy dose of humility for you, smirks Imp from her perch in the corner of my skull.

I try to shut them both out as I shuffle toward my building.

The hall echoes, hollow and cavernous, as I step toward my door. Mechanically, I lift my brass key toward the lock, the one Jack had painted a tiny heart on with my red nail polish, and pause as I realize that the door already stands open.

The comfort of my home, however lonesome, seems to have been swallowed up in a tornado. My eyes flicker from the overturned sofa to a smashed dining chair. Broken shards of glass litter the kitchenette's counter, a collage of green glass and scraps of flowered porcelain. Every drawer gapes open as wide as my own mouth, drooling their contents onto the floor in a frozen look of surprise. Papers and pens, shears and envelopes, silverware and linens.

Each photo on the wall hangs askew in its frame, wearing a spiderweb-cracked pane of glass as though they'd been punched. On quivering legs, I wade through the carnage to the bedroom. Similar to the front rooms, this one's been lifted, tossed, and ransacked as well, only, a single piece of furniture sits upright, untouched, as though a glass dome had protected it in the storm. Jack's night table, his lamp, his letter opener. The photograph of the two of us that had made its home there, however, lies facedown on the rug beside it.

It's as though the entire place hums a haunting tune in unison, *'You don't belong here anymore'*.

The shuddering I feel as I inspect my home is strong enough to cause a natural disaster of its own. In the bathroom I find the claw foot bathtub, my place of refuge from the emptiness of this lonely apartment, overflowing with water and my clothes. Soggy fragments of letters, Jack's letters, float destroyed in this intentional flood.

I can't stay here, I think as I back my way toward the front door. I never deserved to be here in the first place! I never should have let myself become a spoiled brat.

In a roundabout way, I killed Jack. I kept him out from under the protective wing of his mother. I know that if I had never come into Jack's life and pulled him away from her, he never would have enlisted for the signing bonus; he wouldn't have needed it! And the draft? Ruby would've used her dirty, scheming ways to protect both of her boys from going to war. He'd still be alive.

I didn't fight hard enough when he enlisted. I let him go at the train station, even though I knew that war claims young lives! He's dead because of me.

This is what I tell myself as I tack a letter to Lyla to the door, my hasty scrawl explaining why I can't stay in the apartment she had so graciously provided and furnished for us. It's what runs through my head when I stand in the doorway of that apartment for the last time with tears rolling down my neck. Even if it were untouched, everything perfect, I know that I never really deserved this place.

I can't stand to be here, anyhow. There's too many memories haunting these walls. I should swallow my pride and crawl back to the farmhouse, where May and Mama will comfort me and help me through my pregnancy. However, my pride does not want to be swallowed; a thick, stubborn lump clinging to the back of my throat. It's just about the only solid thing about me right now.

If I go home, then I'll be admitting that I was wrong. Mama was right, I am too young to handle all this. Our plans didn't work out. Life did swallow me whole, just like she said it would! And after our marriage, a child is coming indeed.

Why am I so darn stubborn? As hard as I push myself to do the right thing, it feels like shoving both hands against a stubborn brick wall. Or my cow, Tilly. Or something else that just won't budge. It's useless. I am a fool, and I have no home. The gal who shudders in this doorway has made herself a homeless, pathetic fool.

Shakily, I make my way down the block to the Home for Unfortunate Women and Children, a church house for recovering convicts, the homeless, and gals like me: ripe into pregnancy, husbandless, and utterly pathetic. Doris had mentioned this place to me as she recovered from Sweeney's attack: *"At least now I won't have to be one of those pathetic, knocked-up broads in the Home…"*. I'm fully aware of what that makes me as I enter its doors. A pathetic, knocked-up, idiot broad; and a stubborn one.

As I sign the register, Penelope H. Sharpe, the nun behind the front desk informs me that staying in this home not only means two meals per day and a cot in a common room in exchange for my devotion to God, I'll also be assigned some light cleaning.

"All of our girls have been able to fulfill their duties up until the day they deliver," her plain lips insist. The rigid fabric of her wimple and the tight set of her mouth tell me that I would've found more sympathy for my condition at the farmhouse, but I can't go back there.

In my first day here, I learn quickly that the other gals who have signed their names, neatly and prettily above mine, weren't ever married. They greet me with lipsticked smiles like we're old sorority sisters. Their bastard children have been fatherless since conception. Even so, they still fuss over their hair and carry on with bright eyes and gumption for life; still hoping for their stroke of luck.

Well, I've had my luck, and now he's dead. Now my fortune reads a scratchy, stiff cot and kitchen chores, and a lightless future. The grease-stained walls, riddled with cracks, perfectly mirror my feelings.

"Take that bucket of food scraps out to the alleyway," another gal on duty instructs me. I hook my fingers under the metal handle obediently.

"Which way is the trash bin out there?" I ask, planning to push through the door and walk the scraps to a big trash bin.

"Aw, don't bother to heave that bucket that far. Plenty of alley cats and vermin who'll clean it right up for us. Just dump it off of the steps and bring back the bucket."

Swallowing a bitter lump in my throat, I wrinkle my nose at the thought of sleeping a few bricks away from 'alley cats and vermin'. Jack may have tried his best to lift me from the slums, but once a gal in the gutter, always a gal in the gutter.

Perhaps it's the sag in my oomph, but it seems my arms can't remember how to carry something as heavy as a full bucket. I struggle down the hallway with it, and kick the hard metal door open with my foot.

My fingers nearly drop the bucket when I take in the silhouette of a police car against the brick of the opposite building, but I calm myself in time to re-secure my hold on the handle. A gal named Birdie, five months pregnant, sways back and forth with her arms wrapped around another body. Her perky giggling tinkles on the air in sharp contrast to the thick, putrid scent out here. I've shoveled horse poop and juggled bed pans, but the odor out here outdoes them both.

I cough on the thick breath in my throat. The pair turns to me, and I instantly recognize Dalton's face against Birdie's.

"What are you doing out here, Birdie?" I call to her with my nose wrinkled. "Why are you with him? Is he that baby's father?" I wouldn't put it past this creep to have several illegitimate children running all over town.

She bats her lashes sideways at the officer and turns to me.

"Not yet," she giggles as she touches a flirtatious finger to his nose, immune to the stench in the alleyway that clings to our skin.

Dalton pushes her away from him, and she wobbles to gain her footing under her unbalanced midsection.

"Better get back inside now, Doll," he urges her, slapping her on the bottom. She blushes and frolics into the building with her fingers waggling to him over her shoulder.

He scowls at me. "You just cost me a date," he growls, kicking the brick driveway beneath him.

"And you just cost me a decent night's sleep," I return, moving toward him with the bucket hanging from my hooked fingers. "I'll never get that picture out of my head."

"Well, I can't fight crime without taking care of my needs, can I?" He wags his brows up and down in suggestion.

"You don't fight crime, Creep; you are crime. What are you doing here, anyway?" *Who would want to hang out in a disgusting, rat-infested alleyway like this?*

"This is my regular haunt, little Darlin'! And you just crashed my party," he complains.

I wrinkle my nose at him.

"Well, the gals here are obviously looser than a pickle jar, and just beggin' for some fella to pay them some attention, aren't they?" he explains. My mind resists absorbing this new information; how very low a creep like him will sink.

"I mean, they're already knocked up," he laughs, "so I don't need to worry a bit about getting myself in trouble with an illegitimate child." The way his head bobbles on his neck tells me that he's proud of his sordid plan.

"You're a scumbag," I sneer.

"Aw, trust me; I do these dames a favor!" he insists, striding toward me. "All they want is a little attention; someone to remind them that they're still a woman."

My muscles tighten, disgusted.

He grabs me by the waist and yanks me toward his squad car, murmuring, "And now, *I'm going to do* you *a favor*." The bucket falls to the ground, spilling its contents across the brick.

I thrash violently under the tension of his arms as he throws me up against the car door, and stars burst through my blackened vision as my head makes contact with the metal.

"Naw, none of that, Kitten," he grunts, leaning his weight into my back. My head spins with the pain. "I'd say you owe me."

My face presses against the glass of the police car, smashed under the weight of his body leaning against me. I can barely pull air into the tight space left in my depressed lungs. I beg my plea to Jack, wherever he is. I pray he is watching over me. *Help me, Jack. I need you.*

The hiss of metal sliding against metal fills my ears as Dalton slips his handcuffs off of his belt. I struggle against him as he secures a cuff onto my right wrist, works the empty one through the door handle and clamps it around my left wrist. Fat tears push their way from the corners of my eyes. There's no getting away now.

"You may have married up, but you're still just a dirty piece of farm trash," he whispers into my ear.

I drop to the ground and twist myself, thrashing like a caged animal. At least I can breathe, and if I'm trapped, I'm going to put up a fight.

"Stand up, little brat!" he commands through his teeth.

I spit at him. He reaches for me, gripping his hands on my hips. I wriggle, fighting away as I hang from my wrists.

Jack, you've fought him before. Give me your strength right now. I need you!

"Oh, I can see the high life has added a little more woman to you." He groans appreciatively at my fleshy middle as he grabs for it. "All the better to hold on to, my dear."

"I'm expecting, you filthy sack of horse crap," I grunt breathlessly, hoping to deter him.

He laughs.

"Well, that's just a stroke of luck, isn't it? I found myself another Home Hussy to wrestle with. You won't mind another--"

"The child is Jack's," I interrupt. The declaration fills my chest with warmth, and my limbs with strength.

I yank hard on my wrists. The right one slips out, raw and stinging, but triumphant. Immediately, I scramble to my feet, and hoist the bony edge of my knee up between his legs in a swift blow.

Officer Dalton's head crashes into my ribs as he instantaneously doubles over in pain, releasing his grip on my arms. They tingle with freedom. I nod down to my triumphant knee, and shove him off of me. He topples backward, groaning, onto the brick. When the wet ground wallops the back of his head, his groaning suddenly ceases.

I stand frozen in place over his slack face, except for the heaving of my chest. I turn back to the shelter door, wondering what I should do.

Is he dead? Did I just kill him? Fresh fear arrests my anger. If I just killed a policeman, then I'll be thrown in jail! I'm stuck here in his handcuffs. I can't add murder to this, the worst day of my life. Behind bars with a bun in the oven; that'll make me as scrubby and trashy as Dalton claims I am.

But I am not.

I strain against my restricted wrist and reach for the key ring on his belt. My middle finger, the longest finger; barely hooks around the large metal loop and strains to tear it free. My hands fumble through the mass of clinking metal as I hunt for the smallest key; the cuff key. I free my bound wrist, which frees my entire body to choose whether I'll assist this harmed man, or run inside to safety.

I fall to my knees over him. My fingers furiously move over his jaw, hunting for his pulse.

"C'mon, c'mon!" I mutter, digging the pads of my fingers into his skin.

I fall sideways with relief when I find a strong, pulsating beat under his skin. Relieved tears sting my eyes, and my fingers shove his face away. Stifling a sneer, I draw my foot back to deliver a blow to his ribs. His slackened body jiggles, but his face lacks the satisfying look of pain I'd hoped for.

Now run inside and call an ambulance for him, Sense urges me.

Ahem, Imp pipes up. I feel her impish encouragement move me back toward Dalton. *Not before you give him a little payback.*

I cuff his slack wrist, and secure the free cuff to the metal grate under his back. I examine his plight, and decide that I can do much better than I've done to him.

My lips spread into a wide grin as I slide under the steering wheel of his squad car. When I peer into the side view mirror, I notice his leg, directly in the path of the rear tire.

Just pull the car forward a bit, Sense suggests. *Then maneuver in reverse around him.*

I grip the wheel and turn the key, but when the engine roars to life, so does a nasty thought. I lean my head out the window to peer at Dalton's body.

"It's your lucky day, Creep; I'm not going to report you after all!" I cackle.

The engine purrs happily as I bounce over Dalton's ankle and out of the alley. I let loose a maniacal laugh, and a rush of exhilaration bursts in my chest, spattering my limbs, fingers, and toes with glee.

You were right, Mama; Hale gals absolutely do not *do what they're told!*

I fly down the main street with adrenaline coursing through me.

When I find a suitable alleyway, I tuck the squad car inside of it to make it difficult for Dalton to find. I want him to flip his lid with worry. I want his sergeant to scold him for losing the squad car! I want him to scour the streets, anxious that he'll lose his badge for being such a fool! I pull the key from the ignition and run back to the shelter with it tucked in my fist. The night air nips at my earlobes and nose as I run with my hair tumbling behind me.

For the first time in a long, long while, I don't feel the least bit sick to my stomach.

When my keen sense of smell alerts me that I'm back near the Home's alley, I slow myself to a stop. Carefully, I peer around the corner, but Dalton's light moans haven't brought him all the way around just yet. The foot I'd driven over hangs sideways, at an odd angle. The sight turns my stomach with both disgust and delight. My feet pad lightly past him, and I toss his keys just out of his reach. They jingle their applause for me as they clatter against the brick.

"Filthy dirtbag, piece of junk crumb," I mutter on my way to the back door of the shelter.

When I slip quietly into my cot in the dark inside, my eyes swim with stars. That felt *incredible*.

"Hmm?" I mutter as I feel myself being coaxed from sleep.

"What's that noise?" Birdie, two cots away, asks into the darkness. I can tell by the stillness in the air, the absence of street noise outside that we're the only ones in Saratoga awake at this hour. I perk up my ears, and listen hard.

Tat-tat-tat, against the alley door.

"I hear it, too!" Another gal gasps from her bed.

Tat-tat. I recognize the sound of pebbles hitting the metal. I think of Officer Dalton outside, chained with his own handcuffs to the iron storm grate, trying desperately to catch someone's attention.

Tat-tat-tat.

"Aw, cool it, ladies," someone explains, annoyed. "It's probably just a rat trying to scratch his way in. Go back to sleep already."

"Yeah, a rat," I agree as I snuggle back into the cot. A rat, indeed.

March 23rd, 1942

In the morning, I wake arrested with anxiety.

You did a stupid, stupid thing last night, Penelope! You should have called an ambulance for him. You shouldn't have chained him down. You shouldn't have hidden his squad car. You shouldn't have spoken to him in the first place! I scold myself.

Light streams through the windows, so I know that hours and hours have passed while I've been unconscious, but I don't feel well-rested. I feel jittery; I feel guilty. This is why it startles me so when an irritated voice calls my name, cutting through the sound of bubbly chatter all around me like a hot blade.

"Penelope! What in the devil are you doing here?" the crabby, scratchy voice asks from behind me.

"Lyla," I answer before turning. This woman's essence is unmistakable.

"What is this?" she asks, holding up a sheet of paper with my writing all over it; the writing that explained that as grateful as I was for the beautiful apartment and plentiful furniture, it was just too painful to live amongst those memories. Her shriveled fingers tear my letter into pieces, scattering the little shreds in the air. They flutter to the ground like snowflakes.

Her expression tells me that I've somehow offended her, so my chin bounces up and down as I try to find a suitable explanation. She rolls her eyes.

"Come on, then. Let's get you out of this cesspool! Oh, my; what have they done to your hands?" Lyla gasps, gripping her heart like its about to arrest. I pull my sleeves over the raw, red scratches from Dalton's handcuffs.

Before her bony fingers clasping around my upper arm can pull me outside, I stop in my tracks. My eyes comb the room full of gals with a variety of ripeness to their bellies.

"Birdie!" I call to the gal I'd seen wrapped around Dalton, and her blonde curls shake as she turns her face toward me. Her deep brown eyes widen as she waits for my words.

I escape Lyla's grip to scurry toward her. "Birdie, promise me you'll stay away from that creep, the policeman."

She wrinkles her nose at me as she searches my pleading eyes. "Is he your fella?"

"Oh, no. You're better than him, Birdie. You're not his plaything," I tell her.

Her eyes fall to her hands. "I'm not so sure about that."

"Trust me; he's a creep. He's just looking for a tramp, not a wife!" I feel Lyla's fingers close around my arm again. "Trust me, Birdie!" I urge as Lyla pulls me away. "You're better than him!"

As I crawl into the back of Lyla's glistening maroon Duesenberg, I worry that she will force me to buck up and reside in the trashed apartment with Jack's ghost. After all, the woman's skin is thick as a tractor tire; I can't expect her to sympathize with me over something as trivial as feelings. However, her driver breezes right past my building without hesitation, allowing me to sink into the leather of the back seat a little.

"Did you see the apartment?" I ask her.

"When my Hugh came to me with the news, I knew you'd be in a terrible state. I checked the hospital, which they told me you'd checked out of early, against medical advice, *thankyouverymuch*. And I about lost my eyebrows when they flew up my forehead at the sight of your apartment!"

"Who…"

"Who do I think tore it to pieces? A burglar, a thug, or someone who paid a burglar and a thug to frighten the daylights out of you."

"Well, it worked, Lyla. It worked well."

"So I gather," she sneers at me. "Well, you can be sure that whoever did it meant to frighten you away. And I'm not going to let that happen, my dear," she promises as she grasps my hand. "I don't like to let the bully win the match! So, this bully has only frightened you into staying with me. Well, the two of you, so it seems."

My eyebrows lift in unison.

"How did you know?" I wonder aloud. I didn't even know until yesterday.

"I'm a master of coercion, dear. People will tell me anything for the right price, especially underpaid hospital staff!" She cackles gleefully. "No granddaughter of mine will live in the slums!" The driver has taken us far, far away from the slums she speaks of, into the rolling acreage outside of town.

Granddaughter? The words pricks my heart.

"Lyla, now that Jack's gone..." I begin, swallowing a thick lump in my throat. "You shouldn't feel obligated to take care of me anymore."

Her keen eyes steel over, trained on mine.

"Pish posh! Nonsense! You became my kin when my grandson made you his bride. And now, you're carrying Sharpe blood in your belly!"

I open my mouth to argue her point, but her threatening glare halts the words rising in my throat.

"I don't want to hear another argument from you on this, young lady," she scolds.

I nod slowly to her, and she mutters under her breath, "Though I do love a girl who's not afraid of a tussle. Even with me."

The first time I saw the outside of Lyla's home, the "guest cottage" around the back of the Sharpe's house on the Ferring plantation, I'd been sitting next to Jack in the Mercury, and I'd marvelled at its gargantuan size. Today, I see the twin of Jack's parents' grand home again as her driver pulls up in front of the massive structure and its carefully crafted details--dormers and ornamental windows, a sweeping entryway, clean white trim contrasting against the grey shakes.

Somewhere under the blanket of snow hugging this acreage, I know that the skeletons of grape vines run in endless tracks over these rolling hills. I remember them in their full green splendor in the late summer I'd met Jack, spreading as far as the horizon. The bare branches of the orchard around the home remind me of the night we'd escaped from his mother's anger into those trees, and Jack had told me he'd been arranged into a marriage with another girl he barely knew.

This place holds as many ghosts as my apartment. At least I know that under the eaves of Lyla's barn, Tilly is lazily chewing her cud.

Lyla's car door is opened for her, and she extends her gloved hand for her chauffeur to assist her. It appears to be a knee-jerk reaction for her. I scoot across the seat and start to stand, but the driver looks horrified and dives toward me to help me up.

"I'm really okay," I insist.

His eyes tell me that even if I were okay getting up on my own, he certainly is not okay with his passenger getting up without his assistance. He stares at my red, scraped wrists, and I pull them away.

"I'm fine."

When I'm firmly on two feet, he turns to polish the car of my fingerprints. I note that he also wears gloves, and cast him an apologetic look for causing him extra work.

"Don't bother, Beauford. That was Mister Sharpe's baby, not mine." Lyla cackles.

She squints her eyes as though the thought of her late husband's pride and joy being defaced is delicious to her. Beauford looks scandalized, and I wonder what the price tag for such a car would be. Clearly, he knows. Clearly, it's now his baby. I wonder if he thinks this piece of machinery is worth more than himself. His eyes say that he does.

The double doors at the front entrance to Lyla's home sweep open in unison as we step on the first of the stone steps leading up to them. I can't help but wonder if these steps are rigged to make the doors do that, when I see two women in crisp white aprons peek around them.

"Welcome home, Madam," one offers.

"You're looking well, as usual," the other says, curtsying. Her brown fingers contrast against the white of her apron. "I see you have a visitor. May I take your coat, Miss?"

They appear hungry to dote on me. A far cry from the atmosphere of the shelter; actually, a far cry from any of my recent memories. I dote on myself.

"Penelope will be staying with us for awhile," Lyla announces, and I wonder how long my welcome will last. I note an impressive amount of doilies decorating the formal front room. "Choose your room, dear. Whichever suits you best."

Choose my room? I have a choice?

Lyla falls into a large chair in the sitting room and tells the older of the maids, "I'll take my tea now, dear. Please."

"Of course, Madam."

"And offer the girl some medical attention for her hands," Lyla amends.

"Yes, Madam. This way, Miss Penelope; I'll give you the tour!" the younger maid chirps. Her large brown eyes swirl with excitement. "This here's the blue room, and just across the way is the peach one. Each has their own washroom. Yes, kind of fluffy in there, eh?" She winks at me as we peek around the doorframe of the peach room, her full lips stretched into a smile.

I realize quickly that none of Lyla's guest rooms will actually "suit" me. None have been built for a tomboy milk maid who'll surely track in dirt on her shoes and drool on her pillow.

"Up here's the green room; there's the white one, and that door back there leads down to ours. You won't want to be stayin' down there, Miss, but we'll be there if you need anything. Anything, even in the night. I mean, especially in your condition." She blushes as though she's said too much.

I raise my brows.

"I assume… you're in a delicate, er, way?" I run my hand over my barely rounded belly.

"Yes," I confirm. She can tell just by looking at me?

"Miss Lyla's lips are quite loose, you know," she whispers behind her hand, warm brown on top, baby pink on the palm.

I smile in relief. I'd thought it was written across my forehead or something.

"Well," she breathes, her warm eyes aglow. "There'll be a bell in any room you choose. It will alert us downstairs of your need. You ring it at any hour, you hear?"

"Yes," I agree, silently vowing to never wake someone from their sleep to dote on me.

"Come along upstairs, Miss Penelope. Here's the library, over there's the relaxing room. There's a nice porch outdoors with a fine view of the vineyard. Oh! And just over here is my favorite room, the silver room."

She pauses at the entry. I walk in, absorbing the lavish details of the room. A fleeting question passes through my head of why the maid doesn't claim her favorite room as her own, and I realize the absurdity before it dissolves. She's a servant.

"This is your favorite?" I ask.

"Mmm-hmm," she answers. I can see by her held breath and glowing chocolate eyes that she hopes I'll choose this one.

"It's wonderful," I agree with forced enthusiasm for her benefit, claiming the silver room as my new residence. I hope I can keep my dirt to myself in here.

She claps the pink palms of her hands together gleefully.

"Excellent! Lie down so I can bandage your cuts. I'll have Mister Beauford bring your bags up right away, Miss Penelope!"

I exhale and drop onto the bed. In stark contrast to the rigid cot at the shelter, and the compacted feathers of my bed at the farmhouse, this bed feels exactly like a puffy white cloud in the sky. Even though my heart tells me that I don't deserve this, my eyelids flutter closed as I drink in the luxe comfort.

I haven't felt this kind of safety since I laid in bed with Jack. The letter from the Navy read that he has been gone since late February, so nearly a month passed before I knew he was gone. And yet, I'd been loving him every day as though his body still pumped blood through his veins.

How can it be that he no longer takes breaths in through his perfect lips? Warm tears squeeze under my closed lids and soak into the pillowcase. *Where are you, Jack? Where is your body? Where is your soul?* My brain flips through pictures of possibilities as I drift into troubled sleep.

The next time my eyes open, the sun's yellow warmth that had bathed the silver room has changed to a cool blue hue. My case sits open on a chair; my scanty things arranged carefully at the vanity. Someone has removed my shoes for me and laid a thin blanket over my body. I hadn't planned to fall asleep, but I feel wonderfully refreshed for doing so. Strangely, I realize that nothing is required of me here but to breathe. I haven't slept through an important task or a crucial chore.

"Feeling better, Miss Penelope?" the young maid asks as her heart-shaped face appears in the doorway. *Had she attached the call bell to my eyelids? Or has she been waiting out there all along?*

"Yes, very. Thank you...um...what's your name?"

"Annie, Miss Penelope. I'm here for whatever you need," she promises, and I realize that she's as wound up as her tightly as her bun.

"Actually, Annie, you can't keep calling me Penelope. That's what my mother calls me when I'm in trouble." I frown deeply, realizing I may always be in trouble with Mama now. "Why don't you call me Pip instead?" I offer with my hand out.
She looks at it sideways for a moment, then shakes it.

"Pip. Like, Charles Dickens, 'Great Expectations', Pip?" she asks with her eyebrows folded. I marvel that such a young housemaid seems to be well-read in the classics.

"I s'pose. No, I think it was that my dad called me Pip Squeak when I was little. My brothers still call me that," I smile, until I remember that neither of my brothers can call me anything at the moment. The corners of my mouth flatten into a line.

"Oh, good; Great Expecations' Pip is a boy," she giggles.

I look down at my dirty hands and filthy fingernails. "Well, I have always been sort of a tomboy." Her eyes fall to my clasped hands, and her mouth screws up in a poorly-hid grimace.

"Alright then, Miss Pip, let's get you washed up. I believe you have guests waiting downstairs."

My stomach tightens into a ball. *Is Dalton downstairs with the chief of police? Is Ruby waiting to throw me out? Or could it be Mama, insisting that I swallow my pride and return to the farmhouse?*

"Erm, just Pip will do."

"Alright then, Pip, but not in front of the Lady of the house. I'd lose my place here if she heard me calling you that," she insists, seeming slightly fearful.

Oh, Lyla.

"Who… who's downstairs, Annie?"

"Miss Claire and her husband," she replies, and my shoulders relax with relief. "I've drawn you a bath, just through here…"

I follow the maid into the steam-filled washroom, where a large, claw footed tub sits with bubbles spilling over the top.

I stand awkwardly in the room, waiting for her to leave so I can undress.

"C'mon, now, don't be shy," she prods and helps shrug out of my blouse.

My shoulders stiffen when she unclasps my brassiere for me.

"There we go," she says as she slides it off of my arms. In a room meant for relaxation, I feel anything but relaxed. She picks up on my discomfort.

"I'm a ladies' maid, Miss. Nothing can shock me! I've seen bare backsides my whole life," she says as she lays my clothes over a damask chair in the corner. "Here, I'll help you in, now."

She takes my arm and I slide my leg into the heaps of bubbles. Deliciously warm water envelopes my skin. I slip all the way in, sinking into the silkiness. Bubbles overflow and attach to my hair.

Tears spring to my eyes when a delicious warmth crawls up my spine. I don't deserve to be this spoiled anymore; I don't want to feel this good.

I don't want to feel anything at all.

I slink down the grand carpeted steps to find the company Annie had promised. I move slowly, trying to catch the excited words that have floated upstairs from the sitting room. As quietly as I try to move, Claire notices me anyway.

"Penny! Come in here!" she urges, waving her petite hand persuasively. Slowly, I move into the sitting room. Lyla's collection of company includes Jack's father, Claire, her husband Bentley, Claire's brother George, Doris, and my sister, May. My feet pause at the oddity of the group.

"So, it's true," Claire remarks, her doe eyes falling to my middle. "You're expecting."

My hand flies to my belly, barely paunched. I look to May, who grins sheepishly at me, and wonder if she shares Mama's 'spoiled brat' opinion of me. I can't help but feel anything but guilty in her company.

"I guess we both are. You're barely showing a bit, Claire," I comment.

"Ha!" Lyla chuckles, her drink swaying in her hand. "She looks like a regular turtle with its shell on backwards!" Her joke at Claire's expense earns a round of laughter from her guests, but Claire beams anyhow.

When her glow wears off, she turns to me with a little frown. "Am I to understand that a funeral is being planned?" Claire asks in shock.

"I--I don't know," I stammer, touching the wet curls at the nape of my neck.

"I found Bentley working on this!" she exclaims, two sheets of thick ivory paper in her grip. Bentley casts his eyes downward. "It looks a lot like the beginnings of a eulogy! Have you both given up all hope?"

Scolded, my jaw creaks open and shut without words.

"'Missing in Action' simply means they've lost their man, Penny," she insists. "A clerical mistake by the overworked services."

But I saw it happen, I reason in my head. I dream it every night.

"I glossed right over that as well, Dear," Mister Sharpe admits, and Bentley nods his head next to his father. "It's easy to assume your worst fears have been realized when you have a son up against the Nazis."

"He could still be out there!" May cries. She looks to have shed any grudge over our last interface.

"Yes, but what will we do about it? What's our plan?" Lyla urges, redirecting their attention. "Money is no object."

"Indeed, no object," George agrees, and Doris grins at him. I can guess by the wattage of her smile that they must have smoothed things over while my world was busy caving in. I remind myself to ask George about his father's gambling habits, if I can ever stop my head from spinning like it is.

"I'll sail over there and hunt for him myself!" Claire declares, and Bentley cups his hands gently on her shoulders.

"A war zone is no place for a lady," Mister Sharpe contends.

"Pmmph!" Lyla huffs, her hunched, spindly frame barely filling her stately chair. "I'd like to see one of those Nazis give me his best shot!"

"Well, I wouldn't let you go, Grandma," insists Bentley.

"What's Missus Sharpe think?" Doris asks.

"Ruby? Oh, she's had three private investigation teams on it since we heard the news," Mister Sharpe answers. I should have known. "Perhaps their focus has been misguided, however. She, um, she was convinced the letter was a ruse for Jackson to cut ties with the family."

"What?" May and Doris exclaim. No one else in the room seems as shocked by Ruby's sordid assumptions.

"She thinks he faked his own death?" Lyla clarifies.

"No, uh... she's sure that *Penelope* faked his death." Mister

Sharpe's eyes shift to me, apologetically.

I roll my eyes. Ruby thinks of me far more, and with much more cynicism, than I think of her.

"That's ridiculous," I intone flatly.

"I know," Claire, Mister Sharpe, and Lyla all say at once.

"But if he were alive somewhere, wouldn't we know by now?" I ask the group, my forehead aching as I process these new thoughts. *A letter? A phone call?* If I ran the Naval Air Force, notifying families of their loved ones' whereabouts would be a top priority. It just doesn't make sense.

They're avoiding grief by feeling hope, Sense explains.

Several possibilities tangle together as the group excitedly speaks over each other with their theories: Enemy capture? Amnesia? Hiding out in a barn in the French countryside? Wounded beyond recognition in a coma in a Naval hospital?

The latter turns my stomach, and by the looks of it, May's as well. Max is still alive, but unresponsive, at the army hospital in Hawaii. At least we know his face hasn't been maimed beyond recognition. At least the breath of life still fills him.

George wagers that Jack has become a spy, and must shed himself of his former identity and family. "I'd put money on it!"

Doris rolls her eyes at him. "You're as bad a gambler as your father, Georgie!" she giggles.

As far fetched as their suggestions sound, a tiny and frail wisp of hope rises in my own chest. I touch my belly, barely more rounded than a washboard. Hopefully this emotional rollercoaster will end before it blooms fully and this child comes. I know that in order to properly care for it, I need to have things sorted out. I sit down next to Lyla, leaning into the hopeful chatter.

"So, what have Ruby's private investigators dug up so far?"

"They've only had mere days on the job so far. It will be miserable for us, but all we can do is wait and see."

The sun dips below the hillside as we say our goodbyes. Once the hopeful group finally disbands, I ask Annie to show me to Tilly, which earns me one of the oddest looks I've ever beheld. I deduce that Lyla has never requested her servants take her inside of the barn. However, well-trained, she obliges; and walks me to the barn behind the house without questions.

I'm pleased to find that it's not much farther of a walk from Lyla's back porch than the old barn was from the farmhouse. I head straight for Tilly, who lies lazily on her side against a small mountain of hay, and scratch her behind her ears. Her eyes close appreciatively under my fingers.

"Who milks this cow?" I ask Annie.

She shrugs. "One of the field laborers, I suppose, Miss. I never really come out here." With her nose wrinkled, she inspects the soles of her shoes as she speaks.

She hands me one of her lanterns, curtsies to me, and backs out of the doors into the darkness.

Once I'm alone, I curl up on my side against Tilly. I lay my head against the short, stiff hairs of her belly, which rises and falls with her breaths. As I unfold Bentley's ivory papers, I try to push a swirling mass of thoughts from my head--the group's endless theories on Jack's whereabouts, my worries about Max, Ruby's accusations against my character--so I can focus on Bentley's words about his brother. If I wrote a eulogy, or a goodbye to Jackson Sharpe, what would I say? I look down at the words Bentley has come up with:

"Little Brother,
Some say that a parent should never have to bury a child, and I amend that a man should not have to lay his kid brother to rest."

Instantly, my eyes fill, stinging with tears. I shouldn't have had to attend Eddie's funeral, at least not until I was as old and wrinkled as Lyla. I shouldn't have to think about burying my young husband, if the private investigators confirm that he is, in fact, deceased. I read on, through stories of Jack's childhood mischief that somehow seem familiar to me; they sound just like him. My heart stops when I reach the second page.

"You had just come to life this last year when you met your gal. Your eyes have glowed on many occasions, brother, mostly on occasions that I was on the wrong end of one of your pranks, but I had never seen them quite so illuminated as when you spoke of your Penelope. You'd do anything to get a little time with her."

For a moment, I'm whisked away from Tilly's rhythmic breaths, the scratchy hay, and the hard wooden planks beneath me, back to the sidewalk outside of the hospital on a windy September day. Jack had leaned casually out of the Merc window, trying to convince me to abandon my responsibilities and take a ride with him.

"I can't," I'd protested. "It's my turn to check in on the crate boys and collect their earnings. Otherwise they scrape a little off the top before the purse makes it back to Mac, and he gets awfully grumpy."

"Can't you do all that right now, so we can go?" he'd begged, his blue eyes persuasively gleaming at me under the afternoon sun.

"They're never sold out by this time of day, Jack. I have to wait around until all the produce is sold. Look!" I argued. "That lil' fella on the corner still has a whole crate of apples left." I'd pointed to a young boy in a vest and cap dancing around on the street corner like a miniature Charlie Chaplin with two shining apples in his palms. Jack raked his hand through his hair.

"Don't go anywhere, Doll!"

Not twenty minutes later, he was nestling the Merc back up to the curb. The chrome rear bumper sat dangerously low to the ground under the weight of hundreds and hundreds of apples, bundles of carrots, broccoli crowns, eggplants, and bunches of grapes that filled his backseat to the roof, a rainbow of color.

"Looks like your crate boys are all sold out, now, Pip."

"All of 'em?" I stutter with my mouth agape at his rolling

produce stand.

"All of 'em," he confirmed. "Here's the purse; now let's go!" The Merc's heavy load was relieved at the closest bread line, where scores of hungry hands welcomely accepted Jack's edible treasures.

My cheeks burn pink as my awareness sets me back on the barn floor. Jack really would do anything to spend time with me. That is, until he ran off to become a fly boy. The hopeful side of me wonders if he's fighting just as hard right now to spend time with me; to get home. I hope he is.

I continue devouring Bentley's words:

"I suppose many will go through an entire lifetime without knowing a love like that. If that is true, then you have lived enough of a lifetime for all of us. You didn't need any more time to taste of the sweetness that life has to offer us."

As my eyes blur, so full of tears that Bentley's handwriting has gone completely obscured, I conclude that Ruby would never allow these last words to be spoken over Jack's casket. I feel new fondness for Jack's big brother, who I never knew was capable of the softness he's shared on these pages. I'd even somewhat pitied my sweet cousin for the calculated match she had been arranged with, a bland fella, but I was wrong.

Bentley is a good man.

Lyla sits alone at the head of her long dining table. Her wrinkled face snaps up as I pad timidly into the room, and she tosses aside her newspaper.

"Oh, thank heavens! I thought I'd have to finish this all off myself," she croaks in her scratchy voice, and gestures to the spread before her. Croissants, cheeses, carafes of juice and milk, and an overflowing platter of fruits occupy her end of the table. I note the off-season berries and citrus, curious at how she acquired them in late-winter.

"Good morning, Lyla," I say, feeling more inclined to join the help in the kitchen than to sit with the Lady of the house.

"Help yourself," she urges me, and I push myself to sit a few chairs down from her. My stomach gurgles with excitement.

My eyes close gratefully as my teeth sink into a blackberry. "Mmm," I purr. "Where did you get these berries?"

"I have them carted in," she explains, shuffling in her chair. I know from her posture that a long-winded explanation comes. "I have to take in all the vitamins I can if I'm going to out-live Ruby..."

I snort, and a piece of blackberry shoots out of my mouth onto the tablecloth. Its dark purple juice seeps into the fine fabric. "Oh! I'm so sorry!" I blot at the stain with my napkin, but it only worsens.

Lyla waves her spotted hand dismissively. "I have staff for a reason, Dear." Her neck wobbles like a turkey's as she raises her chin to punctuate her words. She tosses her napkin over the stain.

"You're planning to out-live Ruby?"

"Haven't I told you? Since my daughter-in-law can't wait for me to kick the proverbial bucket, I've decided to do the only thing an old woman can do to spite her out of her inheritance. I have decided to seek eternal youth."

"With fruit?" I question with my eyebrows high.

"The specialist that I saw indicated that consuming living things--fruits, vegetables, legumes--will prolong my own life," she explains.

"Oh," I reply. "That makes sense, I guess." I pop another berry onto my tongue, wondering if it will boost the baby's health.

"And if he's wrong, well... his advice was expensive, and so is the fruit. I'll die knowing that *Ruby*," she sneers the name, "will have that much less of my fortune to roll around in."

I giggle behind my hand so that the croissant between my teeth won't escape. A clear picture of Ruby's simpering face fills my mind; she rolls on the bill-covered ground in a room filled with greenbacks raining from the ceiling.

Lyla uses her fork and knife to daintily slice her own berry in two. She spears one half and raises it to her thin, wrinkled lips.

"I just have to keep breathing until she's ready to go. Once she dies, I can slip away in peace," she claims, certain of her absurd plan. "My Hugh will save a fortune on the funeral. Two caskets, yes, but only one service. The mortician won't be able to wrench the satisfied smile off of my face!"

It's a far better plan than poison, Sense reasons.

"Perhaps I can arrange in advance for just one grave to be dug, and her casket to be buried below mine. That way we can spend eternity in the proper order."

"I adore you, Lyla," I tell her, my eyes in half moons slits over my smile.

"So does my grandson," she nods, and the weight of Jack's memory settles over us.

July 29th, 1942

My eyebrows raise hopefully as Claire's round belly appears through the doors of Lyla's barn, following their normal pattern each time she has visited me here over these painfully slow months. They beg the question, "Any news on Jack?"

I sit straight up and let go of Tilly. She moos in irritation, her hooves dancing in the hay, but her head is locked firmly in the stanchion so she can't escape. I shoo away a barn cat from her dripping udder with my foot.

Claire, backlit by the sunrise, is wise to my wonderings. "I'm afraid I don't have much to tell you today, Penny. We know that he's not in a prison camp; there are ledgers for that sort of thing, and he's not listed anywhere. The services all send their mail through the same channel, so the private investigators have combed through the crates of undeliverable military mail. Nothing from Jack. The investigators have collected photos of all the servicemen without identities. Actually, Ruby got the photos into the paper, and three of them were claimed by their families."

I smile, knowing that at the very least, some families have been reunited by Ruby's efforts. I stroke Tilly from the contraption around her neck to the kicker at her hips as I wait anxiously for more information.

"The only two without recognizable faces and lost tags were colored men," Claire frowns, shifting her heels in the straw.

Not Jack.

I gulp, arranging a brave face. "Well, I haven't lost hope." Absently, my hands slide in circles around my bulging stomach.

Claire's eyes well up with glistening tears pooled over her lower lashes, deepening the green of her eyes. "Oh, Penny, I'm so sorry."

"Don't tell me that *you've* abandoned all hope?" I accuse her as a thick tear splashes on her cheek. After all, she was one of the group who convinced me to cling to this hope in the first place.

"No, I haven't," she claims, sniffing. "But I just feel so terrible that your life has been so hard! Every time a gift is placed in your hands, fate just swoops down and snatches it right away from you." Her little frame jostles as she gestures wildly.

What a pathetic synopsis of your life, Imp smirks.

"The hard parts make the good stuff all the more sweet, Claire. Like you and your baby. You will love and appreciate that little thing more than you ever would've if he had come as a surprise."

"That's true, except, I'm fairly certain this little one is a 'she'," Claire insists with a little smile as her petite hand strokes a circular pattern around her belly.

"And the bathroom..."

Claire's wet eyes roll up to the ceiling beams of the barn. "Not this again."

"Don't tell me you still feel guilty over that," I object, the hay crunching under me as I shuffle toward her.

Her shoulders shake. "There's so much more than just a proper bathroom that my mother has stolen from you. Things that can never be made up for."

"Even more than a car?" I tease her.

The corners of her mouth twitch upward. "Just a hand-me-down," she whispers.

"Claire, your mother's guilt doesn't belong to you," I soothe. "You were, and you are completely innocent of her crimes. You don't owe me or my family anything at all, so just keep your little baby nest guilt-free, would'ja?" With my arms wrapped around my cousin, I feel shudders rolling up her back.

"It still tears me up inside, Pip," she sobs. I find myself desperate to ease her conscience.

"Claire, if we'd grown up in the lap of luxury, then May wouldn't feel like a princess every time she stands and gazes at her porcelain throne. It'd just be another 'thing' she would be blind to in her castle. Yes, we struggled, but we gained *so much* from the struggle."

She looks at me oddly. I detect insecurity in the way she curls her shoulders in.

Oh don't feel bad for the gal, Imp jeers in my head. Most people would leave those lessons and all of that growth for half of what she's worth!

"Pip," she begins, and her eyes well up with tears. "I grew up in that castle. And I never once gave a second thought to the washroom. To any of the washrooms!"

"C'mon, Claire; I didn't mean that growing up in a fine home makes you as shallow as a dish, I just meant that--"

"No," she interrupts. "I mean that I grew up in that castle, in *your* castle. The Hale Estate." Her words slam their fist deep into my stomach. I suppose I had suspected this, deep down within my heart. It's sickening, and it's several shades of wrong, but rings in my ears with truth. "I'm sorry, I couldn't tell you before…"

Madge Quinn, my aunt who cut my little family out of her extended family when my dad died, lives in my house. Madge's daily thick coating of shellac is applied in my mother's bedroom. Madge eats in the grand dining room I sat in as a child for meals, swinging my legs in a padded mahogany chair. The hungry suspicion I've harbored that my nefarious aunt arranged to kill my father is fed by the fact that she is living in my childhood home.

Madge is relishing the luxury of that place? My place? Sleeping in the master suite of the man she had killed; her brother?

Naturally, it's the largest home and property in all of Saratoga county, Sense reminds me.

She really is a cold, vile creature. My nostrils flare angrily before I can compose my face to mask my surprise, horror, and disgust. This is Claire's mother, after all.

Once I plaster a cheerful smile on my lips and wave goodbye to Claire, I scramble for the house and beg Annie for the keys to the Merc. My heart pumps eagerly in my veins as she questions Beauford and returns with my prize. I leap a little and scour the property for Jack's car. The engine rumbles in time with my renewed interest in the mystery surrounding my father's death.

I've never driven myself back to my childhood home before, but it seems instinct guides me there. I make my way to the far east edge of town, where the lush landscape is only interrupted by the occasional manicured estates of Saratoga's wealthiest residents. I have to carefully measure my breathing to maintain a calm facade, for my insides are swirling with a mix of emotions. Down a long stretch of road, when rows of trees begin in calculated lines, my stomach flips.

Somewhere in the recesses of my mind, I remember these details. I'm close. But I don't need to rely on fuzzy memories to know that the tall, sweeping arch ahead is the entry to my childhood home. But the familiar wrought iron filigree across it is interrupted by five gold painted letters: Quinn; a new addition since I'd been here last.

The gatekeeper nods to me, apparently the Mercury I drive is fine enough to qualify me for entry without any sort of identification. I pull forward into the great expanse of gardens between the gate and the distant roofline of my old home. A maze of box hedges to my left reminds me of countless games of hide and seek with Max and Eddie, spearing my heart with the pain of Eddie's permanent absence from my life. As I crawl past a circular bed of rose bushes, a picture of Mama, young and soft, humming while she tends idly to these perfect blooms passes through my mind. I duck my head instinctively as water shoots over the car, arcing fountains that spit streams like a rainbow over the driveway. I'd always tried to jump up to touch them, interrupting their streamlined projection. I pass under at least a dozen of these liquid arches. Long rectangles of clear water lead to grand fountains, with carefully trimmed hedges and topiaries circling their stately beauty. The stables far to the right used to hold show horses, riding horses, hunting horses, and my very own pony that Daddy had given me on my third birthday with a giant pink bow tied in it's pale mane.

"She's too young," Mama had protested.

"Let a man bring his little girl's dreams to life," he'd bantered, the lines outside his eyes crinkling into his easy smile. Mama had given in with a grin; not a trace of the stubbornness that has since encrusted her. These physical reminders of the place I once lived stir up warmth for the charmed childhood I'd enjoyed for seven years. I float reminiscently on the memories.

When the tall expanse of home is directly in front of me, and I can drive no further, I wait for the sentimental warmth around my heart to envelop me completely. It doesn't. The house, large, decorated, expertly gardened, seems dead of its former luster.

I jump when I hear a click and my door swings open.

"Park it for you, Miss?" a mustached man in a navy coat and white gloves offers. His brass buttons catch the sunlight as he stretches out his hand.

"Oh, um, please do. Thank you." I use his support for everything it's got; I'm about to see my aunt.

I silently urge my feet to lift higher as I force them up the walkway, up the steps, and onto a wide patio that's carefully designed to welcome the home's guests. For me, it only welcomes fear into my heart, echoing in resounding vibrato as I release the knocker. I nearly faint where I stand when the doors open, and various servants scatter like rats from my view.

Madge stands in the entry, just at the bottom of the stairs, adorned in a mink coat and extremely tall heels for a woman with so much gray streaking her hair. Useless lace gloves cover her talons, which peek through the delicate fabric in a blood red shade. These gloves, the heavy, glimmering earrings pulling on her earlobes, the tiny cap on her head; all useless adornments purchased with my stolen childhood. Her pale blue eyes are piercing, and trained on me like a gun.

"Hello, Penelope. I've been waiting for you."

SEVEN

"Your mother is an extremely attractive woman," Madge hints as we sit stiffly in her living room. Because all of the proverbial bushes have been beaten around, we've finally locked gazes so intense that they'd do a cowboy's duel proud. "Too attractive for only one man to handle all on his own." She doesn't blink, watching the heavy implication of her words sink into my understanding.

"You're wrong, Madge. My parents loved each other very much," I insist, fighting tears back. I cannot appear weak to her, for I know that this villain feeds on weakness. For the moment, she settles for drawing her drink through her lips and smirking at my trembling lip.

"Your mother loved my brother, surely," she agrees, dangling her words over an oncoming caveat. "But she loved so many other men, as well." Her lips curl into a devious grin that boils my blood.

When my hands tremble violently in my lap, I know that I'm about to lose it.

"Liar! You're a liar!" I holler, the force of the words bringing me to my feet. I hadn't planned to lose my composure like this. However, screaming into her vile face without abandon sets free a flock of angry birds from their confinement deep within me. They flap in her face and claw at her skin.

Only her busy nostrils reveal her distress. "Penelope, I know this is difficult to absorb. I know your upbringing must have been quite challenging…"

"Pfffha! Challenging?" *Challenging.* Such a flippant word from the thief of my childhood.

"...but you must understand, I did you children a favor," she insists.

"Wha- what? A *favor*? Please!"

"You'd just lost your father, my dear. What kind of a monster would I be if I sent your sole caretaker to prison for murdering your father?"

"Mama was at home with us when he died," I defend. "Don't try and tell me she slipped out of the house to murder her husband."

"The wealthy rarely get their own hands dirty, Penelope. Surely she compelled one of her lovers to remove their only roadblock to her arms from the picture."

"Who? Do you have names? Who do you suppose was so desperate to land a mother of four that they would kill a good man in cold blood?" I demand sarcastically. Her accusations sound ridiculous.

She holds up her bony fingers to count.

"Charles Parke," she ticks on her pinky. I roll my eyes; I don't even know who that is. She sticks out her ring finger. "Harvey Marshall never could keep his eyes off of her. Grant Pearson, *pffha*! He'd do anything to land that woman!"

I find it difficult to envision this swarm of men vying for the attention of a farmhand in a handkerchief, which is the Mama I've known for years.

"*Oh kay*, made up names, then," I challenge sarcastically.

"Ask your mother! Or better yet, look them up in the directory yourself! I'm sure they'd love to talk to you about the love of their lives. All three of them dripped like a Vermont maple tree for that woman. Saps!"

Sense's words sound in my head, *She sounds jealous. Why would she be jealous of your mother if it weren't true?*

"Like I said, I wouldn't want to be a monster and take your only surviving parent from you, no matter how dreadful a thing she'd done..."

As my fingers dig into a delicate pillow in my lap, I know that I've reached my capacity for her stories and the nagging feeling that they could be the truth. My voice trembles as I stand and interrupt her.

"Oh, you're a monster, Madge. Make no mistake of that!" I sweep the fine pillow across the side table, sending a vase flying through the tense air. It smashes with a satisfying *crunch* just before the door slams behind me.

August 4th, 1942

I shake the pen in my chilled fist, then scratch it on the paper in my journal. *Ah-ha!* It makes a mark. While I lay on the cold ground under the willow at the Spot, I continue my letter to Max.

"I know I shouldn't rile up a recovering patient, if you ever get the chance to read this at all, but I just can't keep this to myself. I'm sorry to say that I sort of doubted your accusations against Madge when you first admitted your suspicions to me. Then, I thought for awhile that they were absolutely correct, that Madge was the person responsible for Daddy's arranged death, but now I'm as confused as ever.

Uncle Harry has a terrible gambling problem; did you know that? I've learned that before Grandpa died, Harry gambled away everything they had. Take a moment to absorb that: millions of dollars lost in a silly game. Are you as surprised as I am? Are you as sick to your core as I am? That fella always made a show of his riches. I never would have guessed they were near destitute! I figure that the threat of the bread lines gave Madge some real motivation to claim all of Grandpa's inheritance; even kill for it.

You'd be proud of your little sister. I confronted Madge. She flatly denied it, of course; pointed the finger at someone else. I don't want to believe it- I really don't. I asked her why she didn't go to the police right away and avenge her brother."

I stare into the depth of the river before I write the next sentence. Scratching it onto paper just might make it true; I'm not sure if I can face that.

"She said she wanted to send his killer to prison, but since we'd just lost our father, she didn't want us to grow up without our mother, too. To hear Madge tell it, Mama had been involved in ongoing flings with Charlie Parke, Harvey Marshall, and Grant Pearson. It's hard to believe, but also hard to ignore, Max. Can we really rule out the possibility that our mother was in love with someone else?"

Madge had made her point as clear as glass: the person responsible for setting up Daddy's death... is Mama. I don't want to believe it. *Mama is stubborn, and Mama can put up a good fight, but could she really take a life?* If my aunt's tales are true, then I've shared a bed with an adulterous murderer for over ten years.

Is my mother really an adulteress?

Could she really be a murderer?

No.

Maybe.

No!

You have to consider the possibility.

As I pull around the corner toward the farmhouse, I'm at war with myself inside. Imagining what Max will think when he reads through my frantic, confused scrawl, I realize, this new story doesn't make any sense.

But then, it *does.*

My legs lumber oddly along like stilts, heavy and jarred, up the walkway to the farmhouse, only soothed by the welcome sight of my little sister.

"P! I thought I'd never see you back here," she says, wrapping her arms around my bulging middle.

"Hi, Sis," I greet her. The corners of my mouth refuse to turn up in a smile for her. "Where's Mama?"

"Out back, talking to the Victory Corps guy," she says, analyzing me suspiciously.

I start to trudge toward the farm, but pause to satisfy my curiosity, "Oh, have you heard anything about Max yet?"

May's smile flattens, and her curls dance over her shoulders as she shakes her head. "Nope," she murmurs.

I stamp my foot in the dirt. The army physician had warned us in a telegram that after three months in a coma, the chances of a patient waking with full brain function slim down to almost nothing. We're so far past the three month mark that the thread of hope I've clung to has frayed significantly. I can't go to another funeral; I can't mourn for another brother.

As I move along the side of the house to find my mother, I realize that ever since I slammed Madge's front door, ever since those possibilities wormed their way into my head, I've been mourning the mother I thought I knew.

I'm doomed to mourn.

When I locate her blonde head amongst the workers in caps, the sting of our last interface shocks my heart. Her thin neck turns toward me, and I watch her large blue eyes widen in shock when she notices me standing stiffly behind the house. She's a natural beauty, even aged, even weather-worn. I consider with new eyes how she could be sought after my eager admirers.

"Mama," I begin, gulping. Her Stare begins freezing my tongue in my mouth. Before I go completely stiff, I push out, "I went to Madge's house." The effect of my words dissolve the Stare. My mother shrinks under them.

"Let's go somewhere more private, shall we, Penelope?" Once in Nell's stall, her countenance falls. "Ugh," Mama grunts, hanging her head. "Are you still stirring up this rotten pot? I thought surely, what with all the other things you have to worry about, your husband missing, a baby on the way, Max still unstable with a massive brain injury, and Eddie gone," her voice breaks; "you'd lay this nonsense to rest."

Several sentences wrestle behind my lips, fighting to come out.

Your nervous defiance of this topic seems rather incriminating, Mother! Eddie can't fight this fight anymore. Finding Daddy's killer was Max's obsession. Max deserves some sort of closure after all he's been through. And when he wakes…

"She claims, rather firmly, that you killed him," slides off of my lips timidly, so I square my shoulders and watch her telltale brow for signs of dishonesty. Brows quiet, it's her nostrils that move rapidly.

"And you believe her?" Mama answers with the Stare trained viciously on an innocent pile of straw.

"Mama." In my tone is her answer: I don't want to believe Madge, but I want an explanation. "You know she said that you and a man named Charles had an affair. And that you asked Charles to arrange the, uh, *accident*."

Mama's fingers instantly fly to the bridge of her nose. "This is ridiculous! I don't even want to dignify these accusations with a response!" She pants. "But I suppose, if my own daughter actually believes that I could… oh, my, *Penelope!* Do you actually think I had anything to do with that?" Her beautiful face screws up in a mix of strain, desperation, sincerity and horror. The sight unsettles me.

"I don't want to." I swallow the lump in my throat. "But, Mama, Claire had no idea what her mother had done to us. Claire, the cousin I love and respect, thought her mother was just as good a person as any. She was blown off her feet when I told her that we'd been thrown away."

"Thrown into the garbage like kitchen scraps, or soiled rags, Penelope! Magnolia Quinn is a *heartless* woman! And a *liar!*"

"It's just that Claire didn't want to believe that about her mom. I don't want to believe this, but I have to at least question it."

"We've lived in that hut for *eleven* years," she breathes, pointing back in the direction of the rickety old farmhouse. "Do you think I chose this life for us?"

"No, Mama. But Madge made it sound like you just wanted Daddy out of the way. Like you thought you could keep living that life on the estate."

Mama pinches the bridge of her nose between her fingers as she shakes her head. "I can't believe I'm still living this. I can't believe this is still happening. I can't believe that my own *daughter...*" she chants, glassy eyed.

"Mama," I beg. "Tell me that I'm wrong! Tell me that it's ridiculous! Tell me that 'Charles' never existed! I want to believe you! Tell me!" I touch the letter to Max in my pocket.

"It's not ridiculous, Penny."

My blood stops pumping.

"It's *ludicrous.* Charlie... he, well..."

"Charlie?" I gasp as my heart restarts. She knows who he is. She'd called her alleged lover by an affectionate nickname. "He's 'Charlie' to you? Mama, did you..."

Mama stands with her eyes shut, her shoulders sagging, waiting for my question to wiggle its way out of my thoughts.

"Did you *sleep* with Charles Parke?"

Mama draws a long breath through her lips before she replies.

"Some things are more complicated than a young girl can understand," she whispers.

"Did you?" I press. "Did you while you were married to Daddy?"

"No, Penelope. I would never cheat on your father," she promises.

She wouldn't sleep with that man until your father was out of the way, Imp amends in my thoughts.

"So what's complicated about it? What can't I understand?" I challenge with my chest heaving.

"Before I courted your father, I had a relationship with Charlie; ahem, *Charles.* After we ended it, and I fell in love with your father, he could never really wrap his head around the fact that I was married, *happily* married. And I... I couldn't..."

Mama's words trail away as tears roll down her dusty cheeks.

"This really is none of your business, Penelope."

My stomach rolls uncomfortably. I feel sick; overwhelmed. This sounds too close to an admission of guilt.

Oh, I can't stand here any longer, bathing in this disgusting information. I back through the hay to the stall door, shaking my head.

Who is this woman?

"Penny!" she calls to me as my feet stumble over clods of dirt on my path back to the car. "Penelope, wait!"

August 9th, 1942

I've been staring at my thumbnails for five minutes, even though I shut off the Merc's engine long ago. My hands have locked themselves around the steering wheel, parked in front of Claire and Bentley's colonial home. Sense prods me to get out of this car and walk up to the door, as I drove here to do, but my body doesn't seem to want to cooperate. So, I just sit.

I don't know if Madge has spoken to Claire since I barged in her door and destroyed her vase. I worry that my cousin will take one look at my face and see the mixed-up doubt screaming from my eyes. I had worked so hard to convince her that her mother had destroyed my childhood, and possibly murdered my father. Only now, the blame swings between her mother, and mine. I'm not sure where it should settle.

Mama had said that man's name, *"Charlie,"* with such comfortable recognition that I know he's real, not a fictional name Madge had made up. It slid off of Mama's tongue like a pickaxe to my sure, hard shell of knowledge surrounding my dad's death. Madge threw out those men's names, and I'd repelled her words as lies; but Mama's eyes flickered with recognition, surprise, and fear when I repeated them to her. *Fear that I've discovered the truth?*

Mama had a relationship with Charles that he couldn't accept the end of. *How hard did he push her? How far did she allow herself to be pushed?* She wore such guilt in her eyes as we spoke. I know there is plenty she's not telling me… yet.

I use the surge of adrenaline that this thought sends through me to throw open the car door and stand up. I hurry to the door, and the maid ushers me back to Claire's bedroom where she sits at the dressing table.

"Hiya, Penny. Did you already hear? Why are you crying?" I sniff and wipe at my leaking eyes, and she abandons her silver brush to stand.

"What? Did I hear what?" I can't imagine that anything she could tell me would lift me from the bed of sticky black tar I lie in.

"About the pilot one of the PI's dug up in a hospital in the city," she clarifies.

"No, please; tell me," I invite her eagerly. I'm willing to set aside my concerns about Mama for this.

"This pilot was there, in the firefight, when Jack's plane went down. They called him Jack 'o Lantern?"

"Yes," I clarify in a whisper, shivering with this unquestionable detail.

"This pilot was down on the ground when Jack's plane hit. He saw the whole thing from a few hundred yards away, from his own wrecked plane. Jack's fuel tank was on fire, and the whole thing went up in flames just seconds after it hit." Her eyes fill with tears, and her lip quivers when she continues.

"I think his name was something like… Savage. Or Savant."

My mouth falls open. It's a perfect retelling of the horrific nightmares I've endured out of worry.

Or were your nightmares a premonition? Imp whispers.

"Savage claims there's no way the pilot could've survived it, even if he'd survived the flak to shot him down," Claire shares with her hands on her stomach. "I'm so sorry, Pip, but I think the best thing we've got is that pair of eyes at the scene. It's likely that Jack really is gone."

I bite down on my lower lip and shake my head. Claire can't sell me his certain death; she's responsible for lighting the fire of hope under me. I won't give up hoping until I see his body with my own eyes. We have a child together. I'll never stop hoping that our child will know their father.

"I'm so sorry, Penny. I'm so sorry."

"Can I speak with this pilot?" I beg.

"Sure, I mean, he's recovering in a hospital in the big city, but I'm sure we could visit," she concedes.

My eyes brighten while the questions I'll beg this poor gent tumble around in my thoughts.

"What a pair we'll make," she giggles, her eyes aglow. "The two of us storming into his hospital with our big old tummies leading the way."

My lips curl upward. This is the first real person I'll be able to talk to about Jack who saw him overseas. Whether he confirms bad news or not, I feel like speaking with him will make Jack feel closer to me.

"Oof," she exclaims, her eyes popping wide open. "She kicked me."

"Thank you, Claire. I know Ruby probably doesn't want you sharing her expensive information with me," I offer.

She shakes her caramel hair from side to side. "What she doesn't know won't harm her," she replies with her rosy lips curled up. Suddenly, her grin falls into a blank, stunned expression.

"Claire? Are you okay?" I ask.

Her hands clamp down on the sides of her round belly as her eyes squeeze shut.

"Oooh, ow," she groans through her teeth. "That was more than a kick. Oof." Her shoulders hunch around her stomach.

"A contraction?" I guess.

She nods erratically as she tries to breathe through her pain.

"Sit down, then!" I urge her. Claire's bottom touches lightly onto the bed before she jumps away, as though her bedspread were made of hot coals.

"Oh, no; that's worse, that's worse! I'll just stand until it passes." She leans heavily into her ornate bedpost, looking pale.

I mumble something like an apology as my hands flutter

helplessly around her.

"It's okay, Cousin. I want this. I can't wait to meet her," she reassures me through her clenched teeth. Her head falls backward in relief as her face relaxes. "Agh, that was worse than I expected." Claire flops backward onto her bed, throwing her arms out in surrender.

Great, I think to myself. *It won't be long before I'm going to feel something like this, too.* If a society girl like Claire feels enough pain to allow it to screw up her perfect poise, contractions are going to be simply agonizing. One of her small feet hangs off of the edge of the bed, so I ease it onto the top of the comforter.

"Claire! You're bleeding," I exclaim, noticing a growing circle of vibrant red in her lap.

"What?" she asks as she pushes herself up on her elbow.

I point to the stain on her dress.

"That's not supposed to happen, is it?" Her eyebrows crumple in concern. "Oh, no…" she mutters as she tries to heave herself up. Her skin quickly develops a greyish quality as the stain widens.

I hold my palms up to her. "No, don't move, Claire. I'll go get your nurse!"

She concedes and falls back on the pillow, muttering, "No, no, no…"

I tear out the bedroom door and down the long, thin rug that spans Claire and Bentley's upstairs hallway.

"Eloise!" I cry out to the on-call nurse that Bentley has hired, though I can't remember which the endless doors lead to her room. "Eloise, Claire needs you!" I hear the shuffle of the house help around the corner, standing up out of their chairs and moving toward my frantic call.

"Is it Missus Sharpe?" a bone-thin, ebony-skinned maid asks with timid worry written all over her face. A portly man who must be Claire's driver catches up with her.

"You need the maid, Miss?" he asks.

"It's Claire. There's blood. I don't think there's supposed to be blood!"

The waifish maid's thin neck supports her dropping head as she shakes it back and forth. The driver lunges forward and pounds on the door just across the hall. The door rattles in its frame from his urgency.

"Eloise!   Missus Sharpe is bleeding!   Please assist her immediately!" he bellows. My eyes fall to his round belly, and I can only assume that he moonlights as an opera singer for how loudly and clearly his voice carries. "Eloise, open this door immed-"

The door snaps open by a few inches. "I was in a *bath*, if you'll excuse me," the pudgy occupant fumes. She slams the door.

The driver huffs out an impatient breath as the tiny maid scurries toward Claire's room. I hurry after her; there's no time to dawdle.

"You had best hurry up with your dressing if you expect to be paid for your time here!" the man scolds behind us through the nurse's door.

I flutter helplessly behind the maid. "What can I do?" I ask her as she stuffs a pillow under Claire's hips and pushes the caramel hair from her sweat-slick forehead.

Her deep brown eyes tell me to calm myself. "Fetch Mister Sharpe. There's a telephone in the sitting room," she instructs. I pass the frowning driver in the hallway as he wrestles the angry nurse down the hall by her arm. Her robe sticks to her wet skin as she tries to tie it closed around her waist with her free hand.

With the phone pressed to my ear, I hear clicks as the operator connects me with Bentley's office, and his secretary leaves me on the open line while she drops the phone to her desk with a thunk. I hear her feet shuffle quickly, and her urgent knocks at the other end of the line. I hold my breath.

"Are you still there?" her voice comes breathlessly through the receiver after a moment.

"Mmm hmm," I confirm with my head nodding up and down.

She can't see you, dummy, Imp jeers.

"Yes," I breathe.

"Mister Sharpe is on his way home."

"Thank you," I warble, and set the ivory-handled phone into its brass forks. The driver rushes around the corner from the hall with a red face.

"Did you reach Mister Sharpe?"

"I did," I confirm. "He's on his way home."

"The missus in in a real bad way. Better call him back and tell him to meet us at Saint Christopher's Hospital."

The hospital's thick antiseptic scent doesn't faze my nose as I blow through the hospital halls toward Emergency Care. The glares of the nurses rushing from patient to patient form an invisible barrier between me and finding my cousin. I know how they feel; nervous family members are just one more person to take care of.

Once I'm told that I can't see Claire, I feel shooed from the hospital by the thing inside of me that tells me that I don't fit anywhere anymore. I hurry back out the front doors under the stone archway with my tail between my legs. I don't want to go far, but I know I can't stay inside.

My eyes fall on the bench just outside of the hospital, near the alleyway. I'm drawn to it. I sit on the cold stone, and as the chill seeps into my backside, so does an all-encompassing memory. I lie on my back like I did the night Jack saved me from the creep in the alleyway, though this time my heavy belly presses uncomfortably up against my lungs. The sight of Jack's face in my head is so delicious that I swat away my physical discomfort like a mosquito. I need to see him clearly, without this distraction.

I squeeze my lids tightly shut to block out the daylight trying to make its way in. Behind them, in memory, I see the soft streetlight touching upon the side of Jack's face as he inspects my wound; his temple, his cheekbone, his straight nose, his jawline. The rest of his face hides in the inky shadows of the night. I'd felt his heartbeat thumping through his skin while we were pressed so close together.

This was the moment I'd given up my fight against him. Lying on this bench that night, I'd surrendered.

I wait for his warmth to fill me, but all that seeps into my skin is cold. The cold of the stone bench, the cold of the air, the cold of being completely alone. The cold of not knowing whether the last bright spot left in your life is hiding somewhere, or if he has burnt out.

I shudder.

"Pip," a feminine voice hisses from the hospital entrance. Immediately, I sit up and tug my skirt to my knees.

"Doris," I reply. "Any news?"

Her lips pinch before they surrender into a frown. When she nods, her carefully shellac-ed hairdo doesn't budge.

"Bad news? Is it..." My chin bounces on its hinge, but the words won't come. *Claire? Is Claire okay?*

"You'd better come inside."

You're here as a patron. You're allowed, Sense assures me as I move under the big stone archway. After being kicked out of this place twice, I'm still skittish as my feet shuffle over the green and white linoleum tiles. Doris pulls me by the upper arm into an empty exam room. I know my eyes are as large as a deer's in oncoming headlights because of the way Doris's expression responds to them.

"Claire is fine. They've given her a tranquilizer, 'cuz she'll be just fine until she wakes up."

"When she wakes up? What... what happens then?" I stammer, afraid of the answer.

"Then Bentley will have to tell her that their baby girl never took a breath. She came out as blue as a blueberry, with the cord wrapped around her neck. Twice."

"A girl," I whisper, and my eyes sting with tears. Claire knew she was growing a baby girl inside of her. "She's dead?"

Doris's jaw stays tight as she gives a curt nod. We've both seen this happen here, just not to anyone we knew before they arrived huffing and puffing with labor pains. This new perspective tastes bitter on my tongue; bitter in my throat as I try to swallow it away.

But it just rots in my belly.

Poor Claire.

No one seems to notice me folded up as best I can around my belly as I sit for hours in the hallway outside of Claire's room. The soles of orderlies' shoes tap past me without pause, and nurses' stiff uniforms just swish on by as they move in and out of her doorway. The only living thing that seems to know I'm here is the cricket wiggling its antennae from three linoleum tiles away. It watches me with its beady little insect eyes.

"*Crrrrrricket,*" it trills, as if to say, '*It's nighttime, why don't you go home?*'

There's no better place to worry than right here, I answer it with my eyes.

It offers a quick, staccato chirp of agreement, and I nod.

The sound of fine dress shoes in the doorway sends a jolt of nervous energy through my heart, and the cricket hops another three tiles away.

I don't think Bentley notices me here, either, as he leans into the door frame with his hand covering his eyes. His shoulders sag like a field worker at the end of harvest day; I know that they've never done that before.

"Um, Bentley?" I whisper. I don't want him to feel embarrassed once he notices my audience to his grief. His hand falls away, revealing the long, tired face of a broken man. I wonder for a moment if he even recognizes me, the pain is so thick in his eyes.

But he sighs and moves one well-polished dress shoe toward me. "Mind if I join you…" he mumbles as his back hits the wall and he slides to the ground.

"Sure," I answer, even though he's already so close to me that I choke on the thick, foul-tasting cloud of his despair.

"They say she'll wake up anytime now," I tell him as an informed eavesdropper. He nods weakly.

"I could give her anything. I could give her everything. She deserves everything," he tells the white, speckled tile in front of him with a blank stare. "But I can't give her this." Tears glisten on his cheeks under the harsh hall light as they run silently toward his chin. His lips barely move as he murmurs, "I can't give her a child." He sighs like he's failed as a husband. Like he's failed as a man.

I take this rare moment of being up so close to Jack's older brother to inspect his face for signs of Jack. It's clear they're related, though Bentley's nose wears a slight bump on the ridge, and his brows sit lower over his eyes. A little paunch pokes out from his belly; probably the result of deskwork. Jack is better-looking, but Bentley's obvious concern for his wife reveals his gorgeous humanity.

"You can try again," I assure him, but I don't think he hears me. He's deep underwater in a pool of grief. I've swum in this pool before. And at the moment, I'm barely doggie-paddling through it.

What seems like hours later, I stir from my uncomfortable sleeping position against the cold linoleum. Bentley is gone, but a thin blanket covers my shoulders. The tapping of several pairs of orthopedic shoes over the hard floor coaxes me toward consciousness.

"...*awake*..." I hear one of them say, and I err my way through the choreography of standing up from sitting with a heavy belly.

On my feet, I use the fact that I've become no more than a light switch or a painting on the wall to my advantage, and slip into Claire's room. I creep toward her, and tentatively lay my hand on her blanketed ankle.

"She was a girl," Claire murmurs, staring at the windowsill.

"You were right all along," I quietly congratulate her with my small smile.

"Mmm hmm," she hums with a nearly imperceptible nod, her carmelly hair dull as it moves against the rough pillowcase. The silence is thick as I gauge her mental state. "I named her before she was born, when she was still alive inside me. Julia," she whispers. I wonder if she knows she's talking to her cousin, or if she means to address that windowsill. She hasn't looked up at me.

"That's a beautiful name," I answer quietly.

"All growing up, I thought I'd name a daughter Magnolia, after my mother," she mumbles like a robot, no inflection to her voice. Her pretty, rosebud lips barely part as she continues, "But then I learned, you can't name a child after someone who's still alive. Because they can disappoint you." *Madge.*

Madge disappointed us all.

"My grandmother, Julia; she's dead. She can't let me down now. So I'd decided to name my baby girl after her."

"That's perfect," I tell her quietly, though she gives no indication that she's heard anything I've said.

She scoffs. "I named my baby after a dead woman."

"Oh, Claire…"

"I doomed my baby girl. I killed her," she mumbles. I know that she doesn't make any sense, but I also know that her mind is swallowed up in the thick fog of grief.

A grieving mind is incapable of sense.

Claire blinks hard a few times, and her eyes shift over to me, as though she's realizing for the first time that another person breathes the same hospital-room air as she does. I watch recognition register in her eyes. Her gaze falls to my rounded stomach.

Immediately, guilt attempts to suck the basketball-sized lump below my ribcage into hiding. It does no good, and I watch as Claire's mossy green eyes moisten with tears before they squeeze shut and her tiny chin turns away from me.

I realize at that moment that as long as I have this person growing inside of me, I'm only going to be a source of pain for my cousin. I came here to comfort her, and since I've only managed to do the opposite, I quickly and quietly pad to the door.

September 2nd, 1942

All evening, I've been trying my best to ignore twinges of pain in my back and hips. Because there is no hope of napping through these aches, I've walked through the vineyard and the orchard in the fading light several times.

Darkness falls over the plantation. I don't trust my awkward, swollen feet to carry me safely over clods of dirt obscured by nightfall, but I can't bear the thought of trapping myself inside Lyla's house with limited room to pace. I make my way toward the barn under the low, yellow moon in hopes of finding a stray lantern to guide my steps.

The burning had come on slowly, like a pot of cold water set to boil, but as I limp through the barn doors, my tailbone sets on fire. I shift my weight from foot to foot to try to relieve the torment in my lower back, cursing the hard ground beneath my feet. I've read that I'll know when the baby was coming when my stomach starts to cramp, hard. My stomach feels fine, but my *back*...

I yelp a ragged cry that echoes in the eaves of the barn. Surely someone is stabbing me repeatedly in the tailbone with a knife. I throw my head from side to side, trying to look for the attacker behind me. I fall to the floor. I can't catch my breath through the sharpness of the pain. Just as suddenly as the knife is plunged, the pain lifts. I gasp for breath. Had I imagined that feeling? I feel my lower back, expecting a wound, and pull my hand away, expecting blood.

Nothing. I am alone.

Minutes later, the stabbing pains return to refresh my memory of their utter brutality, and affirm my sanity. No, I hadn't imagined it, here it is again. Each spell grows stronger and more painful until I can't help but cry out, wailing pathetically like a dying cat.

I become maniacal--wild eyes, gasping breaths--with shorter respites between pains. Four minutes, two minutes. I run my hand across my forehead, which is slick with sweat. I need... I need a friend.

I move over the straw in the barn like a stab victim stumbling to a hospital. I see Tilly's tail up ahead.

"Tilly!" I cry. I know she won't be able to stop the pain or call a doctor, but what I need right now is comfort. And for me, that means Tilly. I stumble to her and lean heavily into my palms on her side. She must think I want her to lie down, because she sinks to the ground and onto her side.

"Tilly… ugh, Tilly," I pant, falling to my knees. As the wracking pain subsides, I draw a deep breath. Without so much as thirty seconds of respite, another blinding wave of pain seizes my body, and I collapse into her, screaming through my teeth. I roll to my side, stiff with pain, and realize that I am going to have this baby. Right here. Right now.

"Lyla!" I scream. "Help me, Lyla!" I don't know that an aged dowager will be much more help than a stubborn cow, but I don't think I can do this all by myself. "Annie… somebody…" Another wave of pain clenches my jaw shut tightly and I scream inside my mouth. It releases its hold for only a moment, and I gasp as though I've been held underwater. A white hot pressure sears between my legs.

Oh, no. No, no, no. No! I will my body to slow down, to stop what it's doing, but it pays me no mind. The pressure is intense. I roll to my back, sitting up against Tilly's belly, and try my best to breathe.

Why won't it stop? Why can't I just have a moment to catch my breath? Only one thought rises above the pain: *Mama was right. I am way, way too young for this.*

Tilly's stillness is so out of character for her that I know she must understand what's happening to me. I'm just not sure if *I* fully understand what's happening to me.

I've learned that women love nothing more than to bond over childbirth stories. I clearly remember pulling on Mama's arm after church service, impatient to get home, but being told to wait as ladies dressed in their Sunday best competed for the prize of surviving the most horrific labor and delivery. It seemed like a thumb war, with several female thumbs trying to top the others. I always assumed that there was a fair amount of exaggeration employed to buoy their womanly accomplishment.

And then in the hospital, observing births in small snippets as I ran errands for the medical staff, I watched women sweat and cry out, insisting with wild eyes that the fabric between Earth and Hell had been temporarily ripped open, and that they were dangling over its unimaginable heat as they felt sharp pains that no one could measure from the outside. Then, also, I figured they screamed loud enough for their husbands to hear them in the waiting room. To earn their respect. Or simply to ensure that their efforts could be used as leverage later. I was wrong. Oh, my, was I *wrong*. The fabric has indeed been torn, and this fire has been stoked just for me.

You owe every one of those women an apology, Sense interjects.

From my ribs to my thighs, my body catches aflame in intervals, searing my flesh with the heat of the devil's pitchfork. I can't breathe when it happens, and I'm stiff until it passes. When the fire goes dim, I pant and shuffle desperately to find a comfortable position, until the heat rises again so rapidly that it would blow the mercury out of a thermometer. Innocent pigeons in the barn flap frantically from their perch as I scream, trying to release the agony through my throat, but Tilly lies peacefully still for me. Between spasms of pain, I try to time my breaths with hers. Two tiny goats look on from their pen, frozen in horror. I gasp as they both fall over into the straw.

I know, little goats; I feel the same way. But, my body will not allow me the sweet relief of unconsciousness. It demands what it wants, and it hasn't asked my opinion.

When I feel depleted of every ounce of energy I possessed, a new, painful pressure presents itself. This pressure insists on action, and it won't take *'I'm too tired'* for an answer. It's time to push. Tears spill out of the corners of my eyes as I reluctantly slide my underpants down to my ankles. I turn my chin to the rafters, howling in agony as I kick the scrap of material from my feet.

I'm sorry, I tell those women through my screams. *I'm so sorry I judged you.* There's no momentary relief like there was with the contractions. I thought that was bad, unbearable, really; but I'd sorely underestimated what unbearable means. Because I *must* bear it. I have no choice.

"*Raaaaaghnaaaaaaaaaaahpppppphhhffffff!*" I scream, knowing my face has never been quite this flooded with blood.

"*Anffff!*" I must be purple by now. "*Ooowaaaaaahgh!*" Surely my hips are splitting in two, but my body won't stop it from happening; it *wants* this to be happening.

"*Eeeeerrgh!*"

Misery. *Misery!*

"*Oooowho!*"

Surprised that I can still see when I crack open my clenched eyelids, that my eyeballs haven't burst inside their sockets as I'd imagined they had, I reach around my inflated belly and feel the top of a hard, slime-covered ball. I draw a breath and realize that there's a baby coming out of my body. A baby!

Obviously! Imp jeers.

Yes, *obviously* I've known for months that I was growing a child inside of me, but I couldn't believe it. Seeing is believing. Feeling is believing. When my body stubbornly persists with another sharp contraction, I throw my head back and whimper. *There's more. More work to do. Nooooo.*

Now I'm certain that my eyeballs are exploding in my head, for the pressure of pushing with all of my might is so intense, that I feel like my head is locked between angry vice grips. When the little body slips away from me all at once, I fall forward in raucous, whimpering sobs. I'm done.

I scoop up the tiny, wriggling person from the hay and hold it to my sweat-soaked chest, nervously checking for signs that it shares Julia's fate. It's a boy; a pink, wriggling, healthy-looking baby boy. His loud cry assures me that he is very much alive. I name him instantly, without registering that I've done it; little Jack.

My head collapses backward onto Tilly's ribs. I'm done. I'm done.

It's over.

EIGHT

After I suck in a recovery breath, I raise my head to take in the tiny body in my arms. Small, wrinkly, and covered in a creamy white coating, he spreads his lips open as widely as they will go with each wailing cry. His spindly arms flail in the air, and something inside of me urges my arms to pull him close to my chest.

My throat vibrates with low, humming words, "Hello, baby; hello my baby boy. It's okay. Everything's alright." His wails soften into tiny, curious croaks as his body relaxes into mine.

"Hello, my boy," I tell him as he opens his eyes. His dark blue irises fill the surface of them, and they peer around with disoriented wonder. "I know just how you feel, little man. This is brand new for me, too."

With a fresh pang, my belly demands my attention, and I'm torn away from admiring him. *Nooo,* I groan, remembering that an afterbirth must be delivered now. When reading about childbirth, I had imagined the placenta sliding right out after the baby, but I can see now that I won't be so lucky.

I need help, I realize. I can't bear more contractions and cradle my little boy at the same time. Tilly has been a patient companion, but I need a person, and I need them right away.

"Lyla! Annie!" I call, my voice hoarse. I'd even take Beauford's assistance at this point. "Help!" I whimper as I roll onto my knees with only one free hand to steady myself with. Shakily, I rise to my feet and clutch my little boy's slick body to my chest with both hands.

I stumble out of the barn doors toward the brilliant lights of the guest house. I know I'm in a state of shock as my legs heave themselves one in front of the other through the brush. I feel the umbilical cord paddling between my thighs as I move.

When I reach the back porch, I lean heavily into the jamb of the open kitchen door, another constriction squeezing the insides of my belly in its vice. I groan.

"Miss Penelope!" Annie exclaims, pushing up out of her chair.

"Take the child," her senior maid instructs her, miraculously calm, as though a bloodied new mother and her naked new son often burst into her kitchen. She coaxes my weight onto her chest. I leave a slimy red smear on the clean white trim as I lean into her. Annie gingerly cradles the tiny child with the clean sleeves of her uniform, and we ease onto the polished floor together.

"You didn't ring the bell," Annie reproves.

"I was… I was out in the barn," I pant, my forehead beading over with fresh sweat. The three of us look up as Lyla's frail shoulders barely fill the doorway I'd just stumbled in through.

"What in the devil?" she gasps as she absorbs the bloody smear on the jamb, and the tangle of four bodies on the floor.

"You delivered out in the barn? Alone?" the older maid chokes.

I nod with a grimace. I don't want questions. This *hurts*.

"Atta girl," Lyla cheers. "Hand over my great grandbaby!"

Annie obediently offers her the child, even though her face is filled with painful-looking reluctance. Lyla snatches a clean, folded dish towel from the counter, and the two of them wrap my baby in the fabric before Lyla hugs her great grandson to her ribs. Annie's fingers pull away from him very slowly.

"You've already proved that you're strong," the maid says, staring straight into my terrified eyes. "You're going to need that again right now. On my count, I want you to push. One…"

"No!" I beg in a weak whimper.

"Two," she continues, not even blinking.

I can't do this. I'm spent!

You don't have a choice, Sense whispers.

"Three. Go!" she urges me. Together, we suck in a deep breath. In Lyla's arms, my brand new baby boy wails along with me as I push with all of the strength I have left.

"Good girl," the maid congratulates me as the pressure inside of me deflates. I hear the metallic rub of a scissor snip, and a clatter as the tool rests onto a dish. "You did it! You're done!"

"You were wonderful, Miss Pip," Annie praises.

"I'd pay to see any man try and do that," Lyla croaks. She redirects her gravelly coo to the bundle in her arms. "Except you, little fellow. You're just perfect."

My heavy lids flutter closed, too weighted to lift again.

Now... now you're done.

When my eyelashes flutter awake, I lie in my luxurious guest bed. With as awful as I feel, I don't feel worthy of the fine fabrics against my skin. *Oh*, does my head throb. I only allow my eyes to open a sliver. The still feeling to the air tells me it is night. The usual lamp is on in the corner, bathing half of the room in its soft light. It's either very late, or very, very early.

My body aches. I open and close my jaw a few times to try to work away the ache that's there, and realize that I must have strained it from clenching my teeth so tightly. I get up slowly, the movement reminding me of what has transpired today. My tailbone no longer aches, but my hips, thighs and lady parts scream with pain. Standing causes my empty stomach to jiggle, and a rush of blood escapes me. I need a bathroom.

The feel of my stomach jiggling as I walk unnerves me. Once taut and uncomfortable, the undulating emptiness feels almost eerie. And my chest, oh! It feels as though tweezers pull the tender skin from the inside; just noticeable enough to be annoying.

In the dim light of the small room across from mine, the soft, squished face peeking out of a flannel blanket is a beacon of light. My heart drops out and a euphoric syrup rushes through me. I kneel beside the tiny figure, hands reverently fixed over its body, not wanting to disturb its peace. So pink, so new. Even though my belly grew, and I felt movements inside of me, I've had a hard time believing that my body was actually making a person inside of it.

"He's been sleeping like a log, Miss, I'm sure you can pick him up without waking him," Annie offers. "Support his head," she directs me. Though the smooth, brown skin of her cheek looks too young to belong to an expert with newborns, she seems confident in her advice. I nod to her as tears fill my eyes and my bottom finds a chair. In my arms lies the most pure, peaceful creature I have ever laid eyes on.

"He looks like a doll," I laugh through wet tears and sniff. The most imperceptible inhales and exhales register under his miniature ribcage. His jaw drops open and he looks like a sleeping old man. I can't remember ever grinning so widely and genuinely.

I am in *love*. Not like with Jack, who slowly wormed his way into my affection, but instantaneously. The intense oncoming of the feeling is like hitting a wall of warm sunshine. I know right away that I will sacrifice anything necessary for this little soul. Adoringly, my fingers run over the soft, dark down on his crown; the creamy pink of his skin; the lilliputian fingernails on his long, thin fingers; the tiny crease between his lip and chin. Even the crust between his lashes has my eyes sparkling.

I don't cringe from the odd stump of umbilical cord that will become his belly button, or the black tar we find in his diaper. I just laugh and smile, happy tears rolling down my warm cheeks again and again. I wrap him and snuggle him, humming with my cheek on his silky soft head until I hear his throat rattle lightly with soft snores.

When I settle him down into a nest of blankets in his little basket, I sigh contentedly. I head to the washroom so I can splash some water on my swollen eyes. I cup my hands to gather a small pool of water that feels as silky as Little Jack's skin and throw it onto my blushed skin. It seems to sizzle on the heat of my cheeks.

I catch my own eye in the mirror and squint my eyes at myself, disbelieving. Dark folds ripple down under my eyes over gaunt cheeks. My grayish skin sets off broken red blood vessels all over the whites of both eyes. My hair is dull, flat and stringy; sagging like my skin. I lift my blouse to inspect my belly. The skin on the sides of my ribs ripple over the bones. A doughy mass suspends just below the spot where Little Jack grew and grew, loose and flabby, like Adler's jowls. My belly button is somewhere within the mass, several inches below its original placement, deep and wide.

My mind supplies the image of my old belly button; the one Jack would run circles around with his finger to taunt me. I used to hate having his finger poked into my belly button. If he were here now, half of his finger would disappear into the cavernous indent surrounded by angry red stripes.

I burst into tears.

It's just your appearance, Sense suggests.

It's what's inside that counts, I hear in Mama's 'sermon voice'.

But, what I see is literally a mirror image of the girl I've been trying desperately to ignore. *If Jack is gone, really gone, then what is left of me?* If he is, then I am not worthy of the tiny, beautiful person bundled up in the next room. That little boy deserves so much more than the broken, mourning pile of despair that I'm hiding below a hopeful surface. I'll have nothing to offer him better than a borrowed room in an old woman's home.

If Jack is dead, what will you do? Sense asks.

I just don't know.

NINE

September 7th, 1942

I awaken to an irritating clicking sound grating against the peace of my sleep. When my eyes flutter open, my groggy senses absorb the sight of a shiny red apple that's just begun to rot; wrinkling and drooping. I blink again. Ruby's red pout comes into focus. *Ruby.*

"Finally!" she sighs, exasperated. She flutters long lashes over her rolling eyes. "Your maid," she emphasizes with annoyance, "wouldn't let me wake you, but I just can't wait to get this done with." She wriggles her fingers, as though shaking away a swarm of Lyla-germs crawling upon them. The squint to her eyes indicates that I am somehow at fault, even though I didn't invite her here. Dark, glossy curls tumble over her shoulders and her blush silk blouse. She shudders and tightens her cardigan over the delicate pink color.

Ruby is here.

I stare at her pale skin. Her jaw gently sags, the droop pronounced by her down-turned, wilting lips posed in an upside-down u shape. Fine lines slither their way out from the corners of her deep brown eyes. Maybe she was beautiful once, but all I see when I look at her are the licking flames of my burning barn. I feel like I could brush ash from my shoulder, the memory is so fresh.

"Well, good morning," she says flatly, dutifully; waving the salutation aside with her hand. "I need to speak with you if you don't mind." Her words are polite, but her tone tells me that I have no choice in the matter.

"I understand you've given birth."

I look at her questioningly. *How would she know?* I become uncomfortably aware of the feeling of a huge, heavy pancake on my belly. It *is* my belly. *Maybe she can tell just by my shape?* I shift under the blankets to obscure my middle. *Ouch*; I'm still very sore, I shouldn't move. However, I've never felt more like bolting for the door.

She waves her hand again. "Really, dear, do you think I would allow a grandchild of mine to come into the world without my being informed?" she laughs, as though the idea is preposterous. I had no idea that Ruby even knew I was going to have a baby.

Mister Sharpe probably told her as soon as he knew, naturally, Sense explains. But, she's made no effort since to contact me or to repair our rickety relationship.

What on earth makes her think she has the right to call him her 'grandchild'?

"I mean, I assume this child is Jack's," she raises a brow suggestively. "Unless…"

I scowl at her, stifling any thought of my alleged promiscuity.

"Well, anyhow, I've had the girls here keeping an eye on things."

"The maids?" I croak dryly. I'd kill for a sip of water just now.

"Of course," she says haughtily, gesturing to our surroundings. I'm astonished that someone as kind hearted as Annie would do Ruby's bidding, or even her senior maid; anyone on Lyla's payroll! Lyla detests her daughter-in-law.

"Anyhow, it's clear that you are in no state to raise the boy. I intend to take him in for you."

A hot flame sparks in my chest. She just affirmed the fear I've been avoiding for five miserable months. But, if this wicked woman thinks I will hand over Little Jack to someone as cruel and scheming as her, she has another thing coming.

"There, *ach*. There…" I try to say, but my throat is so dry it won't come out.

Ruby's long, thin fingers offer me a small glass of orange juice beaded over with condensation. I clear my parched throat painfully. It takes a lot of self control to turn my face away from the tempting glass.

"You can't sway me with *orange juice*."

"Darling, I don't intend to. I intend to offer this boy a life that you simply cannot, one you would be wise to consider for him. Nutritious meals, fine clothing, superior care, first-class schooling." She sips from the glass. There's not a chance I'll drink it, now that her poisonous lips have touched it.

"No."

She laughs and lightly slaps her knee as though we're at a garden party, and I've just told an entertaining joke.

"Darling," she says again. I boil at the mellifluous way it slides from her throat, as though there is any measure of warmth between us. "You musn't be thinking quite clearly."

"It is perfectly *clear* to me that I will not surrender a helpless baby to a woman who would burn someone's barn to the ground just to make her point," I sneer. My words grate like sandpaper in my dry throat.

She blinks against my words, but her expression remains perfectly calm. For some reason, Ruby's serenity is more terrifying than her unbridled rage from my wedding day.

My eyes dart around the room for an escape. She sits between me and the door to the hallway. I'll be much faster flat footed than she will be in those tall heels, even holding my baby; even dragging my aching body behind my will. My hips and pelvis throb at the thought of running, but I vow to *make* my uncooperative body perform.

"Perhaps this will sway you," Ruby purrs before I can even sit up. She tips her handbag just-so, allowing a thick brick of moss-green bills to peek out.

"I don't want your money," I scoff.

"Of course you do, Darling." She blinks at me, apparently waiting for me to change my mind. "Oh, really now; it's just you and I here. I won't tell a soul about the money. It's just to help you get back on your feet," she insists, slipping a few bills out of the bag and wagging them in the air in front of me.

"When are you going to understand, Ruby? I don't want your money!"

She scoffs back at me. "Oh, *please*, Penelope! I've been onto your game from the very start! I'm offering you a golden opportunity here! A chance to start over! To go out into the world and take it by the reins! You'll have everything you wanted!" she urges, the vein on her forehead throbbing. Her calm facade is slipping away.

Everything I wanted? What would I tell Jack when he turned up? "Oh, your mother bribed me, so I took the money and ran." Please.

"Get out of my room," I murmur.

"Think of the child! What's best for the child!" Ruby urges, eyes wide and wild. The silkiness of her voice is gone, replaced with distress. I feel as though Little Jack is a prized jewel, and Ruby's greedy fingers dangle just above him.

I remember Mister Sharpe's words at the hospital when I'd first learned about little Jack. *Ruby aches for a grandchild...*

But I won't give her her wish.

"Scram!"

"Excuse m-"

"Go a*way*, Ruby!"

"Please, Penelope," she pleads, her fiery eyes glassing over with tears. Her melodious voice falls to a sorrowful hush. "You have no idea what I've done to make myself who I am. You can't imagine the things--" she pauses, closing her eyes and clasping her hands together. I find myself curious to know what desperate acts she alludes to.

"I made this family what it is. All of our assets have been preserved and have grown because of *me*. I have absolutely everything I could ever ask for, except for my son safe at home, but if I die without anyone to pass it all on to..." She falters, but I feel as though her head is a glass casing to her thoughts. Bentley and Claire had tried so hard to create a child, only to lose her in the end. It's possible that they never will conceive again. And with only a shred of hope left that Jack is still breathing somewhere, little Jack is her only chance for an heir.

"...then all of it was for nothing." Her clouded eyes seem far away.

As though a scope has been placed at my eyes, sympathy for her rolls over my angry thoughts. This is the first time Ruby has ever lifted her careful mask for me; the first time she's expressed a real emotion besides sheer fury. However, I don't understand is why she feels she must take little Jack away from me to be in his life.

"I haven't given up hope that Jack is still alive, Ruby. Have you?"

She sniffs and squares her shoulders. "Would it matter if he was? He ran away from us, to you," she retorts.

I draw in a slow breath before I reply to her. I've never had an amiable conversation with my mother-in-law before today, and I don't want her shell to harden again with a reminder that she kicked Jack to the curb, not the other way around.

"He's your son, Missus Sharpe; he loves you. Is there any possibility that we could just be a family?" I put forth, hanging my pride over a treacherous ledge. "All of us?"

"As I told you, Penelope, I've worked very hard to make my family what it is. I won't settle for less. I won't settle for *you*."

My face stings as though I've been slapped.

"You can visit him whenever you'd like," I offer, trying my best to remain calm, but she scoffs in return.

"Ha! Visit him in a potato field? Or picking apples? Like I told you, I want to offer him the best life has to offer!"

"You want him in *your* home?" I ask.

"Yes, so I can ensure that you don't run off with him in the middle of the night."

I snort. Ruby has dreamed up a vicious, blood-sucking personality for me that I don't even recognize.

"I'm not going to run away, but I'm certainly not giving him away, Missus Sharpe. Like I said, you can visit him at any time."

"Selfish girl," she murmurs.

"Please leave. You can come back tomorrow for a visit, but I'd like to rest now." Truthfully, all I crave a rest from is her intensity.

She throws her chin to her shoulder, flipping her glossy hair. "If you wish. But I do hope you will come to your senses, Girl. You know where to find me when you do."

"Jack! What do I do?" I urge his lifeless body while sweat drips from the tip of my nose. In Missy's cockpit, we plummet toward the ground at an alarmingly rapid rate. Supporting little Jack with one arm, I furiously work the levers and buttons on the dash with my free hand. "Jack! Help me!"

"Pip. Pip, wake up!" Annie urges me, shaking my shoulder. I fall through a tunnel back into my borrowed bed at Lyla's, and my eyes flutter open.

"Annie," I groan. "I was dreaming," I say aloud as that realization hits me.

"Where's the baby?" I worry.

"He's fine, Miss; sleeping just there in the bassinet," she answers calmly. Though her voice is calm and kind, I feel a hardness in my heart for Annie ever since Ruby implied that a maid was her informant. I sit up, frantic for reassurance. Over the side of the wicker bassinet, I can see his little fist waving in the air. I relax back into the pillows, reassured... for now.

"Oh," I reply, sitting up and smoothing my hair.

"A man," she amends.

Jack? Could it be Jack, returned with honor and ready to meet his son? Sense guesses excitedly. The hardness in my chest melts away to make room for hope. Immediately, my hands quiver.

"He can't stay long, so I'm afraid you'll have to see him as you are," says Annie.

"I don't care what I look like. I want to see him!" I assure her as I bound out of bed. Annie chases me to the top of the stairs with a robe and a brush.

"Wait, Miss! Let me…" I pause momentarily for her to slide the silken robe on my shoulders and run an ornate silver brush through my wild morning mane. As soon as the bristles break contact with my head, I hurry down the steps. My jiggling belly swings like a set of udders as I descend. I hop over the last two steps, my frantic eyes sweeping the sitting room for Jack.

My enthusiasm takes a nosedive when I take in the man examining his thumbs on Lyla's settee. Not Jack. His sandy hair waves across his tanned forehead until his head snaps up, and his large blue eyes absorb my frantic expression. He quickly stands, steps forward and extends his hand to me.

"Hello," he greets me. "Pip?"

"Yes," I reply in a dull whisper as my soul sags with disappointment. "And you are?"

"Jacob Savage, Ma'am. Most folks just call me Savvy," he nods with a polite smile, and I realize that I've dreamed about this person nearly every night. Savage, the pilot who pulled me out of Jack's plane before it exploded, had worn a brown leather helmet, flight goggles, and a thick layer of soot when he'd appeared in my visions.

"Oh," I reply.

Be polite, Sense prods.

"Nice to meet you, Savvy. Or, Jacob. Mister Savage," I fumble as my arm flops along with his eager handshake.

"Savvy's fine," he assures me, and we sit on opposite sides of the settee.

"How can I help you?" I ask him with a sigh.

"I'm sorry that I came so early, I just don't have much time before my train leaves for Boston. Your cousin wrote and asked me to come up to speak with you, and this is the only window I could manage," he explains.

Claire.

I reply, "That's kind of you; you must just be leaving the hospital in the city?"

He nods. Saratoga is well out of his way from New York City to

Boston.

"I'm sure you're eager to get home. So, you're the pilot who saw Jack's plane crash?"

"Unfortunately, yes," he answers, the corners of his mouth turning downward. "Jack-o was one of my best pals in training and on the field. He was a swell pal, though I did grow tired of him always talking about you," Savvy offers a small grin.

"He... *was*?" I clarify. "He... he..." I stammer.

"I'm so sorry, Ma'am. I never would've asked to be the one to deliver this news to a widow."

The title echoes in my brain, *widow, widow, widow...*

"He died? You saw it?"

Savvy nods grimly. "He hit the ground with the nose tipped up, which was good, then he slid about three hundred yards through a clearing. He almost smashed into my plane! I ran to him and threw open the cockpit door. He was slumped over, bleeding; he'd been shot."

In the shoulder, I finish in my own head. Savvy's retelling sounds eerily similar to my nightmares of Jack's death.

"I tried to pull him out, but his gas tank caught fire and exploded. I had to run away before it blew. It still caught the back of me," he explains, reluctantly pulling up the back of his shirt. Angry, mottled red scars cover every inch of his side that I can see.

No, no; this is too real. I bite my tongue to keep from asking him if he'd seen me in the cockpit too.

"He burned to death?" I choke out, tears springing to my eyes.

"I believe the shot killed him before he even landed," he assures me with wet eyes, resting his hand on my shoulder. His touch feels as painful as if I wore Jack's wound on my own shoulder. I shrink away from the feel of his heavy fingers.

This revelation is very convenient timing for Ruby's request, Imp whispers. The rest of me pulls away from him with my shoulder.

"Who did you say asked you to tell me this in person?" I question him with new strength behind my voice.

"Your cousin, Claire Quinn," he answers with a puzzled look. "I don't think she meant it to be malicious towards you." His moist eyes sadden sympathetically.

"I'm sure she had the best of intentions," I mumble, watching Ruby's decorated hand scribble out a forged letter in my mind. "Tell me, Jacob, did she offer you some form of payment for this visit?"

"The letter included train tickets to bring me here, then home," he replies. "I'm sure it was a small price to pay to offer you all some closure."

Ruby, I growl inside. Once again, Jack's mother has resorted to her pocketbook to bring her will to life.

"Thank you for your time," I nod to him, standing abruptly. My stomach wiggles uncomfortably as I hurry back to the stairway.

"Wait! Pip," he calls after me, and I pause on the bottom step with my hand clutching the mahogany rail.

I turn back to him. He stands taller than Jack, but feebly hunched under my icy stare.

"I think you should have this," he says, offering a small rectangular paper to me. I step back to him and accept it; a photograph of Jack and Savage standing happily near their planes. Jack's grin is unmistakable, punctuated by the freckle at the apple of his cheek. The plane behind him wears rolling, decorated script that reads, "Missy" under a painting of a smiling gal. She's blonde, blue eyed.

She's me.

As my heart melts, my ears barely register Savvy's parting farewell. Jack looks so alive in this photograph, so happy. *How can he be dead?* I lift my face to question Savvy further, but the ornate wooden door closes as I do.

Ruby, Imp growls.

It's tempting to funnel my anger toward Ruby for attempting to trick me, but Sense's calm reminder halts me: *Claire shared this account with you long before she gave birth, long before her baby died; long before Ruby had a reason to tell it to you.*

Slowly, I take the stairs back up to my baby. I need to know the truth, but I just don't know where to get it.

I jump when the door to my borrowed room rumbles with a knock.

"C-come in," I call feebly.

The sight of May entering comforts my rattled nerves. She swoops down on the bed next to me and snuggles up to my shoulder.

"Hiya, Sis," she coos into my ear. "Where's my boy?" I lift the blanket on the opposite side of me, where I've made a tiny fort out of pillows around him. I can't rest with Ruby on the loose, without him near me.

"Oh!" she squeaks quietly. "He looks even bigger than yesterday!" Her eyes shine with the glow of new aunthood as he cracks open one eye in a tiny slit for her.

"Hello, Little Jack," she coos. "I'm your Auntie May." She scoops him up into her arms, cradling him like an expert. "Are you going to let Mama meet him soon?"

My eyebrows gather in a scowl. "You didn't tell her that he was born, did you?"

"She's been hounding me like a pack of wild dogs; she just guessed he'd arrived! It's not my fault! I promise I haven't told her where you two are living," May pleads in a string of defense.

"Good," I mumble. I don't want my mother anywhere near this fresh and innocent being after the things I've learned about her, the way we left things.

May bites her plump lower lip as she admits, "But I accidentally let it slip that he's a boy. Can't she see him, Sis? Please? She's a *grandma*, for goodness sakes!"

"Sheesh! Grandmothers are no better than vultures!" After Ruby's visit, I don't feel like sharing him with anyone. I draw a deep breath to ground myself. "Just give me some time to think this through, okay?"

"Okay," she agrees. "Oh! I almost forgot. A package came for you yesterday. I would've brought it over sooner, but I'd already been here that morning, and I was worried Mama would trail me here if I left again, and you'd be mad…"

"Smart thinking, Mayhem." I love how my sister's criminal mind thinks a plan through. "What is it?"

"I don't know. It's over there," she points with her nose. "I'd grab it for you, but I'm sort of busy," she grins, snuggling down into the baby.

"I'll get it," I assure her, though my pelvis objects in pain as I stand and step to the dresser by the door. I ignore the pain and pick up the rectangular, brown-wrapped box addressed '*Mrs. Jackson Sharpe*'. My finger works its way under the string and slides it off. The stiff paper falls away. I hold a small wooden box in my hands. For some reason, the hairs on my neck stand on end as I stare at it.

"What is that?" asks May.

"I don't know," I shrug.

"Why don't you open it?" she prods.

I make to do so, but my body won't cooperate.

"I don't think I can, May," I admit, and a cold shudder rolls up my spine.

"Oh, I'll open it," she groans, setting little Jack carefully in the center of the bed. She looks to me before sliding the top back with her index finger. She stares at the contents without expression.

"What? What is it?" I ask eagerly and claw for the box. A small satchel sits perched inside. I pull back the ribbon and peer inside, and a sledgehammer hits my gut with crushing force. I start retching, and May grabs for the satchel as I release my hold on it. Delicate grey clumps of ash fill the inside; Jack's remains. I've been entertaining the feeble idea that Jack missing in action had meant that Jack was still somehow living and breathing somewhere.

That's not proof! That could be anything! Imp protests. It's true, this could be the burned up remnants of the plane's seat, or burnt wood from the explosion, or anything. There's nothing concrete here that says he didn't scramble away from the wreckage before the explosion.

Ruby could've sent this as a ruse, Sense guesses. *It could be the ashes of a silk pillow for all you know.*

"Oh, there's more in here," May whispers with her fingers over the box. She dips her index finger and thumb inside and pulls out a long chain of silver with a piece on the end. A sooty four leaf clover.

This charm, with the tiny engraved "J + P" in the stem, and the clasp secured but the chain broken where I'd ripped it from my neck at the train station, is one of a kind. Jack told me he kept this in his breast pocket at all times, near his heart.

"And something else," she mumbles, and I shudder. I don't think I can handle anything else.

May's small fingers dance in the air as they carefully lift a ball chain out of the belly of the wooden box. The metal catches the sunlight tumbling in through the windows, and winks of sun glare twinkle as it emerges. Weighting down the chain, at the bottom, two metal tags clink lightly together.

My fingers can't help but close around them. Hungrily, nervously, my eyes drink in the stamped letters, SHARPE, JACKSON H. I run my index finger across the embossing. These tags wear a film of soot on them, just like the charm. The hope Imp and I shared is dashed. If they found these in the ashes, then there's no mistaking that this handful of dust is the remains of my husband.

She couldn't have faked that, Sense concedes.

Jack. Jack is in this box.

What am I going to tell Mister Sharpe? And Bentley? Claire, George, Lyla? All that's left of my husband, and the boy that they all love, fits into the palm of my hand.

"May, help me," I murmur as my hand begins to tremble. The pile of ash will run between my weakened fingers if I don't get them back into the satchel. "Help me, please."

I know that I owe Savage an apology, but I don't think I can deliver it before I slip completely into the blackness that threatens to envelop me. The fingers that have clung tightly to hope go weak. Why shouldn't I submit to the darkness?

Jack is gone. All I have left of him now is a handful of soot. A handful of ashes cannot rock a baby to sleep. A handful of ashes cannot watch his boy take his first steps, or teach him how to throw a ball A handful of ashes cannot be a father to a child.

Jack is gone. He's really gone.

"C'mon, Miss; have a bite," Annie urges me. "It's been days since you've eaten." I hear her words, but it's as if they echo down to me through a dark tunnel. She makes sense, I should eat, but my lips just don't want to open.

"C'mon, please? Your little boy needs his mommy," she attempts. "You need to be healthy for this little man." I can hear little Jack's gentle cooing sounds, as though I'm hearing them through a long tunnel.

Sense screams at me, banging her fists against the insides of my skull, but I can't seem to find the desire to move. My body doesn't want to. I don't want to live without him.

"She won't do it, Madam," I hear Annie tell someone.

"Aw, she'll come around eventually," Lyla's scratchy voice assures the maid. "I did. Keep trying."

Lyla's silken sheets and her expensive fluffy pillows irritate my skin. I don't belong wrapped in this finery. Lyla may have bounced back from her husband's death, but I'm not sure that I can.

TEN

"Ugh," I groan when Ruby saunters into my room. "No babies for sale today," I mutter bitterly through my tears. I don't need her commanding presence near me right now; not when my mind runs on a hamster wheel through what I should do. Not when I can barely find the strength to keep breathing.

She immediately blurts out, "You've heard the news from our investigators? And the eyewitness?"

I muster a nearly imperceptible nod for her.

"Then I've come to persuade you to reconsider my offer." She slams a naked brick of bills onto the night table, with no handbag to conceal her brazen offer this time. It's three times as thick as any book I've ever read, and several shades of moss green. I watch the lamp next to the stack of money teeter from the force of her offering.

"I simply won't take no for an answer," she asserts as she paces the thick carpet. The idea of Ruby raising my innocent little boy rouses me from my state of lethargy.

"I don't want your money, Ruby. And you can't raise him," I contend weakly. The muscles in my jaw ache after days of silence.

She throws her head back and laughs, "Ha! It appears you can't either, Darling." Her dark hair cascades down her spine. "Neither of us will raise him."

I narrow my eyes at Jack's mother.

"*Claire* will."

My mouth pops open. *Claire; of course.* The thought settles on me with the light touch of a falling feather.

Claire.

Claire has just lost her baby, but their bloodlines are nearly identical: Little Jack's father is a Sharpe; his mother has Hale blood. Claire isn't evil like Ruby or her mother, but she and Bentley ooze with just as much wealth. They can offer him a wonderful future. *And me?* I have nothing to offer him but a broken down body and a heart frozen through with despair. In the time it takes for these thoughts drop into place, the corners of Ruby's mouth to turn upward with triumphant glee.

'Nutritious food' rings through my head while the familiar hollow ache stings my belly. I know all too well the agony of hard work with undernourished muscles. A college education would catapult him and his posterity far, far from any of that pain.

This solution glares at me as brightly as the sun. So glaring that I don't want to look directly at it, yet even as I turn away, my back warms by its presence.

Claire.

But he wouldn't know his mother! Imp wails inside of me.

He would also never know his mother's pain, Sense persists. She supplies a vision of a rosy cheeked, dark haired boy running on the dark green grasses of the Ferring plantation; wearing a riding helmet as he trots atop a handsome horse; sliding a forkful of honeyed ham into his mouth and grinning broadly with stuffed cheeks; practicing penmanship with his private tutor hanging over his shoulder; sleeping with a slack mouth on smooth cotton sheets in his own enormous bed; surrounded by stacks of fine toys on Christmas morning; wrapped in Claire's thin arms as she rocks him to sleep.

If I keep him in the name of loving him, then I'm not really loving him at all; I'm only loving... *me.*

"I need to think about this," I whisper through my fingers, my dry throat protesting speech. "I'll need to speak to Claire." Her name hangs heavily in the air while the picture of her rocking him remains in my thoughts, soft and maternal.

Ruby turns and nods to the older maid standing in the doorway. In only a moment the face in my mind becomes real, and comes toward me on the tiny body of shaking, timid Claire. Her ears poke through her honey hair as she shuffles toward us with her head down. My eyes burn at her brightness; despite her timid posture, Claire shines as radiantly as the sun.

"I'm sorry, I couldn't ask you myself," she sniffs, wiping her delicate nose. Her thin limbs shake uncontrollably.

"Claire, why..wha..."

Tears spill over her cheeks. "It's just... if you can't care for him, well; I want him so badly, and I'm afraid that you'll refuse," bounces from her trembling lips. She claps a hand over her mouth, squeezing her eyes shut. Fat tears escape from between her lids. Her face reddens. "I can't believe I'm asking this of you."

She whispers reverently through her fingers, "I held him," as her shoulders tremble. Claire is in love with him.

Is it possible that the loneliness of her empty arms will allow her to love him even more than I do? Mightily, I fight against the clear knowledge that I can't possibly give him anything near to what Claire can.

How can it ever be right for a mother to give up her child? I *grew* him inside of me. I *made* him with my own body!

"He's not your Julia," I whisper.

"I know," she murmurs back with her eyes closed. Two tears race down her cheeks.

As my face falls, Ruby senses the chink in my armor. "What if he gets sick? How will you care for him? Can a volunteer candy striper afford a doctor?" she gushes hungrily. I wave her away and pinch the bridge of my nose. I pull my fingers back disgustedly when I realize that I'm perfectly mimicking my mother's stress tic.

I can barely whisper, "I know it's best. I just don't know if I can do it." Little Jack is the only piece of my Jack I have. It's selfish; I'm being selfish.

Mothers can't be selfish.

Two simultaneous picture shows play side by side in my head.

On the left is Mama with Daddy by her side, chasing after me, May, Eddie and Max. She's youthful and carefree; laughing. She doesn't take her smiling eyes off of us. We are her world. On the right is Mama, probably only six months later. Weather worn and burdened, she can't muster the oomph to raise the corners of her mouth out of her deep frown. Her hands are busy with work. Her weary eyes flicker between her task and her children, but her mind is far away.

I was raised by both of these women, and I must say that from the child's perspective, I much prefer the former version of her. There's no doubt in my mind that while Claire could fall effortlessly into the cheery picture of the Mama I once knew, I am the bitter hag on the right.

Pain sears my heart. The idea of giving him up hurts like nothing I've ever experienced. Worse than starvation. Worse than losing Jack. As agonizing as a red hot poker burning through my chest, straight through my ribs to the red muscle itself, it hurts. Yet, as I look back at the possibility of trying to offer my son a comparable life, I know that I am doomed to fail; and the idea of disappointing that sweet little soul hurts even worse. I'd be giving him *up,* up to something better.

I sit up, and embrace Claire with the coil of a boa constrictor.

I whisper into her hair, "You could take good care of him?"

Claire's tiny fingers dig eagerly into my back. "Yes. Yes!" she squeals in a whisper.

I teeter on the edge of decision when Annie brushes wearing with a huge grin, carefully cradling a tiny bundle. Little Jack. The pain fizzles into soft snowflakes melting over my wound as she hands him off to me gingerly. His eyes are closed, but his tiny mouth stretches wide with a yawn. I can't imagine willingly parting with this velvety skin, or his intoxicating baby scent.

"Sleepy head," I coo to him.

He blinks, and when his eyes open, I gaze longingly into the endless blue of them. I wish, *oh,* I *wish* I could be everything he deserves in his parents! Claire teeters on the very edge of her seat, so far forward that she may even be squatting in the air. I try to ignore the nervous energy she exudes. Little Jack looks at me for a long minute. As his eyes flutter closed again, my decision clicks into place. I'm not enough for him.

"This isn't for you, Ruby. This is for him."

I squeeze my eyes shut and turn my head away from the smell of powder and brand new skin. My mouth puckers sourly, pinching back the words that must be said.

"Take him. Take him now before I change my mind."

ELEVEN

One Week Later

Today, Jackson Sharpe will be buried. Hordes of mourners will gather around his grave. Soldiers will present Ruby with a carefully folded flag, and she will weep in her dark couture clothing for the loss of this young life. The tiny satchel of ashes concealed in an over-large wooden coffin will be lowered into the ground, and shovelfuls of dark earth will rain down atop it, sealing him underground forever. And, I will not be there. I promised myself after Eddie's funeral that I would never stand over a flag-draped coffin ever again, and I won't. I won't make my sorrow for Jack's death a public spectacle.

The muscles that should hold a person's decent expression have resigned, leaving my face drooping low and gaunt. I can see in the faces of the few that meet my sorry gaze that I look haunted. Empty. A monument of hope's absence. Lightless. My insides slowly burn away with the acidic scald of grief from the center of my being and smolder outward. I'm merely a thin shell of grayish skin holding in boiling anguish. It threatens to incinerate me completely before I can exit the bus and complete the task at hand.

"Let me help you," May had begged at my bedside.

"There's no helping me," I'd mumbled back to her, but even I couldn't understand my own words. Those were the last words I've spoken, and it's been a week. My lips have frozen with grief. Now, something inside catapults me toward action, *any* action, any*thing* to stop this aching agony. Something final. Something that will ensure

an end to my pain… I need to die.

I'm not sure what to expect after I do this, but any option seems preferable: if there is nothing but blackness on the other side, then there will be no more pain; if there is an afterlife, surely Jack will be there, reaching out his arm for me to join him. If suicide means Hell, then I dare the devil to deal me something worse than what I feel right now. Maybe I belong there for what I've done. I think I do.

When the bus's brakes finally squeal to a heavy stop, I'm thrown forward with the sudden shift. My chin snaps up, reminding my spindly legs to drag my weighted body to its final purpose. I stand and ghost to the doors. The bus driver watches me sadly as I pass his seat, wrinkling his nose at the scent of misery that trails behind me. I'm the only passenger stopping here at this remote, outskirt stop near the river, and the sky looms threateningly dark grey outside of his bus. If he senses my plan, I don't have the will to care.

An army of maple trees in front of me, aflame with yellow leaves, gently dance in the light breeze of an oncoming storm. Their limbs beckon me forward, and eventually swallow me into the thick of them. My legs trudge forward only by the drive of my purpose. The rest of me teeters atop these stems; lifeless, dead weight. They are soldiers on a mission, undeterred by the stinging and slicing of underbrush into my shins. Blood pours freely from the nastier cuts, allowing the noxious gases inside me to escape like air through a pinhole in a balloon, but does not relieve the pressure of my suffering.

Soon I come to a clearing where the huge river comes into view. It's nearly silent, but I know that torrential waters swirl under its deceivingly calm surface. My arms join in my purpose as I climb up the backside of a large black boulder, and once I'm at the peak of it, I stare down into the swirling water. The shadows of large, jagged rocks loom just under the surface. They will be my salvation. They will be my weapon. I begin to revel in the thought that this dark water will be my grave, and tremble at the same time. I study the large stones underwater and watch my face smacking into them as a short film over and over in my head. I imagine my lifeless body being sucked downstream through the tumultuous current while fish nip at my lifeless remains.

A loud clap of thunder startles me, shaking me off balance. A sudden sob rumbles up from my chest, thundering out with the shock of the roar. I bend at the waist from the force of it, crumbling to the rock. I pound the cold stone with my weak palm, while my tortured howls drive the birds from their perches, a curtain of screeching.

Clearly, God has forsaken me, despite my best efforts to be a good person. My father was murdered. One of my brothers was murdered much less subtly, while the other hangs in the balance thousands of miles from home. After that huge blow up with my mother, I'll never be able to look her in the eye again; never be able to trust that she isn't who I think she is. The love of my life has gone down in flames, and I gave away our child. I gave him up, because *I* gave up. I give *up!* No one can be expected to endure this much sorrow and move on with life! My chest feels just as crushed as though one of these huge, heavy boulders sits right on top of it. My breaths are numbered.

I know, all too well, from Reverend Bell's warning sermons that taking my own life will bar me from going to heaven, but I won't spend an eternity with a God who would deal me these cards. I am forsaking *Him*, as He has forsaken me. If He's even there. *Where is God? Where has He been? Why hasn't His mighty hand intervened?*

Trembling, I pull myself up to my knees. I shake uncontrollably. Anger. Fear. Sorrow. They all drive the torrents of non-stop shuddering, but I am driven to complete the task of ending my miserable journey.

I am just so tired, I think to myself as I try to stand. *So*, so very tired of the heaviness of my heart and the stifling weight it is on my chest. I long for another feeling other than despair. I've been waiting for a glimmer of hope, of happiness; they've never come. I shuffle my weighted feet to the edge of the great rock. My heart thumps with all of its effort. It's as though it knows I am ready to die, and it's trying to show me how useful and valuable it is with its vigorous beating.

My fingers open the bag that hangs near my hip. I reach in and close a fist around a wad of bills. Angrily, I squish the tainted dollars and pull them from the bag with force.

"Aaaargh!" I grunt as I throw them with all of my might into the water. They float down like feathers and touch lightly on the river's surface, which doesn't satisfy my desire to destroy the evidence of what a horrible person I really am.

This poison currency is Ruby's parting gift to me. By accepting it under the pretense of 'furthering my schooling' and 'making something of myself', I've really promised to never poke into Little Jack's life again. Deep down, I knew it when I let her leave it on the nightstand, I just couldn't admit it to myself.

I'm hellbound for sure. I'll bet the devil reserves extra special torture for gals who sell their babies to evil women!

The next fistful of tainted bills gets torn and crumpled and scattered, and the next, and the next, until the marred pieces of one thousand georges are carried away in the current. I dig out the chain and charm from the bottom of the bag, and suck in a painful breath as my fingers close around Jack's dog tags. Sliding my wedding ring off of my finger, I add it to the jewelry in my fist and hold it tightly against my chest. I will expire with all the pieces I have left of Jack by my heart, for he will always be in it. My rapid breath picks up the pace. It is time to die.

Bang! Another loud clap of thunder shakes me to my core. I'm startled by the crash and lose my footing, tumbling forward until I stumble right over the stone's edge. I begin wildly freefalling for the water that I know will be freezing; enough to stop a heart just from the shock of it. I gasp as I smack into a sheet of rock hard ice water and suck in a lungful of the stuff. My chest heaves and spasms, fighting the water, and I fight back against the survival instinct.

Let go, I tell the clawing urge. *I want to die.*

The current tumbles my discombobulated body and hurls me toward a deep, dark stone. My head slams face first into it. My groan releases in a flurry of bubbles racing for the surface, and I slip quickly into unconsciousness; in to death.

Hello, death. I welcome your sweet relief.

TWELVE

I am a child running barefoot through the tall, cool grass of a shaded meadow. The air, sweet and fragrant with wildflowers, lifts my hair behind me as I lope through the trees. Beams of clear blue light reach through the trees to warm my young, soft face. I move without a care in the world. No rocks to trip me, no thorns to snag me, just a blanket of soft green grass as far as my seven-year-old eyes can see.

And then, all at once, a storm: my perfect blue sky marred with ominous black clouds. The trees' leaves wither and die and fall away to reveal naked branches that reach to me like the bony fingers of skeletons. The grass thins to dirt under my feet. Dark, rocky wet soil that I must heave my feet from to step. I shiver in the sudden icy chill to the air, brought on by fierce winds that lift me and twist me, altering me to my very core. My skin stings where staccato drops of tiny balls of ice bite at me; hail rains hard like pitchforks.

My body is ravaged by the tempest. When the downpour finally wanes, my broken form is a tiny heap in the cold, rocky mud. My eyes open anxiously to survey the wreckage of myself.

I am not a child anymore.

THIRTEEN

My eyes flutter, and I realize as my lashes beat against my cheeks that I've been sleeping. My eyes fight against the soft, sudden invasion of pink morning light, eventually willing to adjust so that I can take in my surroundings. No clouds, no mud, no hail; just a veil over my vision that obscures what I see.

The offending light of dawn shines brightly through a dusty, white-framed, east-facing window with no curtain. A worn but intricate quilt holds in the heat of my body against the cold air outside of its comfort. I can tell from the hopeful tips of the most sun-seeking branches of a tree dancing outside the window that I must be on the second story.

I don't recognize the room that I'm in; though my vision is hazy, I know I've never been here before. I try to sit up to further explore, but I find that I'm well wrapped in a blanket below these bedclothes, almost swaddled, which my arms find it difficult to maneuver out of. My damp clothes feel warm from my body inside of this cocoon of blankets.

As I move to try and free myself, my head throbs as though in vice grips, like the worst toothache imaginable. I manage to wrestle one of my arms free, and my fingers fly to my cheek to investigate the source of the pain. Swollen, and, *ow*, tender. The cool air outside of the quilt has a wicked bite. The soggy dress clinging to my skin seems to absorb the cold immediately.

My head feels fuzzy and my body aches for more rest, but a

survival instinct demands that I place my unfamiliar surroundings. I pull the lovely soft quilt around me and slide off the bed. My bare feet continue the dispute as they hit a chilly wooden floor, but curiosity wins over and drives them forward. It is quiet as a graveyard in this strange house, so I try to step lightly against the floorboards.

Where on earth am I? Whose floorboards am I creaking?

I make it to the door with minimal noise. It's barely ajar, and I gingerly pull it fully open. The oiled hinges swing quietly.

The open door reveals a small, square landing at the top of a staircase. My door and the staircase fill two of the square's edges. Two other doors complete the square. One hangs slightly ajar, and I can't help but crane my neck to peek through the crack. A bathroom. My eyes train on the other, closed door ahead. I haven't seen any of this before, I am sure; though my eyes rake every blurry detail for familiarity.

I bite my tongue between my lips and turn the knob as quietly as I can. I feel like the gal in the flicker shows who's in danger, and stupidly seeks out her killer as the audience cringes in their seats at her stupidity. I can finally understand why she does it; curiosity killed the cat, after all. I push the door open with my eyelids squeezed shut, willing its silence.

A symphony of snores muffles the shriek of the hinges as the door swings into the small room, its windows filled with light pink dawn's light. With a fuzzy halo on every object, I can hardly see, but I do make out a bed, and, when I squint…

Oh! I gasp and step back, clapping a hand over my mouth. The movement reminds me of the aching pain in my face.

A single figure lies on the bed. I can't be sure that the lump on blanket doesn't conceal a sharp knife next to the body laying there, but the large dog in complete surrender of his dreams at the foot of the bed gives both of them the impression of innocence. I shield myself behind the doorway, timidly peering around it. The frame of the… man, I am almost certain, lies still except for the light rise and fall of his ribcage. I turn slowly on my heel to leave, but the floorboard creaks. I grimace, and my back tingles with the feeling of being watched.

"Ma'am," the man's voice greets me groggily. My muscles freeze as my veins fill with ice. I've been caught! I try to warm my voice before I speak.

"Oh, uh… hello," I timidly offer, turning back to where he lies, propping his head up on his elbow. I blink twice, hoping to clear my eyes, but it seems that hitting the water with my eyes open has left my vision blurry. I squint. He appears young, though the auburn scruff on his chin tells me that he's not all that young.

"You're alive, then. Ha," he exhales, scratching his head as he sits up. "Well, if you don't mind, I just need to…uh, see a man about a dog," he hints, and it occurs to me that he wants to get up and use the bathroom, and may be too indecent to walk to it with me watching.

Blindly, I scurry backward. "Oh, my, I'm sorry," I say, flustered, and feel my way back to the room I'd woken up in. When the toilet tank whooshes, the fella walks into my room, pulling on a shirt.

It's a good thing you can barely see, Sense giggles in my head. *He's practically naked!*

I wish you could see, Imp counters.

The floor groans under his bare feet as he moves just inside the doorway.

"I…well, did you…" I begin, not sure how to address this stranger, not sure where to appropriately rest my foggy eyes.

"If you're asking if I pulled you out of the river, that was me. Not the fish I was expecting to find swimming around in there, that's for sure," he chuckles.

"Oh," I mumble softly. I don't remember a second of that happening.

"You were all but passed out, so I brought you back here. I wondered if I'd find you dead in the morning, but every time I listened in on you, I could hear you murmuring from the hall. So I knew you were still kickin'," he explains, sounding so cavalier about my life.

"Swimming," I muse with quiet sarcasm, looking down at my hands; peachy pink shapes in my lap. I leapt into what I thought would be the comfort of death, and now I've become a nearly-blind invalid who can't even make out her own fingernails! Warm tears flood my eyes; I blink them away.

"I wasn't swimming, I... I fell in," I lie. "Anyway, thanks for saving me." I look up to find his eyes. Green eyes. I blink rapidly, trying to see him more clearly. He stares back for a moment, cocking his head as my gaze also turns into a deep search.

He chuckles, "Pip Hale." He shakes his head. "You look lousy!"

"Do... do I know you?" I ask, teetering over taking offense. I blink hard, again and again. *Who do I know that could be so rude?*

"Know me? Ha! You've forgotten the fella you hoodwinked into giving you his best marble, Squeak?"

The throbbing in my temples scrambles the pictures that vie for the front of my mind. A fuzzy memory sticks out through the jumble. I'm swallowed up in the faded evening light of early August of nineteen thirty-one, right back into the lap of blissful ignorance. Most of our neighborhood had gathered together at the Collins' estate, our hub for weekend merrymaking; a roundup of the only children left in Saratoga who still had roundness in their cheeks and bellies. The lingering heat of the day had forced our parents to collapse into chaises in the garden, where they sipped sweating drinks and ignored the mischief of their boisterous children. More so, they ignored the nation-consuming economic depression, whose fingers had yet barely grazed the wealthy. It had simply been too hot to make the effort to reprimand children or to engage in deep thought, and that Friday evening, we joyfully ran amok.

Much to my dismay, Mama had once again dressed me in a delicate pale dress, tall stockings to cover my scraped, bruised legs, and shiny patent leather shoes. As usual, I'd sighed with the heavy responsibility on my six-year-old shoulders of trying to stay clean. I dutifully tried to stay presentable by playing dolls indoors with the other girls, but I was quickly bored by the usual script when my doll missed out on the important roles, like "mom" or "baby". From the third-story dormer window, I could see the boys outside shooting marbles, which pulled me like a magnet down to the veranda. A desire for competitive, physical play moved my legs down the stairs and out the door.

The crew groaned upon my arrival; a girl. They'd have to be gentlemen in the presence of a member of the fairer sex, as their mothers had drilled them. How could they know a tomboy hid under this dress? I would've been happier in shorts, as they were, without the restriction of kneeling just-so to keep my delicate panties and petticoats out of sight. The chalk-drawn circle they knelt around revealed that they were playing ringer. These fellas were playing for keeps; I saw a challenge.

"Can I play?" I squeaked in my six year old pitch with curled, corn-silk pigtails swinging on either side of my neck as I bounced down the steps. Their shoulders slumped, knowing that manners demanded they let me in on the game. Even so, most could barely contain their eye rolls and groans.

"Ya got any marbles?" asked a dark-haired boy defending the sanctity of the game. His defiant reply was softened by his wily grin as he crouched at the ready, one eye scrunched shut. This pulled half his lip up, revealing the bud of an adult tooth just growing in. His challenging expression told me that he knew that since I clearly had no marbles, I wouldn't be able to play. *Rascal.*

I was equally cunning.

"Nope, but if I kin borrow some o' yours, and I lose 'em, my daddy'll buy you a whole bag," I bargained, hands clasped, my hip cocked to one side. I'd been perfecting this persuasive posture on Daddy since I could stand. Marble-lust flashed in each of their eyes; an entire bag full of marbles was usually acquired through many tireless games over a period of months, even years! Suddenly, none of them seemed to mind my presence. I could see their impish eyes reasoning that of course a gal would lose, and they could easily win the loot. *Pennies from heaven! Legal piracy!* Everybody knew that my daddy, Mister Hale, was certainly good for a bag of marbles. He could buy them all a marble factory with just his pocket change.

A collective murmur rolled through the pack; I had many eager takers. A tangle of dirtied hands jockeyed for position over one another to offer me their shooter. I chose a large, shiny blue marble with a swirl of white inside from a red haired boy who sported an explosion of freckles across his cheeks and nose. *Phin.*

My very tip of my tongue peeked through my lips as I lowered to all fours to take my first shot. Not a breath was drawn as my finger made contact with the smooth glass and sent it barreling across the patio. When my shooter knocked seven of their eight marbles out of the chalk ring, they groaned, shoved their hands in their pockets, and kicked at the dirt in disgust. To their utter surprise and dismay, I was good. And now I was the owner of a handful of their colorful glass treasures.

The handful I won quickly snowballed into more marbles than I could cradle in my lap. I removed my sock to serve as a marble bag. The rascal who'd challenged me spat angrily on the ground. Losing was lousy, but losing to a gal was just shameful! The game only continued, I suppose, on their hope of winning their marbles and their pride back; but like a bunch of foolishly hopeful gamblers, they kept on playing until both my frilled socks were stuffed with them.

Eddie, half of the matching set of my rough and tumble older brothers, came out the back door holding a huge piece of watermelon. Endlessly hungry, Ed could always be counted on to know where food was.

"Pip Squeak!" he reprimanded. "Aw, guys, don't let 'er play, she'll rob ya blind!" he called from the porch, elbows dripping with watermelon juice.

I shot him a look that defied the sweetness of my pigtails while I stood and tried to wipe the dirt from my hem. The group disbanded, perhaps due to my brother's warning, perhaps due to the suggestion of cool, juicy watermelon in the house, but most likely because they were offered an easy out that didn't include backing down from a girl in a frilly dress. I offered the big blue marble back to its owner as the boys dispersed, grumbling amongst themselves.

"Thanks for lettin' me borrow this, uh..." I realized that I didn't know the marble owner's name.

"Phin," he said ruefully, hands in his pockets, kicking at a dandelion.

"Well, thanks, Phin," I smiled, offering the smooth, round gem again. He nodded his round, pale, freckled head, but didn't take it. I suppose he couldn't be seen consorting with the enemy.

"Aw, you kin just have all of 'em. I don't have pockets," I laughed, looking down at my dress. It was too delicate for functional properties like pockets.

I was offering him two socks full of marbles; surely this was even better than my original bait. Not wanting to be seen collecting the spoils from a girl, he cautiously looked around to be sure none of his buddies were witnessing his shame, and then quickly swiped the lot into his grimy hands. He poured them deep inside his pockets in an attempt to conceal the booty. If you'd asked me, the bulges gave him away.

As he headed up the porch steps to the house with heavy pockets slapping against his legs, he'd turned to me and grinned. That is when Phineas O'Shea began to burrow his way into my heart. The corners of my mouth twitch upward with this memory, but my awareness of our current surroundings returns.

"Phin?" I ask, dumbfounded, blinking away the haze in my eyes. "I must've hit the water with my eyes open; everything's blurry. Like I'm going blind."

"I've landed in the water that way a time or two," he admits. "Feels like your eyelids are made of sandpaper?"

"Yeah," I agree.

"Don't fret; it should pass soon enough," he assures me. I search the visible bits of his face for recognition. Phineas O'Shea, the 'triplet' that I felt anything but sisterly towards. The one I spent all my time following after school, on weekends, and every sunbaked moment of our summers. We lived in the hills, at the river, and in that huge willow tree by the secret spot. Those summers, we'd just roll out of bed, shove in some breakfast, and blow through our chores as fast as possible. Tilly would moo reproachfully at me for rushing through her milking, my impatient fingers tugging too hard at her. Sometimes Phin would roll up in his dad's old jalopy and help us to make things go faster with an extra set of hands. We'd make a break for the hills, not returning until dusk, dirty and starving for dinner. He's grown into his ears, and his freckles have faded a little since. He'd been a pal to my brothers all these years, delving deeper into my heart every time he'd come around.

"Phin," falls from my lips with amazement, my stubbornly blurred eyes blinking furiously. "I can barely see, and you're hiding under all that... scruff," I accuse, pointing to the orange-y blur on his face.

"Yeah, well, no use shaving out here," he says, stroking his whiskers with his chin jutted out.

My mind can't seem to recover. Phin. *Phin.* Phin! I feel the first flicker of something other than fully consuming, choking despair since I surrendered my happiness to Claire. To Ruby. Something that resembles the girl that I used to be.

"Since you're a friend, can I ask; do you, uh, have any dry clothes?" I shiver under the damp quilt.

"Yeah, uh, sorry, you're probably still all wet," he begins. "I didn't think it would be gracious to undress a dame without her permission," he jokes, bowing like a gentleman. Somewhere under the scruffy blur of hair, his familiar mischievous grin shines through.

I return his smile, but I feel my cheeks flare pink. I hate thinking how vulnerable I was, unconscious.

"There're some things in the drawer. No, uh, ladies things, I apologize. But warm at least," he points with his chin toward a tall dresser. He closes the door, offering me privacy.

Through the jamb I hear him call, "I'm starving. Gonna make some grub down here so c'mon down when you're decent." I hear the stairs squeak under him as he descends, and my familiar loneliness fans itself out like peacock feathers in the room.

Decent. I don't know if I'll ever be *decent*.

Alone in this foreign bedroom, I feel so strange. Phin, of all people, pulled me out of the river before I could successfully drown. I'm in the unfamiliar house of a familiar guy, which feels peculiar, but even more unsettling is that hours ago I'd earnestly attempted to end my life.

Yet here I am, breathing in breaths that I didn't intend to take. The strangeness of it all overshadows the thick, tar-like, gut-wrenching anguish that's choked me for so long, like a bug staring into a light. I'm mesmerized, which is a relief from the constant pressure of despair.

A bitter smile twists my lips. Despite all the time I spent trying to impress Phin as a young girl with my toughness, secretly aching for his attention, here I am, the only other person for miles around. I'm finally center stage, and I'm twisted into the worst state imaginable. Mentally, I throw my hands up in the air. Besides sallow skin and baggy eyes, my belly jiggles independently of my body when I move. I'm sure my swollen cheek looks horribly unflattering, but not quite as unflattering as the dead hollowness in my eyes.

But does it matter? I'm so far removed from happy emotions that the glittering dream of my youth, Phin and me, the blissful couple, is just absurd. A cynical puff of air blows past my lips, and I realize that there's no one here to appreciate my cynicism. I think I've read that it's an early sign of insanity to talk to yourself. I stand quickly to dress so I can end my solitude. Obviously, it's unhealthy for me.

I feel no more feminine in the baggy pajamas I find in the dresser, my first time ever sliding my legs into a pair of pants. As I pull them up to my hips and roll the waistband to shorten the leg length, I marvel at the odd sensation of heavy fabric grazing my inner thighs. I've felt the light presence of silk stockings just above my knees before, but this contact rubs me as just beyond strange. It's so alien that it almost feels ticklish against that skin.

My brassiere still feels damp, so I hang it inconspicuously behind the dresser to dry and pull on an oversized pajama shirt. My fingers find that they need no assistance from my eyes to button it up. I run my palms lightly over the boxy shape of the garment. Luckily, the folds of androgynous cotton seem to disguise my figure well.

My fingers cling to the stair rail as my feet descend by feel, though my rapid blinking finally seems to have some effect. The rectangular shape of the door at the bottom of the stairwell becomes sharper with every step I shuffle down. I cross my arms over my chest as I round the bottom of the noisy staircase and enter the kitchen.

"Pip Squeak," Phin says, shaking his head as he grins. "Geez, you'd think…" He stops himself by pursing his lips together.

"Hmmm? What?" I prod as I lower myself into one of the mismatched dining chairs. I can't help but look down at my legs for the source of the strange feeling, realizing again that it's the rub of pants against the skin of my inner thighs.

"Nothing," he replies. "You like eggs?"

I nod. "But you don't have to dote on me, Phin." I blink twice. I can see him a little more clearly now. Though his wild hair is now close-cropped on the sides and in the back, the locks on top of his head still reach upward like flames.

His wide grin nearly splits his face in two. "I think I do. Have you seen yourself? You're practically an invalid," he jokes. My hand flies instantly to my cheek, which stings to the touch. His easy chuckle tumbles out of his mouth.

"What's so funny?" I ask defensively. I rise up to have a look in the tiny circular mirror near the door, and gasp in revulsion. Through fuzzy eyes, I absorb my appearance. My hair, pushed up and flattened in the back, has formed into a crushed beehive shape with rogue strands of hair flying this way and that. My cheek, a canvas of deep purple and blue, wears a bruise that has spread up under my swollen, bloodshot eye as well. My lips pale and cracked, my skin gray and ill-looking. Tears spring to my red eyes. Here it is, the raw, sickly shards of my soul, manifested visibly on my face.

"At least it seems that you can see again," he jokes lightly while my hands flutter around my head. My helpless fingers have no idea where, or how, to begin repairing my appearance. "You're not blind after all."

When he offers me fried eggs, my hands abandon the incurable mess and find purpose in accepting the steaming bowl from him. I keep my eyes down shamefully, focusing instead on the intermingled egg white and yolk sprinkled with pepper.

"You could take a bath, if you want," he offers.

I nod with my eyes trained on the tines of my fork. When I take a bite, the warmth of the food spreads through my belly and chest, calming me a little. It awakens my stomach, now alive with hunger, ravenous; and I pick up tiny bits of egg that the tines can't spear between my fingers. I don't look Phin in the eye when I pass him with my empty dish. It clinks against the porcelain sink. I shuffle back up toward the washroom, drawn to the idea of completely submerging in warm water.

Alone in the bathroom, I undress by the tub as the faucet eagerly fills it with steaming water. A rectangular mirror hanging on the opposite wall reflects what I hadn't seen before: a large, mottled mark spreading from the side of my ribcage to the protrusion of my hip. I slip into the silky water, careful not to bump the dark maroon bruise. My battered body yields to the all-encompassing heat as I drown myself in thought.

 It's strange to lie so motionless in the water now, with my hair dancing independently of me over my shoulders, when only a day ago I had been hurtling toward death as though it were a finish line. Finding an old friend seems to have temporarily snapped me out of my hurry, though I still feel hollow and sick. I sink my shoulders, neck, then my entire head under the surface. It's so peaceful in this quiet warmth. My body sways under the water, and I think of how easy it would be to stay here and finish what I started at the river. I'd turned the lock on the bathroom door with my own fingers, so I know I'll have no unwanted rescuer this time.

Under the surface, Phin's face fills my thoughts. His little boy smile, his ten-year-old grin, his teenaged simper, his jaw crowned with the telltale scruff of manhood.

What is he doing way out here, all alone? What happened to his reliable smile?

Since I've known him, I've watched Phin's mouth curl with mischief, pucker with confusion, spread with humor, frown in thought, part in anticipation; but never just hang limply like it has most of this morning.

You're one to talk, Sunshine, Imp scoffs.

Even though I'm underwater, I still feel the familiar sting of tears pushing through my eyelids. I can't do this to a friend. I can't deepen his frown. Eventually, he'll fight his way through the locked door, find me here, lifeless; and it will scar him.

But I can't go on.

Can I?

A sob rumbles up my chest, escaping my mouth in a string of bubbles. Reflexively, I draw for breath, and warm water fills my throat. My arms thrash wildly, instinctively; and when my fingers finally grasp the sides of the tub, I pull myself up choking on bathwater. In the small, tiled room, my hacking coughs and ragged sobs bounce around the room, loud as a train. The part of me that begs for the end curses Phin in the ugliest way.

Phin bangs on the door within half a minute.

"Are you alright in there?" he calls through the crack, his voice deep and desperate. The handle jiggles on my side of the door. I cough again, but hold back the sob that presses heavily on my throat.

"Yes, fine, thanks," I answer.

"Sure doesn't sound like it from here, Squeak. Why don't you come on out now? Towels are there, on the wall," he coaxes with a frantic edge to his deep voice. I notice a new, gravelly quality to it that wasn't there before he left for Basic.

I hesitate, thinking of the biting cold outside of the steaming tub.

"Got a fire going," he persuades, as though he can hear my thoughts.

"M'kay," I answer, but don't move.

He waits through several beats of my pounding heart. "Coming?"

"Ye-es," I hiss impatiently in two notes, and the swish of the water bounces noisily off the tile walls as I crawl out of the porcelain tub. Careful around my bruises, I dry off and pull back on the baggy pajamas that stick to the damp spots on my skin.

"Happy?" I grumble as I open the door, where he waits with his arms crossed, leaning on the wall.

One of his eyebrows rises as he nods. "You look better without all that dried blood. Fire's downstairs."

I follow his encouraging beckon down into the sitting room, but I have no intention of sitting. It's small but cozy, and the fire's heat has filled the room with a lazy warmth.

"How far away is the place you found me?" I ask him.

"Huh?" he mumbles. With his mouth parted, I can just barely see his straight teeth glinting behind his lips.

"Where I, um, fell in the water?" I clarify. "How far from here?"

"Barely a quarter mile; why?"

"I, uh, I dropped something that I need." I think of the charm Jack had had on his person when his body was eaten up in the flames of his plane crash, the metal tags designed to last through utter destruction, and the diamonds he'd given me as a symbol of his devotion. I'd meant to die with them, and now they're settled in between smooth stones at the bottom of the river.

Phin's eyebrows take turns rising and falling as he watches me quizzically. "I could take you back there," he begins in a tone suggesting a caveat will follow, settling himself into a club chair. "But first you've got to tell me something." I sigh in defeat as I realize that the "something" he wants me to tell him will be long enough for sitting down before we leave. I want nothing more at this moment than to dive back into that river and find those pieces of my husband, so I nod in agreement and fall onto a sofa. Anything; *anything* to find that place.

That chair must be his favorite spot, because his body molds right into it. "What were you doing swimming alone in the middle of nowhere, Pip? Are you in some daredevil club?" he asks in his familiar light banter.

As I stall by taking in the rest of the room's décor, I sense a man's hand in all of it. That is to say, no forethought has been given to this mismatched jumble of furniture. I wonder if I'm the first female ever to sink into this deep sofa.

"Yeah, something like that," I mutter as I pull my feet under myself. "This your place?" My eyes sweep our surroundings.

"My Grandpa's, really. His old hunting cabin," he says and my assessment is confirmed. No wonder I can't find a doily, or any other feminine touch, draped about the place. "Anyway, I've been staying out here for a while, fishing. Nice to have the solitude, ya know?"

I nod slowly, skeptical at his evasive answer. I can feel that both of us dance over the surface of something deeper. I wonder if what lies beneath his exterior shell is quite as grisly as mine.

"You seem different," he says. I sense that this is the first chip at the ice; he's sensed my restraint as I've sensed his. I stare back at him, our eyes in a stand-off.

"Yeah, well, you didn't have a beard last time I saw you," I joke. Under his henley, characteristically unbuttoned at the top, his body seems thicker and stronger than I remember it. It looks like the military has added bulk to his muscles.

"You didn't have that frown last time I saw you, Squeak," he retorts, more serious. "You were always smiling."

"Sorry to disappoint you," I say, shaking my head with a bitter laugh. I look down, because a hitch in my throat warns me that I'm starting to get emotional again.

"So, what brought you way out here?" he pins me down for the answer with a serious tone.

"That's a long story," I warn.

"And I've got nothin' but time," he counters, gesturing to our surroundings. Out the window, the forest is so thick with trees and foliage that no end is in sight.

It takes me a moment to answer. *Where do I begin?*

"Well, I got circled," I start tentatively, wagging my ring finger, to see if more words will follow.

He snorts and sits back. "So I hear. You up and married some rich Joe."

"*Jack* is his name, not 'some rich Joe'," I correct him while my thumb runs over my naked ring finger. "And if memory serves, Phineas, you have the bees, yourself."

He smirks, the apples of his cheeks gathering. "Hardly. My parents have all the dough, not me." His head hangs as he shakes it back and forth.

"He had to leave all that behind for me, you know." I feel a swell of pride for Jack, realizing now how much he must've loved me to abandon his significant inheritance.

Did I even appreciate it then?

"And Mama didn't like it at all. She sure busted my chops about 'abandoning the family' and 'giving up on my dreams', but Jack's mother was so bent out of shape, she burned down our barn." Saying these things aloud makes me realize how out-of-whack things were.

Phin raises a single brow in response. I've always wondered how he's able to do such acrobatic tricks with his brows.

"She was... *flaming* mad, you might say," he answers with a crooked grin, and I notice new lines at the corners of his eyes.

Quickly, I drop my gaze to my hands.

"Then, I guess Jack took advantage of the freedom from his mother's expectations for him. He didn't waste any time before he enlisted as a fly boy," I clarify and look back up at my audience.

Phin's green eyes remain patient and open, waiting for more, so I continue, "O'course, the country was still at peace when he signed on. That was December. And... you know what happened in December." A thick silence fills the room as I nurse a pang of mourning for my brother, and Phin's eyes gloss over with his memories. He was there at Pearl Harbor when Eddie was killed and Max was injured. He *lived* that surprise attack.

Once he's able to swallow a thick lump in his throat, he answers, "Yeah. Yeah I know." His eyes drop down to inspect his fingernails.

"When you all left for Basic, and the boys piled into your truck, Eddie looked right into my eyes and said, *No tears, Squeak. I'll be back before ya know it.*"

"We didn't know." Phin's lips barely open as he murmurs their defense.

"He did come back," I whisper as tears roll onto my lips. "But he came back in a box." Haunted by the memory of my tall, handsome, sandy-haired big brother lying still in his coffin, a chill runs up my spine. The short, blonde hairs on my arms stand suddenly at attention.

Phin's pale eyelashes press hard into his cheeks as he waves his hand blindly at me. "Please, move on," he urges. I suppose if I leave this part of the story, we'll be eased of this pain of losing Eddie, and this gnawing anxiety over Max. But for me, moving forward only pushes me into another place of mourning.

"Okay," I agree. At least one of us should be relieved. "In March, a letter came from the Reaper."

"But wasn't Ed's funeral around Christmastime?" Phin clarifies, knowing that a visit from the man in white can only mean bad news. "Oh, no, Max? But..."

"No, not Max. It said that *Jack* was missing in action. They have to say that when there aren't any, um..." my voice hitches; "*remains* to send home."

Phin's lips drop slightly open.

"He crashed, and there was an ex-ex-explosion," I warble,

shaking. "They think he may have been shot first, and he'd lost control. One of his flight buddies saw the blast firsthand." The blast that incinerated my husband.

Phin stands from the chair that's molded to his body and sits at my feet, placing his fingers tentatively on my knee. The kind gesture breaks the dam that's held back my emotions in a growing pool. Tears stream in rivulets down my cheeks and neck, where they soak into the collar of the ugly pajamas.

"And then... I found out I was going to have his baby," I continue, sniffing back my leaking nose. "As if being abandoned by my husband isn't bad enough, I find out I'm going to have his child, all alone!" As my complaint echoes off of the log walls, I realize that I've escalated to shouting. I tell myself to calm down as my chest heaves, but emptying my head of these things feels like shaking off heavy shackles. Hindsight helps me realize how lousy a lot I've been dealt.

"I couldn't do that to a little baby, raise him without a daddy, sentencing him to a life of meager meals and back-breaking work. He deserves a childhood, a real one! Jack's brother, Bentley, and my cousin, Claire, just had a little baby girl that was stillborn, so it was kind of fate to fill their empty arms. I gave him to them."

"Claire…Quinn?" his brow furrows as he places the puzzle pieces. "I thought the Quinns were in your family doghouse. Deeply."

"That's mostly my Aunt Madge," I clarify. As he nods, I know that his ears must have been filled time and again with Max and Eddie's rants and accusations about her.

"Well, she's Claire Sharpe now. Since she married Jack's big brother, my baby was kinda perfect for them, you know? Same blood lines on both sides, so no one will be able to tell that he's not their own child," I sell to him through lips wet with tears and snot. "He'll grow up looking the part. And he'll never know who his real parents were."

Sharp pains of longing sear my chest. I bore little Jack in a barn without a doctor or a midwife, or even a nurse. There's no certificate to prove that I am his real mother, if I ever wanted to. I'm sure Ruby knows that. She wouldn't have given me those solid green bricks of her wealth if there was any return from what I've given up. A sense of finality settles onto my heart.

What have I done?

"Yeah, I guess," Phin agrees hesitantly. "It's a boy?"

"Yeah. I named him Jack," I whisper, and my eyes swim with the image of the tiny, squirming pink boy. I see his curious eyes blink against the soft lamplight as he searches for my face. I watch his body relax as he realizes I'm his mother. In the present, I ache for his sweet weight on my shoulder, fluffs of his soft dark hair tickling my neck. A cloud of regret looms around me, choking me; waiting to swallow me up.

"I know he's better with them; I know that," I try to convince the two of us. My voice shakes. "It's just... just, if I can't go home, I have no husband, and I am awful enough to abandon my own child... where does that leave me? I'm alone, and I did this to myself."

"He's hardly *abandoned*, Squeak, and you're not alone," Phin counters, gesturing to himself. Sure, there may be another person in this room, but no one can know just this pain until they've experienced it all themselves.

"Well, I know, but I mean alone inside." I look at his sad face as he processes what I've said. This was a large load to dump on a person. He seems to be handling it, his emerald eyes thoughtful. He just looks sad for me. "I just couldn't take it. The emptiness. The gloom. The despair. I couldn't run from it, even if I ran to the ends of the earth! So I decided to just..." Phin's brows rise in anticipation, as if he knows what I'm about to say.

"...end it," I admit.

"The river," he connects. "You didn't just fall in. Not swimming."

"No, no, not swimming," I admit to the afghan between my

fingers. So, there it is, my whole story on the table. I couldn't present a worse front for Phin if I'd tried. I'm disheveled outside, but rotting and hideous inside, hingeing on mortification for all I've revealed.

"I…" he says quietly. "All I can say is that I'm so, so glad I was fishing on just that stretch of river," His head shakes back and forth in slow motion.   "I know better spots than that one."

"I'm still not sure that *I* am glad," I joke with a half-hearted smile, and he grimaces in response. If he hadn't been there, I would've surely drowned in that river. Weighted down with the stones of my despair, my body would've settled to the bottom with the mossy rocks, never to be seen again.

Just like I wanted.

Now, as I sit here with my heart beating blood through my veins, my lungs drawing and expelling breath, I don't know what I want.

FOURTEEN

Phin drags me out of the cabin along with two fishing poles for a session of what he calls "therapy". The sun has eaten through the morning fog on the riverbank, and it sparkles happily on the rolling water. It seems innocent enough as it sings its babble over the smooth rocks and under the surrounding trees, not like the watery grave I'd tried to make it yesterday. I have to admit to myself that reclining on the riverbank indeed soothes my soul. Oh, the difference one day can make for a gal.

"It's only fair that you tell me why *you're* out here all alone," I begin. I know I have leverage to draw out some information; I've bared my soul to him today. "I think I've earned it."

"Yeah, somehow I knew you'd use that against me," he mumbles wryly, and we laugh together.

"Spill," I coax. For the first time in months, I feel kind of comfortable.

"Well, it's simple, really. A guy gets burned in the world, so he shies away from it," he explains minimally. His mouth falls into a line, as though he's done speaking.

I groan at the simplicity. "C'mon, I gave you more than that, Mister Cryptic."

"Maybe try again tomorrow," he suggests, narrowing his eyes at the river.

"Okay, tell me about Max, then. The medical reports they send home are just a tease, and you only wrote us once! How was he when you saw him last?" I coax.

Phin sighs and drops his shoulders. I can almost see a picture of my brothers, his best friends, flash in his eyes. Any mention of Max is also a reminder of the loss of Eddie.

"Last time I saw Max, he was laid out in a hospital cot with white bandages wrapped all around his head. He didn't even look the same with his mouth all slack," he explains, dropping his lips to demonstrate. "I've never known Max not to smile." It's true. Max, though more quiet than Eddie, was never seen without his mischievous grin as an accessory.

"But, he was still breathing, right?"

"Yeah, his chest was the only part of him that moved. I kept sitting there in that infirmary, watching him, waiting for his foot to twitch under the blanket, or his fingers to wriggle. But he never…" he trails off. We exhale in mutual disappointment. I wish I knew if I've officially lost both of my brothers. Having Max hanging in the balance unsettles me.

"I don't want to lose anyone else," I mumble at the water. *Daddy, Eddie, Jack, little Jack, and in a matter of time, Max.* Something tells me that I should add my name to that list. I may have already lost myself.

When the sun sets, allowing the stars to appear above us, we head inside to roast our catch over the fire. Somehow, the simplicity of the meal--not served on Lyla's china with Lyla's silverware, not carefully plated and delivered to an elegant table--relaxes the tight coils inside of me.

"I don't really belong anywhere, Phin," I tell him between bites of trout.

He shakes his head.

"Well perfect, because I don't either." His jaw flexes over and over as he chews. "But you're welcome to 'not belong' out here as long as you need to." A lone cabin nestled in thick woods seems like the perfect hideout for a couple of misfits.

If your Mama thought you were even considering this… Sense scolds.

The thought of Mama's reaction to hearing that her daughter would share a dwelling with a wild fella out in the middle of nowhere curls my lips into a grin.

"I mean, you'd have your own room and everything," Phin amends, blushing. I'm not sure if even that condition would soothe Mama. "I think there's even an extra toothbrush in the medicine cabinet."

"Thank you, Phin. You're a real pal."

"Mayday! Mayday!" Jack cries urgently into his radio mask. When his finger releases the button at his throat, the static of communication ceases.

Thunk, goes the bullet into his shoulder. He gasps in pain.

"No!" I cry out, waking suddenly, bathed in a cold sweat. My eyes rake around my surroundings: dark and barely familiar. I jump as a door swings open and slams into the wall, and the room around me shudders.

"Are you alright?" Phin asks through the darkness. "You were screaming." Dudley's tag jingles against his collar. I can't see him, but I know he's there.

"Yeah," I pant, my chest heaving as I slide into a sitting position against the headboard. "I'm fine."

Are you really 'fine'? Sense questions skeptically.

"I was just having a nightmare," I confirm to Phin, and to myself.

"Oh, I know a little about that. Sleep is supposed to be a safe place, isn't it?" he asks. The floor creaks underneath him as he shifts his weight. "It's not fair."

"No, it's not," I agree, recalling my mother's repeated words. *Life just isn't fair, Penny. Get used to it.*

"Seems like every time I close my eyes, I'm back in that harbor again."

I lean toward his voice in the dark, hungry to hear any detail about what my brothers endured during the attack.

"The swarm of planes, the gunfire, the explosions. Haunts me like a ghost."

"'Haunted' is a good word for it," I agree, feeling the hairs on the back of my neck tingling.

"Luckily, I have just the cure for that," he baits, and I hear the floorboards creak under him as he moves out of the room. The sound of Dudley's jingling tag trails away behind him.

The squeak of the floor planks announce Phin's quick return, and he settles himself onto the foot of my bed. I slide my feet out of his way.

"Okay, here goes," he breathes out in a sigh. Music fills the dark room as his fingers strum a deep humming from a guitar. "*Summertime, and the livin' is easy,*" he sings quietly. The notes settle over my nerves, easing the lingering tension from my nightmare.

"*When the fish are jumpin', and the cotton is high,*" his low voice carries up the quilt. I find myself relaxing the same way that I do when I sink into a hot bathtub, the notes unraveling my spine from a tight coil into the smooth, curved line like it's meant to be.

"*Mmm, your daddy's rich; and your mama's good lookin'. So, hush little baby,*" he croons, "*don't you cry.*"

"Phin," I interrupt. "When did you learn to play the guitar?"

"I picked it up on base; one of the fellas had one in our bunk. My folks always made me take cello lessons growing up, violin, viola."

It makes sense; Phin was at home gaining culture while the Hale kids did chores.

"All that practice translated pretty well over to this thing," he explains as he runs his fingers down the strings.

"Oh," I murmur. "Well, don't let me stop you."

I snuggle down into the pillow and pull the blanket up over my shoulder. Phin's fingers roll across the strings again.

"*Summertime…*"

I submit to the melody, lulling into peaceful slumber. I don't even realize the moment that I fall over the edge of consciousness; I just do.

"Gee, Phin," I greet him in the morning, scratching the side of my tangled head as I settle into a low kitchen chair. "You're a pretty swell bunkmate with that guitar, you know that? I haven't slept so well in ages."

A grin stretches his lips wide.

"Yeah, you slept pretty late. And you were snoring pretty loudly, too," he chuckles.

"I do not snore," I claim, combing through my hair with my fingers; though truly, I'd be unconscious and unaware if I ever did saw logs in my sleep.

"Gals," Phin laughs. "Always gotta be a lady."

"So you were joking," I press as I run the pads of my fingers over the surface of the wooden table.

"I guess you'll never know," he teases, his eyes surrounded in laugh lines.

For the stretch of several days, our comfortable coexistence always includes a fishing excursion. Phin is right; hanging out at the water's edge is, indeed, therapeutic. We explore new bends in the river, always to the south of the cabin at Phin's insistence. Better biters that way, he claims.

Each time I laugh, it takes longer and longer for me to feel guilty for smiling as a widow. The river reminds me that life flows on. The sunbeams on my back make me think that Jack is up there, warming me through the rays, urging me to savor every breath I take in his absence.

Be happy, Pip, he seems to say. *Shake these heavy chains off of your chest for good. Live your life!*

But, how can I breathe so easily without him?

October, 1942

"And," Phin chuckles, choking on his laughter, "remember when we built that fire to cook those little minnows we caught, and..."

"We nearly burnt down the entire grove!" I finish with him,

chortling. As we gather boysenberries and blackberries from a small clearing near the cabin, we volley memories of Max and Eddie between us. My fingertips, purple from the berry juice, wear several puncture wounds from the angry thorns, but I don't care.

"It's starting to grow back around the bank, now," I assure him.

Both of our heads swing toward the bushes as they suddenly rattle with movement. Phin's giant, droopy dog trots into the grove with a limp rabbit between his teeth.

"Dudley!" Phin calls. "C'mere boy. Whaddya got?"

The dog's tail wags as he drops his prize at his master's feet.

"Good boy!" Phin praises as his fingers rake through Dudley's fur.

I turn my head away from the dark stains in the rabbit's coat.

"Aw, c'mon Squeak; it's just a little blood. Weren't you training in medicine? I mean, before your sugar daddy came along?"

I stick my tongue out at him. "I was just a candy striper, and they kicked me out when they found out I was on the nest. But yes, thank you, I saw plenty of blood. I've just never been really comfortable with, um, dead things," I grimace as my eyes land on the perfectly snow-white fluff of the rabbit's tail. "Especially not cute little fluffy ones."

Phin's gaze drops to his feet; he radiates temporary guilt. I pluck an especially juicy boysenberry from my basket and hurl it at his cheek. It finds his face with a wet *smack*, leaving a dark purple smear on his skin. His eyes instantly fire up.

"You will regret that, Penelope Hale," he growls. "Or Penelope H. Sugarbottom or whoever you are now."

"It was *Sharpe*," I gulp as my sense of mischief fades away. "But I don't think I get to be her anymore."

Phin's brow rises. With his gaze locked on me, his fingers drop into his berry basket, and a handful of juicy bullets fly toward me. I shriek and duck, narrowly avoiding half of the flak.

Smack. Plop! Squish! I wipe away remnants of the berries from my cheek, and lick my fingers.

"Stop! These are really sweet, and you're wasting them!" I protest as he loads his fists with more ammunition.

"You can't put a price on revenge," Phin growls through his grin.

"It took an hour to gather those! Aahhh!" I run for cover behind a large oak. As my attacker closes in on me, I hoist myself up into the rough bark of its branches. "I could've made a pie!"

Golly, I think to myself as I climb. *This is so much easier in pants!*

"Ahhh!" I scream as his fingers close around my ankle. Adrenaline shoots through my limbs like a bolt of lightning. I shake my foot violently against his hold.

"Get down here," he roars, "and fight like a..." He stops, loosening his grip.

"Like a man?" I finish for him, smiling. "I know I'm wearing your grandpa's PJ's, but I'm still a *girl*, you know." I kick at him violently, but he quickly regains a relentless grip.

"No fella has ankles this skinny!" he yells, yanking hard on my leg. I scream as I topple out of the tree, crashing onto Phin and rolling into the leaves that litter the forest floor. I surrender to the cold ground, panting from the sudden exertion with a wide grin stretched between my ears. I let my face fall to the side toward Phin.

His body lies splayed on the ground next to mine, his palmful of moist berries sitting invitingly in his loose hand as he recovers from the fall. Quickly, I swipe and close my fingers around the plump, dark fruit. Phin's fingers squeeze over mine, squashing the handful so well that deep purple juice runs through our fingers as we brawl lying on our sides. I struggle to push our hands toward his face, a pale target for the dark pulp.

With equal determination, he urges our fists back toward my face, and I grimace as our arms tremble with effort. My forearms ache, threatening to falter. I grunt in protest.

"When Max wakes up, he's going to hear all about this," I threaten through my teeth as I strain against the force of his counter strength. "You had better watch your back!"

"You've got it all wrong," Phin retorts, his face red with effort.

"I'm acting as his proxy." He's right. This is absolutely the sort of torture Max would subject me to if he were here.

With a final shove of Phin's hand, the purple pulp of hand-crushed berries smears from my chin to my collarbone to the music of his triumphant laughter.

His therapy is working.

November, 1942

This morning, with the sky looming dark and grey, feels different than the other mornings at the cabin. I can feel a storm coming. The air hums with warning, thick and wet, as our feet crash through fallen leaves and brush. With thick rubber soles on the oversized boots I wear, my feet feel powerful, and my strides are long as we make our way toward the rushing sound of water.

Until now, there's been no hurry to get anywhere or to do anything. Until now, I'd felt complacent passing the days as a girl that the world didn't miss. Until now, when my bones tell me that a storm is on its way, and I suddenly feel pushed from behind by some unseen force.

Just as the earth below our feet becomes spongy, the dense trees open up to the river. A pool of water, so clear you can see the trout scatter in it as we approach, empties over a tumble of boulders. I peer over the edge, watching it fall into another crystal pool two stories below us. I've never seen anything like it; it's quite a fall. I can only hope the invisible hands that prod me forward don't push me over that edge.

"It's been weeks, Phineas," I call to him over the waterfall's roar. "I ask you every day what drove you out into the solitude of these woods, and you keep telling me to ask you tomorrow."

He shrugs, stopping ankle deep in the water, and looks back over his shoulder at me. In the dark daylight that the cloud cover provides, his skin looks sallow.

"Well, it's tomorrow!" I prod. "Actually, it's well beyond *'tomorrow'*. Time to spill the beans!" Two droplets of water hit my scalp, and I look up at the opening sky. Light sprinkles of rain freckle my face.

"I don't know what you mean," he deflects, busying himself with inspecting the clouds. His pale eyelashes wink against the rain as the drops become heavy.

"You've been avoiding my questions. But you can't distract a girl from her questions, Phin; you can only brew them inside of her!"

"Good to know," he replies, tapping the information into his temple.

"I want to know why a fella who just *barely* cheated death in a surprise attack on his army base would rather spend his time alone out here than with his family." My hands gesture toward the canopy of leaves behind us, the river at our feet, the dark grey sky above us. With his face flushed red from his hairline to his ears, he peers at me sideways.

"I'm not alone, Pip," he mutters, barely audible over the noise of the water.

I roll my eyes, frustrated. "But you were! Unless, of course, you count Dudley. You said it had been a full month since you'd seen another human being when I showed up."

"And what a way to show up," he teases, finally turning his body toward me. "Facedown and sopping wet."

"Forget me and my pathetic entrance for a minute," I demand, waving the reminder away with my hands. "What's going on with *you*, Phin?"

Phin swallows and wipes his hand over his closed eyes.

I can't imagine what would be harder for him to share than my downward spiral toward a suicide attempt, but he takes his time gingerly setting his pole across a boulder before he speaks.

"When a fella leaves home, he kind of expects time to freeze in place behind him, that things will be just exactly the same when he gets back. In Hawaii, with Ed and Max..." he starts, and hula girls begin swaying seductively across my mind's eye. I scowl as he gestures animatedly with his hands. "...we were having a blast. There are all these dames in the city who want to dance with a soldier, want to kiss a soldier, want to--"

"Yeah, I get it, Phin, go on," I interrupt sourly, rolling my wrist to urge him past this part. I don't want to relive the bitter feelings I felt when I'd read about this in my brothers' letters. Again, I imagine the three of them in uniform, surrounded by eager young gals. In my mind's eye, Max is reserved, but Eddie soaks up the attention and wears a gal on each of his arms.

"Anyway, you know, we're really flyin' high, just doll dizzy, when Ed gets this letter from you sayin' that you'd gone and gotten married. And I think, 'What have I been doing *here*?' I'd totally blown any chance I had with you."

My head snaps up to look at him, my lashes fluttering against the thickening rainfall, but his eyes focus hard on the river water.

"I realized that I shoulda stayed home, in Saratoga."

"Huh?" I blurt out, stunned. The idea that Phin had any sort of emotional reaction to the news of my marriage is a complete surprise. It sounds like he may have been jealous, because… because he wanted me. "A chance with… *me*?" At the moment, inside, I feel like a goofy, scrawny twelve-year-old with a secret crush.

Phin's skin turns as red as his hair. His jaw bounces wordlessly before he speaks again.

"Well, I didn't know either, until then; that moment. Guess it sort of snuck up on me." He smirks, exposing the laugh lines that run through his freckled skin. He still won't look up at me, even though my insides have gone to pudding.

"Anyway, the next Saturday night, Ed's real put out because I won't go to the dance hall with him. He'd lost his best wingman, you know, Max isn't too forward…"

I knew it.

"…and he wants to go to this joint in Honolulu; Jones went with him. So Max and I, we're just sittin' back in the barracks, twiddling our thumbs, when he milks it out of me; I'm a fool for his little sister. His *married* sister. At three a.m., Ed comes waltzing in, fried, and wakes us all up with his boots clomping all over the room. Max says, *'Guess what? Phin's sweet on Squeak!'* and Ed calls me outside to settle it with knuckles."

Nervously, I giggle at Max's use of my nickname; it makes my brother feel close. But still, my heart pounds, and my palms become slippery with moisture that has nothing to do with the rain.

"The next minute, we're throwing punches in our pajamas and Max and Jones are trying to pull us apart. I'm still seething with a bloody nose when we're ordered back to bed by the C.O. And then," he continues, but I cut him off. I want my picture of the last hours of my brother's life to be crystal clear in my head.

"C.O.?"

"Commanding Officer," he clarifies, and continues painting the scene for me. "The next morning, I'm saddled with early kitchen duty, courtesy of that C.O., for throwing the first punch while Ed gets to sleep off his giggle water in his bunk. So I'm in the mess hall, peeling a mountain of potatoes and thinking of what to say to one of my best pals, how to convince him it was all a bunch a' hooey so we can go back to normal, when I hear a buzzing sound outside. Louder than a bee, and gaining on me.

"As soon as I register that I'm even hearing anything louder than an insect, I look out the window. I see this Jap, you know, our eyes meet for a second. Before I can even put together what is happening, he lets it go, and the ceiling rains down on me. Ed, Max and Jones were all back in the barracks when it was blasted by one of the enemy bombs."

I nod bravely, though my eyes sting with hot tears. I've not heard these details before.

"Did you see them that way? In the rubble?"

"Yeah," Phin answers thickly, wiping at the corners of his eyes with his thumb. "I pulled 'em out myself. Max was in a real bad way, but Ed; well, you know Ed didn't make it."

He examines his hands, and I'm drawn into the vision of Phin heaving my brothers' bodies from a collapsed building. Those hands, the hands idly wringing as he tells his story, had saved Max.

"Was he... I mean, was *Eddie* already gone when you found him?"

Phin nods his assent. "He never heard me say sorry. I shouted it at him, I shook his shoulders, but he was gone. Just a shell; no Ed left in him."

I swallow back my grief. It's painful to remember that I'll never hear my big brother laugh again.

"And Max?" I press, even though it's clear that these memories hurt for him to relive. However, I feel starved for these details; I just have to know.

"I climbed out of the rubble with the other boys--Jap didn't get one fella on kitchen duty--but outside, it was total mayhem. Rubble and explosions and wounded men everywhere you look," his shoulders sag. "I ran straight for the barracks, and saw Max first. His whole body was as black as the smoke rising from the rubble, but since the back of his head was bright red with blood, my eyes went straight to him."

Blood. Max's blood, a beacon in the ashes.

"Was he in a lot of pain, Phin?"

"He lay there still, like he was dead, but his pulse was strong. I don't know if he felt a thing; he was out cold." Phin shrugs. "I carried him over my shoulder to the infirmary. Next time I saw him, he was clean and bandaged, but his eyes were still shut."

I nod. I'm grateful to him for dragging these memories up for my benefit, and try desperately to appear unaffected by what I've just learned.

"We lost a lot of good boys," he whispers, haunted.

"So, you weren't harmed?"

"Not physically, really. Surface scratches; nothing that required stitches," he replies.

"So, why did you leave the island, then? I smelled that shriveled lump in your letter; it smelled like heaven. I'd never want to leave a place that smelled like that."

"That was a flower. But oh, no," he protests with a wan smile, "maybe it used to be Heaven there, but after the attack, living on base felt like purgatory." He squeezes his eyelids shut, and gulps as though trying to squelch a bad memory. "After a few months of cleaning up that mess, I guess I couldn't handle it anymore. All the guys in my barracks were injured or dead, so they grouped the survivors into new barracks, but my pals' ghosts were still everywhere. It's rough going on when you're reminded of that every day; not sleeping at night because your ears are too aware, busy listening for that buzzing sound, wondering if you're going to be alive in the morning or if the Japs are coming back to finish the job.

"So I came home. *Formal leave for mental reparation*, they called it. I'm trying to screw my head on straight out here without Ma squawking at me, asking what I'm going to do with my life now. I'm supposed to be seeing a head doc, but I just think there's no therapy like a fishing pole, y'know?"

I nod my head in agreement. Phin's therapy is good therapy.

"I think it's been good, the solitude, but I was all but ready to see another person again besides that greasy ol' guy who runs the grocery over in Sutton's Cross. Then you come tumbling down my river," he finally looks up at me with his green eyes large and vulnerable. It looks funny on his face: sharp jaw, prominent cheekbones.

He's definitely a man now, I think; the softness of his teenage years has sharpened. *Maybe it's time I finally grew up, too.* I watch his face for a moment before I start laughing. I can't control the chortling that explodes from my chest. I lean over with my hands on my knees and try to calm down.

He grabs my hands.

"Why… what's so dang funny?"

I know my face is bright red, and my eyes are running. Their warm, salty tracks disappear in the rivulets of rain water running down my face.

"What? *What?*" he begs, but his uncertainty makes me laugh harder. His expression is familiar: his mouth parted just so, top teeth visible, eyes twinkling with anticipation. But this time, his eyes twinkle with anticipation for me.

The idea hits my funny bone just the right way, and I'm doubled over, crying with hysteria. Words… my deepest secret, sit perched on my tongue as if it's a diving board, ready to spring into the deep end.

"Oh, Phin," I look up at his freckled nose, unable to look him exactly in the eyes. "We're a couple of idiots, you know that?"

FIFTEEN

Phin doesn't follow my declaration of our thick-headedness, so I continue, shouting over the pattering of rain on the river, "Do you know that ever since you carried me home from the river that one day I fell from the zipline, I have been completely stuck on you? Maybe even longer?"

He chokes on a guffaw of his own.

When I dare to look at him, his pale lashes rest lightly on his freckled cheeks, his head shaking back and forth. I know what he sees behind those lids. A puny little gal, trailing the boys on their every adventure.

When his eyelids sweep back open, the color to his emerald eyes seem deepened by the dark grey sky. We stare at each other in silence, allowing the rain to soak through our clothing as we blink against its drops.

"You... you could have asked me to a ladies' choice or something," he finally mutters.

"Well, you could have asked me to *anything*," I growl back, upsetting a stone with the toe of my boot. The gentle rain opens into heavy, pounding drops, and a rumble of thunder punctuates my retort.

"This is a new development for me, Pip," he defends over the roar with his eyes still twinkling. "And, well..." Phin's twinkle dims. "...you know how well it went over with Ed. I didn't even get a chance to make up with him before..."

We're sobered by the reminder immediately, how brutally they were attacked, and how Eddie defending his little sister's honor actually saved Phin's life. *If Phin weren't stuck peeling potatoes… If Eddie had just gotten out of bed to join him…*

"Well, you know," he finishes.

We've just as much as declared our affection for each other, but our feet each remain planted just as firmly in the ankle deep water as they were before these revelations. I suppose that a normal person would leap into Phin's arms and kiss every one of his freckles; his skin warm in contrast to the cold rain. Coil their fingers through his wet, coppery hair. Run their thumbs over the laugh lines by his eyes.

I'm not a normal person.

"Whoa!" we exclaim together as a bright flash of lightning strikes a tree not ten yards from where we stand. It seems to loosen our feet from where they've cemented themselves in the riverbed.

"We'd better get back," he cautions.

"Yeah," I agree, eager to leave this thick weight of discomfort behind. Phin scoops up our poles as another roar of thunder shakes the air. We hurry out of the current, our boots sloshing in harmony toward the bank.

"But we didn't catch anything. What are we going to eat?" I joke. The cabin ice box has enough trout packed into it to feed an Indian tribe for a year. I'm rewarded by Phin's sideways grin, though his eyes remain cast down at the ground as we traipse back to the cabin.

Above the treetops, the gloomy grey sky flashes with light again.

"You'd better lose those poles; they're like lightning rods," I warn him.

He shrugs. "I've already been hit by lightning."

My head whips toward him as we move. "What? No way."

"They say you lightning doesn't strike the same place twice, and I've already been struck," he claims.

I consider his claim while I work my way over a fallen log. My feet move clumsily in the oversized rubber boots.

"By the Japs."

Neither of us speak after that. The only sounds in the clear, wet air are the clomp of our boots crashing through the brush, the delicate cadence of rain finding its way down through the canopy, and the occasional clap of thunder.

It seems that the air of discomfort follows us silently through the trees, and doesn't wash away when we break out of the tree cover and dash through the open field to the cabin. By the time we crash through the front door, my hair has become so thoroughly soaked that it sticks to the skin of my back like it's been painted on. Phin's wild, fiery mane lies matted against his own head.

"At least we won't need to shower today," he laughs, rumpling his hair. Though rain patters rhythmically against the windows, the next few moments fill with silence. My gaze falls on his boots, the back of his hand and his fingertips dripping with water, then to the hollow of his navel where his transparent shirt sticks to his skin.

Stop that, Penelope, Sense scolds me, and my eyes jump to the little pools of rainwater cupped in his clavicles that shudder as he breathes. I feel her blow out an exasperated puff of air in my mind. I shake my head to clear her away.

"So... well, that was a conversation I never thought I'd have," he laughs.

"Tell me about it," I agree with a nervous chuckle. My chin bounces with shivers, and I'm not certain whether it's from my jangled nerves or from the cold.

He lifts his index finger in the air, watching my eyes. Tentatively, he moves it toward my face, lightly touching the pad of his finger near my nose. He runs it around my nostril toward my upper lip.

"You still have that scar," he whispers, his hand falling away from my skin.

"Yeah, I s'pose," I shyly mumble, pressing the back of my hand to that spot. It always turns purple in the cold, along with my collection of old wounds decorating my kneecaps and elbows.

His long, pale lashes sweep over his eyes in a long blink. "Do you remember how you got it?"

I remember. I earned this ugly old scar one spring afternoon before the boys left for Basic Training, and Max had deemed the air warm enough to hit the Spot after the closing bell rang at my school. I rode happily on the handlebars of Phin's bike, not caring that the metal dug uncomfortably into the back of my thighs, feeling the sun warm my face as we flew through the wind. Petals of apricot blossoms fluttered through the air like a spring snow, and I laughed while they flew into my open mouth.

Eddie and Max jogged behind us, losing steam in a race of man versus wheels. Phin called out insults to them to set fire to their heels, but when they'd speed up, so would he. As we sped under a particularly snowy apricot tree, I'd raised both my arms high in the air, closing my eyes in glee. At the very moment I released my hold on the bars, Phin had ducked his head to dodge a flying rock from a sore loser trailing behind him, and he knocked me forward. I flew into the dirt, scratching my knees, palms, and my nose. It took Mama an hour with a sewing needle to dig all of the tiny pebbles out of my skin. I've worn this scar as a reminder on my face ever since, but I only remember it when it's cold out and I happen to catch my reflection in a mirror.

Today, the memory reflects in Phin's eyes.

"I blame Eddie," I growl, and we share a short, tense laugh.

I can hear my own breath in the quiet inside air. Phin's eyes volley between his boots and mine, to the rhythm of the rain pattering outside.

"I have to admit it, Squeak, even though you'll snap your cap at me for even thinking it. I…" his mouth snaps shut.

"What?" I urge; his cryptic remark has me incredibly curious.

He smirks. "Well, I know you've just been through Hell and all, so I have no right feeling this way; but for me, this past month has been a dream come true," he says sheepishly. Warmth visibly floods his chilled cheeks.

I stand across the hallway from him, the shreds of myself left after my soul had been ripped apart, close enough to reach out my hand and place it on the wet fabric clinging to his well-formed chest. I'm pathetic. I feel as though I've been burnt at the stake, and I blew into Phin's life again as a pile of ashes. *Doesn't he mind that I've lost everything?*

The only way he could have you is if Jack was out of the way, Sense points out. *For Phin to win this dream, you had to lose.*

I look up to face the guy who is callous enough to feel lucky like this, and instead, just find Phin's innocent face. His golden-green eyes swim with sincerity. There is no way the owner of these eyes can possess the kind of cruelty it takes to be that selfish, to wish for me to be a widow so he could have me. My brain hurts trying to reason, so I just crumple in the entryway. He bends to help me up, but I swat him away.

"I'm fine," I snap, immediately feeling guilt for shading his hopeful eyes with doubt. I scramble to my feet on my own, kick my way out of his oversized boots, and stomp up the stairs in his soggy socks. I slam the bedroom door, rattling the thin windows, and throw myself onto the borrowed bed.

The rain of the roof intensifies, beating against the window glass, as though desperately shouting suggestions to me that I can't hear. I turn my face into the pillow. Tears burn through my lids, which I've squeezed tight, and the light pain distracts me from the storm in my head.

I'm so confused.

No fairy tale I'd been read as a little girl prepared me for what has unfolded. Hansel and Gretel are saved before they're eaten by the witch. One kiss is all it takes to bring Snow White back to life; to wake Sleeping Beauty. Little Bo Peep's sheep find their own way home. Like me, Cinderella had also lost a parent as a little girl, but Prince Charming came along and swept her out of the jaws of her evil stepmother.

My treasured collection of stories has been lying to me my whole life. Life doesn't deal you easy fixes. There's no fairy godmother waiting in the wings to pick up the pieces. Even though when I look at Phin, the stirrings of genuine contentment rise inside of me, this is no fairy tale.

Am I allowed to enjoy being here with him? I wonder. Am I allowed to feel warm with his declarations, and to bask in the glow of his clear green eyes when he looks at me the way he does? Or will any relationship between the two of us be as dark and shadowed as the storm clouds today?

I'm swathed in the quilt, lost in the betrayal of my favorite childhood books when a knock shakes the door.

"Come in," I call. Phin cracks the door unsurely, poking his head just inside the jamb.

"Just wanted to say g'night," he says quickly, and starts to retreat.

"Wait! Phin," I stop him, and my stomach drops. "Come in."

What are you doing? asks Sense.

I swat the cocoon of blankets away while he walks in, rumpling his hair.

"Come here," I say and pat the bed beside me. While my smile is calm, my pulse runs like a prize racehorse just yards from the finish line.

Atta girl, Imp grins inside of me.

The air is cold outside of the quilt, even in the pajamas. Phin must feel it too, because his bulky arms wrap tightly around his chest.

"Geez, it's cold in here," he shivers with a smirk. "Hang on a sec." When he walks out, the door sways idly. I hear the floorboard in his room squeak and he comes back in moments with a huge blanket eating his head. He tosses it onto me, and my head knocks backward by the weight of the down comforter. I'm fighting my way out of total immersion when he flips up a corner of the blanket, and I see light. He grins mischievously at me under the blanket.

"Is this your blanket from your bed? I can't take this from you," I say, beating down the fluff to find fresh air.

"Look, there's a ring on the moon. It's gonna be freezing tonight," he says. "I can't let you turn into an icicle in here."

"So, you're just going to turn into an icicle in there?" I retort, pointing across the hall to his room. He grins. The mischief in his smile tells me he doesn't plan to freeze.

"Oh, *fine*; get in," I submit crankily and open the covers.

He slides in.

"Just stay over on your own side."

I position the pillows so that there's one between us as a cotton-filled barrier. We punch and flap the quilt and comforter to straighten them, so I think he won't notice the repositioning in the fray, or notice how my eyes have grown as big as saucers. Mama would drop dead if she saw me allowing a fella to slide into my bed. *Dead.* When the blankets have settled, he grabs the pillow and stuffs it under his head.

So much for my barrier.

Dudley stands by the bed, staring pathetically at Phin with his doggie eyebrows gathered up high. He must feel betrayed that he's been kicked out of bed; or maybe he's just cold on the rug at the foot of the bed and wants to make a dog pile with two other warm bodies. Phin assures me that Dudley will survive, but Dudley's droopy eyes fill me with guilt anyway.

"G'night," Phin says, and he's so cavalier that I suspect he moved my barrier pillow on purpose. However, despite his light scruff, the puffy blanket tucked under his chin lends him the innocence of a little boy. His eyes close and he smiles peacefully. You'd have no idea from looking at him that he's just finagled his way into a gal's bed. I click the lamp off and roll toward the window. The moonlight shines too bright, even through my tight lids. I roll back over. I can feel the warmth of Phin's face inches away. I roll back toward the moon.

"Geez, you're worse than Dudley," he says.

"You sleep with your dog?" I exclaim, flipping back over to face him.

"He keeps me from turning into an icicle," he defends. "But he's a terrible bedmate. Flipping over all the time, sticking his paws in my face, dog breath…"

"I'll keep my paws to myself," I grumble into the blanket and start to turn for the moon again.

"Don't, I'm cold," he says and wriggles his paws around me.

Since I'm taken off guard by his sudden touch, my muscles don't have time to stiffen against his arms. Instead, my body responds by nestling into him. His chin rests on my forehead.

I will my pulse to slow down, or at least soften its thumping pace. Surely he can hear the rapid drumming that betrays my feelings so well. I try to tuck my chin to my chest to hide; curled like a porcupine, but his scratchy chin burrows defiantly into my pillow, forcing my face back upward. I know a kiss is on its way.

Sorry, Mama, I apologize in my head as my pulse thrums through it.

Phin's lips move in on my mouth slowly. They feel soft against my skin in contrast to the rough scratch of his facial hair. Their light touch sends my thoughts spinning in a wild tornado, and I become oblivious to my worries, tangled up with him in the eye of this welcome storm.

I exhale, and my breath parts my lips. He presses his mouth in closer to mine. Darkness may surround us, but a burning warmth glows here between us. His fingers slide into my hair, and his other hand wraps around my back. The light pressure of his palm coaxes me closer to his chest. I remember exactly how that chest looked with his sopping wet shirt clinging to it, and a bolt of heat strikes my core.

I pull away from our zealous embrace, leaving him dizzy.

"What? You don't have dog breath," he teases. I roll my eyes. He is still so much like a brother to me.

"This is moving so quickly, Phin," I say, scooting backward on the bed. This feels too close to being with Jack. It's wonderful and magical to have someone touch me with affection, yet eerily familiar. It feels…

It feels *forbidden*.

He laughs, but I don't get the joke. "This," he gestures between the two of us, "has been brewing since nursery school. This is the slowest train I've ever taken, Ma'am."

I roll onto my back, careful not to topple over the edge of the mattress. The thump of my heart echoes loudly in my head as my emotions form into coherent thoughts. If only I weren't such a mess.

"It's just, when you hold me like that, it's like you're holding the broken pieces of me together, and I don't want to need you like that," I whisper thickly. Warm tears run down the back of my throat.

I'm angry at myself for ruining the magic of the night with this. Even in the dark, I can feel my words cut into him.

"I don't want to need anyone like that, Phin. I did once, and he was taken away from me. I couldn't bear living through that again."

He grunts and pulls me back to him. "You don't have to need me, Squeak; but you should know that I need you." I melt back toward him. I rest my head on his shoulder, and he rests his chin on top of my head. As he strokes his hand over my hair, I can both hear and feel a deep, satisfied sigh rush out of his chest.

"You know, I haven't felt right since I came back, with everything so different. But this," he hums, pausing to touch my forehead, brow, nose, and lips with the pad of his index finger, "this feels right at home." He peers deeply into my eyes, and I allow the intrusion.

"And if you care for my opinion," he continues.

I have always cared for his opinion.

"...I think you're healing just fine on your own. Even though the broken you is still pretty breathtaking."

Somewhere inside me rattles a feeling that this can't be possible, that I'm acting out an utter betrayal against Jack. However, that concern sinks deep below waves of contentment. Phin is right; this feels like home.

"Your hair still smells the same as it did four years ago," he reflects.

"Oh?"

"Yeah. Sweet, like... strawberries," he chuckles.

Jack always said that to me.

"Guess I was paying more attention than I thought." I can feel his laugh as much as hear it, with my ear pressed against his shoulder. In the seven months since I got the letter telling of Jack's death, I have longed for this close vicinity with a shoulder. Far longer, I'd been longing for close vicinity with these shoulders; Phin's shoulders. It feels unreal.

He begins humming, and the vibration runs through me, lulling me into a deep, satisfied calm. The dream comes before sleep this time, but I sleep peacefully on him. The first sleep in a long, long time that is true rest for my body, and true rest for my soul.

In the morning, I wake to Phin's open eyes, tousled red bed-head, and a smile playing on his mouth.

"It's real," he whispers, his eyes shining.

I know just exactly what he means. I start to sigh, but quickly press my lips together. I breathe through my nose while I stiffly sit up.

"What is it?" he asks.

"Dog breath," I mutter out of the corner of my mouth while the rest of it stays tight. My tongue has gone as rotten as Dudley's in the night.

I slide out of bed and head for the bathroom sink, but I turn back to steal a glance back at him before I scurry out the door. The morning light catches the red in his wild hair, like the first beam of deep red light of a sunrise. It sheds brilliant warm light on my soul. His head and shoulders peek out from the puffy down comforter. He looks as content as I've ever seen him, even more than at the Spot, with one arm resting on top of the fluff. I can't contain the grin that arrests my mouth and spreads so wide that my cheeks hurt.

I scrub the dog breath from my mouth while I examine the bruise on my face in the mirror. The bruise isn't magenta anymore. It's faded to a blotchy yellow; sort of sickly green. I look hideous. I marvel at Phin's attraction to me in spite of my appearance. A voice inside tells me that's what you get when you've known someone for eleven years- they see right through your exterior. What currently lies beneath my exterior doesn't seem terribly appealing, but his memories of me slowly pull that bright, happy person back to the forefront.

I spit into the sink. *Was it really just a few weeks ago that I was staring into a similar mirror, plotting my own death? I'd been certain that there was nothing left to live for. How could I have known that Phin was an hour's bus ride from me, wallowing in his own despair; that we were each the ladder the other needed to crawl out of our deep, miserable pits?*

My affection for Phin feels so different from my feelings for Jack that it doesn't immediately feel wrong. With a reverberating pang of jealousy for some woman who doesn't exist, I consider the situation in reverse. If I were the angel, I'd be following Jack, whispering '*be happy*', urging him toward someone who could offer him some relief from misery. Someone who is already familiar. Perhaps with heavenly perfection, he is exempt from jealousy, and watches me happily; perhaps he's even directed me here. I'm driving nails into the lid of a box that contains my sorrow when Phin enters the small bathroom. At the sight of him, the last nail slams straight in; my grief sealed in tight.

I wrap my arms around him, reveling in the solid feel of him, and lift my face to his for a kiss. But he's adopted my tight lipped nose breathing and denies my advance.

"Dog breath," he murmurs, and we laugh. I stay wrapped around his waist while he rinses out his mouth. When he's done, he lifts me to perch on the sink and kisses me straight on the mouth. My nose bends to the side, squished against his, and I find that I do not care the slightest bit about its position. I lean into him and the sink wobbles dangerously under me, which breaks our kiss.

"Grandpa's good ol' 'craps'-manship," he says and rolls his eyes. I hop down to the safety of the cool tiles under my bare feet.

"You seem… better," he says, brushing a stray lock of hair from my eyes. That tiny gesture, his care for me, allows me to set down the heavy beam I've been carrying on my shoulders. My soul exhales in relief.

"You're not so bad, yourself," I tease, brushing a lock of ginger hair from his forehead. We've both been traumatized. We're both afraid; we need each other. He can care for me, and I will care for him.

He grins. "Nope, not bad at all," and I know what he means. He fingers the nasty bruise across the arc of my cheek bone. "It's healing."

"Yeah, healing ugly." I look down and try to see my own cheek. I only catch a quarter inch blur of yellow.

"You could be covered in boils and still be a stunner, Pip," he sighs, and scoops me up in his arms. I have zero control over the scarlet that floods my cheeks. We weave through two doorways to make it back to the bed, and he tosses me on top of the fluffy comforter. I wriggle back under the blanket, absorbing the lingering warmth our bodies have left in the sheets. Phin slides in next to me, and I curl up against his chest. The rhythm of his heart beat echoes in my ear, the only sound for several minutes.

...until Dudley's deep *"woof"* shakes the air.

Slam. The house rattles as the front door shuts.

"Hello-oo!" a voice calls from downstairs. "Hey, Lover Boy, where are you?" The voice belongs to Max, and I brighten instantly at the realization.

Max is awake*! He's home!* I slide toward the edge of the bed, ready to tear down the stairs toward my brother.

And you're in trouble! Imp teases.

Phin's fingers close around my upper arm, and his green eyes widen. I freeze.

"I know you're here; I saw your truck out on the main road… Hello?" he calls. My body doesn't know what to do. I'm dying to see my big brother, to hold him to me and smell him and hear his throaty laugh rumble in his chest with my head pressed up to him. But I know if he finds me here, with Phin, my reunion with my brother will become complicated. Soured.

"I found a couple of big bills on the riverbank. What did I miss when I was out? Does money really grow on the mainland trees now? He*lloooo?*"

I look to Phin, who's frozen as well. I hear Max's steps ascending the steps; there's no time for discussion, so I duck under the covers.

"Phi...what the..." Max sputters when he finds us.

"Hale," Phin says. "You're awake; you're back! Hiya, Pal!"

"Oh, sorry, Lipstick, I didn't realize you were, uh, *entertaining*," Max teases, and I hear him take a step backward onto a creaking floorboard on the landing. It's the only sound I hear over the frantic thunderous pounding of blood rushing in my ears.

"Max, wait," Phin says and slides out from under the covers. I feel the quilt shift, and know that the crown of my head is exposed.

"Well, I figured you were here looking for comfort, Pal, but I didn't realize you needed *privacy*. Come by the farm when you're not so--*Squeak?*" Max's tone boils over from sheepish to ferocious. I feel the down blanket pulled away, and with it, most of my dignity. To my brother, this must look so much more scandalous than a sincere kiss and the shared heat of the bed on a cold night. I can only imagine what he must assume.

"Max," I breathe, smiling awkwardly. For a moment, I take in his form with my eyes: he's here, and he's alive. Walking. Talking! "It's so good to see you!" I push the wild hairs out of my face as a rush of relief washes over my head and drips toward my toes. His familiar face has become pale and thin, evidence of his long illness, but to me, it's the most beautiful sight in the world. He's awake!

He scowls. "Pip Squeak, what is this? When I left, you were a gal who needed nobody but herself. Who are you now? You just run into the arms of the closest breathing male?" I should be consumed with embarrassment, but the throbbing of the angry veins at his neck are a beautiful sign of the thriving lifeblood flowing through him.

"Hey, now," Phin tempers.

"And you!" Max turns to his best pal. "Can I only assume you're adding my baby sister to that line of notches in your belt?" Max's face reddens more and more with every word, until he's become as dark as a beet.

"No, Pal, it's not like that," Phin assures him, shaking his palms dismissively.

"Get up, Squeak; we're leaving." As I stand, his eyes rake over the ugly pajamas, and he grimaces. "Oh, please, you're wearing his pajamas? Gross, P!" He drops my arm.

"Max! It's not what you think!" I insist.

"Those are my grandpa's," Phin defends, grasping Max's upper arm.

"Don't touch me," he barks at Phin, shaking out of his hold. "I may not have as much experience in the ring as Eddie, but I have enough fight in me for both of us, and I will pound you into the ground if you tempt me," Max growls through his teeth. I've never seen him threaten anyone before. Even weakened by months of inactivity, the angry set of his jaw looks pretty menacing doing it.

As I stand, pulling away from Max's grip as he pulls me toward the stairs, these thoughts run through my head: *I can't go home to the farm and face Mama. Not yet. Phin clearly has a long list of conquests; was I just the latest one?*

Max pulls hard on my wrist, and I can't fight him. My feet struggle on the stairway, fighting against Max forcing me, but not sure if I want to make my way back to Phin. *Was all that he said yesterday true? Did I bare my soul, only to be taken advantage of with a few smooth lines? Is Phin really cheap enough to exploit a twelve-year friendship just to feel a warm body close to him?*

Am I really the kind of gal to run where someone else wants me to run?

No, Sense and Imp sing together in my head.

With one swift yank, I break my wrist free of Max's grip and run down the stairs toward the door. I hear both of them shouting after me as I run through the jamb and onto the naked forest floor.

"Where are you going?"

"Wait up, Sis!"

Ten yards away, I realize I that don't know exactly where to find what I need. I flip around, looking to Phin.

"Where is it? The place you found me?" The flurry of emotions inside of me has found a purpose, an action. I need to go back in.

A shadow passes over Phin's eyes. "Oh, um, follow me," he says, ducking his head and moving upriver. I allow space between us before I step after him. Max follows with a confused scowl, piqued interest showing in his eyes under low brows.

"It's about a quarter of a mile up this way. Don't you want shoes?" Phin asks without looking at me. Clearly, neither of us wants to set Max off again by closeness or a telling glance.

"I grew up on a farm, Phin," I remind him, rolling my eyes. "I don't ever wear shoes if I can help it." Still, I have to hold up the long legs of the pajamas as I walk so as not to trip on them. *What will I do with them when I go in the water?* I wonder to myself. My hands will be too busy to hold them up.

"Max, when did you get back?" I ask as we walk over a carpet of fallen forest leaves. Lingering moisture from the night-long rain shower squishes up between my toes.

"Last night."

"I didn't know you were awake! All better, and well enough to make the journey home!" I stub my big toe on a rock, but stifle my gasp of pain. I don't need an 'I told you so' from Phin about wearing shoes. "I sent you a letter, months ago, and I didn't hear back... I wondered if you had woken up yet. Or, you had, but you were upset about what I'd written, or if..." I don't want to say that I'd worried his brain was too damaged to be able to read at all.

His expression tells me he knows what I haven't said anyway. "I'm fine. But I have a hard time swallowing ol' Madge's take on things, Squeak. Sounds like a thin cover for her own guilt, and it's a pretty dirty way to do it, if you ask me," he says with disgust. When I hear my big brother say it, it doesn't seem so plausible that Mama could've done those things. But is he just being ignorant, like Claire had been? I don't want to push him when I just got him back, and when he's already displeased with me.

I just nod. "I see." *Swish, swish, swish.* The inner seams of the pajama pants rub uncomfortably against my inner thighs. I'm sure they will be red and sore from the chafing soon enough. Pants can be awful. "Well, why didn't you write to me and tell me that? It's been *months.* All these things swimming around in my head..."

Max halts all of a sudden. "Aren't you training in medicine, Sis?" He holds up his left wrist, displaying for me rows of jagged, ugly scars, mingled with thin, straight ones. Surgical scars.

"Your writing hand," I breathe with barely any breath. Max is alive, but it seems he'd lost a real treasure in the attack. He couldn't write me back. Phin is mesmerized by the sight of the healed wounds.

"Last time I saw that hand, it looked like a pile of hamburger meat," Phin comments. "I'd call that an improvement." I think of Phin digging Max out of the rubble and running him to the infirmary. Max owes Phin his life.

"And I have you to thank for it, Lipstick," Max growls. "Couldn't you have pulled me out of there a little more carefully?" His grin lies thinly veiled under a scowl.

"Sorry, Pal. I was slightly more concerned at the time with that gaping hole in your head."

"Which is precisely why I haven't pounded your face into the ground for womanizing my little sister. *Yet.*"

"Why do you call him Lipstick?" I ask.

Phin and Max look at each other. "You don't want to know." They both laugh. *Lipstick. Lover Boy.* I cross my arms, guarding myself as I realize the meaning of his nicknames.

"How many gals did you romance over on that island, Phin?"

"A better question, Sis, is how many nights did we go to the dance hall. Same number," says Max.

Phin shoots him a dirty look that Max absorbs with pleasure on his face. Phin's shoulders sag.

"I honestly lost count," he admits. Max doubles over in laughter beside us, watching his pal take this fatal nosedive. I'm sure he thinks he won't have to pound Phin to break us up now. I tune out his chuckles as I reply to Phin.

"So, am I to understand that you developed a hunger for women over there? You just feed it whenever you want by whispering a few sticky sweet words and the gals just swoon and fall right into your arms?" He tries to take my hand, but I yank it away.

"What number am I back home on the mainland, Phin? Six? Seven? Eighteen! Or have you *lost count?*"

Phin is only the second guy I've ever pressed my lips to in my life. I wonder which of the Saratoga locals have been on his plate since he's returned. My stomach rolls. I feel cheap. Cheaper than cheap; Phin found me in a vulnerable place in my life, and I just fell right into his trap. I'm disgusted with both of us.

Phin looks to Max. "Do you mind giving us a second?"

Max nods reluctantly and turns away, stepping a few paces into the trees as he nurses the stitch in his side. "I'm still here, you two. Don't forget."

Phin trains the entrancing green of his irises on me, and for some reason, I can't look away from them.

"I didn't know how I felt about you when I'd go out dancing with those gals," he pleads in a hushed voice. "Once I heard you were married, I realized..."

"You realized you wanted what you couldn't have. Just another conquest; it's sick."

"No, no; it's not like that! I didn't kiss another gal after that, even though I thought I'd never actually be able to kiss you," he says, swiping my hair from my eyes. "I just... didn't want to anymore." The wall I'd thrown up against him begins to shake unsteadily under the force of his sweetness.

"Oh?" My eyes invite him to continue.

"I promise, P, you're not a fling to me. I wish I could erase all those dames, but I can't; and I promise, they were all meaningless flirtations."

I'm not sure how I feel about a fella who'd treat a string of gals as 'meaningless flirtations'. My wall against him steadies itself tentatively. I see him register this in my stony expression.

"No gal ever really paid me much attention in high school. In fact, they all pretty much teased me about my hair. They'd call me 'Red', 'Carrot Top', 'Freckles'; mostly just 'Tomato Head'. I was just a skinny circus freak." I never saw him that way.

"I've always liked your hair," I admit, and my hand twitches at my side, wanting to reach out and give his unruly mane a tousle.

"And then suddenly it's something that makes me special. Attractive. It was hard to resist all of that attention. And they were just having fun, too. It never went anywhere. Just smooching in the back alley; no further than that."

You've been way farther than he has, Imp reminds me. I cast my eyes down.

"It doesn't cheapen my feelings for you, Squeak. I never felt anything like this for any of those gals. Not even a glimmer." And just like that, my wall against him crumbles into a dusty pile of rubble. I gingerly place my arms around his waist, nestling my head into his chest.

"The flower in my letter was for you. It was a plumeria, but I guess it shriveled up by the time it made it to your farm." My eyes close. I breathe in the fabric of his shirt, and I can almost smell that heavenly scent on it. Plumeria.

"Gee*eee*, I can't leave you two alone for a minute! This is my sister, Pal," Max growls from the trees. I hear his feet crash through the underbrush back toward us.

"I know," Phin replies, and I feel the warm breath of his words in my hair.

"By the way," he whispers only to me, "we're here." I pull away from him, watching the water in the river flow around large boulders.

Both my feelings for Phin and my excitement at seeing Max are swallowed up by the memory of the last time I was here, in this place, trying to end my life. The mood was so different then; the collision of the two causes a crack of thunder in my insides. It's a jolt to my senses as I try to recall being so low that I would have cheated myself of the rest of my life. I never would have seen Max ever again.

I step into the water. It soaks into the cotton pant legs I'm wearing as I take in this place from a new angle. Through the middle of the river, a quick current hurries downstream, but in a pocket where two boulders meet, the water barely moves. Debris floats there, rocking as gently as a boat on a calm sea. I let out a breath as I realize what it is: fallen leaves, sticks, and crumpled bills.

The money that I threw into the water is still here, or at least some of it. The fact that it floats here, untouched, tells me that this place is so far outside of civilization, so desolate that if Phin hadn't been fishing here, I would've been dead. I was a fool to waste that money. I should've sent it to May.

Give it to her now, Sense suggests.

I wade in, quickly swimming diagonally across the sweeping current, and collect the soggy bills.

"What are you doing?"

"What's that you've got, Squeak?"

"Those are his only pajamas, you know; practically a family heirloom!"

I hold up my fists, and both boys look stupefied. I work my feet over the slippery river stones back to them and press wads of dripping dollars into their palms.

"Is this why you wanted to come back?" Phin asks.

"No. I thought this had all washed away. I can't believe they're still here." Truthfully, the riches I'm seeking here are of the sentimental kind. I scan the boulders on the far side, trying to recognize the spot where I'd stood from a reverse viewpoint. When I spot the boulder where I'd stood, a deep shudder shakes my core. I can't believe I'd felt so hopeless that I'd... I'd just... give *up* like I did. The baggy pants drag in the current as I slosh my way into the icy river, so I slip them off over my ankles and hold them in a dripping bundle over my head.

"Pip," Max growls protectively at the sight of my bare legs. I toss the pants at him, and hear them slap into his chest, thick and wet, behind me. Oblivious to the cold, my feet move slowly over smooth, grey-brown rocks under the rush of the current. The stones cast dark shadows over one another as my hungry eyes search among them for a glint of metal.

"Please be here. Please... please..." I mutter as I squint through the chest-deep water. Finally, I find the glittering things I'm seeking, nestled in the rocks under the surface, but I'll have to dive down to them to be sure. I suck in deep lungfuls of air, squeeze my eyes shut, and plunge myself as far down as I can. While the surface coaxes me to float back up toward her, I kick my legs to push me down as my hands move furiously over the moss-slick river bottom. My open eyes sting while I search, but I can feel the moment that my fingers close around my treasures. I feel it in my fingertips, but I feel it deeply inside of my soul as well. This is what I came here for. Relief escapes me in a string of bubbles.

"Squeak! Get out of there!" Max shouts as I surface and suck in oxygen.

Max's exclamation hits me at the same time as Phin's cry, "*What the...*" I swim to the shallower bank and ignore them both as I examine my prizes with frigid water dripping from my hair, nose, and chin. Holding Jack's four-leaf clover charm feels like holding his hand. When I slide my ring finger through my wedding ring, tears prick at my eyes. The weight of his dog tags hanging from my palm make me shudder. Another shudder follows, and another, until I realize that I'm near freezing as I stand here in calf-deep water on a chilly Autumn day. The current presses against my calves as I wade out of the water.

"Can we go back now, please? I need to lie down." The fight has evaporated from inside of me, and I feel deflated and heavy. I just want to sleep. Phin scoops me up in his arms, as my head bobs as he trots quickly back home.

By the time we return to my bedroom in Phin's cabin and he sets my bare feet on the floor, my chest heaves, upset. *What have I done? Did I just throw that part of my life away when I tossed these things into the river?* Both boys watch me with concern written across their expressions as they pile blanket after blanket on the waiting bed.

"Just rest, P. Take it easy for a while," Max soothes as he pulls back the covers. My body clings to his suggestion, even more tired than I'd realized.

When they shut the bedroom door behind them and I hear the stairs squeak under their descending feet, I nestle my treasures under my pillow before I undress. My shaky fingers lay my sopping wet pajamas over the radiator. I fall heavily onto the bed, and curl into a ball. What seems like moments later, I feel groggier than I previously had, and I know I that must have dozed off. A scent tickles my nose, and I bury my nostrils under the covers to push it away. But I can't hide from it.

Something is wrong.

My eyelids crack open. A thin stream of light smoke rises steadily from the bottoms of the pajama set. I wrestle out of the heavy comforter and snatch them from the furnace, smothering the heat by bunching them in my hands.

I dress in their lingering warmth, and realize, *I'm not shaking anymore.*

At the top of the stairway, I begin my descent. Partway down, I walk into a palpable wall of tension. The air is thicker; heavier than upstairs. At the last step, I turn into the living room, where Max and Phin are posed like two bulls with locked horns. I can practically see white billows of steam blowing from their nostrils as they release biting words at each other through gritted teeth. Necks tense, bodies rigid, I know it won't take much for a scuffle to break out. I worry that Max, weakened by his coma, will be crushed by the tension visible in Phin's muscles.

"What makes you begin to think you can add my *sister* to your list of conquests?" Max sneers, his upper lip trembling angrily.

"You've got it wrong, Pal. Perhaps that broken brain of yours isn't working quite right." He swipes the air near Max's head.

"Boys!" I snap, and their heads swing my direction. With my hands planted on my hips, I feel like a teacher breaking up a schoolyard tussle. "What is this?"

"Ma knows I'm out here to see Phin. I had to thank him in person for saving my skin. But does anyone know that you're out here? Mama said you'd run off in a huff, but I didn't think she could've guessed it was out here with this goon. He's not worthy of you," Max argues, his chest heaving.

"And this guy's not thinking straight," Phin defends.

"And you think ripping each other to tiny pieces will solve things? You're best pals. Best pals don't cut each other up until the other person is nothing but a pile of shreds on the floor. That's the job of the rest of the world! You need each other! Especially right now! The world is trying to tear us up; you can't *add* to that by doing the tearing, you idiots!" As I suck a breath into my pancake flat, depleted lungs, we all crack a smile at the idiosyncrasy. "I mean, you incredible fellas." With our chuckles, the tension in the room falls away. I step toward them and put a hand on each of their shoulders.

"We are more than this, you know. And we're going to need each other to help us rebuild." Both boys nod. "We're so much more than what has happened to us," I state, feeling my soul inflate at my own pep talk. "We've got to remember who we are; who we were before all this."

"I can't ever be that guy again, Squeak. Not after what I've seen," Max says.

"Then be better than that guy. Be the wise guy who has seen it all, and is better for it! No more tearing. We build from here, alright?" They shrug, shifting their feet.

"Now hug. Hug it out." I wait for them to embrace.

"No way, Sis." I sweep a stern look over both of them, but neither will budge.

"Not a chance," they say simultaneously and walk in separate directions.

"Fine! Give it time, then!"

SIXTEEN

The three of us sit scattered along the shore of the river with fishing poles. Max, barely out of earshot, watches peripherally with eagle eyes from his perch atop a rock. He squats, looking uncomfortable and ready to spring at Phin at any moment.

"I thought of something while you were sleeping this morning. I was thinking about this gal, Francis."

I frown at him. With my unwelcome guard, Max, sleeping next to me and Phin back to sharing his bed with Dudley, apparently Phin's attention has had too much room to wander!

"No, no," he laughs, "not like that. I was just thinking about how I was sweet on her in high school."

I look at him flatly. If he's trying to backpedal, this is not helping.

"We spent some time together. She was pretty and all, y'know; real girly," his nose is scrunched. "I took her to the Spot…"

"You took her to t*he Spot*?" That's betrayal.

"Yeah, I know," he says, shaking his head, regret clear on his face. I read that he thinks it's a wasted breach of our spit contract.

"All she wanted to do was lie on the rock and soak up the sun. And I thought, '*wish Pip were here*'. You'd be swinging on the rope, or doing cannonballs, or helping Ed burn down the forest." A smile cracks the grimace on my lips.

"Guess you were sneaking up on me, even then," he smiles.

I work my facial muscles to stifle my grin and scowl at him.

"You shoulda let her try the zip line," I grumble resentfully, imagining the girl splashing into the shallow water. He laughs, and I catch a hint of my smile echoed on Max's face.

Today, we're catching in the river with nets like we did at the Spot, only Phin's grandpa's nets are far superior to our homemade ones. This spot is much shallower, and we don't have to scoop far into the water. The air is unseasonably warm, but still the cold of the water bites at our ankles. I catch two trout, which is two more than I'd ever caught with my crude net at the Spot. Their weight in my net feels like two solid gold trophies.

Tired of canned goods and endless trout, we decide that it's time for a trip to the small, backwoods grocery store. I want to get potatoes and an onion to fry up with the trout. Max confirms that we're down to one roll of toilet tissue. The thought of living one more day in these pajamas makes me claw at the front door to go. We drive Phin's old jalopy to Sutton's Cross. Max watches carefully as Phin maneuvers the gear shift between my knees.

"I want to ask you something, Squeak," Max whispers in a low voice. "But I don't want to upset you."

"Fire away," I invite him, turning my face toward him. His eyes stay locked on Phin's hand over the gear shift, apparently awaiting Phin's fingers to gravitate to my thigh so he can justify breaking each one of them.

"Mama said that when you left…" he clears his throat. "She said you were going to have a baby." That last word lingers in my ear painfully.

"Yeah," I shrug, feeling my soul sag with this memory.

"Did it… did something happen to it?" he inquires tentatively, curling his thick arm around my shoulders. "Did it die?"

"No," I murmur, my eyes welling up with tears. Silently, I mouth, "I did," but he doesn't notice.

"So, I'm an uncle?"

"More like a second cousin," I mumble.

"You've lost me, Sis," he whispers back.

"It's a boy. But, I gave him up to Claire," I admit. My entire body feels weighted by invisible concrete as I say it. A quiet moment passes in the cab of the truck as Max's eyebrows fold over his troubled eyes. A break in the forest ahead reveals our destination coming close. I long to get there, swing the truck door open and breathe something other than his disappointment.

"Well, I'm sure you did what you thought was best," he whispers as we park, and I hear a subtle note of woe riding on his words. I try to ignore it as I slide off of the bench seat. There's not much I can do about it now.

The grocery store is just an old ramshackle building that serves as the post office and gas station, too. While Phin and Max load up, I wander into the little clothing shop next door. It's mostly women's clothes, and the lone salesgirl looks overjoyed to see another soul.

"Can I help you?" she asks eagerly, sizing me up.

Please do! Sense begs.

"Just looking," I tell her.

Her appraising look increases my awareness of the ugly pajamas, and a silent conversation plays between our eyes. '*Please, woman, let me spare you from that awful rag,*' her eyes plead. Without a word, she piles things onto her arm and she walks me by the elbow to the dressing room. I follow.

"Are you sure about this?" I ask through the curtain as I inspect a pair of blue jeans in my hands. Blue jeans cut for a *woman.*

"Honey, they're all the rage! I thought you were keen to that, seeing as how you waltzed in here in pants and all…"

"No, not really," I reply, scrunching my nose at the things.

"Y'know, what with all our boys being called up to war and all, us gals gotta step up to the plate. Can't wear a skirt when you're welding, you know!"

"Women are… welding?"

"Of course," she replies, condescension thick in her tone. "Honey, we've all got to do our part! *Denim,* honey. I can barely keep these things in stock out here!" I can't believe what I'm hearing, especially so far outside of the big city.

When Phin finds us, I'm wearing clean underwear, a camp shirt, and dungarees. "A million bucks," he winks.

Or a thousand bucks, Imp teases as I think of the pile of crumpled bills in my soggy handbag, though surely much of the money had floated downstream to change the fortune of some lucky fisherman. I haven't counted it. It turns out that in this outfit, I actually look like exactly ten dollars and seventy three cents.

"That's all you're going to get?" Phin asks me, and the sales girl's ears visibly perk up.

"Well, I don't know..." I reply.

"I'll be happy to treat you to some new things," he offers. "Whatever you want."

Oooh, you've got yourself a Sugar Daddy, Imp taunts.

I open my mouth to tell him I can buy things for myself with my own damp bills, but in the time it took for those three words to slide over his lips, the gal has shimmied out from behind the counter and taken my arm. Quickly, every one of my fingers becomes a closet hanger for her selections for me. Not twenty minutes later, Phin's shoulder hits the door, and the bell on it jingles as he wrestles two large bags through it. It hits me: I own *pants*.

Jack would call me a rebel. I grin to myself. Perhaps I am.

Outside, my eye is caught on a cork board. The flurry of notices tacked here tell me that even the tiny town of Sutton's Cross is touched by the war. Between the flyer for a boy's farewell and an ad for homemade jam--'proceeds to benefit the Pearl Harbor-widowed Thomas family'--is a typed advertisement:

"Women--War Job With a Future! Join the Cadet Nurse Corps Program! Free training with pay, room and board, and uniforms. There's one for summer and one for winter, and it's hard to say which is the smarter, which you'll wear with more pride! To qualify, you must be between 17 and 35, a high school graduate or a college student, in good health and mentally alert. Enjoy time for

dating while you secure your future!"

I smile at that last line, "time for dating". The plan I'd formed for myself while digging up potatoes as a young gal had me with a diploma in hand before I even so much as looked at a fella, then Jack swooped into my life. Perhaps this ad offers me a balance of learning and loving. I rip it down, fold it up, and slide it into the pocket of the dungarees.

The more I think about it, the more excited I get. I've always wanted to be a nurse. Like a falling star, this opportunity has landed in the palm of my hand. Silently, I apologize to God for being so angry with Him. That was the darkest moment of a hollow black night before the brilliant dawn, where now I can really become a respectable, working nurse with a liveable paycheck. I'll have standing that I've really earned, all by myself.

Of course, I'm also motivated by Jack. Perhaps if he'd had a medic there, they could have saved him; they could have pulled him from the cockpit to safety and treated him; kept his heart beating. If I can save one man, someone else's Jack, then it will all be worth it.

"Don't look at me like that," I scold Phin. Across the bench seat of his truck, he's carefully arranged his large green eyes into a droopy sadness that does Dudley proud.

"How can I just let you slip through my fingers again?"

"I'm not slipping," I insist.

"You're leaving," he argues.

I nod. "I have to do this. Thanks for the ride, Phin." I lean toward him with my chin poised expectantly. He turns his face forward, shunning my offering.

"Have it your way," I say in parting, and slip out of the truck door into the first sprinkles of a light rain. I pat over the folded flyer tucked safely inside of my jacket. I trot behind the truck bed, look both ways down the street for traffic, and jog toward the brick building on the other side.

"Squeak! Wait up!" Phin calls, and I hear the driver's side door of his truck slam. In the middle of the street, I turn back to him, watching him close the distance between us. Just before the yellow line in the road, he halts. His jaw bobs silently as he gathers his words.

With a thunderous crack, the dark cloud above us splits in two, fully unleashing its contents over us. I feel my hair mat down against my scalp, and watch the endless droplets run down Phin's face, over his brows, off of his eyelashes, off of his nose and over his lips. His hair turns from red to earthy rust as it gathers in wet sections, and he finds his voice, shouting over the loud sounds.

"I have to say something… you have to know… something…" He shakes his head and drops his eyes to the street, rain dripping from the tip of his nose. "I mean, I don't want to just say it in a letter." My heart quickens as I stand in the open rain in the middle of the city street.

"I… I love you, Squeak," he shouts over the pounding rain. My rain-soaked shirt and hair provide me an excellent cover as I consider his declaration. I had supposed I was a convenient, familiar warm body who tumbled down his river at the moment he felt lonely, but love?

A fella doesn't just fall in love with a notch on his belt, Imp quips.

"I think I always have," he adds, his chest heaving. If everything had always been so right with the world, and these two puzzle pieces has always fit together so nicely, then I shouldn't have run away with Jack. He wouldn't have run away to the Navy, and we wouldn't have created a child together that I wasn't equipped to raise.

"How can that be?" I shout back to him, over the hundreds of staccato drops splashing around us. "I've never wanted anything more than I've wanted you, Phin. You were always right there, and I never knew." I feel my own warm tears mingle with the cold rain running down my cheeks. The mixture drips off of my jaw and onto my chest, which heaves with my quickened breaths.

"I just didn't realize it," he claims, his brows folded together over sad eyes. "I'm so sorry that I was so ignorant. And now you're leaving." His shoulders fall as he stands pathetically in the open downpour.

"If it weren't for you," I shout back at him, "I wouldn't have remembered what living was for, Phin. I was nearly dead inside when you found me! You blew on the embers and lit my fire; you did this to me."

Phin's boots splash through a puddle as he takes three determined steps toward me, and his warm arms wrap around my cold waist. The sigh I've been holding in since I first realized I was in love with Phin escapes me with relief, and I turn my face gratefully up into the rain. He loves me back. *Let it come*, I think. *Let it pour.*

With our wet bellies pressed together, Phin looks down into my eyes. His fingers gently push the matted hair from my face and behind my ears, and I feel the warmth of his exhales on my chilled skin.

"There's no one like you anywhere in this world, Pip Squeak," he claims, brushing his finger over my nose scar again. His fingers slide behind my ears, and he tilts my blushing face upward. His eyes examine mine, left and right, left and right, as my eyelashes flutter against the falling rain. With water sheeting down my face, neck, and body, I feel completely stripped of any facade. He really sees me. I've told him everything. Phin knows me, the very ugliest parts of me, and yet... he still wants me.

"Come here," I invite him, peering up at him from under my eyelashes. He tilts his head down toward mine, and I lift myself onto my tiptoes. Under a sheet of cold rain, his mouth finds mine, warm and soft as he presses in. I feel the hum of a moan on his lips as he parts mine, his arms wrapping tighter against my ribs.

I rake my hand up his scalp, clutching his wet, unruly hair. I feel his tongue approach mine, and they tumble over each other like frolicking lions. The horn of an oncoming car interrupts us as it speeds past. A sheet of water flies up behind its wheels, soaking me to my waist. I pull away.

"Phin," I blush.

"Goodbye, Penelope. Good luck." He presses his mouth against my wet forehead.

I jog through the front doors of the brick building for the second time in my life, but this time, not intending to stay. This time, not in a downward spiral toward a deep, dark drain. The nun behind the front desk gasps at my sopping wet hair, my soaked blouse, and my daring choice of denim pants.

"Hello," I greet the nun, ignoring her gaping mouth. "I'm looking for a gal named Birdie; she used to live here. Could you perhaps tell me her current address?"

"Annie," I hiss through the back door of Lyla's home. Her dark hair, carefully styled into a chignon, and the back of her maid's uniform are all I can see through the two-inch crack. "*Annie!*"

"Oh!" she exclaims, grasping her chest with surprise. "Miss Pip! How..." Her face falls as her chocolate brown eyes fill with shimmering tears. "You left." Her eyebrows furrow, and I know behind her sad gaze, she must be remembering the morning of Jack's funeral, when I'd slipped out before dawn. I didn't say goodbye to anyone, and I haven't returned since.

A hot ribbon of guilt flutters through my chest. "I'm sorry about that, Annie. I…" My eyes close. I don't want to look her in the eye when I say this. "I thought that you were spying on me for Ruby."

Annie's chin draws into her neck with surprise. "Me? Spy?"

"I know; it's ridiculous. I should know by now that Missus Sharpe lies when it suits her. I'm so sorry, Annie. I didn't leave because of that, though, I left because… because…" I'm not sure I can sum up the raging storm I'd experienced inside of myself during that dark time. *I've healed*, I realize. *Healed.*

Annie waves the expectation of a finished sentence away with her hand. She pulls me into a tight hug, and we exhale in unison.

"It's so good to see you, Miss. Shall I-"

"Annie," I interrupt in a harsh whisper. "How much do you like working for Lyla?"

She shakes her head, taken off-guard. "It's a dream come true, Miss."

"Liar," I laugh. "I do love the woman, but she treats her help like dogs."

Annie's mouth purses shut. I respect her for holding her tongue, because I do love Lyla for the crabby old bat that she is. I urge her onto the back deck, and we ease the door silently shut. I place both of my palms on her slight shoulders.

"I want you to run away with me, Annie. I'm joining the Nursing Corps, and after you helped me with little Jack's birth, I know you'll be great at it."

Annie's eyes widen. "Nursing… Corps?"

I nod excitedly.

She shrinks. "I don't know. I don't make much pay here, Miss. I can't afford to go to college."

"It's *free*, Annie! Uncle Sam picks up the tab for any gal who wants to attend, *and*, they pay us on top of that! And please, stop calling me 'Miss'."

"No charge? *Pay*? How… why?" she wonders.

"It's training for the war. To care for the soldiers," I explain.

"Oh," she returns. "Oh, like in battle?" Her eyes grow wide and fearful.

"Geneva Convention, Annie; medical teams aren't shot at on a battlefield. Besides, there are plenty of positions available back home in recovery hospitals for wounded soldiers. It's perfectly safe, and perfectly patriotic." I'd sold this same line to Birdie when I tracked her down, and found her trying to bravely glue the cracked pieces of herself together after releasing her baby girl for adoption.

"Oh, no, Mi- sorry; I mean, I don't think they'll take a girl like me," she insists, her eyes cast down at her shoes.

"What are you talking about?"

"Because I'm colored."

Taken aback, I scan the girl. Her skin, warm and carmelly like my early childhood nursemaid, Honey, doesn't seem to warrant the title.

"Just from my mama's side," she explains. "But, still, most folks don't like to be too close to one of my kind. Not working as an equal, anyhow."

I shake my head. "We'll go to the registration office together."

Annie catches her lip between her teeth.

"I'm sure it won't be an issue," I insist. "And if it is, I'll gladly smack down anyone who gives you a second look."

Annie giggles, and sucks in a nervous breath.

"When do we start?"

"Right now, Annie. Pack a bag; I'm taking you now."

SEVENTEEN

January 12th, 1943

A first day of school presents familiar emotions: excitement, unease, insecurity, promise. Today feels no different from running into fifth grade, my book bag slapping against my hip. Today, my anxiety is the one doing the running as I take measured steps in order to present a facade of calm and confidence. Today, I begin the Nursing Corps. Today, the gal who thought there was nothing left worth living for begins living her dream.

Nursing is a divine mix of skill and heart. If you don't know the body, no amount of heart can save a patient. But if you lack the urge to do everything possible to preserve a life, no amount of anatomical knowledge can light a fire within you. A good nurse needs both. I examine my hands as I walk toward the training center. *Are these nurse's hands? Do they possess heart, and a desire for skill?*

Desperately, Sense replies.

What seems like a lifetime ago, I knelt in Doris's blood as she threatened to slip away. I saw the life fading from her on that linoleum floor, and I wanted nothing more than to know how to do something to save her. I want this. I will succeed in this. As I draw closer to the entrance, passing clusters of gals wearing Corps-issued hats identical to mine, I wonder if their gum-snapping, giggling heads possess the thoughts I do. *Under their crisp buttoned uniforms, do their chests also burn with the desire to save lives? In all of the training facilities for the Corps nationwide, is there another gal who could save Phin, if it came down to it?*

My heart leaps into my throat when I pass over the threshold into the classroom. Stadium-style seats under harsh lights, long wooden planks of desks, a table of medical instruments next to a stark white roll of gauze. My soul sighs contentedly.

This is it.

I tune out the chatter and scan the room for the perfect place to sit. Front and center seems over-eager, and maybe pretentious, but I'm drawn to it. Another gal sits there, her back straight, leafing through a thick textbook identical to mine. I slip into a seat two spots down from her, watching her in my peripheral vision as I dig for a pencil in my bag.

"Hiya, Pip!" Birdie chirps as she bounces up to the front of my desk and snaps a big bubble of her gum. It sticks to her dainty nose, and she giggles.

"Birdie, we're in the same class! That's lucky," I greet her, and her blonde curls bounce around her face as she nods her agreement.

"I just wanted to say hi. The gals over there are saying the Corps is a free ticket to a knee-deep pool of eager soldiers!" *Snap.* "You wouldn't have had to sell me on this so hard if you'd just mentioned that tiny detail, Silly!"

My eyes close and I shake my head at Birdie's enthusiasm for fellas.

"Hi there," Birdie attempts to engage the other seated cadet. "You hoping to meet a soldier over there, too? Bring ya home and make ya the missus?" She shakes her thin shoulder suggestively as she sweeps her long, dark lashes in a wink.

"No thank you," the seated cadet declares, folding her arms over her chest. With her perfect pout set in a line between her creamy pink cheeks, she almost seems rude.

"I'm sure you'll meet a swell fella or two over there, though," I swoop in, hoping to save Birdie's spirits. She nods gratefully to me and skitters away to find a more amiable group for gossip.

"Save me a seat!" she calls to me over her shoulder. I set my handbag in the empty chair next to me.

"You didn't have to be rude," I scold the cadet.

Her eyelids blink defensively over her hazel eyes. "The last thing we need is a boat full of starry-eyed, squawking gals who were too busy dreaming of china patterns to learn this material," she defends, her finger pointing at her textbook. Her dark, glossy pin curls are wound as tightly to her head as her attitude, but unfortunately, I agree with her.

Her. She is the one you want treating Phin, Sense declares excitedly.

"Penelope Sha… Er, Hale." I stick my hand out, an introduction and a white flag.

She shakes it warily, but with practiced gentility. "Willamena Fox. Pleased to meet you." Curt and sassy, she turns her curved nose right back into her textbook.

I take out the notepad Max bought for me and bounce my pencil against it as we wait for the instructor to arrive.

"I take it you're not here to snag a fella," Willamena says after a moment, squinting at me appraisingly. "If you're not, you're clearly in the minority around here."

"Bah, no. Been there, done that," I disclose, wriggling my naked ring finger.

"You've been circled?" Her expertly groomed brows rise together. "There and back already? You can't be a day over twelve," she says, squinting at me again. I feel like a diamond under the scope at Tiffany's, being appraised by this gal with her keen green eyes.

Under inspection, my heart thrums in my chest, and I declare, "I'm nineteen, actually." It feels funny to defend my age. I feel like a recovering hag inside; doesn't it show? A birth mother, a widow. "You?"

"Eighteen, ma'am," she answers with a salute.

I draw my head backward, raising my eyebrow. "Didn't I just say I'm only nineteen, Willamena? Don't ma'am me; I'm not that old!" I tease her, and we laugh. Some of her rigidness visibly melts away while our laughter thaws the outer edges of my first-day nerves.

"You're still my elder," she smiles. "And please, call me Willa." She extends her hand like the Queen of England would offer it to her subject. It's clear that Willamena has been polished to a bright gleam in a finishing school. I wonder how she ended up in the Corps, a place that promises grit and gore and hard work under tough conditions.

Under her palm, in her open textbook, I see a drawing of a leg wound exposes torn flesh and the mangled muscle beneath it. Having seen such things firsthand as a striper, I quietly wonder if these baby-soft hands of hers will be able to handle the sight of the real thing. Only time will tell.

When our instructor raps her baton against the podium, the flurry of giggling cadets scramble for seats. Birdie drops into the seat next to me, leaving an open chair between herself and Willa. As the crowd thins, I notice Annie seeking a suitable seat. She tries to sit several times, as students fill her chosen chairs with handbags and textbooks, before giving up and walking up to the podium. I glare at the other cadets.

"Annie!" I call out. "Over here!" She swoops gratefully into the seat next to Birdie. "I'm so glad you're in the same class as me," I whisper to her over Birdie's lap.

When Annie meets my eyes, I see that hers shine with tears. "Me, too, Miss Pip." Her gaze falls back down to her hands in her lap. She looks so sullen that I don't correct her for addressing me formally. I pat her leg encouragingly.

"Welcome, Cadets," the instructor greets us, scanning the crowd from behind her horn-rimmed glasses, "to the first day of the rest of your lives."

It turns out that Annie, Willa and I are the only three in the Corps who didn't enlist for the express purpose of landing a husband. I'm not sure about Birdie, but the consensus among the rest of our class is that since all the young men have been shipped off to war, this is the best vehicle to get near them. They muse that their friends back home will be left with the cripples and the old men.

The idea of crowds of eager young fellas doesn't seem to faze Willa at all, though she has made it clear time and again that she doesn't have or need a beau back home. I sense a thick underlayer to Willa that she hides under hard work and superiority, but I don't push her. I really do enjoy her company. I don't want to ruin it by ripping the top off of her box too soon.

Annie seems timid amongst the other Cadets, so I'm grateful that our instructor had assigned her to my dorm along with Birdie and Willa. As we lie in the dark at night, waiting to drift off to sleep, our secrets slip out. Annie's beautifully plump lips tell us that her mother is the maid for a white family upstate in Fairlee. And though she's never told another living soul on this earth before, she divulges that she is the product of a hushed affair between her mother and her mother's white boss. It explains why her skin is more caramel than ebony; she says the name for that is "mulatto". This raises all kinds of questions in my mind. *"Does her mama still work for that same man? Has he acknowledged that Birdie is his daughter? Does this man's wife know that her husband's mistress cooks her meals and turns down her sheets?"* But I know better than to pry open a box of sizzling dynamite.

She only whispers softly, "I think he really loved her," and I'm left to decide whether that's a belief she comforts herself with, or if the world had snuffed out a real love story with its threat of judgment.

Birdie shares glimpses of her life, always peppered with her optimistic giggle. When she makes reference to growing up in the "Hoover House", I instantly remember one Sunday afternoon when Mama had asked our driver to roll past the collection of cardboard huts a few blocks from our church. With tears in her eyes, she asked him to stop the car, and made us all shrug out of our coats and kick off our church shoes. I watched as her silk dress sashayed over the dirty snow, and a collection of smudged faces peeked out from one of the huts. Mama held out our fine things as Daddy jogged to her side, pulling a few bills from his pocket. At just five years old, my eyes couldn't quite register what I watched over the windowsill. I just knew that Mama had urged us that afternoon to be grateful for what we had.

Birdie grew in that ramshackle village. Birdie survived there. And the woman whose heart was soft enough to pull the coats from our backs for the benefit of those in need couldn't possibly be a murderer. *Could she?*

I share my secrets, too; about Claire, Bentley, and little Jack. Willa says that much living warrants the title of "Ma'am", and still calls me that just to bug me. It works; it bugs me.

Over time, as my dorm mates earn my trust, I divulge my past secrets to them without the safety of darkness. They listen like young girls by the radio at story hour, absorbing every detail of my courtship with Jack instead of absorbing facts from our textbooks. When I explain that he'd been unwillingly engaged to a debutant when we'd run off together, Willa sits straight up in her seat.

"*You* are a rebel, Penelope!" she teases, then wraps her lips back around the straw in her 7up bottle.

"Funny, that's what he called his fiancee, a 'rebel', because she was wearing slacks when he went to break it off with her. It turns out she didn't want to be engaged to him, either; although I think she was nuts for passing up a fella like him." Willa snorts and soda shoots through her nose.

"What's his name again? Your husband, I mean, your late husband?" she asks me, switching to solemnity when she mentions his death.

"Jackson Sharpe," I reply.

"Huh," she murmurs with a faraway look in her eyes.

"I mostly just called him Jack, though. Obviously, little Jack is his namesake." My shoulders droop while I remember the things I once held in my hands before the war snatched them away. A loving husband, a beautiful baby boy.

"You have lived quite a life already, Pip," Birdie comments. I suppose I have. But now, I have Phin, and he fills the gaping holes in my soul where the emptiness of my daddy, Eddie, Jack, and little Jack once was. And now I'm finally on the path to the career I've always worked for. The bed pans were worth it. The vomit- no sweat. I carry these experiences under my belt with pride.

In addition to nursing training, we're also fed a hearty portion of war rallying. Not the "*Let's go bomb some Nazi's!*" stuff that the soldiers hear, but the more pacifist "*Our boys need you out there!*" and "*YOU can preserve the lives of our countrymen!*" and such. When the rallying begins, I have to clamp my teeth together tightly to fight against the mass of emotion threatening to spew up out of me. It's as though these speeches were written just to pierce the heart of a gal who's lost her fella to the war. They certainly stir me up.

Telling a gal that she can make a difference is new. Telling gals up and down, left and right in the nation that no longer are they only meant to preen and polish and learn to cook, but they are capable of using their minds and hands for critical work is socially monumental! Even Annie seems confident, and holds her neck straight and strong. We are hungry. We are starving to finish our training and go make a difference. A feast of pride and possibility awaits us on the battlefield.

We've been warned by seasoned army nurses that the work is tough, the conditions can be grim, and sometimes just boring. We've also been told that no job can offer a better sense of achievement. This training can't go fast enough for me. With December's announcement of the draft, Phin's leave of absence is officially spent. He ships out in May; only a few weeks away. Until I graduate the Corps and get an assignment, we'll have the entire Atlantic ocean between us; and Phin will once again only exist in pictures in my head.

Tonight, we're celebrating the end of our first term. Groups of hopeful nurses-to-be skitter to their dorms with bottles of wine and champagne. About a third of the Corps are celebrating high marks on their finals, and the rest look to be drowning their bad-mark sorrows with the stuff.

"Only three more terms to go!" a cadet shrieks happily as she runs by me with a bottle. Three more terms. I groan; *thinking* is more exhausting than farm labor any day. It may as well be three more decades!

Phin has driven up, clean shaven, to spend this rare study-free evening with me. Dashing in a checked oxford shirt with the sleeves rolled up to his elbows, brown suspenders and tweed slacks, he presents me with a fragrant corsage that makes Willa's eyes roll. I suspect she's just jealous, but his gift tingles on my chest anyway.

"Smell it," he urges me.

I dip my head and pull a breath through my nose. My eyes close.

"Mmmmm. Plumerias? Plu-plumerias!" He nods as I inspect the fresh version of the shriveled flower I'd found in the envelope with his update on Max. It's lovely; symmetrical petals of white with warm yellow and bright pink brushed across them.

"How did you...?" I stammer.

His grin tells me that I'll never know. He offers a strong forearm covered in bleached white hairs, the skin tanned and freckled underneath. His hair, neat and pomaded, peeks out from under his cap. He looks like a *man*. I coil myself around that arm, and we stroll through campus in the fading light with my head resting against his shoulder.

"We're invited to practically every one of these parties. Do you want to make our way around, so you can meet some of the other girls I've been spending all my time with?" I ask him, my eyes scanning the dorm buildings.

He pulls me closer to his ribs. "Naw. I'd rather have you all to myself." I blush, and force my weakened knees to keep walking steadily alongside him.

"How does it feel?" he asks me with a grin. He's referring to my high test marks; only the rigidly-studious Willa came out over me in scores; but I barely hear his question. I'm in a loopy state from the smell of his soap and the hypnotizing curved lines framing his mouth. I exhale, and lean into him. I can feel the subtle twitch and pull of his muscles under the shirt as we walk. Imp reminds me that the only thing between my cheek and his bare arm is a thin layer of cotton, and I feel my pulse pick up. I wonder if his long fingers, currently tracing lines on my forearm, can sense it.

"Swell, I s'pose," I answer. Our strides have a matched rhythm. "My brain is about as full as it can manage, so I don't even want to think about next term. Or the next, or the next. But, you know, this means that I'm that much closer to …"

"I know," he interrupts and slows his pace, almost stopping on the path. "When you're done, have you considered... staying home? You'll have the training. You could work here in the U.S…" it trails off like a question.

"The free training is in exchange for a pledge to service. No one's going to hire a rookie," I reason.

His shoulders drop. We both know that there's a hierarchy for stateside jobs; all the fresh nurses will be sent straight to the front lines.

"Are you thinking…"

"P, if you tell me you'd stay home for me, I'll pull out of service right now. I'll shoot my own leg if I have to," he declares, and his sincere eyes tell me he means it.

"I-I," I stammer, but the words won't come.

"We both know what it's like to lose someone you love to this war," he says, fighting dirty. Images of Eddie and Jack flash in my head. He whispers, "I can't stand the thought of losing you," and sets his mouth in a stubborn line.

"Nurses are safe; the enemy doesn't shoot at the Red Cross," I argue. "And hopefully, there's a nurse somewhere who's saying her goodbyes to her beau, even though she wants so badly to stay with him. Perhaps she'll be the one to patch you up if harm finds you. What if *she* stays home? I can't do that *because* I know what it's like to lose someone I love. I need to be there, Phin."

He pulls his arm away and sits down on a bench. He stares at his hands. I step to him, but I can feel that the glowing warmth that existed between us when we started walking has gone cold.

"We're only the land of the free *because* of the brave," I insist. "So, I'm going to be brave. And you're going to be brave, too."

"I could die over there. Does that matter to you and your war rally of one?"

"If you die, I will kill you myself!" I shriek, knocking the cap from his head. The red hair at his crown lies boyishly disheveled. We both smirk at how stupid my comment is, but I burst into tears as well. The conflicting emotions are a hurricane brewing in my belly. I force the upturned corners of my mouth in a serious scowl.

"Are you a fat-head?" I yell at him, falling to my knees in front of him. My delicate, Corps-issued silk stockings tear on the grass, but I pay them no mind as I desperately grip his slacks. My fat, angry tears drop onto them.

"Of course that matters! I've been carrying a torch for you since I was *six*! All that time, I began to love you. And these past months, Phin, I have fallen completely over the edge," I say, much more softly. "I'm gone!" I fling my arms into space to demonstrate. As they fall limply by my sides, I can feel streaks of mascara smeared down my cheeks and neck. My nose runs, and my cheeks have reliably lit up with a deep red flare. My furious gabbing has likely smeared my delicately applied ruby rose lipstick onto my teeth; but as ridiculous as I must look, I know that his gaze sears right through my flesh into my soul. Years of history have bound us far beyond such trifles. I watch the way his tears brighten the green in his eyes while he processes my words.

"Ha. You're that same gal. That same old gal who took a leap into the air on a homemade zip line, even though it terrified her."

He shakes his head, a wry grin curling the corner of his pale mouth. "I s'pose I can't fault you for the fire that made me fall in love with you in the first place." A syrupy warmth drips down through my chest.

"I just hope it doesn't cost me the love of my life," he finishes.

The cold embers between us ignite. They flare back to life in a bright blaze as he pounces, pushing me down to the grass. He presses his lips over mine, fresh flames licking all around us. The quickened beat of his heart permeates my own chest as his weight bears down on me, and my pulse matches his. As my hands press into the fabric of his shirt, I remember Imp's words: just a thin layer of cotton fabric separates my palms from his skin.

I'm too stunned to think, and it's hard to breathe, though I know for certain I'm not mad at him anymore. My fingers weave into the short hair at the nape of his neck. My lips move with his. He kisses me with an eager fervor that's brand spanking new in the book of our kisses. His newly shaven chin skin feels as smooth as a baby's as he parts my lips with his and softly bites my upper lip.

"Ow," I complain, though I'm really not protesting. It feels nice, sort of desperate. Hungry.

"Let's get out of here," he murmurs roughly, scrambling up and pulling me to my feet. We walk briskly through the campus to my dorm. When I throw open the door to my dorm room, panting, my roommates sit inside with a well-depleted bottle of champagne. When they take us in--pink cheeks, bewildered expressions, husky breaths, wild hair--they scramble for their glasses and make hasty excuses to leave. Birdie winks at me as she backs out and closes the door. The frames on the walls shudder, and we're alone.

"Pip, you know I love you, too," he whispers in my ear, answering my declaration at the bench. His breath feels hot on my neck. My mouth is so close to the delicate flesh of his earlobe that I have to pull it in between my teeth. "I've always loved you, ever since you hijacked my best marble." He laughs; more hot breath steams the hollow of my shoulder.

I press my nose into his jawbone, feeling his laughter vibrate in me. Six-year-old Pip couldn't foresee this moment when she placed her marble-filled socks into Phin's grubby little-boy hands. Six-year-old Pip felt a glimmer of affection for him, but she couldn't have known that he would ever smell this *good*.

I haven't had a sip of champagne, but I sure feel drunk. I'm ablaze; tingling all over. He lifts my hips onto the very edge of the kitchen table and presses his torso up to me. Again, I feel his heartbeat pounding against my chest.

Only a thin layer of cotton, Imp reminds me.

"You're squishing my corsage," I mumble, and he laughs. His fingers weave into my hair and my eyes close at the pleasure of the light pull on my scalp. I'm gripping his suspenders when my mother's sermon plays in my head: *"he won't buy the cow if you give away the milk for free."* If her image could read my current response to this reminder, she would be offended. Mentally, I shoot daggers her way for spoiling this moment. However, her nagging has done its job, and I'm sobered. No matter how I feel about her, Mama didn't raise an alley cat. I drop my head.

Phin notices the sag in my fire. "What's wrong?" he asks, head cocked. He looks so cute with his tousled hair that it's painful to give him the quitting orders.

"We've got to slow down, Phin," I whisper. He takes a deep breath, pumping the brakes with grace. He settles for holding me gently, a steady fire crackling between us.

"Pip, I want you to know that if I don't come back, I'll have died a happy man," he says in a low voice. I know he means it.

"Don't you dare talk like that. You *fight* to stay alive! Fight *hard!*" I demand, pressing him tightly against me. *Golly*, he smells good. "And we'll meet back at home when we've won the war." I'm lost in pearly visions: I picture us meeting on the port, slightly weather worn, but elated. I see Phin's truck with aluminum cans and shoes trailing behind it as we wave goodbye to our mamas. A white picket fence encircles our yard, where I watch our ginger-headed children hunt for bugs in the flower beds. We hug proudly as our youngest child walks in a cap and gown to receive his high school diploma. Our wrinkled hands lay entwined on the couch, where a nearly-bald Phin has fallen asleep with his mouth open.

"I think we both know that is a fairytale," he whispers. My fantasy people are gone in a puff of smoke. I think of how I'd thought fairytales had betrayed me.

"This… this time with you has been a fairytale to me, Phin," I tell him. "Maybe you'll come home without an arm, and I'll be a war-hardened hag," I say and we grin together, "but we're gonna make it back alive!" Real fairytales are just a little twisted outside of children's books. If I spend my days pushing Phin in a wheelchair for the rest of our lives, or caressing his scarred, burned cheek; I will count it as a very successful happily ever after.

There's a timid knock on the door. I roll my eyes.

"Come in," I call, and we stand up with our fingers laced.

Annie opens the door with exaggerated slowness. Her head peeks around, and I can tell by her sheepish expression that she had been expecting to find us in a tangle of sheets.

"We're going to sleep over at Blanche's, to give you some privacy," she whispers, and hiccups. "So we'll just grab our pillows, and we can leave you two lovebirds all alone." Her finger attempts a drunken spiral as she points to us with a suggestive grin.

"No, no! Don't do that. Phin was just leaving," I tell her and step forward. "Come in." She opens the door fully and I see my three roommates, plus Blanche and her roommates on the porch. They each glow with knowing grins.

I groan, realizing that the buzz next door has been all about us. They giggle while they stare appreciatively over my shoulder at Phin. I have to agree; without that scruff, he's an absolute knockout. They don't enter; they just stand there with their eyes gleaming.

I turn back to Phin, his fingers entwined with mine, wondering what he makes of this goofy hoard of admirers. He still has my hand, but he's dropped down on one knee. The girls shriek with delight as I take in his meaningful pose. His eyes train on mine, and I'm certain he is immune to their presence.

"Penelope Hale Sharpe, I love you with everything I am. If I die in this war, I want to die as the happiest man on earth. Will you do me the honor of becoming my wife?"

The high-pitched shrieks behind me are deafening, but I barely notice the splash of their champagne that spills onto my back.

My eyes take him in. His green eyes are wide and hopeful; I dive into them. Years of memories flood my head as I swim through his eyes. Eight-year-old Phin grinning at me as he walks up the Collins' steps with his pockets bulging with marbles. Me, straining my legs to run as fast as the boys on the way to the Spot. I'm fourteen, and Phin's spindly arms carry me home. Fifteen, sitting on the riverbank as he cups cold river water in his hands to rinse my fresh scrapes. Sixteen, crying while Max and Eddie pile into the cab of Phin's old jalopy, off to become soldiers. Phin pulling me to him under the covers; the long anticipated first time our lips met, his total acceptance of me in my worst form. The warm air he blew back into the empty, sagging bag of my soul.

I mule kick the door shut on our crowd of observers and kneel on the linoleum with him. "Phineas Emerson O'Shea, you have literally saved my life. I mean, you actually saved my life, but you saved my head, too. I've been dying for your attention my whole life," I laugh through warm tears.

"You have it," he whispers. "You'll always have it."

"Nothing would make me happier," I answer him, and my arms encircle his neck.

"So, is that a 'yes'?" he asks timidly.

"Yes!" I cry. "That is a definite yes!" I nod happily.

He catches me mid-nod with his mouth. We're locked in a soft, warm, endless kiss when the door swings open and hits my feet.

Buzzed on champagne, Willa hollers, "What'd she say?" Embarrassed, I drop my head to his shoulder and my breath hitches with humiliation.

He answers, "She said yes," and strokes my hair.

Deafening squeals pierce the air, as a bouncing ring of twitterpated cadets encircle us.

"We can still sleep over at Blanche's," Annie offers, wagging her eyebrow suggestively.

"He hasn't bought the cow *yet,*" Willa teases. Sounds like

her mother has given her a similar speech to Mama's.

"Just give us a minute to say goodbye," I tell them.

"Ooooooo-kay," they sing together, and retreat in giggles.

I realize as I nestle the door closed that I will walk onto the battlefield with the best medals of honor a gal could ever hope for. I have faithful friends, and I have known love twice in my short life.

I am a fortunate girl.

EIGHTEEN

Now this is living.

This is the life, huh? Imp's words wedge themselves into my happy moment. *A life you almost wasted.*

The gal I know, this happy version of myself, must strain to remember walking the deep caverns of despair that lead her to that dark moment. Though I know I felt I had no other choice as I stood ready to leap to my death, I know now that her heavy soul was blind to the light all around her.

Phin and I have two weeks to obtain a marriage license, and for me to meet his mother officially, as an adult, before he is to report for duty. I try backpedaling to convince him that I'm used goods. The angry red marks on my belly have only just begun fading to pink! I tell him that he can do much better. He waves this off and tells me that his love for me is deeper than the surface of my skin. When my mouth screws up with skepticism, he digs a crisp green bill out of his pocket.

"How much is this worth?" he asks me. The thin green lines of Alexander Hamilton's image are centered on the paper.

"Ten dollars," I answer.

He keeps my gaze while he crumples it up.

"Hey, what are you--oh!"

He tears off the top corner of the bill.

"Phin!"

He drops it into the dirt on mashes it under his boot. He seems to be egged on by my protestations, and dunks the bill into a glass of water. The liquid is cloudy from the dust of the bill. When he pulls it out, he crumples it again. It looks sad and limp in his fingers.

"Now how much is this worth?"

"Ten dollars." Sometimes I hate that Phin is so clever.

"Exactly." He stares at me meaningfully. "Your worth will never diminish for me, P." As the bill dries in his hand, it doesn't look so bad. "Never."

Like I said, this is living.

Phin re-introduces me to his mother, Elaine, who is just as beautiful as I remember her. She has earned a few streaks of white in her brilliant orange hair since I last saw her, and her skin bears the lines of age, but her warm smile brightens everything and overshadows these traits. She is a stew of nervousness and panic, joyfulness and warmth. You can see that she's relieved to see her son so content, that she adores him, and that she doesn't want him to go back into the belly of the beast.

"You just found each other again," she says as she dabs at her tears. "It's so unfair."

His younger sisters hug me, bouncing up and down with the news of our engagement. I must have known them back in those marble days, but I can't drag up a memory. When we moved across town, Phin never brought them with him. Their hair is the same flaming red as Phin's; their smiles the feminine form of his.

"Oh, I'd love to see your mother again," Elaine says. "She'll be at the wedding, hmm?" she asks hopefully.

"Oh, well," I stammer.

"Of course," Phin tells her. My stomach bottoms out. I guess a part of me knew that our return to Saratoga meant that I'd have to face Mama. I know it's only right for a proper marriage to have your only surviving parent at your wedding, but I wonder if she'll even speak to me when I show up on her doorstep.

I manage to contain my nerves until we wave, "Goodbye! See you tomorrow!" to his beaming family. When we pull away, my smile drops away and I start to shake.

"Where to?" he asks lightly, knowing darn well where we must go.

I blow out a heavy breath of surrender. "My old place, I guess." He nods and leaves me to my thoughts while we drive across town. It's a sunny Sabbath day. I know Mama will be home from church, probably enjoying her ritual Sunday nap on the day of rest. Hopefully Max and Phin can control their quarrel today.

I'm twisted as tightly as my nerves can manage while we roll down Radcliffe. I can see my old ramshackle house up ahead. I was hoping for a minute to unscrew my tension before I had to face my mother, but she and May are rocking in the porch swing. When we slow to the curb, May is already bounding down the walk. I open the gate before she can claw through it, and she wraps around me like a hungry python.

"Sis! You're back!" she squeals into my ear.

"Hiya, Squeak!" Max calls, and turns to Phin. "Hey, Playboy, keep your eyes off of the younger one, would'ja? I know how you like the ladies."

Phin slugs him in the arm, and they smile together as they embrace and thump each other's backs. Mama stands slowly, brushing the front of her dress.

"Hello Mama," I greet her with a rigid nod as we move hesitantly toward each other.

As she draws closer, I can see that the last year has left her weather-beaten, and that her clear blue eyes shine with moisture. The lines around her eyes have deepened since I last saw her. I realize, as though the lid of a box has slid off inside of me, that I can't possibly hold Mama to such a rigid standard when I have made so many mistakes of my own! I don't have any proof of her innocence, yet I have no evidence of her guilt, either. I only have my heart, which longs for peace between us. Suddenly, my greatest desire is to embrace her.

"Penny," she breathes and welcomes me into her arms. I'm a

child with a skinned knee, and I long for the comfort of my mama. Our embrace is like a magical healing light, and the wounds between us are mended in it. I can barely recall any bad blood when we pull back and look at each other. "I understand you have some news for me," she says, a knowing tone in her voice.

My eyes shift to Phin, who grins sheepishly with his hands in his pockets, and he explains, "I had to ask her permission." Phin shrugs his shoulders. I can't help but forgive him and his lopsided smile, so I fish a hand out of his pocket and squeeze it. Somehow he knew this is just what I needed.

"I can't tell you how this heals my heart," Mama says with tears, eyes on our clasped hands. "It's just right, you two. Eddie would be pleased as punch," she's nodding to herself.

"Well, to be truthful Missus Hale, when I told Ed about my feelings for her, he punched me in the face." Phin smiles at the memory, no bitterness in his expression. Mama's temporarily stricken.

"Actually, Max gave him away," I laugh. Max shrugs, smiling, and my shoulders relax further.

"So, when's the big day?" Mama asks, clasping her hands and raising her thin shoulders excitedly.

"As soon as City Hall opens their doors tomorrow," Phin answers. "We ship out next Thursday, so I want as much time with my *wife*," he squeezes his hand with the word, "as possible".

"Rotten luck, soldier," Max sighs. Luckily, his past injuries will keep my brother far from the battlefront.

"Next Thursday? So soon?" Mama asks, shoulders falling. I am eternally grateful that her expression doesn't react to his mention of our honeymoon. I feel a flash of discomfort as our original "birds and bees" talk plays in the forefront of my mind, and my feet shuffle beneath me.

"Yes, Ma'am," Phin answers sadly. I don't think he has ever addressed my mother so formally in all the years he practically lived at our house.

Mama and May draw shocked breaths and swoon together. "Oh, no," May says quietly.

"So, you can understand our hurry," Phin says.

"Yes," Mama answers quietly, her mile-long lashes resting on her sallow cheeks. The general happy glow about the reunion has dimmed, but my heart sings with contentment.

Whatever lies ahead, everything is now in place.

NINETEEN

Phin insists that I stay the night with May, Max and Mama on my last night as a single gal. For a few hours, I feel nervous that the glow of reuniting will wear off and our old arguments will seep to the surface, but things go butter-smooth as we catch up late into the evening. It's all the lighthearted teasing and laughing that I missed out on before Jack secretly whisked me away to City Hall; the way a gal's wedding eve should feel. It feels good, like I'm doing it right this time.

"I can't stomach all of this giggling about ol' Lover Lips," Max complains with a grimace. "I'm sleeping in the treehouse. G'night, ladies." He scoops up his blanket and pillow from the ground at the foot of the bed.

"Goodnight!" we chorus back to him, grinning.

I feel perfectly content sleeping beneath the old quilt with May and Mama, with the same old leaky draft of cold air from the corner tickling my exposed arm, which falls off the side of the bed in just the way it used to night after night. I think the mattress has held the impression of my sleeping body all of this time.

I wake with a smile and comic urge that makes me want to meet Phin on the steps of City Hall in his grandpa's old, crusty pajamas, but they are an hour's drive away at the cabin. I guess I can't test his claims that I look stunning in anything, but truly, I hadn't thought of what to wear today before now.

Just as I feel the revving hum of mild panic, Mama walks toward the closet with a grin. It seems to have been originally built as a storage cupboard for food jars, but when we moved here during the peak of the Great Depression, the shelves inside had only held dust. Mama's first move in this house was crafting a closet rod out of a battered broom handle so we'd have somewhere to hang our things. As Mama shuffles the hangers back and forth across the splintering wood, May and I exchange a meaningful, worried glance. Her panicked eyes beg me to keep our secret: we already know what's in those garment bags. She had raided Mama's old gowns frequently, and stole one for me the night I was supposed to meet Jack's parents. Oh, little Mayhem. I assure her with my eyes that I'll act perfectly, convincingly surprised.

My heart misses a beat while I watch Mama slide out the familiar bag that contains the navy blue satin. I try to arrange my face and scramble for something gracious to say, because I can't possibly put that dress on my body again. The scent of Jack will be too strong, even if his smell has long-faded from the fabric. I won't be able to give her a truthful excuse without exposing May. Sweat bathes my palms at the thought of The Stare.

My nerves are unnecessary. A dramatically slow unzipping does not reveal dark blue satin, but creamy ivory silk that is inlaid with diamond-clear and sapphire-blue gems at the waist. She hesitates. "I was saving this for May, you know, when you left, but..."

May pounces on the bag and tears it away to reveal the garment. "I can share!" she exclaims, and I'm worried she's about to combust. This must be her favorite. She grasps the hanger with greedy delicacy as though what hangs from it is the lost treasure of the Nile, breath seized in her lungs. "Try it on!" she finally breathes.

"Wait! Not yet," Mama halts her and begins removing the pin curls May put in my hair last night. She pulls me into a chair, where I am a mannequin in a slip for them to toy with. May applies Mama's best lipstick and rouge to my face. I can tell she's done this to her friends countless times; but Mama seems none the wiser to her 'natural' skill. I think if she were, she had realize her makeup has been used on giggling teenagers time and time again. Mama toys with my hair and affixes pin after pin until my head is heavy with them. They hand me a mirror.

The girl with the sickly, yellowing bruise and the dead eyes has gone. In her place, a glowing angel beams back at me. A crisp, smooth bill again-- bright eyes, pink cheeks, full red lips. Soft waves across my forehead end in an elegant chignon at my neck. I look spectacular.

"Now, the dress," Mama says.

She lowers it over my head, careful not to muss my hair. I press my lips together to keep them from staining the delicate fabric.

"Come see!" May squeals and pulls me to the standing mirror. The fabric floats on my shoulders, dropping down in a deep "v", almost to my sternum, where a cluster of the white and brilliant blue gems catch the sunlight. From them, the empire waist drops a sheet of the luminous silk to where it dances at my calves.

"Something blue," Mama whispers, touching a sapphire. Then she turns and disappears into the kitchen, returning with a box.

"My own veil," she says with a coy curl of her shoulder, removing a little scrap of cream-colored netting, "...borrowed." She secures it over my face with more pins, then adds a broach to one side. Scrunching her nose, she dips back into the box and cups a hair piece of delicate ivory feathers. Once secured with pins, she claps her hands together. "Old. Voila!"

May looks stricken. "Where've you been hiding those?" Mama laughs, but if I know May, she's scoured the house for just these sorts of treasures. Maybe Mama has been more wise to her poking around than I'd realized.

May and Mama share the gift of tiny feet, so my only option for footwear is my old heels, still nestled in our closet. I slip them on, and I'm complete.

"Phin's never going to get on that boat," Max says, sighing proudly, and scratching his head.

If only that were true.

TWENTY

I see Phin before he sees me. When I spot him on the steps of City Hall, he looks dapper in a crisp white shirt, black pulleys, and grey slacks. His fiery hair is mussed, as usual; his chin is clean shaven and his cheeks bear a tinge of anxious pink as he rocks from toes to heels, heels to toes in his wingtips. When May leans over me and honks the Merc's horn, he turns, and the corners of his mouth immediately turn up into a grin. We park, and I try not to wobble clumsily on my heels as I step out of the car. His emerald eyes are wide and appreciative as I approach him with my entourage.

"You, Dame, are a stunner," he whispers in my ear. The warmth of his compliment reaches all the way to my toes.

"You're not so shabby, yourself," I answer. I feel light as air in the dazzling sunlight as we take the steps with locked arms.

Willa trots down the steps at us. She wraps her arms around me and whispers in my ear, "Did you get everything on the list?"

"Huh?"

"You know, the *list*." She rolls her eyes and blows out a breath. "Something old, something new, something borrowed, something bl--"

My nerves twinge. Something *new*! I forgot something new! An almost imperceptible thought nags: I hadn't bothered with these superstitions when I married Jack, and so our marriage was doomed from the start. With Phin shipping out in just days, I feel frantic to get something new on my person.

"Oh, *applesauce*! I forgot to bring something new!"

"Oh, let your best pal take care of that," she hints, digging into her bag. She produces a brand new stick of Wrigley's gum and holds it up like a trophy. I snatch it from her fingers and stuff it into my bra. She gives me a funny look.

"It's my breast pocket," I explain, patting the rectangular package wedged under the silk. "Does gum count?"

"I'm sure it does," she assures me in a whisper, squeezing my arm. "You're still shaking."

"I'm sorta nervous," I whisper back. My lips barely move; anyone around us might think we were just sharing a long, meaningful embrace.

"Nervous? Sheesh, it's not like you're a *virgin* or anything, missy," Willa taunts, poking my ribs.

"I know, but I think that my virginity has grown back," I whisper with a giggle. She sighs with mock exasperation, giving me a little shove. She pulls me across the sidewalk toward a flight of stone steps that lead to the courthouse. We giggle together, weaving like drunkards as we climb them; drunk on our own silliness.

When my eyes adjust to the dimmer light inside, I see small clusters of familiar faces. Uncle Mac and Aunt Faye stand just inside the doors. Phin's sisters and parents are gathered near the reception desk. Annie listens dutifully to Lyla as her bony hands gesture wildly with some story, and Birdie's face appears bewildered as she takes in the spunky old woman. My cousin George's hand laces through Doris's, who glows over her round and pregnant belly.

"Don't muss her dress!" May scolds while I hug my former co-worker, and over Doris's shoulder, I take in a little cluster of figures sitting at the far wall. Willa pulls down her hat and slips away. Claire comes into focus. Bentley. And sitting on his lap is little Jack, no longer wrinkled and pink, but brilliant. My head supplies the fact that almost nine months have passed since I last touched his soft skin. He's awake and alert, wiggling in Bentley's arms. The couple smiles at me timidly. Little Jack busily gnaws on his daddy's finger.

My belly fills with a mix of utter joy and searing pain at the sight of them. They look just right, sitting together; everything I could have had. Even with the agony of loss bubbling back up, the ripped part of my soul that had once flapped loose and sore, refusing to heal, fuses back together when I see my son thriving in his parents' love. Claire is a glowing mother. Bentley has never looked more alive than he does now, with a trail of little Jack's drool dripping down his hand. Even as my heart aches with loss and pain, it also swells with joy. I know I've made the right choice by giving my child the complete family I couldn't offer him. I rush to them and stop short in front of his round, bright face, marveling at his resemblance to Jack while he looks up and claps his chubby hands at me. I kneel down so we're eye-to-eye. Tears sting mine and I summon Phin with trembling fingers.

Bentley offers little Jack to me, and I scoop him up tenderly. A rush of motherly affection washes through me as I take in his light blue eyes, fat pink cheeks, and shock of dark hair. This is my child. His arms and legs are so chubby that they appear to be a stack of marshmallows, one on top of the other. Plump fingers stick out from his little, puffy hands, and the effect reminds me of a tiny starfish. His dimpled hands reach up for me. My mouth falls open in reminiscent wonder as his tiny fingertips graze my face. He grabs a lock of my hair and pulls it out of the chignon, and he stuffs it into his mouth. My nose starts to run, and I laugh as tears dance down my face and splash on his cheeks.

"Phin, I'd like you to meet baby Jack," I say softly, paying no mind to the stinging of my scalp or the destruction of this morning's makeover. Phin puts his huge, freckled hand in little Jack's tiny, flawless one, grasping and shaking the tiny, chubby fingers.

"Pleased to meet ya, lil' gent." Little Jack scowls at him warily and Phin and I laugh. Little Jack buries his face into my shoulder, pulling every heartstring I have at once. I can't discern between his drool on my skin and my tears.

"He's beautiful," I say to Claire, sniffing. She looks extremely nervous. "Oh, I won't drop him," I assure her.

"No, no; it's not that," she says and tears spill into her lap. "I'm just wondering if, you know, since you'll be married and all, if you're going to want him back," she admits and a sob escapes before she can catch it. She resumes her nervous smile.

I glance at Bentley, whose furrowed brow tells me they share this worry. I realize that they must have been gripped with fear over losing him since I invited them to our wedding.

"Well..." I start, considering the idea. By the time the hour is up, I will be able to offer little Jack a father. Not just any father, but one who could love and cherish him. Phin earns a salary from the army, but has enough family money to support us without it. Little Jack could have a very good life with us, once we return.

But no, I firmly believe I'd made the right choice. Heaven only knows if Phin will come home to me. Heaven only knows if *I'll* make it back in one piece! Since Ruby will never allow another son to join this war, I know little Jack will be offered the best of everything in Claire and Bentley's care.

"You know, I'll never stop wanting him. I'll never stop mourning for the family we could have had." A bolt of hot pain strikes my heart. "But I've made my choice, Claire. What I want more than to hold him like this forever," I affirm with my eyes squeezed shut as he snuggles his ample cheeks against my collarbone, "is for him to have the happiest, most fulfilling life that he can. I know that you can give it to him better than I would. I know that he's better off with the two of you," I tell her earnestly, and tuck the stray lock of hair behind my ear. "And imagine how it would upset his world to be passed back and forth."

Claire seems overrun with relief, ducking into Bentley's shoulder to compose herself.

"Thank you," she breathes, peeking up at me. Her eyes are relieved as she dries them. "You have no idea how sick with worry I've been!" Claire clearly loves this baby boy with all of her heart.

Ceremoniously, I pass his warm, chubby body back to them, and Little Jack goes back to gnawing away on Bentley's knuckle. I want my friends to meet my son.

I turn to them and call, "Birdie! Annie! Willa!" across the room. The sound of my voice bounces over the marble floors and columns. When Willa looks my way, her smile drops and she quickly turns back to May.

"Hey, come here!" I call again.

Slowly, Willa sucks in a breath and shuffles after Annie and Birdie with her head ducked. I turn to Claire, who wears a look of astonishment, then I whip my head back to Willa in time to see her shaking her head. My gaze snaps back to Claire, who now appears friendly and composed.

"Hello, I'm Claire Sharpe," she says as she offers her hand to the girls. "And this is my husband, Bentley, and our little boy, Jack." Annie curtsies while Birdie shakes Claire's hand.

"Annamarie Jennings, Miss."

"Bernadette," Birdie says. I wrinkle my nose at her full name. Birdie is better.

Willa takes Claire's hand mechanically. "Willamena... Fox. Pleased to make your acquaintance." Willa gives a tiny curtsy.

"Likewise," Claire replies, barely moving her red lips over her teeth in a plastered smile.

"Willa, we call her," I say, bumping her hip with mine to soften the stiffness between the two of them.

"Now that we're all acquainted, shall we?" Phin asks, hooking his arm through mine. "I'd like to marry this girl today."

The clerk mops his shiny head with a kerchief as we all file into his cozy office. While the small group we'd originally planned on would've fit comfortably around the curves of his grand wooden desk, the man's eyes bug out as our family and friends pack in around us like sardines. He has far too many witnesses to fulfill his request for one, so he settles for Max, the only one in our party who didn't raise his hand to volunteer.

With more annoyance in his tone than grace, the clerk conducts a short ceremony. The room rattles with cheers when Phin lifts my little veil and plants a celebratory kiss on my lips. Everyone's eyes are wet, save Uncle Mac's, who's grinning widely, and little Jack's, who has fallen asleep on Claire's shoulder. We sign the document that declares that we're wed.

Max slaps Phin on the shoulder. "Guess we really are brothers now. You'd better take care of my little sister, Loverboy," he tells his friend with more than just a hint of a warning in his tone.

"I will, Pal. Thanks." Phin's cheeks flare bright pink.

"Shall we go for a bite to eat?" Mama asks the group. There's a general assent among the party. But Phin, whose lips now wear a smear of my lipstick, seems hesitant.

"Go on without us," I tell them, with my arm around Phin's hip. A suggestive roar bubbles up from the little crowd as they file out the heavy door, and I glare heavily at Willa. *Why had she acted so strange around Claire?* We are about to follow the stream of people when May stops us.

"Wait! Wait," she shrieks. "Hang on." She's halted Phin and me, but shoos everyone else outside. She offers Phin a handkerchief, reapplies my lipstick and checks me over. "Okay, you can come out now," she permits. We step out into the brilliant sunlight, hands clasped, as a hailstorm of rice pelts us. We run for the old truck, escaping the falling torrents of rice.

Mama calls out to me, "When Phin ships out, there will always be a pillow at home for you."

"Thanks, Mama."

"Have fun!" Willa and May sing in unison in a teasing tone, arms wrapped around one another. I ignore them as I hop into the truck next to a small pile of wedding gifts, and Phin shuts the door after me. As we pull away, we wave happily to our family and friends. I catch Mama's eye and hold her gaze until she's out of sight. I sigh contentedly and melt into the seat, working the heels off of my feet. I plop my bare feet on the dash and the silk pools at my hips.

"Look at them gams," Phin ogles distractedly, eyebrows wagging, and he wolf whistles.

"Drive," I tell him, pushing his smooth face forward. A memory flashes in my head. Almost one year ago, it was Jack's chin I was pushing while we raced to our honeymoon. It stings my heart, but a swelling rush of contentment replaces the sting. I think, wherever he is, he approves of the soaring happiness I feel in my chest right now.

I pluck a small box from the pile between us, and busy my hands by tearing the ribbon and paper off of it.

"Who's that one from?" Phin asks with a quick side-glance. I pick up the discarded paper and detach a little card.

"Um… oh, 'Love, Claire, Bentley, and little Jack'," I read.

"What is it?"

"Let's see," I murmur as I lift the top from the box. "It's a key." I loop my finger through the ribbon tied to it and hold it up. "Oh! There's a note! 'Dear Pip and her new husband, Whatever you decide today, your new family should have a place to call home. Please accept the key to 37 Wadsworth Lane, Saratoga, New York.'" My fingers weaken with surprise and the note flutters to the floorboard. They bought us this home without knowing whether or not I'd insist on taking little Jack back, and the idea sears my heart.

"We have a house," I whisper. When we return from war, we'll have our own place to call home.

Phin digs under his side of the bench seat. "It's not a house, but I got you a little something, too." He produces a wrinkly brown package and places it in my eager hands. "And I'm sorry, I don't have Claire's wrapping skills."

"It's okay," I assure him with a grin. "I didn't marry you for your wrapping skills." I break the seal and unroll an excessive amount of paper. When my prize drops into my lap, I quickly scoop it up. I can't speak with my throat full of the tears that instantly come to me.

"Oh, Phin! Is… is this…." I stutter. At the end of a delicate chain hangs a large, blue marble with a swirl of white in the center. This is the marble we'd met over. I had no idea that he had hung on to it all of this time. And he's made it into a necklace!

His eyes shine with moisture as he nods his head. "I've always kept this, ever since the day I met you. I never played it after you gave it back to me. And I realize now that somehow, I knew that from that day on that I would always love you. Penelope, I love you so much," he declares, his voice hitching. "I love you in every way. I still can't believe that you love me, too."

"I love you so much, Phin," I tell him, but words can't articulate the profound affection in my bursting chest. My heart is full.

With a grin spread across his face, Phin drives us into the hills. We bump along a dirt road that is rich with potholes until it becomes impassable, and he throws the truck into park with a sigh.

"It's walkin' from here," he says. I wiggle my bare toes at him and wonder what kind of motel has such terrible road upkeep that patrons have to walk to it. Surely not a very busy one; I haven't seen even one other car.

"Don't worry," he assures me. He gets out and comes around the truck, opens my door, and scoops me up. Though I'm longer now, it feels similar to my rescue when I was fourteen.

He sniffs my hair. "Strawberries," he says, and I curl into him and close my eyes.

I jostle a little in his arms as he walks. It's not long before the dark of shade is visible, even through my closed lids. I'm expecting to be standing in the shade of a building, a rough little motel, or even a cabin; but my eyes open to the brilliant green leaves of a willow tree.

Not just a willow tree. The willow tree. Our willow tree. Phin has carried me back to the Spot.

"My heart is racing," Phin breathes into my ear.

"Mine, too," I whisper back to him. I try to keep my breaths even, but I can't help the mild tremors rumbling throughout my body. When he sets me carefully onto my feet, I keep my arms wrapped around his neck. With our chests pressed together so closely, our hearts create a syncopated beat.

Phin nuzzles his mouth into my neck, and I let my head fall to the side. When his kisses move over my jawbone and find my mouth, my hands slide down to his waist. By the time I untuck his shirt and run my palms over the smooth skin of his back, a nervous thought has woven itself into my brain. I stop him, and pull my face away from his.

"What if someone sees us?" I whisper, as though we're already being watched.

Phin chuckles. "The only other living person who knows about this place is Max, and I'm pretty sure he's seen enough of my backside to last him a lifetime."

My fingers press deeper into his skin. "He knows we're here?"

"I may have given him a hint," Phin laughs. "So he knows to steer clear."

I narrow my eyes. "What about that girl you brought here, years ago?"

"Oh, Francis? If she shows up, we'll just have to start charging admission." With that, he brushes away my concerns with the softness of his lips.

When evening falls, we drive into New York City. I know that what next Thursday holds will dampen this joy, but I'm perfectly content curled up on the truck's bench seat with my head nestled in Phin's lap. He strokes my hair. I swat the thought of our separation away like a pesky fly. For the eight short days we have together in our hotel room, I'll try to block out the looming shadow of what's to come.

TWENTY-ONE

On the morning of May thirteenth, I wake up with my limbs entangled with Phin's. I'm just gripping the edge of contentment, until waking's full awareness rips it from my fingers. In its place, a horrid thought haunts me: this may actually be the last time we wake up together. I grasp at Phin, pulling his heavy, fair body toward me, panting with anxiety.

His eyes flutter open, focus, and read the angst in mine. "I know," he soothes. "Me, too." We wrap ourselves together and thin tears roll down his chest. My tears.

"If this is all we get, it's enough for me," he whispers into my hair. His fingers drag up and down the skin of my back.

"Not enough for me," I moan. "Not enough at all! I want to stay with you for every minute of every day." Phin's old suggestion of deserting the service sounds delicious and doable in this moment; for both of us, not just me. We could just run away. We could be Canadians! Or go far south, and flee to Cuba.

Freckle face will never pass for a Cuban, Sense interjects.

Argh! I *hate* Nazis. I hate Hitler!

"I want to have babies with you! *Lots* of babies with you!" I'm nearly throwing a tantrum. Little Jack's face flashes in my mind and suddenly I know where this fresh, urgent desire comes from.

"Then we'll just have to stay out of harm's way," he tells me resolutely, dragging his fingertips across my shoulder.

I blow out a puff of air. Unlikely, as he's headed to war, and I won't be far behind. Grotesque images of bleeding wounds and missing limbs flash through my head. I try mightily to stuff these demons deep and out of sight. I can feel the struggle in my stomach.

"Land of the free *because* of the brave, remember?" he whispers. I hate to be corrected with my own words.

In the late afternoon, when we're walking to the harbor, the panic grips me in a fresh wave. Once again, I'm allowing my husband to slip right through my fingers into the thick of the fight.

"Hey there, Missus Sharpe," a low voice calls.

I whip my head around, scanning the faces in the crowd for the one that's fixed on me. When I find it, my lip curls up in a sneer.

"Officer," I nod tersely to Dalton, who leans lazily against a bench, and urge Phin forward.

But Dalton halts me with his words, "I heard about Sharpie. Too bad." His voice is hollow of genuine sympathy. "But, I see you haven't wasted any time filling the empty space."

I feel Phin's muscles stiffen against my arm as our steps pause simultaneously, and work to calm the tiger claws inside of me that wish to strike back at Dalton's mean spirited jeers.

"Perhaps we'll get lucky, and we'll see your name in the obituaries soon enough," Phin growls. Dalton flashes a wooden walking stick as tall as his hip, and knocks it against his boot.

"Your little slice of cherry pie there made sure I won't see a battlefield any time soon," Dalton grins back at Phin with his lids half-closed. "Or, ever."

Guilt floods my chest as I recall mowing over his ankle with his own squad car. At the time, I'd thought I was striking back at him, but it seems I've given him a free pass from the draft. At least, it seems, he won't be pressing charges against me.

"What are you doing here, then?"

Dalton leans into his walking stick. "Seeing off my brother. He wasn't as lucky as me; he never met the likes of *you*, Kitten."

As Phin's pulse pounds through the thick veins of his arm, I pull him forward.

"That scumbag isn't worth a fight, Phin," I murmur under my breath.

"Thanks for the freebie, Dollface!" Dalton calls after me. If I hadn't just steadied Phin, I might have dragged Dalton to the harbor and held his greasy blonde head under the water.

As we hurry away, a huge ship looms in the water before us, its own continent. To me, the ship may as well be Hitler himself for all the danger it symbolizes, and I wonder which foe we stand between I detest more. Phin's explaining how they've converted this ship from a cruise liner to an army transporter, but as we step into its looming shadow, his words fall on deaf ears.

We halt under the weight of its shadow. Phin wraps his arms around me.

"We'll come back when it's over," he says with a brave face. "No need for goodbyes."

I hate goodbyes. I wonder how experienced one has to be before he can handle them with Phin's grace.

"However, this will have to last me quite a while, Darlin'," he says, and smothers me in a kiss fraught with desperation. He's bent me so far over, I can feel the tips of my hair brush the pavement. Wolf whistles call out all around us as soldiers and medics swarm for the ship. I'm dizzy from the sneak attack and the passion his body exudes.

He's handling it, alright, Imp snickers.

"You saved my life, Phineas O'Shea," I whisper into his ear.

"And you saved mine back," he whispers back and brushes his lips on my forehead. I feel the hum of his voice vibrate my skin as he purrs, "It's been an honor to be allowed to love you, Penelope." For perhaps the very first time, I don't mind the sound of my full name.

I'm left cold in the sunlight as he marches away.

Annie, Birdie and Willa do their best to soothe me.

"He's just in training, no real combat, Pip."

"We're on the strong side. He'll be safe!"

"Just try not to think about it."

I'm having a tough time coping with the passing days. While I'm happy to be distracted by my studies, even happy to take tests again, Phin had been a balm over my past wounds. They fester in his absence; those I've lost, the mistakes I've made, the fool I am for letting Phin leave for battle.

What was I thinking? My track record for loved ones surviving is terrible. I've just sent another off into the bowels of the enemy. My nerves fray to shreds from constant use. On the weekends, when I visit my family at the Wadsworth house that Claire and Bentley generously gifted Phin and me with, Mama, Max, and May attempt to distract me from my gnawing worry. Mountains of Kerr jars full of jam, three quilts plus one that's nearly done being tied, baskets after baskets of mending, and a newly-sewn skirt for May are the evidence of their distraction efforts, but the mindless work has kept only my hands busy. My mind has been free to race.

May digs deep, finally using Daddy's words against my angst. *"Worrying is like a rocking chair; it gives ya somethin' to do, but it won't get ya anywhere."* Her booming imitation resonates through my thoughts, blending with the memory of his deep voice uttering the words. Only minimally soothed by the memory, I'm still a wreck. Phin creeps his way into my thoughts all the time.

Needless to say, when his letter arrives at my Corps dorm, I pounce on it like a housecat on a mouse. My eyes drink in the small, square-ish characters of his penmanship on the envelope. Annie giggles when I sniff the paper, but I don't care. I dive in.

"Dearest Pip,

How anti-climactic it was to leave you, then sit on a ship that didn't leave for hours. I wish now that I had stayed with you just awhile longer. It seems like that time was wasted. I'm sorry I've stolen it from us."

Tears roll down my cheeks at the memory of saying goodbye.

"I suppose it's really Hitler who's ripped you from my arms, and for that, I intend to do all I can to personally be his demise.

A lot of Joes here talk about their sweethearts back home, how they just had a few days with them before we shoved off of port. Some only knew their wives a week or two before they married them. I've decided not to rub their nose in it, but all I can think is that I'm the luckiest fella on board. I've had my gal for twelve years!"

My heart leaps. It's difficult to allow the miles and miles between us to remain with his sweet words that renew my need for him. I want to stand up and run to him; to swim if I must.

"We're training for something big. Drills all day long, and when we're ready, we're headed to a staging camp. They hardly leave me any time to miss you, so I've taken one choice memory of you and put it in my pocket so I can miss you anyway.

It's you, asleep, in our hotel that last morning. The sunlight streamed in, and your hair was on fire in its light. There's nothing here to compare with the softness of your skin, so that memory will have to keep me going for now."

I curl the edge of the page up so that my roommates can't peek at his intimate words.

"I never knew that being so far could still feel so close.

Yours forever, Phineas."

This war can't pass quickly enough. My only hope is that when it does, I'll have more than this letter left to cling to.

TWENTY-TWO

May 1944

I'm frustrated by Willa, Annie, and Birdie's short steps over the wooden planks toward the harbor. My legs ache to run full out toward the ship, bump aside the captain, and steer us to France with the speed of the birds. Finally, *finally*! We're doing something!

Three large ships loom ahead. They are still, as the gentle swell of the harbor water can't move them. I look back and forth at them, wondering which one will be my new home, when I realize there are no more certain steps to take without deciding between them. We stand in the cold shadows of the huge ships, and it's familiar in a sick way.

"Which one is ours?" Birdie asks.

"I think it's that one, to the left," Annie guesses. We all look to the left, where two gals in cadet uniforms wave like beauty queens to greet oncomers.

"Well, c'mon Nurse... well, what do I call you these days, anyway?" Willa asks me.

"O'Shea," I tell her. "Nurse O'Shea."

"Well, O'Shea, look alive; we're off to save lives!" she teases, bumping her hip into mine. I grin at her, lengthening my stride to the boat.

"Penelope?" a woman calls, and I turn toward the voice. A tall, stately woman in a suit and heels stands from a bench near the marina. She shakes her long, dark hair behind her shoulders.

"Ruby!" I exclaim, halting. "What are you doing here?"

"I came to say goodbye," she explains as she moves toward us, and I force my facial muscles to hide their surprise. Of all the friends and foes I'll be leaving behind in the United States, my former mother-in-law is dead last on the list of people I'd expect a farewell from. After all, Ruby has what she wanted from me, her grandchild.

"That's sweet, Ruby. It's been a long time." I haven't seen Ruby since she offered me a bribe for little Jack. She nods.

"That it has," she agrees.

"How's little Jack?" I inquire. I think about him every day; wonder about him.

"He's very well. A roly-poly thing, he is!" she laughs, then her brows furrow. "I- well, I…" she mumbles. "I'm just surprised, Penelope; I thought you had crawled into a dark cave somewhere, but here you are, living your life. Living it with purpose, it seems." Her eyes graze over my uniform and cap. My own eyes swoop down at my crisp white apparel.

"Yeah, I guess so."

"You seem so… happy," she states, confused.

"I suppose I am," I agree.

"It's just… I always thought…" Her lovely face wrinkles with confusion, and I realize that Ruby has never really known me. She's only known the version of me that she's made up in her own head-- the gold digger, the son-stealer, the 'farm trash'. I realize that she can't understand how I can laugh and smile when I'm headed off to work. To her, any kind of labor must mean drudgery. To her, a blue-collar job isn't 'living'. A pang of sympathy strikes my chest for Ruby; I wonder if she'll ever know true happiness.

"I'm happy, Ruby. Jack wants me to be happy, and so I am." My lips curl up as his face appears in the forefront of my mind. I haven't forgotten him.

"So you are. Safe journey, Penelope. I hope you return safely," she claims. I offer my hand to her, and she takes it with her own buttery-soft one. Our very first handshake.

"Goodbye," I say. My heart reaches out to her in gratitude for loving my child so well.

Willa tips her head toward the ship to urge me on. I follow her to the smallest of the ships, where we stand in a long line of heeled, uniformed ladies waiting to check in. We're given strict instructions to stick to the ladies' side of the bunkers, especially after lights out. Birdie laughs at the implication. We lift our elbows to maneuver through the swarm of girls to find our cabin, toss our cases onto our beds, then set off to explore the ship. I'm in awe of how large it is.

As we pass by the rec room full of male medics, Birdie enthusiastically pulls Annie by the arm through its doors. A room full of fellas is certainly Birdie's kind of recreation, but Annie's eyes pop wide open as she's dragged inside. Willa and I shake our heads and continue exploring. In the fresh air on the top deck, we stand in the shadow of the larger ship, carrying soldiers.

"Willa, remember at my wedding, when I introduced you to Claire?"

"Mmm hmm," she replies, pursing her lips.

"You both were acting so strange. What was that all about?" Slowly, she swallows, as though the truth is uncomfortably thick.

"I knew Claire, from before," she offers. I allow an empty moment to pass, hoping the silence will coax out more of an explanation.

Her lips don't move.

"Oh?" I try arranging my features into the intense look Mama gives me when she wants to interrogate me without words.

"What?" Willa says with the annoyance of swatting away a fly. "What are you doing with your face, there?" I drop my effort and my face relaxes into its normal expression.

"I'm trying to dig the real answer out of you."

"By looking like you just bit a lemon? Nice try," she laughs.

"Seriously, Willa, I don't like being lied to. You both pretended that it was your first time meeting each other. What's between you two?"

"I'm not lying to you."

"Withholding the truth is the same thing as lying," I scold, withering at the echo of an argument with Mama on my lips.

"Fine! We knew each other when we were younger. Same debutant pool, so to speak."

Ah. I knew Willa was well born.

"And my parents would rather I'd stayed home to marry well than run off to join the Corps."

"You *ran* off?" I repeat with wide eyes.

"Yes. A debutant no more. I've been snipped from the family will for my 'reckless behavior', as my mother calls it," Willa admits. I can almost see a thin, scaly layer falling off of her with this revelation. I'm getting deeper, and sensing an odd parallel between her story and Jack's. Perhaps I'm attracted to a "type": Friends and lovers of the rebellious, reckless kind.

"I guess I wasn't sure if Claire would speak to me anymore, now that I'm a common street rat. No offense," she adds quickly.

"Ha! I've been a common street rat for years, and Claire's one of my nearest and dearest. Don't worry about her. 'Sides, when has Willa Fox ever worried about someone's opinion of her?"

She quietly mulls over my question while her mouth puckers.

"You're right," she agrees, squaring her shoulders. "I don't."

My mind drifts far away into thoughts of Jack.

"We're doing a good thing, you know," Willa reminds me when my brows go so low that they rest atop my cheeks, as though she can read my thoughts. We've become so close in the Corps that she probably can. She pulls me down into a deck chair next to hers.

"Of course," I tell her. It's rotten that sometimes the best thing isn't the thing that makes you happiest. I'd be happiest lingering forever in Phin's arms, soaking wet and curled up under the willow tree, but there's not a willow tree in sight. It's been a whole year since its tendrils grazed my skin on our wedding day.

Willa has closed her eyes and left me to my thoughts. She's the best girl friend I've ever had. Accepting, understanding, a great listener...

Soft snoring floats out of Willa's open mouth.

So, while I was mentally praising her friendship, she actually fell asleep! I snort, and she comes to.

"What?" she asks grumpily, still hiding under her lids.

"You fell asleep," I tell her.

"I can't keep my eyes open. Birdie and I were out hoppin' at a gin mill 'till the wee hours," she admits.

"You? The studious over-achiever?"

"I was *achieving* a memorable send-off," she mumbles. "It's what we rebellious types do." We grin together.

"Well, don't let me interrupt you," I tease, and watch the soldiers on the other ship. They all look so similar. Same uniforms, same haircuts, same hats. Even the same proud stride. Except one. My eyes squint at him. Dark hair, clear blue eyes. That's a Sharpe if I've ever seen one! My entire body stiffens along with this stunning discovery.

"Bentley!" I shriek like a curse word, and Willa shakes awake. Her expression reads annoyance.

"Sheesh, P, it's not like I had the hiccups or anything!"

I run to the railing. "Bentley!" I call again with all of my breath. *What on earth is he doing in a uniform on a ship? He's supposed to be home, with little Jack and Claire. Hadn't I been satiated only by the vision of their happy little family? Little Jack is supposed to have a father. Wasn't that the point?* My chest heaves with anxiety, and Willa lays her hand on me.

Oh, I realize. Ruby had come to the marina to say goodbye to Bentley, not to me. My cheeks flush with delayed embarrassment. It makes my voice crack when I shriek his name once more.

"Bentley Sharpe!"

"You're drawing a crowd," Willa mutters and steers me away, but I don't think Bentley had even heard me; he remains still.

A chubby, eager looking girl stops us in our path back to the bunker. She gives me a sympathetic smile.

"Too bad we're not on that ship, huh? Or the medics' ship; lotsa lookers and future doctors on that one!" She giggles. "Fellas only, y'know, on those boats. Guess they don't want us ladies standing in the crossfire of *Operation Overlord*," she says importantly and rolls her eyes.

"What's Operation *Overlord*?" I ask, interest peaked at the mention of 'fire'.

"Ooh," she giggles, covering her mouth. "Guess I said too much. Let's just say they're gonna need that other medic ship trailing close behind those soldiers!" she whispers through her fingers.

"When? When is the operation?" I press eagerly.

"No one knows, not even the Commander-in-Chief himself. They're waiting for the right moment to strike. Plus, I wouldn't know anyway; what if there was an enemy spy on the ship?" she giggles.

I manage a tense smile in return.

She rests her hand on my arm. "Oh, don't worry Honey, we won't be anywhere near the fighting. We'll swoop in to clean up a day or two afterward." She pats me and walks away. I'm sure she thinks she has soothed me, but she's done anything but.

Willa resumes pushing on my back. "You need chocolate, honey."

Once in our bunker, I shut the door and turn to her with wild eyes. "I've got to get on that medic ship."

She rolls her eyes and digs through her bag. "Aha! Here's your medicine," she says and offers me a gold-wrapped chocolate bar.

I don't take it. "I'm serious, Willa, I can't be miles away in safety when this operation thing goes down. Little Jack's dad is on that ship! I've got to know what's happening, or I'll go insane!" I'm pacing and twisting my hair. What can I do? I wonder how far our ship will be from the operation. I scramble for ideas.

"I can't pass as a soldier; I don't even know how to hold a gun!" I think aloud. I hate the feeling of adrenaline coursing through my veins with no way to physically expel the nervous energy. I scan over the information the giggling gal leaked to us, and suddenly, an idea illuminates the entirety of my mind.

"...but I *do* know most of that medical jargon," I mumble excitedly.

Willa looks stricken with the idea that she's stuck in a bunker with me, in this state, indefinitely. I'm like a crazed bird in a house, recklessly flying into a closed window over and over.

"Okaaaaay, what's your plan?"

"I don't have one. I mean, if I can pass as one of them... well, I guess I have to hide my…" I'm gesturing to all of me.

"Girl-ness?" Willa answers.

"Yeah. How do I do that?" I ask her frantically.

"Well, first of all, wipe off that lipstick."

I smear it onto the back of my forearm.

"And lose the stockings."

I toss them aside. She looks down at my chest.

"Gotta do something about those, too," she nods toward my bosom.

"No problem," I tell her, and I wriggle out of my brassiere in no time.

I button my uniform back up, the perkiness the brassiere had offered gone.

"You still need some binding," she assesses with a scrunched nose.

I pull the sheet from my bunk, rip the corner with my teeth, and tear off a long strip. Willa's brows reach higher up her forehead than I've ever seen them, but she helps me bind my chest down anyhow.

"You're an animal," she remarks.

I grunt, taking it as a compliment. "I'm a rebel, Willamena."

"You'll need a medic's uniform," she says, grinning.

"Alright, I'm headed to the laundry," I answer.

Willa comes with me, but we're both overly anxious about the laundry mission. With nervous eyes skittering about, we slither, backs to the wall, down to the laundry unit. The heavily armed guard I'd been expecting is nowhere to be seen. It's simply a matter of tiptoeing in and snagging an armful of the stuff. We lope back to our room with adrenaline coursing through us.

She sighs. "You're really serious, aren't you?"

"Yes. Dead." I assure her.

"Then we've got to chop off that hair."

I swallow hard.

"You have any scissors?"

I dig in my bag. "Yeah, a little sewing kit." I produce the kit and hold it up triumphantly. I'm still panting.

"Those things are tiny!" she complains. The scissors are shorter than my pinky finger.

"*'Sometime in the field, you'll be required to do something you don't think you can do. Do it anyway.*" I feign the serious voice of our instructor, who'd been amping us up for action in the field hospitals. "Rich girl," I add for effect.

She sighs, rolling her eyes. "Sit down." I sit obediently. She holds up a lock of hair. "You're sure that you're sure about this?" she checks again.

"Absolutely," I answer, holding still for her, though my heart pounds defiantly against my ribs.

"Good," she says as the first lock of my hair falls to my feet, a long, curved Corpse lying dead on the shiny wooden planks. The cabin door bursts open, and the sewing scissors drop from Willa's fingers and clatter to the floor.

"Hey, roomies! Wha-" Birdie exclaims, her eyes raking over my outfit.

"Pip's gone nuts," Willa informs her.

Annie raises her brows. "Why are you dressed like that?"

"I've got to get on the medic ship," I tell them. They listen intently as I explain why I must watch over my child's adoptive father.

"Well, these will do much better," Birdie claims, drawing a long pair of sharp scissors from her bag.

"Where did you get those?" Annie gasps, drawing her head away from the glinting points.

"From the arts and crafts table," Birdie explains. "These skirts are waaaaay too long to catch any attention. I planned to give mine some alteration back here in our bunk."

"Thief," Annie giggles. Willa snatches the scissors from Birdie and shears an alarming amount of lengthy strands from the side of my head.

"No going back now," she warns.

I straighten my neck. "I don't want to. Finish it, please." I try not to wince with every snip of the shears. Still, hot tears threaten to push through my tightly-squeezed eyelids. I had no idea that I was so emotionally attached to my hair! I purse my lips as tightly as my eyelids and scold myself to be strong, because my baby means more to me that my silly *hair*. I won't let little Jack lose another father.

With a final snip, my crown of femininity lies in a pile at my feet.

"You look like a boy!" Birdie gasps.

"That's the idea, dummy," Willa groans, pressing the handles into my palm. "Now, do mine."

"You... You're coming? With... with me?" I stammer. She turns around, pulling her hairpins from her carefully styled mane. She tosses them into the waste bin, where they ping lightly against the metal.

"I can't let you leap over the edge of insanity all alone," she claims. Birdie's hands drop to her sides as Annie's eyes grow bright.

"I'm coming, too," Annie claims, unclasping her brassiere under her shirt. "You made me enlist in this crazy adventure. I'm going to see it through at your side." She glares at Birdie.

"Oh, *fine*," Birdie groans. "Count me in."

TWENTY-THREE

As night falls, my loyal pals and I are all bra-less, bound, and dressed in the drab uniforms of the male medics. Willa thinks we're hardly passable as men, but I remind her of our laundry-retrieval mission.

"No one's going to be looking for two dames dressed as medics," I assure her. "You know how some fellas are sort of... feminine?"

We slip off the ship without a hitch. Like I'd thought, everyone is here voluntarily, pumped full of the pride of the Nation, so there's no need to watch for strays planning to run off. As we creep across the dock, avoiding the large pools of lamplight as best we can, my heart swells with affection for these girls. How many friends would chop off their hair for you? We scurry through the darkness, passing the Army's soldier ship, tossing the pillowcase full of our hair into a waste bin, and make our way to the medic's ship. The cover of the darkness allows us to blend right into the crowd of medics milling around the ship deck.

I find a Private lazily holding a clipboard, and I tell him in my most gruff voice, "Uh, I think I've lost my room assignment." Willa nods behind me and he asks for our names. I glance at the sagging clipboard. Rows of tiny, typed names have check marks next to them. About a dozen are unchecked, and I squint hard to make out the characters upside down. A group of unchecked names are sandwiched together.

"Uh, Grouse," I answer, jabbing a thumb at my chest, "and this here's, uh, Hamil, Hardison and... um, Marsden."

Birdie and Willa nod. Annie stands frozen between them, and I can see that her hands dangle, trembling, at her sides. The Private tilts up his clipboard and scans down the list.

"Grifter," Willa mouths at me accusingly. I do feel a bit like a con woman.

"Grouse, Grouse, Grouse," he mutters around the stub of a cigar in his teeth as he scans the list. "Oh! There you are. Good man. We thought you weren't coming. We need every warm body we can get," he pats me on the back and checks off my name. It's more forceful than anyone's ever patted me before, and it *stings*. I'm almost offended, when I remember that I'm a man now, and men don't pat each other's shoulders lightly.

I grunt in response, kind of Neanderthal-like.

"Hamil," he says. *Check*. "Hardison; Marsden; looks like you all can squeeze into 32A, second deck." *Check. Check.*

Swell; we can stay together.

"Thanks," Willa coughs deeply into her fist.

We skirt away and find our cabin, hearts pounding. When we push the cabin door open, the air inside swirls with thick smoke. Two men stretch out on their beds with magazines, each holding a lit cigarette between their lips. When we cross to our bunks, three high, the grey air visibly moves with us. I cough. Apparently, these cabins hold six to a room, instead of the privacy of just four that we'd enjoyed on the small nurses' ship.

"Evenin', gents," a fella greets us from the lower bunk.

"Hi," Willa and I grunt in unison.

"Thought we were gonna have the palace to ourselves," the bigger fella in the upper bunk says, gesturing around the tiny cabin with three-high bunks lining two walls. The walkway in between them barely fits two of us, shoulder to shoulder.

"Yeah, uh, sorry," I respond gruffly and cough again.

"Hey, no worries, Pal," he responds. "These biscuits we sleep on aren't much for keeping all to ourselves. The name's Striker."

"Grant," the lower bunk offers. His voice cracks like a pre-pubescent boy's.

Willa, confident from our close call on the deck, answers for us. "I'm Hamil," she says, her voice low and gravelly, "and this here's Marsden, Hardison and Grouse."

The fellas nod and get back to their magazines.

We sigh collectively and flop onto our bunks. As my back hits the bed below me, I realize what Striker meant; the mattress is made up of three square cushions that do little to pad the hard wooden board beneath it. Still, I welcome my current surroundings, however uncomfortable. With two male bunkmates, changing clothes will be a real challenge. Even so, I can't contain my smile.

We're in!

Things indeed get tricky with details like changing, showering, and having any privacy whatsoever to discuss our strategy. We wait for Grant and Striker to clear out in the mornings before we change into our uniforms, which can be tricky with a bully like Striker pulling us out of bed by the ankles.

"Get up, lazies!" he usually shouts at us. "Find your sea legs!" It's always a task finding things to do in a cramped bunk to wait out his impatience so we can change in privacy.

Lathering up with shaving soap alongside the medics and cutting away our nonexistent facial hair makes me feel like we've blended in well, even though most all of the fellas shave shirtless. We obviously can't join the routine topless, and we have to kick at Birdie's shins to keep her from openly ogling down the rows of bare, muscled chests.

"You're a man, Birdie," I whisper harshly. "Play the part!"

It's not difficult to wake in the dead of night to guard each other for a shower, because nerves keep our sleep light. That, and our baritone roommates snore loudly enough to keep anyone this side of unconsciousness. However, it's a comfort to hear; we know they don't notice our absence when the symphony is still playing upon our tip-toed return.

It's a real luxury to let the hot water wash away the layer of cigarette ash that bathes us in our cabin. We'd be completely exposed if someone were to enter, but we haven't had a close call yet. Our nerves are soothed with each successful encounter with our shipmates, who seem to accept us without question as bona fide fellas.

Annie tells me, "You're so good at this, it's scary."

I shrug my shoulders. "I grew up with two older brothers." It's easy to slip into Eddie's mindset. Sometimes I play Max, but he is a little more soft-spoken, and somehow I don't think that will go off well here. So, Eddie is my main inspiration.

After thirty-six hours on board, we're glassy-eyed from the endless monotony of the open ocean. It helps a bit to hang over the rails on deck and watch Bentley's ship ahead of us; we ride in its wake, but time still seems to creep by like a turtle. So, when some hot shot calls out for a contender at the ping pong table, I pounce at the opportunity to play him, pulling me from the safety of the shadows.

The opposing fella grins as he appraises my slight frame, but once the game begins, he doesn't know what's hit him. I take to the paddle quickly, and I'm much more spry than he is. It's easy to fake him out and send a ball just out of his reach three times in a row. I'm victorious.

Willa watches me with wide eyes as I pound my chest with the paddle and assume the role of calling out a challenger. We've sort of had an unspoken agreement to lie low. A glance at her worried expression sobers my loud arrogance, until someone has stepped up to the table to contend. I wipe the floor with him.

This happens twice more, and I yelp in victory.

The wounded washout grumbles, "You scream like a dame," and I know it's time to turn in for the night before I allow my guard to slip any lower. I keep to the bunk a lot after that close call, which is bearable only when Striker and Grant are out of the room.

One night, I'm in a coughing fit and I've had it with the thick, smoky air. "You're medics, right?" I begin.

"Yeah," they say. Obviously.

"Haven't either of you read Hoffman's Report?"

"Huh?" they ask.

"Ya' know, '*toxic tobacco smoke impairs the immune system*'? I'm tellin' you boys, if I catch some disease from a festering battle wound and die because my immune system is impaired, I'll haunt you sorry greebies!"

"Well, ain't you hard-boiled," Striker huffs. "Yeah, I've read it, but it's questionable."

Grant puts out his ciggie and honks, "I don't want to die from the cooties from a festering battle wound, Strikes. You know, they call these things 'coffin nails'?"

Striker cups the air around his ciggie like a premature baby. "This is the only lady friend I've got on this ship, Grant!" he says out of the corner of his mouth. If he only knew he was sharing a cabin with four lady friends.

"Listen, I'll play you for it," I tell him.

Grant groans again. He was there the night I smashed three guys in a row.

"Cards?" Striker says hopefully, his fag wagging in the corner of his mouth.

"Not my game," I say.

"Not his either," Grant smirks. Striker swings at him, but he swerves out of the way of the blow. In my mind the connection clicks- 'Striker' isn't his given name, it's a nickname he has earned for his easy punches.

"Ping pong?" Willa suggests. Again, she's read my mind. I love her for it.

Grant groans.

"What's the bet?" Striker asks.

"You win, you can blow all the immune system crushing slop you want down my neck and you'll never hear me complain. If I win, this cabin becomes smoke free," I bargain.

Grant objects. "He's real good, Strikes."

Striker looks offended. "So am I, Goober," he defends and punches Grant's arm.

Grant cradles his bruised arm. "What's in it for us? We smoke all we want now," he argues.

"Pride. And I won't have to hear his girly whining anymore," Striker says. "How 'bout, I win, and girly Grouse here has to smoke down one of these Cubans?" He wags a thick brown cigar in the air at me.

My eyes narrow as I consider the long hours it would take me to suck down that thing. But as it stands, breathing the air in this cabin is the same as holding a cigar between my lips anyway. This is a chance to clear the air.

"You're on, Striker. Let's do this."

Grant looks defeated as we trudge up to the game room.

Striker wasn't bluffing. He's really very good. I'm panting and down by two when we trade sides. But, I quickly gain back the lead, and a crowd gathers to investigate the source of Striker's heated swearing.

I note that the trio of chumps I'd beaten is cheering for Striker, but I've got a good following behind me as well. Way in the back, in a short row of doctors, a familiar face stands out. My stomach rolls as I realize I'm in the same room, on the same boat, sailing toward the same mission as the slimeball creature who attacked Doris; Doctor Sweeney. I shudder in revulsion.

Sweeney.

My eyes blur out of focus, and my head spins wildly, as though the lever on a merry-go-round has been pushed to its maximum inside of my brain. When Striker's small cheering section explodes into a chorus of cheers, I know I've been scored on. The sound pulls me back into the present, but it's looking grim for me. I'm pretty sure that I'm going to live in a constant cloud of smoke. Striker is a quick, spry, and dirty fighter. He raises his arms in triumph, soaking up the crowd's cheers, and I send a shot just under his paddle.

"I wasn't ready," he complains.

"Don't be sore," I contend gruffly. I try to keep my eyes low, out of Sweeney's line of sight, though I know he only has eyes for a curvy feminine figure. Right now, I'm just a skinny fella that he's probably as blind to as the rest of our shipmates.

"We're even now. Keep on your game," I tell myself as much as Striker. The sight of Sweeney has shaken me up. Badly.

Striker shuts his eyes and beats his paddle against his chest after another dirty score. I capitalize on his arrogance and once again return the ball just under his elbow. I score the winning point, and the crowd roars appreciatively.

I'm victorious!

Striker yells, but I can't hear his complaints over riotous cheering as the crowd presses in on me. A pumping fist with a coffee cup accidentally sends a dirty brown splash onto Willa. Her eyes fly wide open. I fight my way to her, but I'm lifted proudly onto their shoulders and passed over the crowd. The procession rounds the corner and I lose sight of her. Someone hands me the winning ball, and I stuff it into my breast pocket over my flat, restricted breast. I crawl off of their shoulders when we pass my cabin. They haven't seemed to notice, and the cheering procession continues down the hall as I push through my cabin's door. I guess I'm not the only one happy to see Striker lose.

I stretch out on my bed, basking in to the glow of victory. Willa waddles into our cabin, holding her shirt all wet with coffee away from her body. I draw a deep breath.

"Smell that?" I ask her with my hands behind my head.

"What?" she asks, sniffing the air.

"Neither do I. Clear air from here on out!" I smirk and close my eyes.

"I need to change out of this shirt," she tells me. I hop up, immediately alert.

"Okay, I'll guard the door," I assure her and stand right by it. It doesn't have a lock. I've become so comfortable here that I feel fairly confident that we won't be discovered, so I stand somewhat slack as her guard.

"You sure were hot-doggin' it up there," she tells me while unbuttoning her shirt. The brown stains have permeated the white fabric wrapped around her chest.

"Aw, it's all over your *restrictor*," I giggle, using the nickname for the 'non-bra' we've coined.

She laughs. "To Hades with this thing," she curses and rips off the 'restrictor'. She's bent down, bare-chested, onto her bunk to grab her spare and I'm doubled over with laughter and shock at her boldness.

The door flies open, knocking into my rear. "Bird-" I begin to growl, but I stop short when a very large boot swings into the small room.

I'm stunned, wondering if this is really a nightmare, while a very sour Striker and one of his cronies stand at the door with shock spilling out of their gaping mouths. Willa shrieks and throws her arms over her chest, leaping onto her bed. She balls up to protect herself, like a porcupine.

"My, oh my," Striker grumbles, stepping in the door fully. I don't like the smile that blooms on his lips. He's obviously seen enough that our cover is blown, and given our recent interaction, he's not likely to keep our secret out of roommate loyalty. But what really upsets me is the way he licks his lips as he steps over to Willa.

TWENTY-FOUR

Striker grabs Willa's arm and yanks her up to her feet. She manages to hold one forearm tightly against her chest and squeezes her eyes shut. Unfortunately, this gesture that was intended for a protection of her modesty accentuates her flesh, like a corset. She leans her weight heavily toward the ground, so Striker has to strain to hold her midair.

"Looky here," Striker laughs to his buddy, who looks like he may have frozen solid where he stands. He points at Willa like he's just found a box of candy. "You two some sort of secret lovers?" he asks.

I snort.

I can't let Willa be exposed alone, so I admit in my normal trill, "No, I'm a gal, too." My voice sounds steady, despite the ice in my veins.

Willa lets out a little puff of air. *Was I supposed to let her go down alone?* After her grand show of loyalty in following me here, I would never abandon this friend.

Striker's eyes shoot up at the sound of my feminine voice.

"Prove it," he goads, looking directly at my chest as though undressing it with his eyes.

"No way, Goon," I snarl. "I'm a married woman. And even if I weren't, I wouldn't waste my girls on a slime like you." Even though I'm still clothed, restrictor still firmly in place, I cross my arms tightly over my chest as though he can see through every layer. "Let her go, and get out of here!"

"Ha! Monty, hear that? I've been bunking with two dames this whole time!" He throws Willa to the floor. She scrambles to her knees and crawls to her bed, clawing the thin blanket and hastily wrapping herself in it. She shakes like a leaf underneath it.

"Go away!" I scream again.

"Not until you prove it, Sweetheart," he says. He slams me into the wall and leans his weight on my forearms. I can't make any progress as I fight against his weight. "Monty! Get her shirt!" He calls to his friend, who doesn't move.

I squirm, turning my head away from his hot, sticky breath.

"C'mon, kid, help me out here!" He looks around the tight cabin, scanning for a way to unbutton my shirt while still holding my wriggling arms. "*Montgomery*! You can have the broad on the bed when you're done,. Just give me a hand!" I'm sick at his words. Monty stands as still as a statue. If Phin were here, he'd throw both of these creeps overboard and leave them to be picked up by a Nazi sub.

He isn't here, so I'll have to fend for myself. I spit in Striker's red face and aim my knee for his crotch. Immediately, he releases my arms and doubles over in pain. I pull the ping pong ball from my pocket and stuff into his throat. He gags on it before falling back and spitting it on the floor. I'm not sure what to do next. If I scream for help, then fellas will swarm in and see Willa's bare, feminine figure; but I can't physically take him alone.

Luckily, Monty grows a conscience and thaws out. He keeps Striker down, which can't be difficult in his writhing state, and pins him to the ground. Monty is smaller than Striker, so I'm amazed at how he's able to contain him.

"Two-time wrestling champ in high school," he grins up at me with a wink.

I roll my eyes. While I'm enormously grateful for his late help, I can't help but detect the notes of flirtation in his voice. I'd almost forgotten that fellas were capable of charming phrases, after all the garbage I've heard this week. His attempted charm is deflected off me and bounces to the floor. If he were truly gallant, he would've stepped in much, much sooner.

"Well, get him out of here!" I bark at him, irritated. Striker nurses his crotch and is easily led into the hall. I slam the door behind them and pile mattress biscuits in front of it.

I dive down on the bed next to Willa and wrap my arms around her. Her entire frame shudders.

"It's okay, it's okay," I whisper into her ear. But it's not at all okay. We've been discovered, and there's surely punishment to follow. I'm fairly sure they don't throw stowaways overboard, but I can't be certain. Over and over, my mind plays a scene of our flailing bodies pummeling toward a torrential sea. *How will we survive the rest of our journey rooming with that foul pest?* I know Willa won't be able to sleep a wink; neither will I.

Something must be done. I can't very well go to the head medic and tell him, *"There are a couple of dames on board who need protection from a dirty pervert. And, oh yeah, I'm one of them."* I decide that our only option is to sleep in hidden spots around the ship. We can take turns on watch so the other can catch some winks. I'll have to swipe a knife from the kitchen. I don't want to have to use it, but it would at least hold Striker off, if it comes to that.

"Willa, I've got a plan. Let's get you dressed." I shake her; she's sobbing. "Hurry! Let's get all of our things. And grab your pillow," I direct her. She's in shock, and she follows my words robotically. There's no sign of the brute in the hall, so we scurry up to the top deck and stow our things behind a thick hanging hose.

"We'll just have to wait for Birdie and Annie to find us. Hopefully they do before Striker," I tell her, trying my best to sound confident.

"Or worse," she amends. "The captain."

I was right about our shipmates disliking Striker. To my horror, our secret has spread through our row of cabins like wildfire, the extreme boredom on board fueling the gossip flames like dry straw. Now at least fourteen men are keen to our real identities. Though I feel nervous that so many on board know about the gals on board, most of them express absolute loathing toward the bully. Somehow, instead of fourteen enemy informants, we've gained fourteen protective allies.

Striker wasted no time blabbing to the Orderly that two dames were aboard ship impersonating fellas, but our loyal shipmates were at his heels, making him out to be a boy who's cried wolf. A *drunken* boy, spouting an alcohol-induced tall tale. At first I was amazed at their loyalty to us, until truths came out that made their motivations more clear.

First of all, many eagerly shared their own tales of being at the wrong end of Striker's temper. One medic had had his gal's photo thrown into the sea, compliments of Striker, when he'd accidentally spilled gravy on Striker's pants. His large nostrils flare with fresh bitterness as he tells us his story. That photo was meant to give him strength in his inevitable moments of fear. Two victims join the conversation with incensed accounts of being beat up in the showers; towels stolen. Striker is a *mean* bully.

Somehow, Monty had managed to re-assign Striker's bunk to another level. He tried to assign himself to our bunk, but Willa threw him and his duffel bag out along with Grant.

"We can sleep in our own underthings again," she explains, brushing her hands together. "No more GI boxer shorts hanging between my legs!"

"Oh! I've missed you!" Birdie sings to a pair of ladies' underpants that she's pulled out of nowhere, and hugs them to her chest.

Annie chews her fingernails nervously. Monty and Grant settle for claiming two empty beds the next door over. Each of our small group of 'supporters' looks at us with appreciation, taking in our femininity with newly keen eyes. Around them, we've given up the gruff voices. Birdie's lashes flutter as though they've been imprisoned for weeks, and my throat sings with the sweet relief of higher notes. I make a point to let our fourteen fans know I am very happily married. So, as the only available females on board, Willa, Annie and Birdie have become more interesting than a secret cabinet full of liquor. I'm pleased. After following me down this path of insanity, they deserve a little fun.

Our cabin quickly becomes a social club. While I draw a group of guys to our bunk who need "a dame's opinion" on letters from their sweethearts, such as, "What does she mean when she says, '*If you still feel...*'"; the unattached boys are positively dancing in circles, vying for the girls' attention. One fella with a ukulele has hastily written a song about Willa's beauty.

"You'd foo-ooled me, but excu-use me, you're the prettiest dame on board. Swee-eet lips; I'd love your swee-eet kiss; be my lady, I'll be your lord!"

He has a terrible singing voice, but I love the comic relief.

The four of us move with a human barrier around us in the mess hall to protect us from Striker. Encircled, poor Annie and Willa are the recipients of sneak attack kisses on their hands and foreheads. Both of them are quick to turn away from attempts at their mouth. Birdie, ever seeking attention, accepts the affection with her gate wide open.

"Miss Wii-iilla Fox, knocks o-off my socks, you're a foxy little lady it's truuue! Refuu-uuse me, it will abuu-uuse me, I'll just diiie or I'll for-ev-er be bluuue." The uke gent follows us everywhere.

Willa rolls her eyes at his songs, but I think she secretly likes being recognized as a female again. His strumming reminds me of Phin's fingers rolling over guitar strings, so I like it, too.

But even with all of the new entertainment, I cannot wait to reach our destination, in spite of whatever evil awaits us there.

The white ripples lined up on the open ocean seem as endless as my racing thoughts. To calm myself, I try to time my breathing with the rise and fall of the boat. It's gentle enough to coax long, deep breaths. I rest my elbows against the railing and stretch my chin up until the massive ship disappears from my view, and I'm alone on the dark water. After awhile, the rapidly-spinning cogs in my head slow to a stop. My heart welcomes the new, relaxed pace as I lose myself in the low-lit giant sphere of a moon among scattered clouds. This is the closest as I can be to the Spot, my old thinking place; the closest a person can come to being alone on an enormous army ship.

My eyelids relax into slits. The swirl of light allows my harried mind to wander to better times, better memories. Alone here, on the water, I yearn to share this beautiful moonlight with my love.

My glassy eyes blur with a daydream until I can nearly feel his arms resting against my sides. His breath, or the wind, fills my hair with sweet words, and I sink backward into him. He shares the burden of my mission with me, lightening my load with his presence. My eyes sink closed, relishing the feeling, drinking in the rare comfort.

Protect my brother, he whispers.

I will, I promise silently. *I will, Jack.*

Ahem, Sense interrupts. *Jackson is gone. Phineas is your love now.*

I allow my forehead to fall into the metal railing as self punishment for being an idiot. I slipped so far into my thoughts that I slid right past the warmth of Phin, back to the comfort of Jack. The terrible part is that I didn't even notice.

Eh, neither of them are really here anyhow, Imp shrugs. *They'll never know.*

But I'll know. I don't know how I could've mixed them up when my feeling for each has been so different. My feelings about *myself* when I was with each have been so different. Jack loved a young, perfect version of this body, a gal like an unbroken horse who stubbornly resisted affection. Phin's gaze goes right to my heart, noticing but ignoring the scars I'd gained over the years.

I'm an awful person. They both deserve better than a wife who can't keep her husbands straight.

Sheesh, gal; give yourself a break, Imp chimes in. *Your love for Jack didn't die with him. It would be wrong if it had.*

My eyes fly open again when the sounds of approaching boot steps register in my ears, and I quickly shove my shame out of sight. If Willa knew she had lopped off all of her lustrous hair and survived an attack by a creep like Striker just for the sake of some two-bit floozy, she may never trust me again.

The boot steps stop. I carefully arrange my face in innocence before I turn to face her.

"I know who you are."

I stiffen at the sound of the voice, familiar; as sticky and persuasive as a fly trap.

Not Willa.

No, this voice is a man's deep tone, and dips much deeper into my memories than those of Willa. Deeper than Jackson, even. And these memories are stained with dark red blood, making me wish Willa had already managed to slip me a stolen kitchen knife.

Doctor Sweeney.

"And I know *exactly* who *you* are, you wormy creep. Don't touch me or I swear, I'll throw you right into that black abyss," I threaten, my tone as my blade. "You're a *murderer*."

"I acted purely out of fear," he explains. "I knew that if that child grew and was born, I'd be saddled with a woman I didn't love, her greedy family, and the result of that relationship for the rest of my life. I didn't love her."

"If you didn't love her, then why did you *make* love to her?"

"Oh, what we made was pure lust, I assure you," he insists with a smirk. My stomach rolls in disgust as he adjusts his waistband. My face must show my distaste for him, because he immediately defends, "Oh, don't pretend your friend was in it for love. She was only after my name and my pocketbook."

"You cannot justify what you did, you creep."

"I'm not. I came here to tell you that I'm haunted by that little soul every single day of my life; even more so at night, when I try to sleep." Even though the authorities didn't charge and punish Sweeney, it seems his guilt still holds him prisoner.

I know a bit about a person feeling haunted as they attempt to rest.

Almost sympathetically, I whisper, "There is no escape from your ghosts, is there?"

"No, there really isn't. That's why I'm here; to save lives. It won't bring back that child, but perhaps it will keep him from haunting me." Guilt isn't noble, but it still soothes me to know he's been punishing himself all this time. Apparently he hasn't gotten off scot-free, after all.

"Doris is doing fine, no thanks to you," I tell him, and he winces at her name. "She's happily married to her high school sweetheart, and they're expecting a child. You didn't manage to destroy her completely."

"I'm glad to hear it. I truly am."

I nod curtly, barely accepting his words. However repentant he seems now, I've spent a long time truly loathing this man.

"Thing is, I can't figure out what you're doing here. Last I checked, you were a dame, Missy." I wince as I wait for the stroke of my cheek that would always accompany his terms of endearment, but it doesn't come.

"I have my reasons, Sweeney," I say stiffly. "And they're none of your business. Just know that we're working toward the same goal right now. We're here to save these brave men."

"Fine by me. I don't expect you to forgive me, but would you do me a favor, please?"

"Depends on what it is."

"When you return, would you kindly offer Doris my sincerest apologies?" he requests.

"Sweeney, offer them yourself."

TWENTY-FIVE

June 6th, 1944

Cool drifts of morning wind sweep over the ocean and tickle my naked neck as I lean heavily against the railing. My eyes, still crusty with sleep, haven't caught up yet with the pounding of my anxious heart. Even with all the talk, all the preparation, my soul is twisted with unease. I recall Daddy's words: *"worrying is like a rocking chair..."* His face and May's loom above the images in my head, speaking in unison. *"...Gives you something to do, but it sure doesn't get you anywhere."*

The sea below us moves as roughly as my thoughts. I have to grip the slick railing to remain standing as a rain as fine as mist falls on us. I'd rather be wet on deck than dry inside, where stifling fumes of vomit permeate the air. Fellas fall like bowling pins to seasickness. Even Birdie can't keep up her flirtatious wink as she curls up in a ball on the deck. Those who aren't dry heaving have taken to chain smoking to calm their ragged nerves.

This is the day. The last strings on Operation Overlord tie up neatly as we move toward the distant cliffs, the shore of Normandy. The endless herd of craft we're moving with is only a small piece of a gigantic attack from the air and sea, all along the coastline of France. Our assignment is to tend to the tens of thousands of brave men who'll storm the beach they've nicknamed 'Omaha'.

"The word is, the air assault is happening right now. They'll wipe out the enemy, and they'll have a clear path up the beach. It'll be fine, just like they said. Taking candy from a baby." Willa has read the lines in my forehead like a fortuneteller. Even with her soothing words, anxiety binds my chest as we pull toward the wide beach. It's as crowded as a public pool; ships, tanks and boats are everywhere I look.

Only two hundred feet from the sand, the bow of a gigantic ship blows upward out of the water. When it lands, it sends wading soldiers tumbling sideways in its wake. Their cries mingle in with the great splash of the craft.

"Whoa!" I scream and hit the deck with Willa, even though we're hundreds of yards back. The vibration from the blast echoes in my chest.

"Did you see that?" I hear behind me.

"Mines! They've got sea mines!"

Boom!

Again. And again.

Boom!

Boom!

"What are they... *why* are they... they're still headed to shore!" I shriek, watching small metal boats loaded with men move toward the pillars of rising smoke. I've tangled myself up in Willa's limbs.

"Yeah, Dummy; we're not giving up. This is *war!*" She holds her fist up in a perfect imitation of a war rally poster gal. Annie nods bravely behind her, and I can see that both of them are far more mentally prepared for this than I am. Their terror seems to be stifled by their patriotism, but I can barely believe my eyes. Those fellas are willingly riding toward the gunfire and the mines. I squint my eyes. Under their helmets, any one of them could be Phin or Bentley. I have no idea who they are among the thousands.

Pop! Pop! Pop! Three soldiers fall off their boat into the water. *Boom! Pop! Pop!* A wall of water shoots up with the blast. The boat slows, and the rest of them file out into waist-deep water. *Pop! Pop!* It sounds like rattling in a tin can. *Pop!* At least a dozen soldiers drop. The others move forward, pushing toward the beach, even though the shooting from the cliffs is relentless. I don't want to blink, because I've never witnessed anything like this. Boatful after boatful are heading into the fray. If I were one of them, I would've died of fright before they'd even let the ramp down. These are brave boys.

"Is this what you wanted to be here for?" Willa groans in my ear. "Squeezing my leg isn't going to keep your boys safe, you know."

I heave my legs out from under her and tuck them under me, not taking my eyes off of the beach. "This is murder," I mutter, slack-jawed. *Boom!* We're steadily crawling far slower than a snail's pace toward the beach. Useless adrenaline pumps through my still body while I watch the surf darken with blood at the shoreline.

"How can we just stand here?" I wonder aloud to Willa. She is busy shoving away a starry-eyed medic.

"Not *now*," she barks through her teeth at him. She sighs. "What can we possibly do, P? We're not in charge."

She's right- we're not in charge. I feel as helpless as a baby. Somebody's son, grandson, maybe brother or even father just fell backward, dead, off his ship when he was hit twice in the chest. A whole boatful of sons blast into the air when they cross a sea mine; most float face down on the water. It's hard to see any point in the massacre. I try mightily to recall the war flicks we'd watched back home. *Why are we doing this? Most of them are dying before they even reach the beach!*

Hours of this horror tick by before we're called to action. By this time, my muscles are fatigued from trembling.

"Alright, gents," Sergeant Bates barks gruffly when our ship settles four hundred yards from shore. "This is what you've been trained for. Hold your medic's bag high, and you'll be clear of fire." His assurance assumes that we won't hit a sea mine. I don't assume that.

My breath will not steady; my eyes won't focus or blink. Though I know the cross on my bag will keep me from being fired at, my body is convulsing with fear. "I don't think I can do this," I stammer through quivering lips. My eyes and nose are pouring. "I don't want to go."

Bates slaps my shoulder, hard. "Pull it together, Grouse. Those boys need us."

My eyes close. I picture Phin on the beach, wounded. I imagine Bentley, calling my name. I can help them, I encourage myself. These images move my shuffling boots down the rungs. When my right boot dips under the surface of the water, my terror escapes through my lips in a ragged yelp.

"Chin up, Grouse. Keep walking." I've never felt so out of control of my body.

The cool water laps all the way up to my ribs. The bag I hold over my head provides a shield for my eyes, so I follow the sound of Willa's body sloshing through the water in front of me. I strain to pick out the noise over the tin can rattling, the hum of planes and shouting, but I won't open my eyes. Panic and dread have sealed my eyelids together.

I'm forced to pry them apart when the water gets shallower and waves push at our calves. I need to see now.

"Agh!" I shriek when I spot mangled, uniformed bodies rolling in the blood-tinged surf. I'll never be able to wash this memory from my head.

"Oh, I'm gonna be sick," Birdie moans ahead of us. While I teeter dizzily behind Willa, Annie holds her chin up and marches straight for shore. Annie's strength clears my head, motivates me to push myself forward.

"Medic! Medic over here!"

"Aw, thank heaven!"

"Please! I need a medic!"

"Medic!"

A chorus of desperate cries rings all over the beach. Their pleas breathe life into me. Suddenly, my ears are deaf to the blasts and gunfire, and my legs become steady. I run for the closest voice calling for help near the tide line, a soldier with no legs. Dark maroon streaks on the sand lead all the way to the lapping salt water.

I scoop my hands under his armpits and pull him up the beach.

I read his tags. "Marks. I'm going to take care of you, Marks." I tear away his sleeve with hasty fingers. The material rips in clean, frayed lines, just the same way a bolt of cotton tears in a straight line for a weekend sewing project. The similarities of the two experiences end there as I tourniquet the stumps of his thighs with the fabric, numb to the charred red flesh there while I apply sulfa powder. His face looks sickly pale.

"Does this hurt?" I ask, not bothering to lower my voice an octave. He doesn't seem to notice me or my question through his haze, but I know his body must be in agony. I pull a tiny syringe from my bag and stare at it queasily. The oranges I injected in training haven't exactly prepared me to stab human flesh, but I swallow the lump in my throat and quickly bury the tip in his thigh anyway. I feel sick and my head starts to swim, until I see his shoulders relax with relief. The shot must have helped him. This feeling, the feeling of contributing, gives my body instant vigor.

I wipe my hand over my eyes. *What's next?* The ghostly pallor of his cheeks reminds me that he has lost a lot of blood through his leg wounds. The tourniquets will stop him from bleeding out, but he'll be stronger with more blood pumping through his body. I pull out a plasma bottle, find a plump vein on his arm, and slide the needle in. He doesn't even seem to notice the invasion. I hold the bottle high, allowing gravity to keep plasma flowing into his body.

The pitiful call for "Medic! *Medic!*" echoes all across the beach, as though the hatch to Hell has been cracked open, and the wailing cries of the tormented are escaping. Cadets are taught that one person should hold the plasma bottle up while another tends to the wounds. As my instructor's voice repeats this in my head, my eyes sweep over the beach. There just aren't enough of us to waste that kind of time.

My eyes dart around the littered sand for something tall and stable to hold up the bottle for me. I pull a rifle from the cold grip of a face-down soldier, and slam the barrel into the sand. It seems steady enough, so I tear the cold soldier's lace from his boot, make a loop around the bottle, and hang it over the trigger. Satisfied, I move on.

To move anywhere on this beach, my wet, sandy boots have to step over the mangled bodies of fallen soldiers. Though I'm careful, my toe catches on the arm of a splayed, face-down body, and I stumble. As I catch my footing on my thick rubber soles, I hear him moan. My head whips back around to him, and I instantly drop to my knees. My trembling, blood-smudged fingers hover over him as my mind goes blank. I grunt to myself, trying to jog my memory. It feels much like coaxing Ollie, my old tractor, to life on a cold morning.

Assess, I remember as my brain's engine chugs to life.

Okay, I think. *He has a pulse.* It's weak, but steady. I roll him onto his back, and drop my cheek down by his mouth. When I feel the sticky moisture of an exhale on my skin, I scan his body for wounds. He's covered in wet sand, so it's hard to see. That is, until I notice that the sand on his shoulder and belly are saturated with blood. Gunshot wounds.

I pull yards of gauze from my bag like a clown with an endless scarf. I press it firmly over his wounds, which leaves my hands occupied until this bleeding stops. I blow out a frustrated puff of air. I can't help anyone else with my hands busy like this. Even though we've been strictly taught never to stop pressure on the wound, I've got to keep moving.

I push myself up to standing, and squat down over a body lying face down in the sand. My fingers press into his neck as I check his pulse from the back. No pulse. Perfect.

With my elbows hooked under his armpits, I drag the dead man over to my gunshot patient. I quickly lift my patient's soaked dressing, sprinkle sulfa over the wounds to prevent infection, and redress them. Then, grunting, I heave the dead, dirty body over my patient, providing the constant pressure he needs on his wounds. The face of the still body flops to the side, and I gasp in horror as I realize that I recognize its owner. My body shudders of its own volition.

I tell myself to slow my heaving breaths. The body with no pulse, the body I'm using as a tool, belongs to Doctor Sweeney! It seems I'll be the one to offer his apology to Doris after all.

In the Corps, they repeated over and over that nurses and medics are immune to fighting; that's the rules of engagement. But looking around at the horror on the beach, I realize just how innocent I was in training to believe that any sort of gentility existed on a battlefield. This is barbarism, not a gentleman's duel! The soft cloud of safety I'd felt around me, because I'm wearing a red cross on my uniform, evaporates at the sight of Sweeney and his blood-soaked cross.

At least he can't hurt anyone anymore. At least he's good for something, now.

I try to block images of the bloodshed Sweeney caused Doris back home, and I turn my attention back to the bloodshed on the beach. My hands tend to the soldier underneath Sweeney's dead weight. I give him water, a morphine shot, and a plasma bag, which I set on Sweeney's back so that gravity will allow it to flow into the wounded man.

When I stand and quickly swat the sand from my palms, I realize that I no longer feel afraid or queasy. Adrenaline coursing through me makes me feel like a powerful machine, bestowing life upon wounded men. I work quickly, marveling at how strange it feels to apply classroom knowledge to real-life wounds. This is nothing like I expected; my imagination could never dream up such sheer horror.

Annie calls out to me, "Pip! I've got your man here!" I don't know which man she's referring to, but my boots tear up the beach to her. My heart falls when I see the dark hair of her patient. I guess I'd hoped she'd found Phin, but I'm relieved to see that she's located Bentley amongst this endless sea of uniforms. After all, it was the idea of preserving a father for little Jack that drove me here in the first place.

This is what I came here for. A strange mix of satisfaction and terror wash over me as I fall to my knees and slap his cheek.

"Bentley! Bentley, wake up! It's Pip; do you hear me? Bentley!"

Annie has to move on; there are too many lives hanging in the balance for two "medics" to focus on one patient.

"Go ahead," I assure her. She nods and rushes toward the sound of desperate pleas calling out to us.

Bentley coughs, spraying blood onto his chin and my face. I make no effort to wipe the dark red spots off of my skin.

"Bentley," I smile triumphantly. "You're going to live. Do you hear me?"

TWENTY-SIX

A deep gash in Bentley's neck threatens against my promise. He groans, and the effort pushes more blood from his neck.

"Shhh, don't talk; just stay with me. You've got a little boy back home, Bentley. You've got a wife. Claire needs you. Little Jack needs you. Stay with me." My fingers work quickly to stop the bleeding. I compress the wound on his neck with my iron determination fueling my every move. Little Jack's father needs to make it home. With my free hand, I give him my last syringe of morphine.

Whoever packed these medic's bags wasn't planning on this many wounded, I think to myself.

"Hey you!" calls a soldier. I realize he's been calling me for minutes now, but I have been tuned in only on Bentley. He's standing up, obviously well enough to breathe, but moaning like a dying cat. I'm about to tell him, *'In a minute!'* when I get an idea. If he can compress Bentley's wound for me, I can tend to him.

"Can you move on your own?" I shout to him. He shakes his head. I look down for the source of his apparent paralysis. I shudder when I see the barbed wire around his foot, which stands directly over an antipersonnel mine. We were carefully warned about this hazard in the Corps. No, this soldier isn't wounded, but if he moves to escape, the mine will explode. He'll be blown up, with Bentley and me in the blast radius. My eyes close, defeated.

Think, Pip, think! Sense urges me. *You can't just give up on him*!

"How wide is the blast radius?" I call to the soldier.

"I don't know. Twenty feet maybe." His voice sounds terrified as I drag Bentley by the shoulders farther away from the mine. My own terror strengthens my arms for this feat.

The trapped soldier cries out, "Hey, you're not gonna just leave me here, are you?"

As Bentley's body jostles over the sand, I see his left foot turned at an unnatural angle.

"Please! I've got a family!" the soldier cries to my back. "A little girl!"

"Keep breathing, Bentley; I've got you," I say softly to him as I move away from him, jogging toward the mine. "I'm not leaving you," I assure the trembling soldier. "I'm not an expert on explosives, but I think that that land mine won't blow up if we keep pressure on it, right?"

"I think; but I can't be sure. Do you got a ciggie?"

I roll my eyes. I'm not going to let him light a smoke over an explosive.

"Just to calm my nerves," he explains shakily.

"I have a plan," I assure him. I need another body. I find a still soldier with brown curls in a heap on his side, and feel for his pulse. Nothing. My arms protest as I pull him toward the mine.

"Aw, no, that's my pal Grayson," the trembling soldier protests. He looks like he's going to be sick.

"What's your name, soldier?"

"Teagan. Private Teagan." he salutes. I can hear his teeth chattering together.

"Well, Private, your buddy Grayson's gonna save your life right now, okay?" He nods, and gulps. "Help me lift him. But don't take your weight off that foot. This could be a dud, but we're not taking any chances today, you hear me?" He nods nervously. Somehow, between Teagan's arm strength and my straining with all of my might, we get Grayson's body upright.

My jaw is clenched, my face bright red, when I say, "Drop him on three, and run like the dickens. One... two... *three*!" I stretch my legs to their absolute widest leap and run hard. My feet sink into the sand with each step. When I'm almost to Bentley, I hear the mine tick.

Teagan throws his body onto mine and we flatten onto the beach. My face presses into the gritty sand under his weight.

Boom! Sand showers down from the blast.

"Grayson!" Teagan screams through his gritted teeth. He wraps his arm around my chest to pull me up and gasps. "You... you're a..." he stutters with wide eyes.

I brush his touch away from my chest, realizing that in the fray I haven't bothered to keep up my disguise in the slightest. I stare at Teagan.

"...a *dame*," he finishes. He steps toward me slowly, then grabs my face with both hands and plants his lips over mine. Sand, ash, and blood are the only barrier I have between our skin. Disgusted, I swat wildly at him and throw myself backward.

"And a *married* one!" I cry, though my cheeks are pink. I wipe away his kiss, which leaves a smear of sand and blood on my face.

"You saved my life," he says. "I had to thank you." His eyes shift to the blast, and his shoulders fall. "Grayson," he whispers, slipping into shock. His eyes glass over. I try to distract him from the exploded remains of his buddy. Though he's grieving, I need his hands to help me save Bentley.

"You can thank me by putting pressure on this guy's neck," I direct him sternly. "Your pal was already gone. Let's make sure this one makes it, okay?"

Teagan merely nods. Shakily, he drops to his knees by my brother-in-law and presses his palms over the side of his neck.

I scramble to Bentley's foot to assess the damage there. When I lift his pant leg, I gasp, "Oh, no."

His ankle is attached to his leg only by about an inch of stringy flesh. I squeeze my eyes shut and run my sandy, bloody forearm across my brows. I have no idea how to save or preserve his ability to walk. Images of Bentley chasing after little Jack, tossing a football in a grassy field, and wrestling on the rug flash through my mind. He needs this foot. Quickly, I dust the wound with a thick coat of sulfa powder and wrap it in gauze.

The foot's no good to him without a beating heart, Sense reminds me, and I turn my attention back to his neck wound.

"Don't you dare die on me, Sharpe; I've been through enough trouble for you!" I growl at him while I stuff more gauze on under Teagan's fingers. Brilliant red soaks to the surface as though it's gasping for air.

"Claire," Bentley murmurs.

"Is this your husband?" Teagan asks, apparently noting that the soldierly professionalism I'd treated him with has melted away to reveal the frantic desperation of a loved one. "Are you Claire?"

"Claire," Bentley murmurs again.

"No. But he's the father of my child," I say hastily, "and he needs to live, do you understand me?" Teagan's brows fly up, surprised. In a glance, I can see his perspective in my eyes: I'm a married gal posing as a man, dedicated enough to refuse his kiss, but rescuing the father of my illegitimate child, who moans the name of another woman. I don't have the time or care to tend to this soldier's curiosity on the matter.

I look around in the haze of carnage, frantic. As though it shines like a bright beacon, one of the nets that carries wounded men back to the medic ship catches my eye as it's lowered five yards away. I know that endless packages of clean medical supplies, real doctors, and piles of boxes of morphine injections await them on the ship. Ten bodies, some twisting in agony, some as still as death, lie between us and that net.

As the net settles into the sand, boots step over Bentley's face. Medics all around us move their wounded toward it. I have seconds to move him into the net before it's full. If we don't make this one, Bentley's chances of survival are slim. I can't very well tourniquet his neck and cut off the blood supply to his brain. He's bleeding profusely and every bandage from my kit is piled on the gash, soaked through and dripping into the sand. I don't even use the sulfa. It would be wasted, running off his neck with the blood and soaking into the sand.

"Help me move him," I bark at Teagan, who won't meet my eyes.

Thunk. I feel a spray of sand litter my lower leg. The next thing I know, Teagan gasps, letting go of Bentley's wound.

"No!" I cry as blood stains Teagan's chest.

His eyes roll backward, and he topples to the sand. "Help," he coughs. He sucks in a breath, and I hear it whistle out through the hole in his chest. The shot must have passed right through his lung.

"Help me, please," he wheezes, blood dribbling from his lips. My breath quickens. I'm out of supplies! I don't even have a drip of morphine left to ease his pain.

It's too late anyway, Sense points out. *Teagan is dead.*

"P!" a high voice screeches desperately.

My head snaps up, and the struggling forms of Willa and Birdie working together to heave a body toward me steals my attention. Weak, lifeless arms dangle from over their shoulders; an unconscious head bobs between them. The soldier is almost completely covered in soot, though a few strands of his brilliant hair show through the ash.

Coppery gold hair.

TWENTY-SEVEN

My heart leaps.

"Phin!" I gasp as Bentley's leg slips from my hands. I murmur an apology through the rush of relief that blows through me, and I pick up the mangled foot I've let thunk into the sand without taking my eyes off of Phin. I grimace as I see that my mistake has covered Bentley's clean bandage in clumps of bloody sand. My newly invigorated legs work fast to get to that net. I hastily place Bentley next to another body, his head rocking listlessly.

Birdie and Willa look strained under Phin's dead weight, but their eyes are steeled with iron determination. My calves scream as I run back toward them. The sand under my boots feels like melted marshmallow, sucking my heels down into it with each labored step. Phin's eyes are closed, but there is no mistaking it's him. His jaw is slack, and the feet that drag through the sand behind him are charred black. Angry red flesh is exposed from his heels to his ribs through his burned clothing.

"Is he…?" I can't finish asking the question, in case the answer is too awful to bear.

"I can feel him breathing," Willa tells me breathlessly. Her pained expression admits that she doesn't know how much longer his breaths will last. "But he's been burned badly." Unconsciousness has been granted him by some merciful angel.

Once, I burned my wrist on a frying pan-- the raw, red flesh had pulsated with heat for days, exploding into waves of relentless pain at the slightest touch of my sleeve. That feeling, multiplied over most of his body, would arrest him if he were conscious. It would kill him. Phin needs a real medic, not three rookie nurses pretending to know what they're doing! My box is empty of morphine syringes, as empty as my limp, exhausted shell of a body. I whip my head back to the net. Its ropes start to close over Bentley and the two other bloodied bodies lying beside him.

My shriek, "Wait! One more!" echoes with enough desperation to halt the pilot. No one has ever screamed with more fervor. As the three of us carefully lower Phin next to Bentley, I notice that Bentley's pallor greys by the second as a deep red puddle grows steadily under his neck. He needs pressure on the wound to staunch the flow, or he'll die before he reaches the ship.

Hoarse cries ring out behind me of, "Medic! Please, medic!" but at the sight of Bentley's life oozing out of him, I realize that my mind was made up long before I made it to this beach. I came to watch over Bentley, and I can't let him die. Without pressure on his wound, he'll bleed out in transport. If I leave the beach so I can save a life, *this* precious life, then I am worthy to have fought my way here. I fling myself over his body, belly to belly, and slap my dirty palm over the soaked gauze to staunch the flow while the net tightens around us. For once, my mule-like stubbornness will count for something.

With my left leg stretched over Phin's body, I push the net away from his hip with the toe of my boot to keep it from cutting into his raw wounds. While my body screams with the discomfort of this pose, we begin to rise from the beach. The net forces our bodies in more tightly, and I grunt through my teeth as my foot strains the rope away from Phin. I find Willa's and Birdie's faces below us.

"I'm out of supplies," I pant through the ropes to my friends. "Please, help the rest of them!"

Willa nods. Her eyes look stunned as she watches us lift. Bentley's blood drips onto the shoulder of her dirty white uniform. She doesn't even notice, as the pull toward the hundreds of wounded men still on the beach snares her.

"Keep him alive," Birdie's mouth forms. Her face, streaked with sand and blood and the dirty soot of Phin's head, disappears into the shrinking mass of figures below me on the beach. I'm not sure who she means, but I don't intend to let go of either of them.

Being carted through the frigid air is the strangest sensation. I could feel like a bird, if it weren't for the bodies mashed close and the cut of the net into my skin. The rush of cold coagulates the blood on Bentley's neck. I can't feel relieved, because adrenaline courses through me.

I continue encouraging Bentley, "Stay with me. You can't go yet. Stay. Think of Claire; think of little Jack." There's no way he can hear me over the roar of the chopper, even with my lips at his ear, but the words tumble out regardless.

My leg over Phin's body hugs his thigh. I wriggle, grunting, with my free hand outstretched to feel his sooted skin. Pale and freckled; dead under my fingers.

"Phin! Don't you go anywhere!" I urge through clenched teeth, using my voice as extra arms.

Keep fighting!

I force my body weight to roll toward him, clawing my outstretched fingers toward the hollow just below his jaw. The tips of my fingers absorb a weak, intermittent thudding just below his skin.

Bee-dum.

Bee-dum.

Bee-dum.

He's still in there, but he slips further away with each long pause between beats. My own pulse hops erratically, as though it can make up the difference for his weak one with its vigor.

Bee-dum.

"Phin!" I screech at his slack face. "You can*not* do this! You can*not* go now!" My fist thuds into his chest as a howl rips from my lungs. It may as well be silent for how quickly the sound is swallowed up in the other noises--the rhythmic sweep of the chopper blades, the staccato pop of gunfire, the chorus of desperate cries for medical attention--all swallowed up in the whistle of the frigid wind. I squeeze his cheeks between my angry thumb and fingers, jostling his face, trying to force life into it. He's so still, but not like sleeping, where life simmers just under his sleep-slackened face. No, the dirtied, singed face with me now almost seems like a different body without Phin lighting it up; terrifyingly hollow.

You're losing it, Sense warns me. *This is exactly why you shouldn't treat your own man.*

I curse at her soothing voice to shut her up. There's just no room inside of me for sensibility at a time like this! The voices in my head fall quiet, leaving only the rattling of a frantic hamster wheel turning inside.

Bee- dum.

"Phineas O'Shea, you stay with me! We're almost there, you see? There's the ship. And the doctors! Don't go yet, Phin!" I feel my stomach drop as we begin to descend.

Bee-

"Don't do this to me, Phin! I can't lose another husband! I swear to you, I just won't survive it! Do you want me to rot away and die without you? Phin!" I scream, clinging to his neck.

dum.

Our clump of bloodied bodies lower onto the deck, and the gripping hold of the net releases my indented skin.

I rise to my knees, straddling Bentley's middle, and I shriek, "Two wounded here!" I wave my free hand frantically, hoping I can get the clean, rested medics on deck to see my boys first. I will them to be blind to the other bodies, just as I'm blind to the two other men. I continue to press down on Bentley's wound with one palm and hold hooked fingers under Phin's jaw with the other.

Bee- dum.

Clean, uniformed medics rush toward us with a stretcher. I sigh with relief, perhaps even deeper than the relief I'd felt after delivering my baby.

Bee-

However, the remaining breath left in my chest is knocked out by some invisible wrecking ball, stealing the warm blanket of relief along with it as they reach for one of the other wounded soldiers. Not Phin, not Bentley. Someone *else*. Not my husband. Not the man I'd chosen to be my child's father. Empty of breath and warmth, I choke on my own cold stupor.

dum.

The medics carefully lift the stranger's limp, bleeding body, and I give one of them a nasty, perplexed look. They are supposed to rush Phin away for care, and rush back for Bentley. That was the plan!

Your plan, not their plan. Sense's words sound off in my head.

"What are you doing? These two are dying!"

"Triage," the medic huffs out in a crusty voice that surely matches the disgusted look on my face. To him, Bentley has what he supposes to be a medic treating him, not the less-trained nurse I really am. If I thought anything I'd learned in training would save him now, I'd feel comforted, but my mind races with anxiety and any useful knowledge is lost in the tumbling blur of exhaustion.

Phin lies stone still. However, I can tell that the fourth man, lying grey and perfectly still, hasn't survived the net transfer.

Free from this fight, Imp observes. *Lucky fella.*

A fresh set of medics rush in right behind the first, looking to me for direction on which soldier to take. Their eyes ask me to choose who gets the better shot at surviving.

I balk at the responsibility of such a choice. I'm frantic as my eyes dart between Bentley and Phin. The two mangled men under me represent my full and happy life, and little Jack's full and happy life. If I choose Phin, and Bentley dies waiting for treatment, then I have killed him for my own selfish purposes. If I urge them to take Bentley first, and Phin's body gives up fighting the immeasurable pain, then I'll wither back into being a widow, as empty and fragile as dust in a storm.

Neither option allows me the freedom of happiness.

"This man first," I direct them to Bentley with my nose. His thickened blood seeps through my fingers. "I used up all my plasma before I found him. He'll die if you don't treat him, *now!*" He's stopped moaning; I think he's passed out. While they load Bentley, I keep my hands tightly clamped over his wound.

A second stretcher follows, and when the medic's eyes scan over the blood covering my body, I quickly explain, "Their blood, not mine," so that even a second isn't wasted tending to me. My heart pinches hard, but I have to leave Phin behind so I can keep pressure on Bentley's neck. I'll have to trust the next team of medics to care for him without my hovering presence. My heart whispers an apology to Phin's still form as I shuffle alongside the stretcher. My eyes are glued to him, my feet guided blindly by my hold on Bentley.

This could be the last time that I see Phin alive.

My arms move along with the stretcher, merely as a medical tool for Bentley's neck wound. As a dozen boots hastily clomp across the deck toward the treatment area, I hear the Naval commander's direction to the pilot behind us: "Take the deceased man back to the beach to be buried." I glance back and see his arms are gesturing wildly.

"Are you crazy?" shouts the pilot. "That's a *suicide* mission! I'm not risking my neck or theirs!" he counters, jerking his head to indicate that there are at least hundreds more wounded waiting. The commander standing comfortably on deck in his clean uniform, has no idea what it's like on that beach. Blood, horror, fear, carnage, wailing, despair. You can't have any idea, unless you've witnessed the horror firsthand, up close and personal. I hope my friends still wading through the fray will make it through this.

Bentley and the team swarming around him move as one into a small room on the ship. I assist while a senior medic furiously tends to the ugly gash on his neck. I'm handed a syringe.

"The thigh, please," I'm directed. I plunge the needle into his upper thigh, watching Bentley's slackened face not even react as I do. I take in the room. Certainly no sterile operating room; just a medium-sized table with two feet of clearance around it. Perhaps it's a small kitchen or a lounge. At least there's a sink.

Somehow, the medic has stopped the never-ending flow of Bentley's blood.

"Sulfa," he directs, and I dust the wound with the powder.

"Must've hit the carotid artery. This fella's lucky you were there," the doctor observes behind his mask. I can't see his mouth, but his eyes show his admiration for my care of this patient. If only he knew what this patient means to me! Still, my guilt for leaving the endless need on the beach subsides with the doctor's comment.

Now that the parameters of the gash are visible, I'm shocked to see that it is not very large. A medic covers and wraps the wound, while another secures a plasma bottle to his arm and steps back. I stare at him.

"It's all we can do for now," he says. "Got dying men waiting, and he'll keep for a few hours," he explains, though he also seems disturbed by how little we can offer the injured. I don't want Bentley to "keep" for a few hours. I want him to keep for years and years, so he can watch over and protect my son!

"Check his ankle first," I press them, scurrying to Bentley's feet and exposing his dirty bandage. Like flies to honey, they swarm in on the wound.

After a fresh bandage, Bentley is carefully settled into a line of treated soldiers on deck. Their fresh white bandages look stark against their dirty grey skin, and most of them lie eerily still. One uniform doesn't match the rest: the surviving soldier from the net who was given priority over Phin and Bentley.

The dark tan of his uniform and the red band on his arm suddenly seem like a beacon to me. He's a *Nazi!* I bristle at the realization that this life took precedence over my boys. *Aren't his comrades busy picking off our countrymen? What were those medics thinking?*

I'm reminded by Sense, *Geneva Convention.* I remember this concept clearly from my training in the Corps, only it's jarring when it's real. Once an enemy soldier is wounded and can't fight, they can surrender and become a prisoner of war. It sounds gentille and pretty in a textbook, humane, even; but who's to say that this man didn't cause Phin's burns, or shoot a bullet across Bentley's neck?

I quickly examine the others laying side to side like soldier sardines on the deck; American soldiers. With Bentley secure, I rush to find Phin.

"O'Shea? Where's Private O'Shea being treated? The burn victim?" I beg the medical teams.

"Burn vic's in there," a medic with a gruff bark answers with a jerk of his head. My feet carry me in that direction before I even realize that I'd asked them to move, but I'm stopped before I make it to the door.

"Grouse!" the senior medic shouts. "We need you here!" It takes a second too long for me to remember that I'm Grouse.

"*Grouse!*" he barks, louder. I run toward his crouched figure with my eyes still trained on Phin's treatment room doorway.

"Assist us here," the medic directs, and I hurry to the unmanned corner of a stretcher. We lift it together, and move away from Phin's treatment room. I feel my heart reach out for his doorway, while reason tells me I've got to move forward. I have a duty to perform.

The faster we treat this man, the faster I can get to Phin, I assure myself.

TWENTY-EIGHT

"Wash your hands, Grouse," the medic says when we reach the operating room. "You're filthy." I look down at my palms. Sooty, bloodied, barely recognizable as my own.

Hastily, I rinse my dirty palms and fingers at the sink, where sand and rust-tinged water circles the drain. Without saying much, we get to work treating soldiers' wounds hastily, but effectively, one after the other. My mind slips into a clinical mode as I work alongside the medics. After our third patient is quickly treated and carried away, I don't even bother to look at the victim's faces anymore.

When we settle another patched-up soldier in the same line as Bentley, I check on him. His rising and falling chest and clean bandage reassure me; his wound has finally stopped bleeding. I rush back to the treatment rooms to find Phin.

"Where's Ph- Private O'Shea?" I ask, deepening my voice when I remember that I need to pass as a man.

"Still on I.V.," I'm told, and I sigh with relief. They wouldn't bother with him if he'd died. My aching legs run to find him. I peek inside the door, and watch a medic picking small pieces of shrapnel out of Phin's calf.

"Can I give you a hand?" I offer hopefully.

"There's another set of these in the dish," the man replies without looking up from his tweezers. His hands seem steady and skilled as they work, probably far steadier than mine will be working on my husband. I reach for the second set of tweezers.

"Grouse! Over here!" a different medic calls before my hands close around the instrument. "Whatever you're doing, this is more important!" I grit my teeth and turn my back on Phin.

Again, I tear myself away from Phin uncertainly, hoping those steady hands I left him in will care for him properly. Hordes of soldiers await treatment, but I know that the carnage worse on the beach. I wonder how Annie, Willa, and Birdie are managing, and squeeze my eyes against the images in my head. As dirty as the soldiers, especially with the soot from Phin smeared on Birdie and Willa, I hope their bright red medic's crosses are still visible enough to keep them safe from enemy fire. I feel miles away from that nightmare, though it has been less than thirty minutes since I've escaped into this one. The need is endless; we work without pause. I've become a machine. I don't see the torn flesh for what it is.

Many missed meals later, I'm trembling all over while I open my sixty-third packet of sulfa powder of the day. My muscles ache with the effort, and I realize the last time I've eaten is four-thirty a.m.; nearly twelve hours ago. Officer Luszeck notices my exhaustion when I drop the legs of a soldier onto the table. I am immediately ordered to eat and rest. I simply nod in assent.

Free from duty, I rush down the long line of bandaged men to find Phin and Bentley. My burning curiosity drags my limp body toward them, giddy with liberation. When I see most of the soldiers sitting up, smoking, and talking in the twilight, my stomach bottoms out with relief. I skid to my knees beside Phin's feet, and hastily crawl up and straddle him. I press two fingers under his jawbone. Weak, steady beats thrill my fingers. He's alive!

"It's touch and go with that one, eh?" a medic comments as he passes us, lighting a cigarette.

"Huh?" I ask. I examine his face, and realize he's the man who had been carefully removing bits of shrapnel from Phin's leg hours ago.

"Let's just say the doc's counting on his spot on the deck opening up anytime now." He gives me a pointed look before moving on, muttering, "Guess I wasted my time cleaning him up."

Tumultuous tremors shake my limbs with his words. *If the doctor doesn't expect Phin to make it, then how can I?*

"Wait!" I shriek after him. He turns back to me, annoyed, as he sucks a long drag from his cigarette.

"What do you mean? What's so wrong with him that it can't be treated?" I beg.

He scoffs as though the answer is obvious. "Third degree burns, miles from any real medical facility? We can't perform debridement here! And the risk of infection in all those open sores is at at least one hundred percent, if you ask me." He takes another drag, squinting at my shocked expression.

I rack my brain for solutions. "Did you give him penicillin?"

"I administered it myself," he replies.

"And sulfa powder?" That combination should annihilate any bacteria.

"Of course. But if the poor guy wakes up, the shock of the pain will kill him before any infection could set in!"

"Morphine?" I squeak in desperation.

"The maximum dose!" he grits between his teeth. "What, is he your girlfriend or something?"

"Actually," I mumble, "he's my husband."

The medic's cigarette falls to the deck, forgotten. With my admission, his frustration melts away, and his eyes go soft.

"Sorry, I didn't mean to be so harsh, um, Ma'am. I'm sure there's hope for him."

"Thank you," I whisper quietly as he turns to leave.

"Uh, um, may I ask…" he starts, his question trailing off.

"No, I'm not supposed to be here," I admit. "Please don't tell anyone about me."

"Are you the only, uh, lady on board?"

"Yes," I lie. I don't want to incriminate my friends after their sacrifice on my behalf.

"Oh," he replies, looking stunned and slightly disappointed. "I'll get your man another bag of fluids."

"Thank you," I whimper, my chin trembling uncontrollably. I squeeze my eyes shut, and wipe the tracks of tears from my cheeks. I'm not doing a lick of good blubbering. I crawl to Bentley, and find him awake and talking to the soldier offering food and cigarettes to the patients. His eyelids flutter with disbelief as he examines my face.

"Penny?" he questions as his head turns carefully toward me. My new tears, tears of relief, splash onto his chest.

"Yes, Bentley; but *shhh*," I urge him as I press my finger to my lips. "I'll explain later." He sighs and closes his eyes, looking slightly more content than when I'd found him.

When the medic returns with a fresh I.V. for Phin, I try not to hover as he inserts the large needle, slips in the tube, and hangs the bottle from the railing. He's being cared for. All I can do is wait.

With this knowledge, the adrenaline has drained away and fatigue cramps my legs. I stumble to a coil of rope across from Bentley's feet and I snuggle into it. Before I can even register how uncomfortable I am with my face pressed up against the scratchy coils, I'm unconscious.

The next morning, consciousness greets me with a sheen of sweat and a rolling stomach. The sun tells me it's been over twenty-four hours since I've had anything to eat, but bile presses on my throat all the same.

A boot nudges me.

"Oi," says the owner. "Spam and eggs?"

The savory smell of breakfast eases my nausea, and my fingers gratefully accept the tray. I shovel three forkfuls into my mouth before I remember the boys. My eyes search for them, and I find Bentley propped up with a nearly empty plate. If he's eating, he's on the mend! I swallow a partially-chewed, baseball-sized mouthful of Spam and smear the tears from my face with my forearm. A resounding sigh of relief escapes me. Bentley's storm has passed.

Phin. Phin still seems unconscious. I crawl to him and feel for his femoral artery. I can feel that blood still moves through him. I jostle his leg, but he doesn't respond. *Why isn't he awake yet?* I start to crawl up to his head, so I can whisper some encouragement to him. *Wake up,* I'll whisper into his ear. *I'm here. Come back to me.*

"Grouse," a familiar voice calls. I look up to find Willa striding toward me, a rueful grin dancing about her lips. She is absolutely filthy.

I embrace her, and she uses our closeness to whisper, "We're found out," into my ear.

My chest tightens. "The girls?" I whisper.

"They're fine. Busy. C'mon."

"But Phin's still unconscious," I say.

Willa stops a passing surgeon by gripping his upper arm. "Private O'Shea is still unconscious. What do you make of that?" she asks in her gruff voice.

The exhausted-looking surgeon looks Phin over, feeling for the drum of his heart. "It's better for him to be out. Burns are sheer torture. He's still breathing, and unless he gets an infection in those wounds, he'll make it back to the States for proper treatment." We wait for some kind of direction. "Nothing can be done for him right now," the surgeon confirms. "Just keep him clean and treated with iodine and fresh bandages. And if he wakes… God help him. He'll need all the morphine on this ship."

Nervously, my feet follow after Willa's into a room where Officer Luszeck sits at a small table, drumming his thick fingers.

"Please, sit, ladies," he directs us, obviously displeased. My breath catches in my throat as he says, "ladies". Willa gives me a sideways glance, and my chest is about to explode with anxiety.

"I don't even know where to begin. This sort of infraction-ugh." He shakes his head as he removes his cap. He leans forward and runs a hand through his thinning hair. "This is a serious breach of policy. I can't say we didn't need you desperately here yesterday, but if it goes public that we had women amongst our medics…" The struggle in his voice calms me a little; punishment does not seem imminent.

"This mission is already going down in history as largely flawed. If the papers get word that we had girls on that beach," he says as though he's going to be sick, "and that you weren't caught on board beforehand? Aggh! We'll be the prey of the American public; the world! Women? Oh, *my*..." He shakes his head. "They'll eat us alive for this. Not to mention the fact that this country needs to know that they've thrown their support behind the best and the strongest. We need to provide them hope, not foolish pranks!" He sits back in his chair. "The nurses' ship is due here within the hour. If the two of you can quietly slip back into their numbers, we need you on that beach. There's more to do than that shipful of girls can manage."

Our combined sighs of relief are audible.

"Do I have your word that you'll keep this under your hats?"

We nod eagerly. I don't know about Willa, but my nerves can't handle much more of this.

"Tell the other ladies to go with you and keep their traps shut. Now get out of my sight!" he grumbles. We skirt eagerly out of the room.

"And, uh…" he adds before we clear the doorway, "maybe dunk a few times in the water on the way over, both of you. You look like hell."

TWENTY-NINE

There is no rest for the medical teams. The beach, now eerily absent of gunfire, is littered with the bodies of fallen soldiers. Corpses roll in the lapping waves. It is our job to sort through them, and recover those still clinging desperately to life. Willa, Birdie, Annie and I, battle-worn and exhausted, must fight to keep up the appearance of nurses who have freshly arrived. The clean jackets we have acquired are the only things fresh about us. Yesterday was soul-sucking; the four of us are drained.

Tents have been erected to treat the men. It is complete mayhem inside ours, with barely enough room to shuffle sideways in between cots.

"There's not much that can be done for the ones in the cots near the back. Just reapply the sulfa and find the ones who need another round of morphine. All you can do really is hold a hand and lend an ear," the head nurse directs us.

I look down the line of cots, hopeless cases who have been suffering through the night, just waiting to slip away into death. I sigh, flooded with feeling, wondering if Jack had had a hand to hold as he died. In honor of him, in his memory, I would willingly remain in the horror of this tent. Each bed holds a boy whose family awaits a return that may never come.

I begin with a small soldier who could very well be a boy. Sergeant Daniel Crane, his tag tells me. He moans quietly while his hastily-applied bandages become soaked with his blood. He is wrapped like a mummy, only his left shoulder and arm and one sleeping eye visible through the fabric.

"St-stay with me." I make out the plea from his dirty, trembling lips. I still myself, willing my ears to hear the words. His exposed eye flutters, and the limp hand I hold suddenly grips mine. "Don't... leave... me." His frantic message comes in quickened breaths. The small patch of brow above his eye beads with sweat. His boyish desperation causes my heart to clench painfully.

"I'm right here," I soothe. His hand relaxes; his breaths slow. As I dab the sweat from his brow, his chest deflates with a heavy breath. He does not refill his lungs.

I'm so stunned that I can't release my hold on the boy's hand. I'd never touched a dead person before yesterday, let alone held one as they passed on. With tears staining my cheeks, I lower my head and raise my hand, signaling that the bed will become freshly available.

A pudgy hand rests comfortingly on my back. "Moof on to da next. De all net you," a nurse prods with sympathy in her voice. I slip my hand out of his, and the Sergeant's hands falls limply onto the sheets, fingers splayed. Though I am horror-stricken at what has just occurred, I choke back the sobs that try beating their way out of my throat. *There is nowhere I would rather be than with this young boy, so desperate for comfort in his final moments. If I can be of use, some sort of death angel, I will. For them, and for him.*

For Jack.

When I turn to stand, I see the face of the fellow nurse who had encouraged me to keep working. I know her!

"Nurse Adler." I nod to her. This isn't the moment for a happy reunion.

"Hello, Hale," she replies, making my maiden name sound like "*Hell*". Indeed: *Hello, Hell; we've entered your gates.* Watching the bravest of young boys in pain, slipping into death is absolute purgatory.

"I alvays knew you'd become a nurse. You vere von of da good ones," she offers, nodding. "But, don't lose your focus; menny neet you. Get to verk."

Treating the others isn't so hard after that first patient, once I have adopted a purpose. Some of them fall into sleep instead of death, and I can move on to provide comfort to another. While the dead are carried out of the folds of the tent, triaged soldiers take their beds while the leftover warmth of life still lingers there. I begin seeking out the worst of the hopeless, guiding them to a comfortable death.

The very worst case under this tent is in the bed at the far wall. A man lies there, not posed neatly as the other men are, with their straight legs tucked under a thin blanket, calm arms over the blanket, but thrashing and tangled in his coverings. Even as he sleeps, he twists in agony, one arm held tightly to his chest, the other hanging limply over the side of his bed. His legs have been restrained to keep him from tumbling off the cot. His arms should be restrained as well, but the shredded, burned flesh surely can't withstand the firm hold of tightly-wrapped fabric, especially when he is conscious. Every time he touches upon consciousness, he thrashes and screams, making the monstrous appearance of his red flesh all the more frightening. The long, tangled hair peeking out of his bandages makes him seem all the more feral.

"Can't somebody spare a little morphine for that poor gent?" I whisper to another nurse.

"He's had a whole box! Five is the limit for this dose. It won't touch him," she shrugs.

"Yeah, if you can't stay ahead of the pain…" I begin.

"It'll eat you alive," she finishes for me.

I shudder for the poor soul lying in that cot. Nurse Adler tends to him herself, repeating the same gentle words with each fit, palms clasped over the healthy, unscathed spots on his forearms. She leans over him, effectively holding his arms down with the weight of her body, with her face very close to his, whispering to him. When his body is forced to be still this way, his breathing slows, and he's lulled back to sleep by her soft words.

It's difficult to keep from looking his way. Such a tortured soul lies in that bed. Each convulsion is merely a physical manifestation of how everyone on this beach feels. This is by far the most gut-wrenching experience of my life. The depths of hell, ripped open, licking flames all about us. People, little boys, are mangled and dying here. These are not *criminals* in agony, which might seem just, but our country's bravest young men. Not surrounded by loved ones; just a feeble group of nurses trying in vain to soothe their wounds and their souls.

Hours pass by. I don't watch the time. Surely my subconscious has been counting the loud ticks of the clock, but I keep time by the soldier's fits, which occur about twice an hour. They become shorter and milder as we break through midnight and into the next day, almost unnoticed. Nurse Adler's round head begins to bob, eyelids fluttering. Without the immediate danger of his disturbing shrieks, her adrenaline will no longer carry her. She trembles, sits straight up, then fades again.

With my own patient now sleeping soundly, a fresh dressing on his head, I slip over to the bed at the end of the room. I rouse Nurse Adler and urge her to go and catch a bit of sleep. Her eyes are unfocused as she nods and leaves, and I know that she could easily sleep on a coil of ropes without a problem. Sitting so close to my newest charge, I can see that his sleep cannot possibly be as restful as it appeared from across the tent. He pants; perspiring, balling his fists. The ragged locks of his dirty hair are slick with sweat. From time to time, his exhausted body goes completely limp. The respites are not long.

I can see how Nurse Adler was so quick to catch an oncoming convulsion. Though his face is nearly covered completely, I see it coming when his chest deflates with an exaggerated exhale, then he sucks in a sharp breath, again exhaling far more breath than he had taken in. Three quick pants later, his body begins to thrash. I position myself as I had seen Adler do, holding the only patches of his arms with healthy pink flesh. I had not heard her words to him.

I will have to use my own.

The only comforting words I know are from songs. "*Summertime, and the livin' is easy*," I begin to sing in a whisper.

The bandaged head stops rocking side to side and his arms relax under my weight.

"*When the fish are jumpin', and the cotton is high.*"

A labored, muddled croak comes from beneath the bandages. Nurse Adler had gotten him to calm and sleep with her words, but he seems alert at mine. He moans again. I can tell it is difficult for him to make the sound, so I gently shush him.

"Whiskey?" Willa appears beside me with the common bottle of liquid painkiller, her voice much louder than my song. The most imperceptible hum comes from behind the bandages. The way she's styled her pixie haircut looks adorable, while I'm sure that mine looks like a mangy dog who's had an unfortunate run-in with some clippers.

"Let's see here," I say, cautiously unwrapping the lower half of his face for my examination. There is no telling what's under these bandages. A gaping hole where an eye should be, like Colonel Wade, exposed teeth with no lips, or a shrapnel-severed skull.

Oh, these poor fellas. The quick death so many of their comrades were granted was so much more merciful than slow death, or disfigurement.

Patchy facial hair covers this patient's chin. I wrinkle my nose.

"What do you make of this?" I whisper to Willa. All these soldiers are pretty dirty and battle-worn, but this guy looks downright neglected. The blood-crusted end of a large gash peeks out from the still-bandaged upper portion of the soldier's face, but his lips are intact. I slide an uneasy hand behind his head and raise it slightly.

She shrugs and lifts the bottle to his lips. "The head nurse insisted he get this."

His adam's apple bounces as he swallows, grunting.

"Whiskey!" a hoarse voice pleads out from across the tent. Willa hurries away toward the sound.

With cotton and alcohol, I dab at the wound through his facial hair. The chin winces as he draws a sharp breath.

"It needs to be clean to heal," I whisper to the visible earlobe.

He exhales in surrender. Tentatively, the cotton makes its way toward the gash. I feel the pricks on my neck that alert me I am being stared at, and when I look over my shoulder, I notice that a nurse has her eyes trained on me, appraising what I'm doing. I can see that she would disapprove of anything I could do that would provoke a fit, especially something as long-sighted as preventing infection in this hopelessly doomed soldier. His thrashing and moaning fits upset everyone in the room. But at the moment, he is not fighting me, and something in me feels protective toward him. I have to do something, so I continue.

I work especially carefully near the gash. With tweezers, I remove small pieces of shrapnel from the part I can see, and then I dust on the Sulfa. It is not horribly deep, perhaps only an inch, but it will need stitches.

"Doe needs stitches," I tell the cynical nurse. She rolls her eyes and crosses her two index fingers, silently indicating a hopeless case that medical attention should not be wasted on.

My stony glare communicates that I do not believe in hopeless cases. She throws up her hands and retreats out of my eyeline.

"Listen, I have to go away for a minute," I whisper to him. "I need you to be good, okay? I have to go get a doctor to fix up this cheek, and I can't have you throwing yourself about and yelling, hear me?"

He doesn't audibly respond, but shows his obedience with stillness.

But as I had suspected, every doctor is busily engaged in crude surgery. I have to remind myself that while this soldier is my charge, other men need care more desperately. I am promised that they will check in when they finish. I return to Doe, still lying still. His sooty chin is clenched though, and I can see that his stillness is a real effort for him.

"That's a good fella," I say and recognize a maternal note in my voice. "I have to cut away this hair before we can patch you up." I hold up a straight razor in my hand. "Have you ever met one of these?" I tease, even though his eyes are covered. "You don't want to get in a fight with a straight razor, Pal, so hold still." My tongue peeks through my lips as I hunch down and carefully shave away the facial hair surrounding the wound.

I begin to unwrap the upper half of his face with care. Ever so gently, I cut away stripes of fur with the straight razor. A small heap of dark hairs grows on the blade. I dip the blade into a bowl of water to clear it, and the lump dissipates into hundreds of single hairs floating on the water's surface. On my third stroke, I stop short. Just next to the gash's widest gape, at the apple of my patient's cheek, I've uncovered a large, distinctive freckle. The straight razor clatters against the cot and falls to the sandy floor as my hands fall slack.

I know this face.

THIRTY

Realization hits me like the blasting updraft of Niagra Falls. The truth roars like tumultuous falling water and blasts me in the face; my limbs stunned by the electric jolt coursing through me. My hands, still posed over his face, tremble while my mind's eye flies through a tunnel of pictures. I catch my breath, but I cannot control its rapid shallowness. This man, this tortured soul who mirrors my own shredded core, who is suffering this cruel, brutal ending, is… *him*.

My mouth, held in a bobbing "o" shape, releases a croaking shriek. Clumsy fingers tear away the remaining bandages, shaking wildly as I stammer, "J-Jack?"

He hums with effort, "H-hmm!"

I throw the nest of dirty bandages carelessly to the ground. Sooty, battle-worn and bloody though his face is, it is like seeing a falling star.

"Jack!" I cry, grasping his head between my hands. To the naked eye, the head I hold looks ridiculous: blistered, red skin from his cheekbones to his hairline, where stringy, dirty hair hangs long and heavy from his scalp. The long scruff of a beard on his cheeks look like a different man's beside the clean lines I've made with the razor. Under the beard, in stark contrast to the upper half of his face, the skin is pale white where it was protected by the matted fur. His eyes crack open with feeble effort.

"Jack, it's me!" my voice is shaking, I realize, because my entire body is in tremors.

He hums again, sighs, and promptly passes out. His breath is steady, so I rake his features for confirmation. His lashes, long and straight, are familiar, though singed to the lid on the left. I have seen this straight, strong nose from every angle. His sun-parched lips are swollen and disfigured, but unmistakably his. As I examine his features, memories of them flood my head. Tears stream from my eyes; I don't blink them away. The light feel of them is nothing against the elation that fills my chest.

When he wakes again, he's more alert than I've seen him. He has abandoned his thrashing and holds himself relatively still, except for a giant grin that widens the gaping gash on his cheek.

"Don't! Don't smile!" I cry out at him with nurse's concern. It is not me who says it, because all I have wanted for years is to see that grin again, somewhere outside of my head. And here he is.

"How... I thought," I whisper through the hand clapped over my mouth. "I got a letter... it said your plane was shot down. Savvy said you'd been shot before your plane took a nosedive; that it wasn't twenty seconds before the whole thing exploded! You were presumed dead... I mean, they have to say that when there are no... remains except for a handful of ashes. How can you be here? How are you *alive?*"

My voice rises as close to a shriek as the whispering will allow. My brain struggles to reconcile the person in front of me against the pilot who died in an explosion. Suddenly, another hot emotion bubbles up through the happy ones. The difference in temperature creates a storm in me. A building, raging storm. My brows settle deep into anger, low over my eyes.

"*Why* are you alive?" I accuse. It occurs to me that if Jack has been alive all this time, he should have contacted me. I realize with growing heat that the deepest aches of raw sorrow I lived in could have been spared, if he had just cared enough to notify me of his well-being! All of the tears that dripped off of my chin for him were wasted! How could he allow me to have shed them? I watch his Adam's apple move, and the pain it causes on his face as he tries to form an explanation. The anger I feel crushes the ribbon of sympathy I want to feel before it can fully form. He does not deserve my sympathy; he has had enough of my emotions.

I punch his shoulder, and strain through my teeth, "*Where* have you *been*?" I see the pain on his face, from my punch or from my question, rising above the influence of the morphine in his veins.

"I fought," he strains, coughing. His voice is painfully hoarse. I want to know exactly what that means. I want him to recount every minute that I mourned for him; my chest burns desperately for an explanation like my lungs burn for air when I am underwater for too long, but speaking is clearly painful for him. Even the two words he has offered grated his throat. The thin ribbon of my sympathy for him fights to my surface, now thick as a braided cord of rope. He really is in terrible shape. Threads of guilt weave into my already complicated emotions. It seems my body just does not know how to react to what is happening. How can someone prepare for something like this? His throat rattles as he draws in a deep breath, but I silence him by gently pressing my fingers to his lips. They feel dry and cracked.

He sighs gratefully, and falls asleep. I comb his face for the familiar pieces of him that remain against the sooted and broken ones. Jack's hair has always been neatly trimmed, if not expertly combed. Now it a tangled mass of dirty cords. His smooth, pale skin is red and blistered under a thick coating of black soot. His eyelashes, now resting atop his cheeks, no longer match as two threads of long, dark fans. One hedge of them is perfectly intact, just the way I remember them looking as he slept, while the other is singed to the nubs. At close inspection, I see that they've been reduced to tiny clumps of burned hair at his lids. Next to the outer corners of his eyes, unfamiliar wrinkles have etched into his skin. When I touch them lightly with the pad of my index finger, white lines of skin reveal from where they are hidden in the crevices. The only lines I remember on the nineteen-year-old fella I met were the ones around his mouth that would appear when he would smile.

While his face relaxes into the expression I loved to gaze at so many mornings in our bed before he would wake, the poison of reality starts to trickle in. It is not long until I am in a pool of the stuff, choking and gasping for air. This is *bad*. This is really, really bad.

I don't know what Fate has against me, but this is a cruel game she's playing. As I consider the hands I have been dealt, I feel like a ragdoll in the careless hands of a toddler throwing a tantrum, slamming into the wall again and again. *Bang!* Jack is off to war. *Bang!* He's dead. *Bang!* There goes our child. *Bang!* Phin's there, and he loves me, then *bang!* he is teetering on the edge of death. *Bang!* Jack is alive. I have two husbands. I'm married to Phin *and* to Jack.

I think this is illegal back in the United States, Imp teases.

All's fair in love and war, Sense chimes in. There is nothing 'fair' about this. Inside, this is its own war. I cannot decide which one is worse.

I don't know if my exhausted body is sucking the juice from my brain, but I just cannot wrap my head around this. My husband is lying a foot away from me; but yet my latest husband is lying in a cot on the medic's ship, about to make its return voyage to the United States. Both are in bandages. Both have survived the first night of this hot, burning hell. I desperately hope both will survive the week, then the month, and then the years to come. Even though... oh, even though that puts me in a terrible position.

Jack has no idea that I'm married to Phin, and Phin has no idea that Jack is alive. With my eyes squeezed tightly, I bang my fist on my forehead in frustration. A heavy hand lands on my shoulder, and I leap to my feet with a shuddering gasp. I'm like a spooked cat.

"Sheesh, Hell; I jest thought I'd releef you." Head Nurse Adler, fresh after a few hours of sleep, looks as though she suspects I have been drinking the whiskey. I think of the possibility of getting away from Jack; getting away from this choice.

"Yeah. Thank you," I mutter, taking long strides out of the tent. Out in the dark, my strides shorten immediately. Most of the bodies have been collected and taken to the ships to return home for a hero's burial, but the images in my head of the sickening way their bodies had landed in the sand haunts me. I'm terrified that I'll stumble over someone as I walk toward the distant lantern lights of our pup tents.

I can barely see ahead of me in the dark, but I become completely blind when my eyes start to tear up. Sadness. Frustration. The feeling that something completely wonderful has been spoiled, and it's my fault. I want these emotions to pour out of my tear ducts and soak into the sand. *Go away; go away.*

"Agh!" I shriek. My fear has come true, and my limbs recoil in horror; my nose and chin hit the sand. I have stumbled over someone. A strong retch builds in my throat, ready to heave my stomach when...

Sniff. The body made a noise. *Is this the death rattle we learned about in training? Has this soldier been lying here on the beach for over a day? Or has he just barely returned to the beach from the mission?* I sit up and start patting around for my bag.

Sniff. "Sorry," the body says. It's a gal's voice. A *gal.*

"Hello?" I say into the dark, relieved that the body isn't dead.

"P?"

"Willa?" I cry out, crawling through the sand toward the source of the sound. My hands find her, patting her lightly until I orient her body parts and wrap my arms around her. "Are you crying?"

"Yes." *Sniff.* "Is that so bad, considering?" Her body trembles. I think of how unaffected she was on the boat when we watched the mines blast and bodies fall. Brave. It seems she is just now allowing herself to realize the full scope of the horror we have witnessed.

"I mean..." she continues in a thick voice. "I'm exhausted. Not just tired, not just body-tired, but..." she wordlessly gestures to her ribs. I read in the movement a mirror image of how I feel, *soul* worn as well as physically drained.

"Shhh, no. I know. I know." I rock her as though I'm soothing May. Her arms around me feel like Mama soothing me. In this way, we calm each other. However, in light of the past days, and especially the past hour, I cannot be fully soothed.

"Willa, I have something to tell you."

"I have something I have to tell you, too. I mean, I want it to come from me, and Bentley will tell you soon enough..." Willa says, but in my desperation to share the news about Jack, I speak over her.

"Hang on, it's about..." My throat chokes with emotion before I can finish my sentence.

"Oh no, who is it? Bentley? Phin? *Both?*" she cries. "Why didn't you say anything before, in the tent? Or did they just tell you now?" Her concern reminds me of my fortune in having both Phin and Bentley alive. For now.

"No, not them. Bentley's foot is no good, I think, and Phin's still unconscious," I tell her as a fresh pang of worry about Phin hits me. I can hear her sigh of relief. "It's--I was tending to a patient in the tent, and, um, it's Jack."

Willa sits straight up. "Jack? *Jackson* Jack? What?"

I burst into tears.

"Is he alive?" she begs.

I nod. "For now. He's in pretty bad shape. He's the one you gave whiskey to."

"The *Neanderthal?* No! But he..." she gasps, wiping her eyes with abandon. "Did he see you? I mean, was he awake? Did he recognize you?"

"Mmm hmm," I confirm. "Then he passed out."

"Whoa, nelly,!" she pants.

A little wail escapes me.

"You know, a lot of gals wouldn't be crying over this," she scolds as she pulls me up by my arm. "Let's go see him."

THIRTY-ONE

"Jack," I whisper as the sun rises over the dark canvas tent. His eyelids flutter. "Jackson, it's me."

Willa's hazel green eyes rake over his face, as if looking for something in particular. *What could she be looking for? Perhaps she is trying to align this man with my careful descriptions to her of my late husband? Claire knew her before she ran away from her family. Does Jack know her, too?*

"C'mon now; come back," she prods, poking him in the ribs.

"Hey," I scold her with my eyes.

The other nurses in the tent shoot severe looks at us. Jack's fits were disturbing to everyone; they don't want him awake.

"Hmm," he moans. When his eyes flutter, Willa dances lightly into the shadows. His brilliant blue eyes focus on me, and he smiles weakly. It makes the gash start to spread open.

"No, don't; you still need stitches," I warn, brushing the gash on his cheek lightly. He winces. "Sorry." The morphine really did nothing for him if he could feel that soft touch.

"This is Willa," I begin, and his blue eyes move to her shadowed face for a moment; "...my very best girl friend in the world."

Her darkened face nods, satisfied.

"Willa, this is Jack."

We all feel the absence of a title- "my husband", "the love of my life"... something along those lines.

"Pleased to meet you," Willa nods, and I feel her back away.

Jack and I are alone at the end of the tent.

"I thought you were dead," I say quietly, recalling the depths of despair I had wallowed in when I was told that.

"Me, too," he agrees in a raspy voice.

"Huh?"

"I *was* dead," he wheezes.

"What are you saying?" I press. He clears his throat and winces.

"They can't know that I'm alive," he croaks. With a quivering hand, he fishes his dog tags out of his bandages. I read the stamped name, 'SAVAGE, JACOB R'. I look at his face again, trying to reconcile this incorrect name with his familiar face. This is Jack, not Savvy. I have *no* doubt that this is the face of the boy who rescued me from shutting the world out just to keep myself safe from being hurt again. He drew me from the thick, protective layer I'd built around myself, helped me slough away my thick skin, so I could experience real joy. Real love. And unfortunately, real pain.

His eyes plead for my discretion. "Later," he mouths, dropping his tags and grabbing my hand. I realize that I will do anything for this man, even grant him my patience. But he's in such bad shape, I wonder if there will be a "later". I don't know if I can wait for his explanation!

Where has he been?

THE END

Learn more at **alissabright.blogspot.com**
and be sure to 'like' the **Hale's Storm Fan Page**
on **Facebook** for the latest information on the
Hale's Storm series!

ACKNOWLEDGEMENTS

My heart is bursting with gratitude for every person who helped raise this barn! I could not have done this alone. Well, I probably could have, but I would've gone nuts, and I would have a lot of trouble signing books in a straightjacket. My helpers helped me keep my sanity. Wait, have I kept my sanity? I'm not sure...

Natalie, it means the world to me that my daughter has you (and "Wyan") in her life. Ashley, thank goodness for your trampoline, and thank goodness you're so cool about potty problems! Leah, Farm School has been a win win win. You, Bob, Bonnie, Bucky, the chickens, and your farm-fresh popsicles allowed my writing to bump up to the next level. Thank you so much for opening your doors (and your hearts) to her so I could work!

Looky Loo Photography blows my skirt up. Seriously, like Marilyn- Monroe-standing-over-a-street-grate skirt blowing! Cindy, you are (and forever will be) my favorite photographer on earth. Your gorgeous photos elevated this project. Thank you, my dear Cindy. And, on that note... models! Or... parents of my models! Thanks for creating and raising such beautiful people. I know it was a personal favor to me, and for that, I am grateful. We had a ball shooting this cover, and I will never forget how hard I laughed in the process! Thanks for your valuable time and valuable gorgeousness.

Carson is my hero. That is all. (Insert curtsy here.)

Mom, thanks for relentlessly voicing the correct way to use "lay" and "lie" (although I'm still not sure I've got a handle on the concept...). You are a smarty-pants. Grandpa Jim, please note that I did not use 'like' in that irritating valley girl fashion anywhere in this series. Perhaps you drilled that into me along with your every poke at my dimples.

Thank you to every pair of fresh eyes that proofed for me: Amy, Natalie, Leah, Ashley, Kristi, Kayde, and Stephanie. You made sure that the story in my head came across in print. Amy, you are the proof-reading queen. Thanks for pushing me to be better. Natalie, your attention to detail is stellar! Ashley, your super-charged preggie hormones haven't failed me yet. Each of you made this story better.

SLO Apple Store employees, one to one was killer during this project. I'm so impressed that you're a group of customer service personnel that actually like working with people! You're all geniuses to me.

Ben, every time you make me laugh, I know I picked the right guy. Every time I hear your animated voice reading to the kids at bedtime, I know I married the right man. Every time you move mountains to give me a little writing time, I know I'll keep you forever. I'm a lucky girl.

Maverick and Rees, Mommy loves you more than she loves her keyboard, I promise! Your snuggles and wet kisses power me up to face the world. Thank you both for granting me my dream job, mamahood, 'cuz I couldn't have it without you. You both are very special kids, and I can't wait to see where your creativity takes you.

Once again, I thank my Creator for His innumerable blessings. Each of us have a gift to share with the world, and these gifts come from Him! Use them!

ABOUT THE AUTHOR

Alissa Bright lives on the Central Coast of California, 126 steps from the sand, with her husband, two children, and their dog, Brutus (who escapes to the beach whenever a window has been left open). She loves being a mom (her dream job), and seeks a creative outlet wherever she can find one.

Alissa is not an English major, nor a college graduate, but she does believe creativity and drive can leap traditional hurdles. Her favorite quote is, "Whether you think you can, or you think you can't, you're right," by Henry Ford.

www.ingramcontent.com/pod-product-compliance
Lightning Source LLC
Chambersburg PA
CBHW070644180626
46817CB00006B/2235